Queen Delilah

and the

Encroaching Gloom

Queen Delilah

and the

Encroaching Gloom

Nikki Peone Pison
&
Niko Peone

Published in the United States by Little Heart Press, Rosendale, New York.

ISBN: 978-0-9892459-3-7

Cover Art: By Nikki Pison and Layla Cummings Peone

Inside Art: By Nikki Pison

Family Photographs: By Lonnda Sullivan

Little Heart Press
Rosendale, New York

This book is dedicated to our respective spouses: Jeff and Layla.
It is not always easy being married to us. This is why we married Pisces.
We sometimes need the calming temperament of the fish.

The Queendom of Delilah & Surrounding Territories

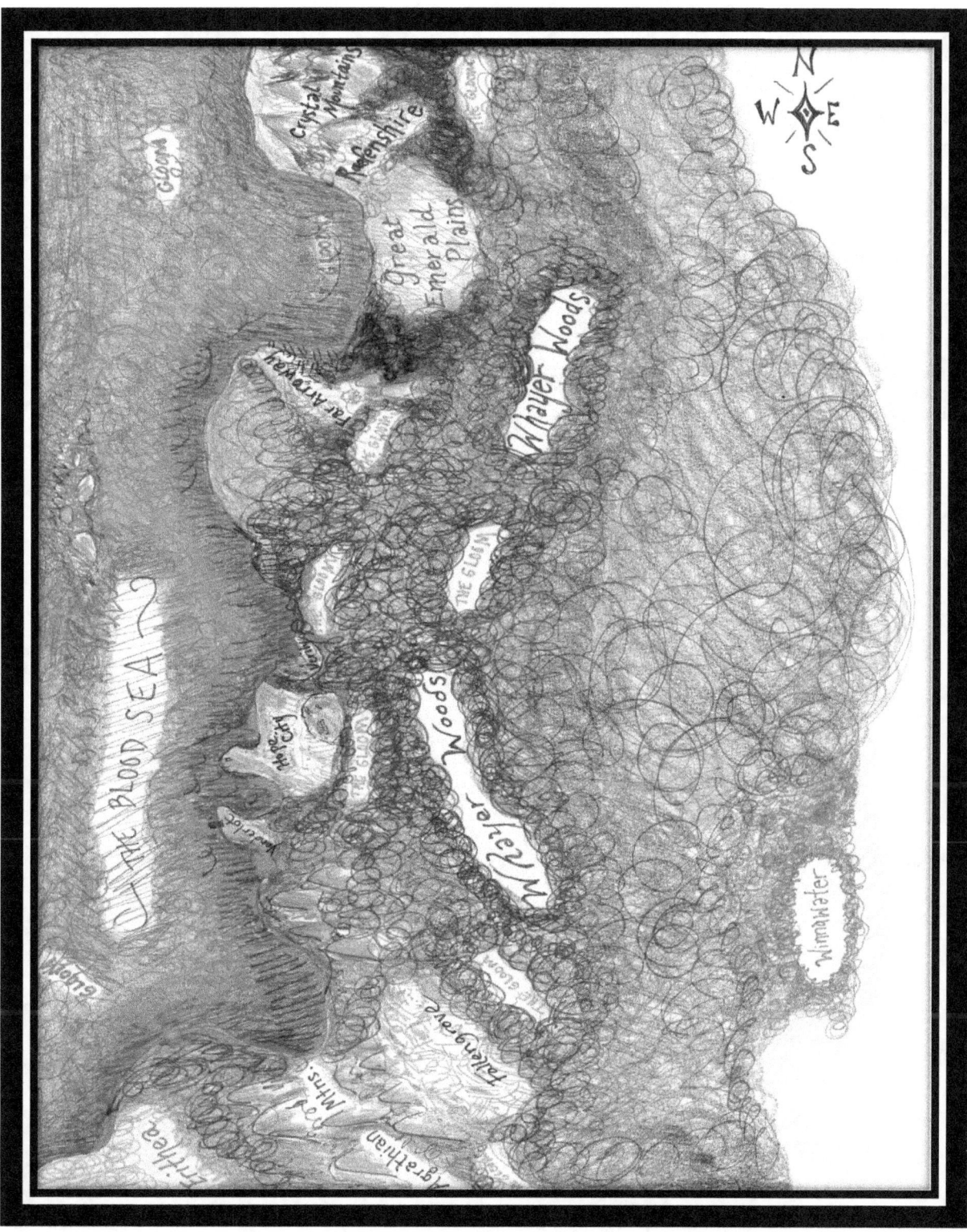

"In the Queendom of Delilah,
all are loved and wanted.
Those who wander will despair
and those who stay are haunted."
-The Ghost Scribe

Chapter 1: The Year of the Pumpkin

Delilah was only going to stay for a moment, feeling the ocean breeze upon her sturdy face, when the spiky blue thistle caught her eye. The plant had a curious name: *Aelves' Blessing*. Like the aelves Delilah had seen, the flowers were intimidating. They had tall, bristly stems, jagged leaves, and needle-sharp blooms, yet this was the first time she had stopped to wonder about how they had gotten their name. Jarvis would have known. Her brother had been an expert on all things aelven, but Jarvis had plunged down the cliffs and into the Blood Sea, right below where she now sat. She looked down and recalled her last glimpse of him, his cape floating above the waves for a moment before being pulled under, into the swirling eddy. She tried not to remember, and still the images appeared to her. As they had for the past fifteen years, the moments before Jarvis' leap to his watery death flashed in bright frozen moments in Delilah's mind: first her father falling with his throat laying wide open, rivers of blood pooling on the stone; the surprised look on her mother's face when the sword was thrust through her; Jarvis circled by armed guards backing him toward the cliff edge; and then the moment when her brother leaped back into the air and disappeared silently from view. The last Delilah would ever see of Jarvis was his cape twisting down beneath the water. Why had she thought she could come here to enjoy some fresh air and peace from her daily troubles? This would always be the place where her childhood abruptly ended and her life changed forever.

Shaking her head free from these thoughts, Delilah lay her cloak on the hard stone of the cliff and sat to examine the curling tendrils that rose from the heart of each spiny blossom. Their woody stems grew straight out of crevices in the rock, and still they were vigorous and strong as the rainbow corn at harvest. Only the tiniest vibrations along the hairy stalks and storm-cloud blooms revealed any deference to the windy sea. On an impulse, Delilah reached out and ran her fingertips across the top of a needle-like bud, prepared to pull her hand away. She almost laughed: the thistles were soft! She ran her hand back and forth across the tops of the plants, wondering at their downy tickle. The flower was not as fierce as it seemed.

The water seemed angry today, roiling and crashing below with foamy crimson peaks. By habit, Delilah looked out and scanned the horizon for large ships. There had not been any in months, which could be bad or good depending upon whether approaching crafts had the dreaded black sails of marauders or were trading vessels carrying desperately needed supplies. As much as they needed fresh food, the sight of nothing at all on the horizon was a relief, since she did not feel she could face the challenge of another scuffle with the pirates. They had enough to contend with at the moment.

Sighing, Delilah pushed herself up and left what she had hoped would be a tiny reprieve from the pressures of her daily life. She turned back toward the winding trail leading through the Pine Barren. Back to the city and to her work, which never seemed to end. Her duty compelled her, as it always did, to return to the urgency of the tasks at hand. She reached down and snapped off one of the blue flowers, putting it through the buttonhole of her cloak before departing. The thistle had no scent, but Delilah imagined it had an aura surrounding it that somehow protected her, whispering its secrets to her. The Pine Barren was not much of a forest—not like the opaque and terrifying Whayer Wood on the other side of the city. The Whayer Wood was a dark, lush, and impenetrable jungle, sheltering wild, unthinkable creatures. It secreted those who used to be human but became poisoned and transformed. In the Whayer Wood, people turned into horrifying demons with no souls who lived without living and survived by sucking blood from any prey they could find: animal, human, or beast. The Pine Barren was sparse and tame by comparison. A fringe of briars tangled along the edge of the path, filling Delilah's nostrils with the fragrance of wild roses. She savored it while she could.

Approaching the shanties at the edge of the city, a foulness of human sickness and rot permeated the air. Delilah reached into her pocket and pulled out a dark scarf, wrapping it across her nose and mouth. There was little movement in the city. Most of the residents were sheltering indoors, hiding from the *Mungus*. The illness had recently devastated the territory. Houses with infected members were marked with crossed laurel branches tied above the doorways. Delilah's contacts in distant lands informed her that the Mungus was spreading quickly across the world. It had been six grand moons since the disease swept into Hope City. Already Delilah had trouble remembering a time when children played in the streets and hawkers sold their wares, pushing carts up and down the uneven cobbles, yelling to each other and laughing, faces uncovered. Those who scurried about had cloth coverings, like hers, that disguised the exchange of normal human expressions. Delilah longed to see someone smile again.

"Rexion!" Delilah called across the narrow street to a man she recognized as the head of the vegetable market. "I need to speak to you about the pumpkin delivery from Verily!" The merchant backed away from her, holding one hand over the scarf on his face and the other out in front of him to stop Delilah from coming any closer. He shook his head and turned to flee down an alley. Delilah stood for a moment looking after him, then kept walking.

The first person infected with the Mungus was a sea merchant who had docked by the wharf to sell live seafood to the fisheries along the coastline. The seafarer was covered in bumps, but it was common for those outside the sheltered city of Hope to have some form of physical abnormality. The buyers did not think much of it until they, too, broke out in rashes and lumps several days later. Many of those who handled the fish from the sea merchant also become covered in knobby pustules. For the unlucky ones, those boils would eventually cover their whole skin. The person's mind became more and more demented and they were possessed by a vile temper. Loved ones would have to tie down the patients to prevent them from harming their own families as they screamed profanities and made mad accusations. The pustules would eventually burst into clouds of smoke like puffballs, leaving dried, empty husk of skin behind. Others—the lucky ones—merely had an itchy rash that was impossible not to scratch. They, too, became delirious, hallucinating spiders under their skin that could only be released by tearing at the bumps. The smoky substance released by scratching the awful rash was infectious, so they needed to be isolated. No one knew how long a sick person needed to stay away from others, or if the infection could spread in other ways, so almost all activity in the city had ceased. Each household dealt with their fate alone.

The streets were dusty, as they always were. Once emptied of people, one noticed the dust more. The buildings here were constructed practically on top of one another, relics of when Hope first grew and became populous, at the beginning of a time when it was a city of refuge. Now, shop windows were boarded up. All business had come to a halt and those who were hungry grew hungrier still. The fields lay untended and overgrown, the crops having been neglected when the populace fell ill; hence, no harvest that season. Delilah used to be greeted by smiles, pleasantries, and requests when she walked through the streets. Now, a quick nod and skirting widely around her, or fleeing completely like Rexion had, was the most she could expect from the city dwellers. Delilah heard a commotion. Two skinny dogs skirmished over an old cheese rag that still held the scent of whey. The stronger dog pulled the cloth away and held it with its paws, licking and ripping the fabric with his teeth while growling at the smaller fellow. The little guy had a ragged, notched ear and a mutated third eye. All three glassy eyes trained piteously on the bigger dog's bounty. Delilah reached into her pocket and found the end of a crust of bread and fed it surreptitiously to the tinier mutant pup. She felt guilty as she did it, knowing that on the other side of the doors there was probably a child who would have relished even that crust.

Delilah had grown up rarely leaving the confines of Hope. She had been born here, and perhaps she would die here, too, hardly glimpsing the rest of the doomed world. Even before the Mungus arrived, their planet was not an easy place to live. A meteor had struck about 100 years prior, creating a pervasive toxic fog that spread across the seas and over the low valleys. The purplish smog became known as the *Gloom*. People who entered the Gloom turned into undead creatures, demons, or mutants. This made travel almost impossible. Hope City had essentially become an island, with the raging red sea on one side, the dense forest filled with Beasts on the other, and the Gloom all around. Hope had become a sanctuary because previous generations of sorcerers had used ancient magick to create a giant enchanted bubble around it to protect it from the Gloom. The invisible dome prevented invasion by the undead and mutant beasts on the perimeters that lived in the forest and ocean. There were other refuge cities, but they were spread out and separated by vast woodlands, inhabited by monsters, and surrounded by toxic sea. There were few who attempted to travel through the Gloom to reach other outposts.

The effects of the Gloom were unpredictable, yet almost always terrifying. Animals who encountered the murky smog turned into monstrous beings or freakish oddities. Those who made it from one safe place to another told nightmarish tales of sea creatures, poisoned by the Gloom, or fiends lurking on the fringes of the cities. It was virtually impossible to safely leave any of the small peaks of mountains that rose above the smog. Each isolated community was its own ecosystem that had developed almost entirely alone over the century since the Gloom descended upon the earth. Now, because of the plague, each household in this place of refuge had become alienated from every other. Six moons ago, the biggest problems in Hope were the Gloom, whayerwolves from the forest side, and invading pirates on the ocean side. Yes, Hope had enough to contend with even before the Mungus took hold.

As Delilah neared the gated keep, two masked Sister Guard stepped aside. She recognized them as Kaolin and Geneve even with their covered faces, but only by their red braids. It was hard to know who was even serving in your own army these days! Fortunately, Delilah had never had to deal with subterfuge in her ranks, yet it occurred to her now how easy it would be for someone to sneak in and cause mischief, or worse. She brushed off the thought, since she would be sure to sense something amiss if it would come, which it probably never would. Most people were preoccupied with putting scraps of food in the mouths of their families. Despite how easy it would have been for the populace to fault Delilah for the pestilence, there was not even the tiniest whisper of blame in her direction. She had their undying devotion, even while dying. Or in some cases, even when undead.

"Your Majesty." She heard the gruff voice of Olavfin before she saw his burly form.

"Evening, Olav. How goes the watch?"

"All is quiet, except for the flies. They are having quite a feast these days."

"True. Sad, and still so true. They are the only ones eating well."

"Have you had any signs on your walkabout? Anything reveal itself to you, Your Majesty?"

"Come now, Olavfin! You know me better than that. I am hardly the superstitious type."

"Times like these can make anyone superstitious, Your Majesty."

"Not I. Times like these make me turn to science. I seek cures from the greatest minds, not from the skies."

"Yes, of course. Which reminds me, you received another scroll from Doktora Ilvana. This one had so much wax and binding cord it might take a year just to bust through it all."

"It must be important. Thank you, Olav. I will take it in the library."

"It is already there… on your desk."

"You know me so well."

"Will you eat *anything*?" Olavfin's nurturing eyes implored her.

"No, I do not feel right eating when so many are starving. Just… maybe some tea?"

"A pot of dandelion root tea is also hot on your desk."

"How did you…?"

"As if you could go anywhere in this city without people knowing when you leave and when you return, Your Highness."

Delilah's study comforted her with the smells of old leather-bound books and ancient hardwoods. The ornate furniture had been in her family for at least five generations. The tea was laid out in the center of a massive crescent-shaped desk. The jade teapot was a gift from a long-dead emperor. A scroll was placed next to it, and was, indeed, bound with so much wax it took Delilah a good long time to release it. She did so with the help of a gem-encrusted letter knife that her father had given to her mother as an engagement gift. Doktora Ilvana leaned toward the dramatic, so Delilah was not entirely convinced of this letter's importance. The eccentric researcher might be just as likely to confine an invitation to a scientific lecture in that way. Ilvana lived in an outpost of Hope called Verily that could only be reached by a clandestine vine-covered tunnel that ran through the Whayer Wood. The tunnel had a habit of moving, and the entrance was a carefully guarded secret. The enchanted bubble–called the *Vector*–that the ancients had invoked to keep Hope safe, extended through the tunnel to the small mountaintop village of Verily on the other side. Verily was also encapsulated by the Vector in a smaller sphere of protection. Few lived there except for some farmers and Ilvana's assistants and acolytes. It was a small territory with steep cliffs on one side and the frightening Woods on the other. One could get nervous with the snarls, howls, and glowing eyes from the forest-side. This did not bother Ilvana, who lived at the top of the mountain in an old observatory that was built in Delilah's grandparents' days. Like many of the old buildings in Verily, the observatory had deteriorated, yet still had a viewing tower and lots of space for Ilvana's laboratory and extensive library.

There were a few families who grew amaranth and swamp rice on a marshy terrace on the far side of Verily, and some goat farmers on the back side that overlooked the sea. The farmers grew oddly formed pumpkins, long twisted eggplants, and bulging gourds in the pockets of cliff gardens protected from the vicious wind. In Hope, many people refused to eat the unusually-shaped fruit from Verily. However, these days, any food was good food. The gourds, which grew with barely any attention, were some of the only produce available in Hope City these days. Pumpkin soup had been ubiquitous. Even when sick and weak, a family could throw a pumpkin into a pot of water on the fire and eat the orange gruel in a few hours. It was not much, but it kept away the gnawing in one's belly. The entrance to Verily was hidden, a tradition harkening back to when Science and State were first separated. In the past, royalty had often tried to interfere with scientific enterprises: they could destroy key discoveries, if it suited them to keep the world mysterious. Withholding information that might undermine their divine right to rule was a tactic for control that was banished with the Science/State division. The scientific integrity of Verily could only be kept pure if it was seen as sacred and separate and therefore not a tool of the nobility. Since the Mungus, it was fortunate that the location of the food coming into Hope was kept secret, since starvation may turn even the kindest folks into criminals.

Others might have felt isolated in Verily, but not Doktora Ilvana. She was devoted to her studies, and was also responsible for directing a squadron of apprentices, monks, and novice scientists, preparing them for vocations in the scientific arts. She used all her resources to focus completely on her work, which right now was committed entirely to finding a cure for the Mungus. The sickness had spread quickly to the livestock in the farms surrounding the city. Some of the first infected fish had been used to feed geese and ducks, who then mingled with the chickens and turkeys. The poultry became erratic and attacked their caretakers, only stopping once they exploded into clouds of dust and empty skins. The pigs, cattle, and sheep were next, having been assailed by the fowl. The animals that did not appear sick were still not eaten for fear of contamination. As if Hope did not have enough troubles, the plague came and made survival in the city that much harder. Now Ilvana was on to something. The doctor had sent Delilah several messages letting her know she was getting close to a cure.

Delilah unrolled the scroll, which was on a strip of old fabric since paper was so scarce these days. Ilvana sometimes sent pages and pages of her ponderings, thoughts on causation and musing on how to contain and kill the virus. The deaths had slowed after the Time of Great Isolation, but they were still losing people every day. The oldest and weakest died first, then those who took the greatest risks to help others. Those who cared for the sick, buried the withered fragments of bodies, or ventured out to find sustenance were most vulnerable. Delilah had the current numbers showing that in six changes of the moons, the city had lost almost one quarter of its population. Almost everyone had lost someone to the disease.

The scroll did not contain the usual ramblings, scientific words that Delilah had to look up in her mother's obscure reference books, or frustration about the alarming pace of the sickness. Instead, there were just two words scribbled in Ilvana's impatient hand: "*Goat Milk.*" It was hard to know if Ilvana had intended this to be informative or was purposely trying to be cryptic. Regardless, Delilah went back out to find Olav.

"I leave for Verily at dawn," she said.

"Are you sure, Your Majesty?" he asked. "It is not the safest time to travel."

"Yes, it is urgent."

)(

There was only one person who could bring Delilah to the protected location of the tunnel to Verily. A retired member of an elite division of the Sister Guard was entrusted with the secret. This reclusive sect was made up of holy scientists, sworn to protect the sacred arts of the scientific craft even while serving the Crown. Doktora Chastice was called out of retirement whenever the need arose. It was said that only Chastice's daughter knew the way, and would take over her mother's duty once she passed over into the realm of the Ancients.

Queen Delilah and the Encroaching Gloom

Even Delilah could not know the way. She was blindfolded and led by the doctor, who was slow, but still strongly grasped the queen's arm. Delilah felt like a mummy with her eyes covered and a scarf across her mouth and nose to protect from the Mungus, yet she was strangely comforted by the woman's touch. There had been so little physical contact for months. They walked a winding route. Delilah never could never tell if the old Guard just brought her around in circles for an hour. The entrance could be in one of her own gardens for all she knew.

"'Tis right in front of you, Your Majesty," said the woman, placing a torch in Delilah's outstretched hand.

"Thank you, Doktora Chastice," Delilah said, but she could hear the old Guardswoman disappear into the darkness behind her before she even removed her blindfold. It was barely daylight, yet pitch dark in the tunnel. The path wound inside part of a mountain and then opened to a trail through the forest. There, Delilah extinguished the torch, since her eyes were already attuned to the dark, and continued to feel with her feet along the trail. The vine covered walls of the tunnel were so dense that nothing could be seen on the other side, yet all the forest sounds echoed through the leaves. Light filtered in from the top, but the Vector's enchantment made those in the tunnel invisible. They could still be smelled by creatures from the other side, however, which was the most unnerving part of the journey. Delilah heard the howls and snorts of beasts through the layered growth of the tunnel's walls. They could sense her presence there and came to the sides to sniff at her through the leaves, and yet they could not see or access her.

The walk through the tunnel took Delilah at least an hour. All the while she heard hoofbeats, shrieks, and the wails of the whayerwolves on the other side of the dense black-green growth. Finally, Delilah could see light spilling in from the end of the tunnel, and she realized she had been holding her breath. She came out into the morning light of Verily and saw the verdant, rocky hills sloping up toward the observatory. The remnants of old buildings that had been used for experimental enterprises in ages past were tucked into the surrounding cliffs. The ramshackle structures were mostly overgrown with weeds and wildflowers taller than a person, arching heavily under the weight of their enormous seed heads. Delilah had worn her face covering through the tunnel, but she removed it now and breathed in the wet morning air. The clear breeze was punctuated by the saltiness of the ocean on the windward side of the cliffs and the fresh aroma of healthy growing things.

This side of the tunnel was not secret, as no one who lived in Verily was a security threat. Besides, the tunnel moved unexpectedly to open up in different places in Verily. When it was time to leave, a volunteer would escort Delilah back through the tunnel and then deliver her blindfolded back to her castle door. The population of Verily was small and they could not always find matches among their own. When one married into Verily, part of the wedding ceremony included the new spouse being told how to locate the tunnel's entrance in Hope. The bride or groom was brought to Verily blindfolded, as Delilah had been, and then after the handfasting, the couple would walk the journey through the tunnel to Hope, there and back, to solidify their union and entrust the new community member with the secret to finding the ever-shifting entrance.

There was no Mungus in Verily. Nothing got in or out that was not safe, and those delivering vegetables and goods into the city wore scarves over their faces and dropped the merchandise in an agreed upon location in the outskirts of the city, picking up stashed payments. The coins were soaked in vinegar upon return and the bags holding them were burned. Due to these precautions and the insular nature of the populace there, Verily had barely been touched by the sickness. Delilah felt a wash of relief flood her as she breathed deeply and walked the rocky path up to the observatory. Even during her morning ventures into the unpopulated parts of Hope, she always felt the imposing threat of danger on every side. Here in Verily, Delilah felt a small measure of safety that she had not felt in months.

The climb was vigorous. She saw a few monks practicing their morning exercises and some people working at a distance, carrying water for the crops and leading animals to graze. It was nice to see the ordinary tide of life, uninterrupted by the fear that pervaded Hope. Delilah approached the giant shoak door of the observatory, which opened before she reached it. A young girl, who was dressed in apprentice's robes, led her into the anteroom and served her tea. To sit in a parlor awaiting a visit seemed such a common thing. Yet to Delilah, this tiny semblance of normalcy almost brought her to tears.

Ilvana burst in, her wild hair barely restrained by an unkempt braid, glassy eyes darting about. "Good, you are finally here!" The scientist began at high speed: "I have not slept. I am running tests, but it is certain now. We have protection here! Verily is protected! At first, I thought it was because we avoided bringing in the infection. But no! Not that! We had a case or two come through the tunnel. We even lost a few souls, and yet it does not spread!" She looked at Delilah expectantly. "The cure is here! It is something specific to Verily!" The doctor paused, as if she wanted a response.

"Something in Verily?" Delilah queried, since it seemed a reply was expected.

"Yes! There is… protection here. Not an enchantment or magick, or even just the remoteness of the place. It is… an *innoculus*."

"Apologies, Doktora, I am not familiar with the term," Delilah admitted.

"Something that makes one resistant to sickness from the inside out! There is something in Verily that makes us stronger so that we are less likely to get ill. When the Mungus slipped in here, it was not passed to others! Of those who got sick, a few died and many recovered. But it did not spread!" She got close to Delilah and her eyes got intense. "Why?" she demanded.

"I… I, I am not sure, Doktora," Delilah fumbled. She was not used to being imposed upon in this way. Still, one of the things she appreciated about the scientist was that Ilvana always treated her like an equal, not like a queen.

"No, neither am I," Doktora Ilvana confessed, looking away. After a moment she held up a finger and shouted: "But! I have some ideas," and she smiled, an event so rare that Delilah could not help but smile with her. "The innoculus is in the goat milk!"

"So, you *do* know!"

"No, not exactly. It is not just any goat milk. There was goat milk in Hope before the Mungus and they were not protected, right? Goatherds and farmers from Hope got sick just as quickly. It is only goat milk from Verily!"

"What… why? Are they a different type of goat?"

"No, same breed. Exactly! Why?"

"And more importantly, how do we treat the citizens of Hope? How much Verily goat milk is needed?"

"Well, we interviewed the people in Verily who recovered from the sickness. We also interviewed the families of the people who had died. We made careful records of everything they had done, how they were treated and what they had eaten and drank. When we compared the lists, we found that those who recovered, more often than not, had some gruel mixed with goat milk, or a little warm milk with cinnamon, or milk in the teas they drank. Those who died had no milk. Anyone in the family who also drank milk stayed healthy while those who did not got sick, too. The Verily folks tend to eat a lot of dairy products. Lots of yogurt, creams, and you know our cheese is famous. Our love of goat milk is what protected us here."

"My goodness, Ilvana, that is remarkable!"

"Simple scientific methods, Your Majesty."

"Yes, but this is so important! We just need to get a little bit of Verily goat milk for the sufferers, and…"

"No," the Doktora interrupted. "It is not possible. There is not enough to treat the whole city. I am working out dosages now, which is what has kept me so busy these last days. Once I realized it was the milk that protected us, we took detailed accounts from Verily's residents, what they eat on a regular day, and more specifically if they recalled what they ate when the Mungus came to Verily."

"That alone must have been an enormous task!"

"Well, I had Aaranon to help me," Ilvana said and gestured to the corner of the room. Delilah noticed for the first time the slight young man, barely more than a boy, at a small desk in the corner scribbling away at some notes. He was an apprentice to Ilvana, taken in when he was very young. Delilah had only ever seen him serve tea and clean the observatory. Ilvana continued, "Aaranon was very thorough in collecting the data I needed from the Verily residents." The youth did not look up, but a blush spread up his neck as he continued to write.

"Nice work, Aaranon," Delilah said.

He glanced up and fumbled, "Th-thank you, Your Majesty," and quickly returned to his work.

"So, what did you find?" Delilah turned back to Ilvana.

"I found we do not have enough milk to treat all of Hope. You could choose to treat a small portion—say everyone who lives and works at the Castle—but not the whole city."

"You know I could not do that. We all have the cure or none of us does. I will not take any before my people can have it."

"Well, you are probably protected now from the small amount in your tea," Ilvana gestured to Delilah's cup. Delilah instinctively pushed the cup away as if it had poison. "Your Highness," Ilvana chided, "if some of the people in Hope are protected, they are more capable of helping those who are not. You could always give the treatment to the healers and clerics in Hope first. Then, as we produce more milk, we can treat the others over time."

"How much time?"

"It would take about six moons to produce enough to treat the whole city, in phases, starting with the people who need it most—the midwives, the healers, those who care for the sick and bury the dead. Next the merchants—all who will start the wheels of the city's trade and commerce moving again."

"That is too long, Doktora! The Mungus has already taken a quarter of our people in six moons. We can hardly afford to lose another quarter. We could lose half the city by the time we have enough milk for everyone!"

"Yes, it is not a perfect solution."

"So, what is the answer, Doktora Ilvana? We must find a way to get the cure sooner! There must be a way!"

"Well then, I will need your eyes," the Doktora said and looked at Delilah pointedly.

On the far side of Verily facing the sea, past the monks' dormitories tucked back into the cliffs, there were homesteads built amongst crumbling walls and foundations. Small, ramshackle structures gave livestock protection from the wind and rain, and irregular paddocks with stone pillars and cedar pasture fences zig-zagged across the uneven slope. Modest, robust-looking homes were low and wide with thick stone bases and heavy planks, built to withstand the ocean gusts. Ilvana led Delilah to a weather-beaten cabin and stood speaking to the farmer in the doorway. The old woman bowed her head to Delilah in greeting, and then spoke intently to Ilvana. Delilah stood at a distance and her gaze took in the rugged landscape. There were pastures with goats, a few donkeys, and poultry sheds with fat hens scratching up the dry earth to reveal grubs for frenetic chicks. The fields tumbled over with the oddly shaped gourds. Dry arching grasses spilled in cascades over the protruding gold and orange skin of the bulging fruit.

Delilah shuddered with an image the fruit invoked. Her mind was invaded by the memory of Harribold, or, more accurately–of Harribold's head. Harri, as Delilah had called him, was one of the few men inducted into the Sister Guard. He was a favorite soldier of Delilah's since childhood when he would toss her into the air and battle her gingerly with blunted wooden swords. He had been one of the first at the castle to become infected with the Mungus. Against the advice of her Council, Delilah had gone to see Harri where he was tied down and restrained in the barracks on the palace grounds. The worst boils were on his head: they poked out of his straw-colored hair, looking to burst, almost pulsating with the living spores inside them. This was before anyone had any idea what to expect from the virulent fungus that would release through the skin in bursts of sickening clouds. Those who breathed it would become infected, but that was not yet well-known.

The room was foul with rotting flesh and there was blood on the floor from self-inflicted scratches. Harribold's wife stood watch, tightening the straps around her husband's extremities as required by sudden violent outbursts where he dug at his own flesh, howled, and screamed obscenities. The Advisor who accompanied Delilah tried to dissuade her from standing too close, but Delilah stepped in to provide what comfort she could, unbuckling a muzzle-like contraption across Harri's face while trying not to touch any of the boils. To her horror, Delilah saw that the muzzle had a wooden bit, like for a horse, to prevent him from biting off his own tongue. Harri's wife tensed to have the Queen remove this device, torn between her instinct to protect the queen and her desire not to insult her monarch by telling her to step back for her own safety.

Delilah took cloth soaked in boiled Talon Tree bark and put it on Harri's head to soothe the offending mountains of blisters. He began to cry like a baby, wailing and whimpering, like no soldier she had ever seen. "Is that my lily-flower, little Queen-flower, little bee-blossom, honey-Queen?" he gasped, peeking through eyes slitted between swollen welts.

"Please forgive him, Your Majesty, he is not himself!" Harribold's wife seemed mortified.

"Nonsense. Harri and I are old friends. I am not small anymore, though, Harri-man. I am a big lily-Queen now, do you not remember? Remember the ambush of pirates last year? We fought armband to armband and I wielded a heavier weapon than even you!"

"Yes, I remember lily-Queen," he said tenderly. You are a fierce warrior, a fierce... a fierce... You... you," his voice shook and changed: "You are a stinking whayerwolf she-bitch, foul, evil wench! I will kill you! Kill you!" he thrashed and tried to gnash his teeth at Delilah's hand, which she pulled back from his forehead in alarm. "I will kill you! Kill you! Kill you!" the sounds of the soldier's voice retreated as Delilah's Advisor ushered her from the barracks down the long hallway. It echoed with outraged shrieks behind her as she gulped back bile and tears. She was grateful for the strong grasp the Councilwoman had on her arm. Harri died only hours later.

Now, among the stones, grass, and gourds, Delilah felt the revulsion all over again. The fruit looked obscene and unhealthy to her, despite her knowledge that the Verily squash harvest had kept much of the populace of Hope alive these last months. She could not help but see the grass as bristly hair standing up and flopping over vulgar swollen blisters. She shook away the memory and stepped to the flagstone walk snaking through the hilly garden patches. She needed air. She bolted along, careful not to trip on the uneven path but eager to break free from the sight of those wretched gourds. Over the peak of a hill, Delilah came to a cliffside meadow, dry and windblown, thriving with hearty grasses and flowers. She sat on a rock and took some gulps of salty air. Goats grazed among the weeds, nibbling vines and seed pods and pulling roots out to chomp every last bite of a favored plant. The goat kids ran circles around their dams, jumping up on their mothers' backs and launching off to pronk and spar with one another.

Delilah's mother had her train for a time under an herbalist, so Delilah could name almost every one of the diverse plants along the ridge and the ailments they could treat. She looked about and challenged herself, cataloging the flora and reminding herself of their benefits. How wonderful, she thought, that the natural order of things provided the cure for most illnesses right in most back fields, if one knew where to look. She watched an old nanny goat with a long beard lay on her side, sporting a tremendous udder and eating all that was within reach without any urgency to rise from a desirable sunny spot. Having cleared the grass around her, the goat reached her sinewy neck across a boulder and came up with a bluish stick, which she slowly inhaled like sucking in a straw reed. The plant came up and up, only for each new segment to disappear into the old lady goat's jaw at a lazy, persistent pace.

At the end of the long stick was a fluffy star of spiky petals, dull blue like a stormy sky. Delilah recognized it at once as the Aelves' Blessing thistle she had admired on the cliffside the day prior. Funny, she had never paid much attention to the flower before, but she did not spend much time on the edge of cliffs. The goats, on the other hand, spent most of their days browsing in this very place. How nice to be a goat, she mused, with nothing more to worry about then where to pluck your next piece of foliage to chew. Or at least, how nice to be one of the Verily goats, anyway. She had seen the dry lots where the goats of Hope were housed, grazing only on small pastures and eating vegetable scraps from the kitchen or bundles of straw, if they were lucky. None had the luxury of roaming free like these goats. It was no surprise Ilvana had discovered the Verily goatmilk to be something special. The animals here had such a diverse appetite, their milk would be infused with all the healing properties of the plants they ate. Like a flash, Delilah's vision zeroed in on the she-goat's mouth as the last of the thistle closed between her jaws, a piece of blue fluff escaping to drift over the cliff on an upturn of wind. Jumping up, she ran toward the startled goat, who wobbled to stand on knobby legs to jettison from Delilah's path.

Leaning over the boulder, Delilah found a patch of thistle spraying out from between rocks on the other side. She broke off a bloom and ran back toward the homestead on the other side of the ridge. She saw Ilvana walking toward her, having finally left the conversation with the woman from the cottage. The doctor was watching her feet, carefully avoiding twisting an ankle. She looked up to see Delilah barreling upon her, holding the flower proudly aloft.

The scientist had a look of puzzlement upon her face. "Well, thank you, Your Grace," she said. "I am flattered, but…"

"It is the thistle!" Delilah blurted out.

Now the confusion left Ilvana's countenance and was replaced by a wide-eyed reverence. "Yes!" the scientist shouted and grabbed it from Delilah's hand. "The Aelves' Blessing! Of course! How could I have missed it? You see, I needed your eyes!"

It turned out that Aelves' Blessing was rather rare in all places except where plants had the hardest time growing, most notably on salty sea cliffs. Once the key was discovered, Ilvana quickly determined that the goat's milk was not needed at all. It had been but a vehicle to deliver the cure for the Mungus to the fine folks of Verily. The flowers themselves, which were in abundance on the Verily cliffs, could be pulverized and converted to minute doses of powder that were much stronger than the micro-doses ingested through the milk. This delighted both Delilah and Ilvana because the problem of inadequate supplies of goatmilk to treat all of Hope was no longer an issue. Instead, they discovered that a few grains of the dust from the thistle could reverse the Mungus in all except the most advanced cases. Furthermore, those who took it pre-emptively were prevented from getting sick in the first place.

Ilvana had befriended a tribe of goblins who lived along the sea edge that ran from Verily into the dark forest. Years before, an evil goblin king had dominated the colony through cruel and brutal methods. Ilvana's monks had led an attack to help overthrow the demon and replace him with his daughter, who became a fair and just goblin matriarch. This helped the tribe and made for better neighbors for Verily. The community was peaceful after the defeat of the king, and indebted to the Doktora. They were pleased to perform odd favors for her, such as fetching herbs from the depths of the Whayer Wood, where humans could not venture. This time, Ilvana employed the goblins to help process the herbs needed for the Mungus cure. The residents of Verily were occupied for a straight week, standing at raised tables and separating the stalks from the flowers and packing these into pouches. Even the children helped, running back and forth to the cliff, gathering more of the plant and delivering sacks of blossoms to the gates of the goblin village. There, the creatures used their muscular arms to wield mallets pounding the flower heads to dust. The powder was then returned to Verily, where it was weighed and measured out carefully by Aaranon and other fastidious acolytes. It was sealed in little paper dosing packets and delivered through the tunnel to Hope. As was fitting, a few trusty goats pulled carts of the boxed medicine through the dark tunnel. The path was not wide enough to drive a regular-sized cart with horses, and the goats did not spook as much from the frightening sounds on the other side of the viny walls.

Delilah organized a party of Sister Guard to distribute the medicine through the streets, starting in the poorest and hardest-hit areas. No one was denied if they wanted an extra packet or two to take to a sick relative or to save for someone who was not at home. With Ilvana's calculations, Delilah felt confident that there would be more than enough to treat the entire city. Ilvana also recommended a precisely calculated quantity to be dumped into the city's water cistern to passively treat the populace. Within a few weeks, the streets started to come alive again, shopkeepers took the boards off their windows, and hawkers walked the streets with the wares they had crafted and stockpiled during their isolation. Common gathering places were frequented again. There was still a desperate need for food in the city, since it would be some time before new crops could be grown and livestock replenished, but there was a spirit of sharing. All gave what they could to their neighbors.

A steady stream of gourds and pumpkins continued to flow from Verily into the City of Hope. As much as all began to loathe the sight of the vulgar fruit, it became a point of fierce competition to make the most creative dish from the flesh. Pickled squash, pumpkin dishes, gourds roasted and seasoned, disguised and flavored to resemble a portion of meat, and all sorts of soups, pies, jams, and curries began to emerge. All had their preferred way of eating the unusual fruits, and all insisted that their recipe—or their grandmother's—was simply the best. Contests emerged and alliances formed over a particular method for roasting, stewing, baking, broiling, or even shredding and fermenting them with savory seaweed and spicy peppers. Forever afterward, that time was lightheartedly known as the Year of the Pumpkin. This euphemism emerged as a way to avoid saying out loud the horror of what had occurred the year the Mungus killed one in four people in Hope. Delilah was grateful now to those awful fruits for monopolizing the conversations as she walked through the streets. Once again, people asked her for favors and advice. Only now, her opinion was mostly solicited related to how to best get the thick stubborn skins off those giant beige-colored squash!

Delilah sat in her study, reading a scroll from Ilvana, who had set Aaranon and his young peers on the task of constructing a greenhouse to grow more of the blue thistle. The structure was almost complete. It was the Doktora's intention to restore the plants that had been diminished from the cliff sides and replenish the stores in case of another outbreak, but also to send thousands of doses to her colleagues in other lands. Delilah was amused by Ilvana's most recent communique, where the scientist described how she had gone around to all the Verily farmers collecting goat manure for the project.

There was a solid tap on the door. "Enter," she said, recognizing Olav's large-knuckled rap anywhere. Her stomach grumbled at the sight of the tray he carried.

"Some sustenance for you, Your Majesty," he said.

"Let me guess. Pumpkin soup?"

"Of course, Your Majesty," he said, laying the tray on the low table beside her with a steaming bowl of orange pulp. There was a dab of cream on the top and a few seeds, but it was still pumpkin soup.

"I believe all of my insides have turned orange," Delilah whined.

"You, along with all the lot of Hope City, Your Majesty."

"Yes, I should not complain, Olav. We all suffer together. Even if we must eat pumpkin soup every day for a year, we are alive to do so!"

"That is correct, Your Highness. We are here to complain, and that is a blessing."

Yes, it is a blessing, Delilah mused after Olav departed. She swirled the cream into the soup, suddenly curious once again about the name of the plant that had saved her city. Aelves were a sore subject in Hope, so it was strange that the plant should carry such a name. "I will have to ask Ilvana," she thought. "That woman seems to know everything!" Delilah downed her soup quickly out of duty to her stomach. She put her scrolls and books away and went to her chambers, where she proceeded through her nightly rituals lost in thought and was in bed without being able to remember if she had even run a brush through her thick hair. "Mother would be so annoyed at me if I forgot to brush my hair." The thought of her mother was a punch to the gut, still, after all these years. Delilah wondered if the former queen would be proud of her, running the city and helping to find a cure for the Mungus.

It did not matter. Her mother was gone. She had been gone since Delilah was little more than a girl. It was just Delilah now. She turned over in her bed and felt something crunch under her. It took her a moment to identify the flower head of Aelves' Blessing that she had stuck into her cloak buttonhole so many weeks ago. She had hung her cloak on the hook by the bed and had not worn it since. The thistle must have gotten knocked out as she was getting into bed. She held the starry bloom up to the dim light coming through the window. It was a miracle, this flower, just like all things in the natural world. They held secrets and solutions that were not always visible. As she put the flower under her pillow, she felt a sharp poke to her skin. As she withdrew her hand, she saw a drop of black blood smeared across her pillow in the moonlight. She chuckled to herself to think that her original instinct that the thistle was sharp had been true after all, even with all the good it had brought. She sucked the small puncture on her finger. Then she fell into a strange half-sleep where she dreamed of mushrooms that sang haunting melodies and trees containing doorways to other worlds.

"The world is full of thirst and greed;
Of this one thing, you may trust, indeed.
Hunger makes a soul retreat;
Replaced by a monster's evil feats."
-The Ghost Scribe

Chapter 2: Pirates!

It was not typical for Delilah to awaken with a knife to her throat, but clearly this was not going to be a typical day. Delilah's mind could not process who might be holding the blade, or why, before her training kicked in: she grabbed the wrist of the assailant with one hand and reached behind their head with the other. Using her body as a lever, she catapulted the attacker into a tumble across her bed, their full weight thudding against the far wall. Delilah heard the blade clatter against stone. She scrambled up to stand on her bed, swiping away a trickle of blood from her neck, and looked down at the figure as it gathered itself to stand. In the gray light, Delilah could see a hood and alarmingly muscular arms rounded by snaking tattoos. The creature launched itself at Delilah's legs, knocking her off balance and smashing her head against the unforgiving floor. Blows from powerful arms rained down on her as she struggled to get an advantage. The creature was straddling her, heavier than it should have been. Delilah felt hands close on her neck and panicked as her airpipes crushed. She fanned her arms out in a sweeping motion, like making snow faeries when she was a girl. Her fingertips brushed against the hilt of the weapon that had landed under the bed. Desperately wiggling her fingers, Delilah pulled it toward herself until she could grasp it. With all her strength, she plunged it up into the creature's side, hoping it found its way under ribs into something vital.

For a moment, she thought she had failed, since the grip around her throat did not lessen. There was no sound to indicate the blade had met its mark. Yet in a moment, the heavy body fell forward and trapped her beneath its mass. Delilah gasped and struggled to breathe as she wriggled to get loose from the dead weight of the assassin. The door flew open then, and Olav and two other Sister Guard ran in. The Guard dragged the assailant's body from Delilah as Olav pulled her to her feet.

"Your Majesty!" Olav shouted, "Are you harmed?"

Delilah looked down to see that she was soaked in black blood. "No, it is his," she said.

"Hers," corrected one of the Guard, as she held a torch up to show where leather armor had been shaped and fitted to protect the woman's substantial chest. "You got her right under the armor, Your Majesty. A very lucky blow."

"Lucky," agreed Delilah, still shaken with the sound of blood rushing in her ears. "How did this happen? How did she get in?"

Before anyone could respond, movement on the corpse caught their eye. The tattoos around the woman's giant biceps came alive and began slithering across the floor. Delilah gasped as two glistening serpents raised their heads and hissed at her. The Guard wasted no time chopping at the demons, but the blades went right through them as if they were ghosts, metal ringing out on the stone. The snakelike apparitions hissed again and slipped over each other, disappearing into the corner of the room to vanish through the floor.

"What in the world…" Olav uttered.

"Sea Magick," one of the Guard proclaimed, and pointed with her sword toward the body. The body of the woman, who had easily been twice as wide as Delilah, seemed to be shrinking. Her muscles rippled and contracted, giant hands flickering in the torchlight. At each flicker, her fists became smaller with increasingly slender fingers. The contortions distorted her whole form and lasted but a few moments. What remained was a petite young girl of no more than 17 in the clothing and armor of a woman many times her size.

"Is that not… Savrow's daughter?" the other Guard asked. The girl had disappeared two years prior, and no one had heard from her again. It was largely assumed she had entered the Whayer Wood and turned Beast.

"How strange. She must have joined with the sea folk… pirates probably," Olav mused. "But why try to assassinate the queen?"

"And back to my original question, how did she get in here?" Delilah looked accusingly at the Guard, who shifted under the unusual temper of their monarch.

"A full inquiry will be launched, Your Grace, you may be assured of that," Olav asserted.

⚓

Delilah sat at her desk in the study, a book and a warm cup of spiced goat milk in front of her. The tome was one her father had given her: *The Seafarers of the Netherdeeps*. It had been many years since Delilah had even thought of this text. She mused now, turning the ancient pages. The borders were illuminated with richly colored depictions of wild sea creatures and magickal items, possessed by those who had haunted the waves over centuries. She stopped on one page with a diagram of a strange multi-pronged implement that was described as a "tattooing trident" used to brand those of a particular sea tribe. If regular ink were used, it stated, the recipient of the tattoo would have a traditional inked design on their skin. If, however, the ink was from the giant sea creature, the *Thundercracken*, it had a different effect entirely. The monster rarely needed to use its ink to defend itself, since its 100 tentacles were lined with razor-sharp barbs that easily sliced anything that came within reach. However, on the rare occasion that someone could make it past the Thundercracken's undulating fortress of arms, its last resort was to shoot deadly black smoke through the waters. Nothing could survive the toxins. If, however, the ink could somehow be collected, the liquid contained unthinkable power. Used in a tattoo, the wearer would take on magickal properties and could be transformed into a fighting machine for the tribe: they would become a living manifestation of the Thundercracken's fearsome strength. The tattoos became living things, inhabiting their wearer and feeding off its lifeforce. If the host died, the enchanted tattoos would sap the remaining life from them to become even stronger, returning to the tribe to adorn and possess another member.

Olav interrupted with a light tap on the door before coming in with a few other key members of the Guard. "Your Majesty, we have a report as to how the assassin got in."

"Yes?"

"Ahem, yes, well… She, um… She came through the floor."

"Pardon me?"

"I know it sounds unlikely, but the Guard from the front gates saw a pair of snakes coming over the wall and did not think much of it. A few others reported seeing the snakes and dismissed them, thinking that they were the nightserpents that sometimes come out at this time of year to breed. The pair was last seen by one of the bakers who was making the day's bread in the kitchen, but they disappeared into the corner of the wall that is several floors beneath your chambers. I… uh, I know it does not make sense."

"No, it makes perfect sense," Delilah countered, and pushed the book toward Olav.

"Oh!" Olav said as he skimmed over the pages.

"And what of the girl?"

A senior Sister Guard member, spoke up: "We returned her body to her father. Savrow was distraught, naturally, yet had no idea why his daughter may have joined a sea band. She was always a restless girl, so he did not think it odd that she sought an escape of some kind. Growing up trapped in Hope can be hard on those with a lust for adventure," the elder Guard said wistfully.

"Indeed," Delilah agreed. "Still, the question remains, why would the sea bands want to kill me? We have always been fair in our trading, and we signed that truce with them just last year. We leave them to their piracy so long as they do not harm the citizens of Hope. Why would they jeopardize the good relations we fostered?"

"This, we do not know, Your Highness," said the officer. "However, our entire Guard is now on the alert, especially at the port. They are watching for anything out of the ordinary, any creatures, or even shadows that seem unusual. The Vector may keep out most Beasts, however, sea magick can somehow still allow our enemies to sneak through. We must not take any chances since we do not know what they want or when they might return, or what enchantments they might have at their disposal. This was a pointed attempt on your life, Your Grace. Since it failed, the next assault may not be a single attacker in the night."

"No, I doubt it would be. But they had to try, right? Why send an army when one assassin will do?" Delilah chuckled and the others joined in halfheartedly. The group ushered out except for Olav, who lingered behind.

"Honestly, My Queen, are you alright?"

"Of course I am alright!" Delilah said. "I am alive, am I not?"

"Yes, but I feel we have failed you."

"It was a mistake, Olavfin. Last I checked, we are still human. We may be surrounded by vampwhyres and dessicators, but on this side of the Gloom, we are all still human."

"You are too generous," Olav said, "but I swear to you we will not be so easily sidestepped again."

"Or side-slithered," Delilah snorted.

"You are truly too much, Your Majesty."

"So I have been told."

Delilah returned to bed, as it was still dark. She was not surprised that sleep did not come. The face of the dead girl invaded her mind. She recalled her as a small child in the palace gardens, collecting flowers for a wreath at the Spring Rites. Delilah squeezed her eyes together to remove the sting of tears there, knowing fully that she had no choice but to kill the creature the girl had become. She made herself think instead of the seafarers and why they might want to kill her. They were a loosely organized band, all following a fierce leader. The pirate queen, Jezschmel, had been terrorizing the seas for decades, long before Delilah was born. Delilah's parents had spent much of her childhood defending the ports and waters from Jezschmel's ships. Usually this meant a vigilant watch on the sea, but in one of the worst raids, the pirates had snuck onto land and sacked half the city before the Guard had gotten the upper hand. The threat of assaults from the ocean had been an ever-present reality in Hope. Jezschmel was a frightening presence. Still, Delilah had somehow made peace with her by agreeing to terms of a truce the previous year, way before the Mungus had taken hold. She had found an opening when she learned that Jezschmel was seeking an enchanted necklace that had made its way into Hope's treasury. It was made from braided dryad hair and sea glass from a mirror owned by a fearsome sea witch, named Lahuri.

Delilah could hear her mother's voice telling her the story when she was a girl: "Lahuri was once a human princess who fell into the toxic waters. She was transformed into a powerful sorceress. Sprouting a fish's tail, Lahuri swam until she reached one of the volcanic islands in the middle of the ocean. There, she feasted on sea merchants who were pulled to her like a magnet, her size and power increasing with each meal. Lahuri sat there for years, hunting sailors and growing bigger and more terrifying. One day, a young man who was about to become Lahuri's supper offered to give her a golden mirror to set him free. When Lahuri looked into the mirror, it shattered! She disappeared into the ocean and was never seen again."

"What did she see?" Delilah always asked her mother at this point in the story.

Queen Delilah and the Encroaching Gloom

"She saw the monster she had become. Still, she was a hero to the merfolk who lived in the waters around her island. They worshiped her like a goddess because she kept them safe from the human hunters. The Mer people even called themselves the "Lahur" in her name. The Lahur collected the pieces of the broken mirror from the bottom of the sea and braided them with one strand of hair from each member of their tribe. This created an enchantment that contained Lahuri's power. They gave the necklace to their queen, Nayhami, who was the last great sea queen before Jezschmel."

"What was the necklace's power?" Delilah asked.

"Nobody knows, yet it ended up in our royal treasury when my grandmother, Queen Pharrix, defeated the sea tribes."

The story of the man-eater Lahuri haunted Delilah's childhood dreams. It made sense that the pirate queen Jezschmel yearned for this item, with its legacy of dark magick and its connection to the last sea queens. Having no fondness for the thing, Delilah was glad to have something to negotiate terms of a treaty with the pirates, and more than eager to have it out of her possession. Since the parley, the attacks had ceased. Now Delilah worried that she had been naïve to think that the trinket would keep Jezschmel satisfied for long. It would be more lucrative for the pirates to go back to pillaging and taking anything they wanted. As the terror of the night sizzled out of her veins and questions swirled through her consciousness, Delilah found herself quite sleepy. She dozed into a dreamless slumber.

"Pirates!"

The alarm roused Delilah. She arose instantly and threw on her leather armor, with no time to adorn her usual plate mail. She was out the door, scimitar in hand, before she was fully awake. Delilah barreled out to find the passages of the castle roiling with clashing swords. Her Guard were fully engaged in fighting half-mutant seafolk.

"Your Majesty, fall back!" A senior guard member shouted to her. The soldier was fighting a pirate with six arms, each holding sharp knives.

"As if I would do such a thing!" Delilah growled, jumping in to slice off two of the attacker's arms with one blow. She continued to chop her way through the passage. She pulled a woman with giant ears lined with gold hoops in front of her to block a thrust toward her heart. The woman took the brunt of her sea-comrade's blade. A door flew open, and a pirate dragged out one of the royal advisors by the hair, holding a bone-blade knife to her ribs.

"Is this one important to you, Maggot Queen?" the pirate snarled, her foul fish-breath assaulting Delilah even from yards away. Before Delilah could respond, a silver flash from above rained down, cleaving the nasty creature's head in two. The advisor gasped and pulled away as the ruffian's body crumpled to reveal Olav standing behind her, battle axe dripping with blood.

"They are *all* important to Queen Delilah," Olav said, his chest heaving from the effort.

"Nice work, Olav. Watch out!" she pointed behind him to a pair of ghastly slender creatures who looked as if they had just come from the sea. They dripped with ocean stench, tangled blue-black hair plastered around their translucent faces and pale pink fish-eyes. Their grimaces revealed pointed yellowish teeth as they stalked in unison toward Olav and

Delilah.

"You go high," Delilah nudged Olav, and they ran forward, with battle cries curling from their lungs. Delilah did not see Olav make contact but felt a deluge of blue blood splatter down across her face as she used a double-fisted grip on her weapon to slice up into the monster nearest her. She knew it was a fatal thrust, but as she pulled back, saw the creature's evil face come close. The monster's teeth sank right through her armor into her shoulder. Sharp claws impaled her arm. Delilah grabbed the mess of hair and ripped the head away from her then sliced off the hand that grasped her forearm. The offending hand stayed put, severed from its master yet attached to Delilah's arm by the sharp nails which perforated her skin. She shook it free and as the loose appendage tumbled to the floor, Delilah saw the large gashes that remained on her arm pooling with blood. She ripped a strip of cloth from a tapestry that had been on the castle wall for a century to use as a makeshift bandage.

"That was one of your mother's favorites," Olav said, pretending to scold her. Delilah snickered, yet said a silent apology to her mother as she wrapped and tied the fabric tightly over her arm. She ignored the seething pain from her shoulder, although the leather there was soaked in blood as well with a few of the monster's teeth hooked firmly under the skin.

They heard the pounding steps before they saw her: a massive pirate covered in scars and tattoos wielding a double headed battle axe. Two Sister Guard intercepted her and she easily knocked one out of the way just by raising up her giant elbow. The Guard who fell tried to get up, but Delilah could see her shoulder was dislocated and she could not get a grasp of her weapon. The second Guard got in a good swing with her sword, but it clanged onto the woman's plated shoulder and she, too, was tossed off, crashing her head into the stone wall, her skull irreparably shattered. The dead Guard slid to the floor, leaving a smear of pink blood and brains. As Delilah got closer, she could see that two of the pirate's tattoos, the ones encircling her arms, were serpents like those that had entered her bedchamber that morning. They raised their heads from the woman's biceps and hissed at Delilah, recognizing her.

Despite the urgency, Delilah felt she needed to at least try to find out why they were here. "What does your mistress want?" she shouted.

The woman snarled, "Vengeance!" and ran at her, swinging the axe in large arcs.

Olav exercised an impressive feat that Delilah had only seen once before when he was younger and playing Bladder Ball for a championship match: he ran at the pirate and slid, feet first, his entire weight launching forward like a missile toward the encroacher's legs. The pirate became tangled and, losing her balance, began to fall forward. Delilah took the opportunity and slid also. As the weight of her large opponent came tumbling down, Delilah propped her weapon up with all her strength to impale the woman between her chest plates. For the second time that day, Delilah had the weight of a dead attacker on top of her, this one truly crushing her frame as she struggled to get free. Olav and the injured Guard rolled the corpse from her. They began to witness a warping and gyrating of the giant pirate's skin as it shrunk and contracted. This time, Olav was prepared and stepped on the neck of one of the snake tattoos as it departed its host, handily slicing off its head. The serpent's parts dissolved into a puddle of ink. Olav went after the other one, but it was too fast and slid into a corner of the castle, disappearing into the wall.

A young boy was left in the shell of the she-pirate. He could be no more than fourteen, Delilah observed sadly. "Do you recognize him?" she asked Olav and the other Guard. They shook their heads. They looked up, hearing a commotion at the end of the passageway. Several of Delilah's soldiers came in with a prisoner: a gnarled old pirate with one big eye in the middle of her forehead.

"The others are dead, Your Majesty," the most senior Guard announced. "There were fifteen of them on the lower floors."

Delilah counted quickly, "Six up here. Are you sure there are no more? It seems a measly number for an attack on a heavily guarded palace."

"The Guard has secured the compound. There are no others to be seen, but that does not mean there is not a second deployment in wait somewhere. We are scouting the coast."

"Our fallen Guard—who is she?" Delilah looked remorsefully toward the casualty, the woman who had given her life defending her.

"Varren," said Olav. "Fifteen years in service."

Delilah shook her head. "Notify the family and give her a hero's burial. Her family will be taken care of." Olav nodded in acknowledgement. Delilah continued: "I will go to the Healer's to get cleaned up. Then bring this one to the Throne Room," she gestured toward the gnarled old pirate. "I would like to have a word with her." As she said this, the woman spat in her direction and received a slap from a nearby Guard. "Try to behave yourself," Delilah warned the one-eyed brigand, and walked past her, holding the blood-soaked bandage on her arm.

"What have you done to yourself this time, Your Majesty?" Helanza had been roused from bed. A few of her young apprentices were still in their nightclothes, attending to the injured.

"Do you think I would do this to myself, my friend?" Delilah tried to laugh, but the wounds were starting to burn and bubble.

"The weapon must have been poisoned," the healer observed.

"The weapon was fish saliva," Delilah muttered.

"Ah, that makes sense," Helanza said, reaching for some pliers to pick out several hooked teeth from Delilah's shoulder. Delilah winced as the healer carefully wiggled the sharp barbs to loosen them from the flesh. "These are hollow," Helanza remarked. "Probably filled with venom. These mutants usually have toxic body fluids."

Now that Helanza mentioned it, Delilah felt the burning across her face from the blood that had spattered on her during the battle. She had hardly noticed it with the searing in her arm and shoulder.

"You should really get into a full bath," Helanza suggested. "Ladies! Draw a bath for the Queen! Fill the tub with Orgwort and Hellsbane. It will counteract the poison. It will hurt, though, Your Majesty. I apologize."

"See to the others, Helanza," Delilah gestured to members of the Sister Guard who were holding arms and heads nearby.

"Nonsense, they will wait. Nothing is as serious as your injuries."

The bath did hurt more than Delilah could have anticipated, but it was also a relief to remove the scorching that seemed to be burrowing through her skin everywhere the sea-mutants' blood touched. She was left with large welts across her face and arms, as if she had been burned by hot oil.

"They will heal. I doubt there will be scars" said Helanza, as Delilah turned her head to look at the marks in the mirror.

"Well, you must know by now I am not that concerned about my appearance," Delilah said.

"Yes," Helanza said with a sniff, "it is well known that you are careless in your… queenly presence."

"Somehow, that did not really sound like a compliment," Delilah noted, and they laughed.

Helanza had been her mother's Royal Healer, and Delilah's own from the time she was a little girl. The medicine woman was one of just a few of the royal household that had been retained after the coup that took her parents' lives. There had been too much corruption and betrayal; most of the advisors and entourage that had surrounded the Queen and King had to be purged. It was one of the more brutal things Delilah had ever done, although it was necessary to establish trust and legitimacy for her own rule. Helanza was an exception because she had never shown any interest in politics or gaining advantage with the Court. She cared only about medicine and this had saved her.

Freshly clothed and with clean bandages on her wounds, Delilah sat upon her throne and called for the prisoner to be brought to her. She had asked that they feed the pirate first, which the Guard had argued was too humane treatment for the "fish-gilled barbarian," but Delilah had insisted. The woman did, indeed, have gills, Delilah noticed when she was brought before her, limping.

"Bring her a chair," Delilah said, looking steadily into the pirate's single eye, which blinked under her gaze.

"But Your Majesty…"

Delilah turned her eyes to the Guard who spoke out, and the woman quickly retreated and returned with a chair for the old sailor. As the crone sat, a huge groan escaped her and she tried, unsuccessfully, to suck it back into her puckered mouth.

"You must have been serving Jezschmel for a long time," Delilah said.

"Yes, Cretin- ooph!" a nudge from a Guard corrected her. "Yes, *Your Majesty*" she said, with an exaggerated wave of her arm.

"What it is about Jezschmel that you find so worthy of loyalty?"

"Why would you care?"

"Well, it is curious to me: soldiers like you, willing to die for a pirate. She must be quite a leader."

"She is our *Queen*, not that you would know what that means, you whining infant."

"I do not quite remember… How is it that she became your queen?"

"You know very well, child, how she became queen. Your great-grandmother, Pharrix, killed the last great Sea Queen before Jezschmel."

"And then how did Jezschmel rise to power? Oh yes, that is right: by slaughtering everyone who might have tried to take the throne, including her own sisters."

"A legacy we are proud of, *Your Majesty*, as none of those crawling vermin deserved to be in power. You see, unlike you *humans*, we do not believe in myths like a "divine right" to lead by succession. Those who can take power by force deserve to lead. Those who get slaughtered deserve to die. But then, maybe you believe that, too? Did you not participate in the coup that slaughtered your own parents?" Her one eye was trained on Delilah with fierce intensity.

Delilah could hear intakes of breath around the chamber. She blinked but did not drop her gaze from the one glassy eye that stared intently at her. "Of that, you are mistaken, lady. But let us not quarrel about ancient history. Tell me, what is it that your queen wants?"

"Vengeance!"

"Yes, I have heard that, but for what?"

"For poisoning her, of course."

"Poisoning her?"

"Oh please," the pirate scoffed, "do not play at innocence, Queen, it does not suit you."

"I am sorry, but of this I have no knowledge. Trust me, if I had attempted to poison your queen, she would be quite dead and not around to make false accusations."

"Lahuri's necklace—if you insist on feigning ignorance. The necklace is cursed, and you knew it! Nice work, by the way, getting her to believe it was a coveted treasure. She unfortunately trusted your integrity enough to make a pact, which I am sure she will never do again."

"What kind of curse?"

"Please, must we carry out this charade? Really, Majesty, 'tis beneath you."

"What kind of curse?"

All in the room tensed. "The curse of the Lahur, the followers of Lahuri. Do you not know how that item came into your treasury? You must know!"

"No, I do not. I was told tales of Lahuri as a child, but I know nothing of how the necklace came to be ours."

"Then you are oblivious as well as entitled."

Delilah spoke slowly to steady her response: "Perhaps this is true. There are a great many things I was not told as a child upon which I wish I had been more educated."

"Well then, I will enlighten you. It was your great-grandmother, Pharrix, who slew the Lahur ruler, Queen Nayhami. The necklace was made for the Mer-queen. Do you know that it contains a strand of hair from every one of the merfolk who lived in her entire queendom? If you have a hair of a Mer, you have their soul, you know? Can you see every one of your subjects giving up a piece of their soul to make you a gift, Majesty? That is true loyalty, true love and devotion."

"And why did Pharrix kill Queen Nayhami? I know a bit about my great-grandmother, but have never heard this tale."

"Oh, it is not a tale. It is fact. Pharrix killed the Mer-queen for rights to fish those waters. It was after the Gloom had begun to spread around the world, and those parts still had a few areas that were not tainted. Pharrix was selfish and greedy. When Nayhami argued that her own kind needed to eat from the waters, too, Pharrix chopped off her head and took the necklace. Your people have never been merciful to us sea dwellers, and that was only the beginning. Pharrix chased the merfolk from that region and then fished until there was nothing left. There was nothing for the queendom already living in the waters there and then nothing for Pharrix's people either. Nayhami would have shared with her, too, that is the ridiculous part. The Mer-queen was ready to negotiate terms to divide some of the region's bounty, but that was not good enough for Pharrix. She wanted it all, so she just slaughtered Nayhami and took what she wanted."

"And what is the nature of the necklace's curse?" Delilah asked.

The old woman tsked and shook her head, clearly not believing Delilah was not informed on this topic, but she responded: "It is the mirror that is the secret of the necklace's curse—the mirror that destroyed the giant sea witch, Lahuri. It was enchanted, you see. The boy who brought it to Lahuri did not do so by chance. He brought it to her to destroy her. He was just an apprentice then, but he later became a great sorcerer. The mirror was one of his first successful acts of magick, and he created it to impress his mentor. It worked! He followed in that mentor's footsteps to become one of the most powerful magicians this world has known." The pirate paused and looked at Delilah, her one eye stern and accusing.

"Who?" Delilah asked.

"Aldruid the Wise," the old woman said, leaning in to watch Delilah's face.

"But Aldruid was Pharrix's father! My mother's great-grandfather!"

"Exactly, and Pharrix came back to finish her father's dirty work. Aldruid destroyed the great Mer Goddess Lahuri with the enchanted mirror, and then his daughter destroyed the Mer who worshiped her. This is why it is so strange that your family kept this from you. It is the ruthless legacy of your foul birth."

"Perhaps my mother did not know," Delilah hoped out loud.

"Or perhaps this was a secret you were not trusted with," the pirate said pointedly.

"If the mirror was enchanted to cause harm," Delilah thought out loud, "why would the necklace made from it not harm Queen Nayhami?"

"The mirror's magic is that when one looks upon it, they can see all the pain they have ever caused to others. When the sea witch, Lahuri, looked upon it, she could see the monster she'd become, feasting upon innocents. It destroyed her. The necklace made for the Mer-queen Nayhami was created from pieces of that mirror, rounded by the sea, but still containing the same magick. Nayhami's tribe called themselves the *Lahur* merfolk, because they were followers of Lahuri, yet they were a peaceful kind. They Mer people worshiped Lahuri as a Goddess because she looked like them and protected the waters from fishermen and adventurers who might harm them, but they themselves were a rather timid sort. The Lahur queen, Nayhami, had done no horrific deeds. Her subjects loved her, as she was a kind and fair ruler. Therefore, she had nothing to fear from the mirror. Her only danger was a human murderer, your great-grandmother."

"Pharrix. And what of Jezschmel? Should she not have anything to fear from the mirror if she is truly the leader you say she is?"

"All pirates have histories of dark deeds, Queen. You must know that. But the necklace is affecting her in quite a different way."

"How is that?"

"It is making her… sensitive."

"Sensitive?"

"Yes. She is a changed woman. She cries at the death of a moth in a candle and weeps for puppies she had as a child, long in their graves. It has made her an ineffective pirate."

"I see. And she views this as my fault?"

"Well, clearly, she blames you! She assumes you knew of the necklace's power and gave it to her to disarm her."

"She obviously did not know the necklace's power either, so why would she presume I did?"

"It is your family's legacy! She assumed you tricked her."

"So why did she want it so badly if she did not even know its power?"

"It is a symbol of the sea folk: Lahuri was one of the most awesome sea goddesses of all times, and the necklace was made by Lahuri's merfolk followers for their Mer Queen. It was gruesomely taken from that queen of the sea-tribes, as has always been done to us by your kind. Jezschmel felt that it should be returned to us. When it started to affect her so… deeply… she began to believe that it is because the person who is heir to the necklace's traitorous inheritance is still living and that the curse could only be broken by killing you. She blames you and thinks you tricked her to disempower her, another betrayal by your kind. She thought the spell could be broken once the last link in the chain of deception was destroyed."

"Kill me and regain the power to kill without mercy or feeling: Lahuri's legacy."

"And Pharrix's legacy, too. Recall that she killed the Mer Queen without any thought. Her act infused the necklace with even greater magick that Jezschmel hoped to reclaim."

"I wonder if Pharrix was haunted by the necklace?"

The old woman sputtered and cleared her throat: "Why do you say that?"

"Well, she hid it away in the royal treasury. She did not boast of it, and I swear my mother must not have known. She was only passing on legends she heard from her own mother. I do not think her grandmother, Pharrix, ever told anyone the real story. Perhaps she glimpsed the horrors of her own deeds and hid the necklace away. I wonder how I can regain Jezschmel's trust? I did not attempt to fool her, I swear it. Might there be another resolution? What if I took the necklace back and replaced it with another item from the treasury — anything Jezschmel might choose."

Delilah heard muttering and gasps from the onlookers, whom she had forgotten were even present. "What?" Delilah asked, looking about at the faces of her Guard and advisors. "There is nothing in those chambers that I care for! There is nothing more valuable than preserving our queendom. Did anything in the royal treasury protect us from the Mungus when it came? Gold and jewels do not keep us safe! They do not keep the Gloom at bay and they do not fight our battles for us! We are living in a different world from the one where my parents and their parents accrued wealth of diamonds and objects. Only loyalty to each other, Science, and cooperation with others on this forsaken planet will protect us now!" Delilah saw heads shaking and skeptical looks upon the faces in the room, although no one spoke up to disagree.

"Well, Jezschmel believes that the curse can only be removed if the giver is killed," the old pirate spoke up.

"Or if the giver agrees to take on the curse herself," a voice said from the doorway. Helanza had appeared to check on the Queen.

Delilah looked at her, surprised to hear her interject. Helanza never expressed anything publicly that did not somehow involve healing, especially anything involving matters of the past. "Helanza—you know about this curse?"

"Yes, Your Majesty."

"Is it true? I can take on the curse myself?"

"Yes, but I would not advise it."

"Well, it would not be the first time I have gone against your advice," Delilah smiled.

"No, Your Majesty. In fact, you make quite a habit of it," the healer observed.

The old pirate coughed: "You are not the woman I thought you were, Queen Delilah."

"Well, thank goodness for that!" Delilah exclaimed.

The castle was preparing to receive a royal guest: the Pirate Queen, Jezschmel. It could very well be a trap, but Delilah had insisted upon extending an offer of peace, once again. In good faith, they had offered the hospitality of Hope to Jezschmel to help her with the problem of the enchanted necklace. Delilah had reminded her advisors that there had only been one fatality on their side from the assault on the palace. There were twenty-one dead pirates on their side. The one-eyed pirate, Admiral Razzle-Eye, had been safely returned to her waiting ship. As speculated, there had been a slew of other pirates sitting in wait off the coast, ready to attack. They were watching for a signal from Razzle-Eye, who had a trained silver seabird under her cloak the whole time. If she released the bird, it was the sign for them to proceed with the attack, sending thousands more pirates toward the castle to fight.

The first group had been scouts. They were led by the Admiral and sacrificed themselves, trying to accomplish as much as they could with consolidated resources. Delilah had wondered why they sent the old lady: an infirm pirate seemed a liability. Razzle-Eye had been a soldier, serving Jezschmel's sea-army her whole life and rising through the ranks. She was willing to lay down her life before releasing the sea bird to inform the attackers lying in wait that they should come on land and continue their offensive. Now, the old officer was an emissary of peace, bringing a message back to their pirate queen that there had been a misunderstanding and that Queen Delilah wished to reclaim the cursed necklace and re-negotiate terms of a truce.

The Lahur weavers had created a charm to make the necklace contract on the wearer's neck, only to be detached through death. The necklace was securely fastened to Jezschmel, and no tool, spell, or weapon had been able to remove it, though they had tried. Now it became known, based upon Helanza's familiarity with the subject, that the curse could be removed by the giver of the necklace, if she were to take on the curse herself. There was not much time to prepare, especially with clearing the palace of the dead ruffians and scrubbing the passageway of sea-slime and blood from the battle. Still, the kitchens prepared a hurried feast in Jezschmel's honor. It was laid upon a banquet table in the Great Hall. The Guard were in attendance and prepared to defend against an onslaught if the pirates decided to use the invitation for foul play.

Queen Delilah stood at the far end of the table, flanked by her advisors and Guard as Jezschmel was announced and entered the Great Hall. The imposing warrior strode in, dressed for battle, with her scruffy entourage in tow. The women of Jezschmel's army were known for their fierceness, definitely not for their beauty. The beastly crew were an ugly lot, some with tentacles or other deformities, giant lumps that sprouted eyes and extra or missing limbs. A fishy stench encircled them. After their visit the prior year, Delilah had joked that their smell was the scariest thing about them, as it took weeks to air out the palace from the lingering rot. Jezschmel strode across the hall. Her black leather armor looked as if it were made from strips directly woven onto her large, muscled form. Delilah could not help wondering at the application of it and how such a complicated garment would be removed. It was well known that a disadvantage of life at sea was that metal rusted in a fortnight, so battle gear was generally made of wood or leather. However, it was also said that Jezschmel's armor was made from the hide of sea monsters she slew, with scales that were flexible and yet tougher than iron. What was odd about the pirate queen's dress today was a black fishing-net veil that she wore over her face, as if in mourning. It shrouded her eyes and made her look somehow less intimidating than when they last met.

"Queen Delilah," Jezschmel growled, extending a formidable calloused hand. Delilah grasped the pirate's arm at the elbow and they clasped forearms in the seafarers' greeting, staring into each other's faces. Delilah was not a small woman, yet she felt dwarfed by the sea queen. Jezschmel's strong body was trained by a lifetime of fighting the sailing lines, heaving the cables and heavy ropes that forced the ships across the wind and waves. The sea queen pulled her in close so that Delilah's eyes became blurry trying to see past the netted veil into the pirate's eyes. During this exchange, the Guard tensed with hands upon weapons, watching the pair of queens, but also keeping eyes on the motley assemblage of oddly-limbed pirates.

"If I had more time to prepare, I would have baked you a cake," Delilah said.

"Oh, Sister, *please*, let us not pretend to be so civilized!" Jezschmel laughed and released Delilah's arm, pulling out the nearest chair and flopping heavily into it. Spatters of forced laughter came from her party and echoed among Delilah's guard. The moment of tense engagement relaxed into a more typical state visit and the guests began to find places to sit. It had been expected that Jezschmel would sit in the large chair at the opposite end of the table, so it sent the servers into a flurry to suddenly have her seated right next to their queen. Delilah was caught a bit surprised as well to be so close to her rival. Platters of food began to arrive and the ravenous pirate crew began ripping into anything that was placed before them. Jezschmel lifted her veil back over her head before grabbing a passing turkey leg and gnawing upon it. "Sea birds are just not this meaty," she said between large mouthfuls, rivulets of juice dripping down.

The pirates seemed to be starving, observed Delilah, who had no intention of eating during this event and was instead sipping a glass of ale. Over the cup, she noticed that Jezschmel's eyes, now uncovered, were puffy and rimmed with red. "Queen Jezschmel… may we talk of the necklace? If you would like to wait until after we feast, we can do so, but I see no reason to delay our most important conversation."

"Please!" said Jezschmel, wiping a smear of grease from her chin with her arm. "I want nothing more than to be rid of this accursed thing," she pulled at the braided band with a forefinger. It seemed to come awake, sparkling with ripples of light across the particles of mirrored glass, then growing and snapping back as if a living thing upon the pirate's neck.

"First," Delilah said, "I need you to know that I had no idea of the necklace's powers. I am ashamed to be so unfamiliar with the legacy of my ancestors. I only recently learned from your admiral of its enchantment."

"Yes, my trusty Razzle-Eye!" Jezschmel raised a glass to the old pirate, who was seated across the table. The admiral kept her single eye trained on the two queens, with one hand around a weapon on her belt and her other hand scooping mounds of roasted vegetables into her mouth.

"I was glad to meet the Admiral, despite the… unfortunate nature of our acquaintance," Delilah said. "She enlightened me to how the necklace has harmed you."

Jezschmel stopped eating and pushed her plate away. "Harmed me? Harmed *me?* Ha! You must be joking. It is *I* who have done the harm. I have been harming others my whole life since I stabbed my two older sisters in their sleep to remove them from the line of succession!" A deep gurgling sob escaped Jezschmel's throat. "They were in the way, and I… removed them… my own *sisters!*" She threw the veil back over her face, which she buried in her massive, greasy hands, her shoulders wracking. The other pirates, on cue, looked away and began uttering loud remarks to one another, suddenly becoming deeply involved in banter with their neighbors.

Delilah leaned in and placed a hand upon the solid rock of the queen's shoulder. Eyes of the seafarers closely attended her movements amidst the ruckus of their distraction. "Let us not delay," Delilah said, and reached both hands gently around to the back of Jezschmel's neck. A few pirates pushed chairs back and stood alert, but Jezschmel seemed unconcerned, consumed by her grief. Delilah fumbled to find a way to release the necklace's hold. As she reached to see if there were bindings on the back, the band seemed to relax and fall loose into a wide oval. What had been braided and woven tight was now a large, messy loop of twisted strings. Delilah easily pulled it over Jezschmel's head and placed it over her own. The limp ring of a necklace came alert and re-braided itself to be taught once again on Delilah's neck, humming and flickering flashes of light from mirrored fragment to fragment. It calibrated and the flashes quieted and became still.

Jezschmel looked up then. "But… why? We have not negotiated yet."

"There is no need," Delilah said, fingering the braids, now tautly encircling her neck.

"Your trust is all I require. I had lost that, and I am willing to do whatever I can to restore it."

Jezschmel stood and pulled the veil from her head, flinging it to the stone. "I did not think it was possible, but you have restored my trust, Queen Delilah!"

"I am grateful for that and hope there will be years of peace between our queendoms. But Jezschmel, there is just one more thing that I must ask you," Delilah said, looking closely at the pirate queen.

"What is it?" the brigand looked perplexed.

"Your sisters—How do you feel about them now?"

Jezschmel sneered, animation returning to her beautiful face: "Those bitches had it coming!"

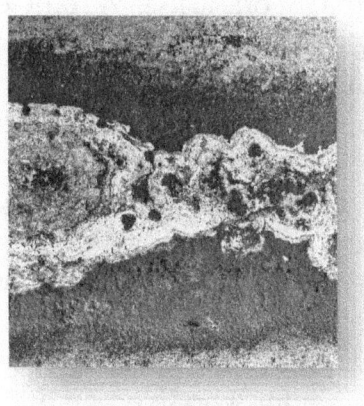

"Life is sweet, and life is sour
Around and around, at any hour
It may be rancid at half past noon
And then turn succulent under the moons"
-The Ghost Scribe

Chapter 3: The Encroaching Gloom

With things returning to relative normalcy after the Mungus and the pirate attacks, Delilah took once again to visiting her subjects and wandering her extensive gardens. Jezschmel had surprised her by returning several weeks after their treatise to deliver a rare flowering bush from across the ocean. It had suffered the journey and the sea air, yet Delilah was able to plant it and restore it to health. New blossoms, swirled with gold and peach, were beginning to form. Delilah smiled now, thinking of the pirate queen, who had blushed when she had delivered the plant. She wondered how old Jezschmel could be, since she had been terrorizing the sea back in the time of Delilah's parents. Perhaps the sea queen was immortal? That had been known to happen to some royalty with dryad lineage who only aged when on land. So long as they kept adrift the massive ocean and no mortal injuries befell them, they would never die. If that were true, Jezschmel risked much by returning to Hope. This last visit, Delilah had noticed a new strand of silver hair tucked back into the pirate's leather hairband.

On this morning, the sky was clear with only wisps of smoky gray toward the sea. One could believe there were no troubles in the world in the refuge of a fragrant orchard, like the one Delilah ambled through now. She had awoken in the dark to take care of royal business, affixing her seal to several documents and responding to letters from royalty, great thinkers, and scientists in other realms. Much of this correspondence traveled by sea, with the bumpy and malformed seafaring folk. They risked the Gloom that hovered near sea level, bringing mail from port to port for a few coins. It was mostly reliable, but there was always the risk that ships could become lost at sea or captured by marauders. Other times, those who transported the letters became more feral and unpredictable with each visit. One sea merchant was a misshapen woman with one arm and some patches of scales on her face. The lone sailor seemed more shrunken each time she arrived at Hope's docks in her beat-up vessel. Her neck disappeared until her head merged into the top of her shoulders, her eyes becoming redder, teeth growing pointier, and eyelids doubling. The last visit, the sailor had snapped with her sharp jaws at Delilah's hand when she reached out to pass her a bundle of scrolls. The queen sent her away and told the Guard at the wharf not to let her into port anymore. The effect of the Gloom was unpredictable. Some could live in strange transformations with no real disadvantage for decades while others became monstrous overnight.

Delilah carried a letter that she was quite nervous about. She was writing to a reclusive biophysicist named Lord Xanfar who lived on the other side of the Whayer Wood. He had turned Beast and was reputed to have the countenance of a whayerwolf. He had been a noble before entering the Wood in search of his true love who had been devoured by creatures in the dark forest. He returned but was forever changed by the Gloom. Now, Lord Xanfar lived in a stone castle and dressed in elaborate costumes like the courts of centuries prior. In his lonely refuge, he sat speculating about tree dreams and how plants talk to one another. He had a strange theory that one might be able to tap into the communication of plants to find out the secrets of the universe. The plants themselves had changed with the Gloom. Many became moving creatures with arms of vines, some with faces and mouths, and some that were even reported to speak. In consorting with those, the lone scientist had discovered that the trees had a sophisticated messaging system that allowed them to know what was going on in all parts of the forest. If a new whayerchild was born on the other side of the Wood, the trees knew about it before anyone else. It was getting them to tell the story that was the trick, Xanfar reported.

Delilah had gotten a long letter from the scientist, telling her about a conversation he had with a great Andromeda tree deep in the woods. The ancient tree had told Xanfar that the stars spoke to trees just as they speak to the animals to tell them to migrate. The patterns in the stars are encoded in their bark and help them to know when to slow down their juices to go into slumber through the dark months. Delilah found this intriguing and wrote a long and wordy essay back to Xanfar about the sentience of trees, a topic about which she had much to say. Now, delivering the thick, wax-encrusted envelope, she wondered if she had said anything at all. She hoped the scientist would not find her ramblings to be that of a foolish queen who thought herself to be an intellectual. Delilah was confident in most things, but when she engaged with the thinking elite, she felt the shortcomings of her childhood of luxury.

As a child, tutors had instructed Delilah in archaic languages and warriors had trained her in battle, but she learned little of true relevance to the world around them. Her early education taught diplomacy and how to hold a crystal chalice when dining with an ally versus a potential rival but did not explain the secrets held in a dying leaf or the meaning of one owl call versus another. Give her a scimitar and Delilah knew exactly what to do. Ask her how the spider knows when to build and when to dismantle her web and Delilah was filled with the gaping awareness that there was so much of her world she did not understand.

Queen Delilah and the Encroaching Gloom

All Delilah had learned about leadership she had learned on the battlefield, and all she had learned of science she had learned from magicians and lonely geniuses.

At the end of the orchard on the southeast corner of the palace grounds, the tumbling fields of flowers and old bent apple trees gave way to the dark woods. There, a giant bell was hung, suspended from a gnarled white shoak tree. Delilah rang the bell, and the sound reverberated throughout the landscape, echoing off the hills with its silvery voice. There was a visible purpleness to the Gloom; one could see the mass of it as it gathered around the trees at the edge of the forest, its grayish cast spilling out and vanishing in the light where the sun fell on the grass. It was almost as if the forest contained the Gloom. Still, Delilah had heard some disturbing rumors about the Gloom beginning to spread. Usually, it stayed mostly in the lowlands and across the ocean. The higher territories, such as on the hilly bluffs where Hope was settled, were typically safe from danger. The Ancients, a shamanic sect worshipped by Delilah's grandparents, had helped to create the Vector with a powerful enchantment around Hope. It placed the protective bubble around the city when the Gloom was formed. No one knew exactly how it worked or its true structure, but it seemed to help keep the Gloom and Beasts from spilling in, while also making it harder to leave. Those who passed through the Vector out of Hope felt a startling tingling and warping of sensations that made it seem as if one's mind and body were being pulled and bent. This way, if a resident of Hope accidentally got too near to the Gloom, the Vector would let them know they were in dangerous territory. Visitors who entered from the ports would jolt and distort as they passed through, their faces and bodies bending as they struggled to push through the charged barrier.

Perhaps the enchantment was losing strength, Delilah considered as she watched the fringes of the Wood tremble and vibrate. She had received reports that there were places where the Gloom seemed to be expanding and even crossing the barrier of the Vector, growing into areas it had never been before. A farmer in the south said she woke up one morning and her sheep shed was enclouded in Gloom, the animals turned demented and wild. The livestock had to be released into the Wood before they hurt anyone. The thought of those mad sheep filled Delilah with dread now, as she waited for her message to be heard. Delilah had befriended a satyr, who was her usual form of mail delivery. Belk was a kind soul: his hooves and furry haunches and horns were the only beastly things about him. He spent most of his days trying to run from the monsters in the forest that would make a meal of him. He was fast and could become invisible at will, so he was generally safe from harm. He would sometimes appear out of thin air just on the other side of the Gloom, startling Delilah. She waited for such an appearance now, expecting the light to shift and for the satyr to be there, like usual, alighting out of nothingness.

Delilah saw something back in the trees. There was a darkness like a form there and she heard branches snap. She thought her eyes must be fooling her, because for a moment, she thought she saw Jarvis. Although her brother had been dead for fifteen years, he was always in her mind, so she was sure it was playing tricks on her now. The figure vanished into the gray air. Delilah stared into the shadowed gaps between the trees, trying to focus on the fuzzy outlines. Out of that very spot, a shape emerged, dark and furry. It shot like an arrow directly out of the Wood toward Delilah, buffering in the air for a second as it crossed the Vector and leaped toward her. Delilah saw its furry frame launching on all fours with a strangely human head and pale face. Giant fangs opened and Delilah's body responded with her instinct to fight. She unleashed the scimitar that hung from her belt and held her stance as the creature advanced. She had but a moment to angle her weapon and slice with both hands toward the monster, feeling the impact as his muscled body encountered the blade. She felt hot liquid pour over her and the weight of the beast knocked her off her feet to tumble backward. She quickly scrambled back up and held the scimitar aloft, ready to strike again.

It was not necessary. The beast lay dying, a large gash across his neck and chest. He panted, with his yellow eyes trained on Delilah seething hatred. It was a vampwhyr, she realized, seeing now how his veiny bald head was almost human atop a wolflike form. Two giant teeth gleamed as blood spilled from the corner of his mouth. He lay gasping, then opened and closed his mouth, looking as if he were trying to say something. Delilah leaned in, trying to hear if he had final words for her. The creature jumped at her with all his strength, mouth open and teeth aimed at Delilah's neck. She felt herself being pulled backwards, just out of the path of the creature's fangs. The monster tried to pull himself up on his front legs, but they buckled under him and he fell forward onto his stomach with his face in the dirt. He lay motionless.

Delilah turned to see whose hands had saved her only to see Belk's sweet face twisted with horror. Her friend was shaking, his bare torso heaving with the effort of pulling her out of harm's way.

"What excellent timing you have!" Delilah said, her voice unsteady.

"Oh, my dear, this is all my fault!" said the fawn, dancing on furry legs, his hooves pattering the earth in his distress. He wrung his hands in front of him. "Please forgive me for touching you, Your Majesty. I meant no disrespect, I promise!"

"Silly! You saved my life!"

"Yes, but it is my fault! I was being tracked. This vampwhyr was following me all morning. I thought I had lost him, but I led him right to you!"

"Belk, please! You must not blame yourself for the evil nature of monsters. These things will suck the blood from anything they can sink their teeth into." She went over and with her boot kicked the vampwhyr over onto its back. "Huh. I have never seen one up close before." She began to lean in again to inspect the ghoulish face and felt the satyr's hands on her shoulders.

"Sorry, sorry Your Majesty, so sorry for my hands, but you must not get close. They are *undead,* so who knows what they are capable of. They have been known to regenerate."

"Not this one." With a flash, Delilah severed the ugly head from its body with her blade. At this moment, three Sister Guard ran down the hill, weapons drawn. "You are a little late, ladies," said Delilah.

"Are you alright, Your Majesty?"

"Yes, thanks to my friend here." The Guard looked Belk up and down with distaste on their faces. Delilah gestured toward the corpse: "Take this body and burn it. Burn the head separately and make sure to throw the ashes back into the Wood."

"Shall one of us stay with you?"

"That is not necessary. I shall finish business with my friend and then return to the castle."

"I am sorry we were not here sooner. The Guard on the wall saw what was happening and deployed us. We got here as soon as we could." The young lady looked uncomfortable. "Perhaps you should bring a Guard with you when you venture down here, Your Majesty?"

"Hah! In my own gardens? I have been walking my estate alone since I was a girl. I will not stop now because of a measly vampwhyr."

"Yes, Your Majesty, yet it should not have been able to cross the Vector and still it did."

"I will not let fear control my life," Delilah said. "Take the Beast away."

The Guard carried the carcass off. Delilah searched for the large envelope she had dropped during the fight. It had dirt in the creases and some spattered blood across it. Delilah shook it out and wiped the blood across the grass.

"Is this for Lord Xanfar?" Belk inquired. Delilah nodded. The satyr said, "He will smell the blood."

"Yes, I would imagine he would."

"I will tell him what happened."

"Please."

The message back from Xanfar came within days and was as fervent and excited as Delilah's letter had been, reassuring her that he did not think her foolish at all. He expressed appreciation for her impressions and shared his own ponderings about the way the trees were transforming. Delilah caught her breath at the end of the letter, where Xanfar invited her to his castle. He explained that Belk would be informed of a secret method of transport that would keep her safe on the journey and untouched by the Gloom. When she assembled her Council and informed them of her intentions to go on the journey, they flatly refused. It was not like them to tell Delilah she could not do something. They might try to reason or dissuade the Queen, but rarely did they express outright rejection of her ideas.

"Well, I do not believe I need your permission," Delilah countered, reminding them who was the monarch in the room.

"No, Your Majesty, you do not need our permission," said one of the younger members of the Council. "Still, we do not agree with this plan at all, and we will not support it." The woman was not much older than Delilah and had been selected into the group of elders because of her seriousness and excellence in the field of monstrology.

"Doktora Sinsarel, you know I hold your opinion in high regard. I have not ventured out of Hope in years, disregarding my occasional trip to Verily. I can bring a small detachment of soldiers with me. Lord Xanfar's family have been our allies for decades! Remember when the boerbeasts packed together and were threatening the periphery? They gored dozens of our livestock before Xanfar sent out centaurs to hunt them and bring down their numbers. He did us a great service then and has been a friend at other times when we needed intelligence passed from the other side of the Wood. Do you recall that he was the one who got the message to Queen Ebonne from the Great Desert Plains when we ran low on antitoxin to fight batel-bite poison? He assisted with that transaction and even took the time to decode the antitoxin so we could fight the venom with ingredients we have here in Hope. Other than my safety, what is your objection?"

"Other than your safety!" Sinsarel exclaimed. "The Council's primary task is to protect and advise you so that you can be of service to Hope! What is there, Your Majesty, other than your safety?" The doctor shook her head. "I am not even concerned about your trip across the Wood. There are many secret ways to travel through the forest without harm. It is Xanfar I am most worried about. Once you are alone in his castle with him, with your defenses down, who is to say when he will transform further and decide you are worth eating?"

"Really, Doktora! Xanfar has been in his current form for ages!" Delilah protested.

"The Gloom is unpredictable, Your Majesty. It can sit dormant and pop up when a threat appears or when one is overly… excited."

"Is that what you all are really worried about?" Delilah looked around the room at the faces of her Council. Some dropped their eyes. "Are you worried that Xanfar will get too 'excited'?" Delilah began pacing. "Well, I have to say, I did not take you for a bunch of prudes. Really! I am not a child, people. I can handle myself if anyone becomes 'too excited' in my company! I have fought alongside most of you. You know I can defend myself. Hell, I have defended you and saved a few of your lives, if you have forgotten!"

"We have not forgotten," it was an elder member who had been on the Council since Delilah was crowned. "…and no one cares with whom you get 'excited,' Your Majesty. We care only for the welfare of your person. If you become… distracted, it may be deadly for you. Who is to say Xanfar is not a spy or does not have evil intentions? He writes pretty letters, it is true," she gestured to the papers Delilah had brought to share with the Council regarding his discoveries. "We just do not know if we can fully trust him, and we know we do not trust the Gloom. It can stay inert in one who has been affected. Temperaments or intentions can change and become deadly. You have seen it yourself in those we thought were safe."

This was a direct reference to Jarvis and no one in the room missed it. It was a low blow, and Delilah knew it would not have been weaponized unless the elder was truly worried. "I hear you. I hear you all. Yet I do not think you understand what is at stake! If we capture this technology, if we can somehow send messages through the trees, think how that could change our whole troubled planet! Maybe others have figured out how to dissolve the Gloom elsewhere, or fight plagues like the Mungus. What if there is a city on the other side of the Wood now that is struggling with the Mungus as we did—We could help save them! We would no longer be stuck sending messages over waters filled with terrors or sending scrolls with trusted beasts who could turn at any moment or be eaten along the way. Our communication is stilted—primitive! If we can find a way to converse with people in other sanctuary cities, other enclaves, think of the scientific discoveries we could share! It could increase our knowledge a thousand-fold!" Delilah saw some nodding from around the room.

Doktora Sinsarel spoke up again: "Talking through trees is not my area of expertise, Your Majesty, although I do find the prospect compelling. Monsters are my area of expertise, and that is the reason I am on this Council. You seem to have forgotten that Lord Xanfar is Beast. Beast is Beast. He is not trustworthy because of that, even if he has shown himself loyal in the past. It could flare up at any moment."

"We must not mistrust everyone who is different from us, Doktora. We have partnered with Horks and Ogreds in battles and trusted them with our lives when we had shared goals. Could they have turned on us at any moment? Of course! Yet the risk was worth it because of what we had to gain." She walked again circling the room and meeting the eyes of her colleagues on the Council. "Lord Xanfar is no Ogred. He is safer than any Hork. I would trust him with my life."

Despite the Council's grumbling, they finally gave in to support the journey. Belk was made aware and assisted with the preparations. Arrangements were conducted in secret in case there were spies who might sabotage the endeavor. Even Delilah was not informed of how she would be transported to Fallengrove, the estate across the Whayer Wood where Xanfar lived. Belk simply directed Delilah to go to Verily at an appointed time without disclosing further details.

"You are late." Doktora Ilvana was customarily gruff, meeting Delilah at the exit of the tunnel. Aaronon was there with a tray of hot spiced cider, which he offered to Delilah and to the three Guardswomen who were to accompany her to Xanfar's realm. They reached for it, but the Doktora pushed Aaranon back and grabbed Delilah's arm. "No time. Really, Aaranon? This is no time for hospitality. The winds are changing."

Delilah sent a grateful look to Aaranon, who backed away as Ilvana rushed the four women down the path. They followed the winding foot trail toward the cliff, where they saw an immense form hulking against the sky. It looked, at first, like a giant pumpkin hovering in the air. Strong acolytes in burgundy robes scurried around the bottom, busily making final preparations. Delilah was temporarily distracted from the floating monstrosity by admiration for the fit shapes of the young assistants. The Doktora's apprentices were said to be intensively trained in Qi-Kai, an ancient martial art that allowed them to learn to kill while barely touching their opponent. Furthermore, the physical demands of providing the small community of Verily with food, herbs, building, repairs, and fuel, kept them all in peak condition. The Doktora herself led training exercises at sunrise before they embarked on the daily chores and whatever scientific enterprise they had on the docket for that day. The novices became deadly, spiritually sound, practicing monks who were expected to meditate on the side of the cliff for one full day each new moon. This was in addition to having their intellects exercised by the Doktora, who held vast and obscure scholarly lessons each evening in the great lecture hall. Some said the rigors of tutelage under Doktora Ilvana was a test in body, mind, and spirit that only the hardiest souls could endure. After their tenure, some would go on to be recommended as senior officers for Delilah's Sister Guard or other esteemed professions, taking a sacred oath to take the secret location of Verily to their graves. Delilah almost got caught up in trying to pick out which of the monks were the strongest and most agile, when she snapped out of her reverie to the gourd-like object hanging against the sky.

Delilah's stomach dropped when she realized that this was the plan for how she would be expected to travel. "What… is it?"

"It is an airship, of course!"

"I have never seen one." Delilah began to walk around the craft, which was made from hides stitched together, its surface crisscrossed with a massive fishing net and a large woven basket attached to the bottom. It was tethered to the mountain with great cords.

"No time, Your Highness!" Ilvana grabbed Delilah's arm again and practically yanked her back to the door in front of the basket. The Doktora waited impatiently as two apprentices dragged a giant metal urn filled with embers out from inside the basket. "We cannot wait a moment longer. The airstreams are changing! I have calculated your trajectory for the trade winds to carry you precisely to Fallengrove."

Not wanting to appear fearful, Delilah stepped inside onto planks of wood secured to the bottom of the basket. Her three Guard looked nervously up at the great balloon before entering as well. Ilvana shut the door and yelled instructions to her team, who ran around unhooking the bindings one by one and throwing the cables over the rim into the basket. With each rope that was loosed, the basket lurched, and Delilah and the others grabbed to the sides to steady themselves. When the last two riggings were untied, the beefiest of Ilvana's apprentices let them out, hand over hand, keeping either side of the craft steady as the hot air inside lifted the vessel and the acolytes could no longer hold it. The last two ropes were left to dangle, and Delilah felt the hold of the earth release them as they rose into the air.

"Doktora," she called over the side, feeling a panic take hold of her. "How do we get *down*?"

"Do not worry, Your Majesty! It will not stay aloft forever!"

This did not seem reassuring, and Delilah regretted taking her time putting her things together that morning. She wished she had more opportunity to ask the Doktora questions. She looked to her Guard, who were feigning nonchalance as they looked down, grasping the lip of the basket, their knuckles white. They floated up at an alarming pace. Wind gusts came up the cliffs from the sea below, blasting them and pushing the craft aggressively from one side to another. The draft seemed to be pulling them out in the wrong direction to float above the waves far below. For a moment, Delilah thought they would be carried out to sea or crash against the cliffs. Then, just as the Doktora had projected, the winds shifted and they changed course. For several minutes, they could not see anything at all. A whitish mist surrounded them and blocked visibility, dampening their skin and leaving the taste of salt on their lips. Then, the fog separated, and they could see that they were traveling away from the vast ocean and over the dark woods.

Delilah and her Guard let out a collective sigh and smiled at each other, breaking into relieved laughter. She had chosen these three because they were some of her most skilled warriors, yet also because she liked each of them greatly and enjoyed their company. Sergeant Oravica, who led one of Delilah's most elite squads, was intensely loyal, strategic, and smart. She was approaching middle-age and had become stronger and more capable each year of her service. Batelnut and Torrence were cousins, and close as sisters. Batel was a slightly gawky young woman with ridiculously roped muscles under her lanky form. She was trained as a Pan Bo fighter, excelling in hand-to-hand combat, and rarely carried weapons. And what hands she had! When she made a fist, it was the size of a small melon. Delilah pitied anyone subjected to one of those bludgeons. Batel's rounded shoulder was marked with a flaming fist tattoo, belying her exclusive training and the secret Pan Bo guild that was said to infuse sorcery into its members' appendages. Batel's cousin, Torrence, was quiet and studious, a little overshadowed by her kinswoman, yet Delilah had seen them in action together and loved Torrence's graceful and lethal swordplay and their compatible fighting style.

They were still rising, and Delilah and the Guard watched as the forest squirmed with life in miniature below. A three-legged whayerwolf was in pursuit of a shrieking maiden. The maiden suddenly stopped, turned around, and grew three times her size into a hulking troll-like creature. She pounced, promptly ripping the wolf to shreds. Several ghostly forms clung to the treetops, following the craft's journey, looking up with pale, curious faces. A demonic centaur tracked them over a span of woods, turning his glowing eyes toward them and yelling in a voice that sounded like a twisted old ballad, echoing through the forest. The monster took an arrow from the quiver on his back and blew on it until it burst to flame. Delilah watched with horror as he aimed it at them and let it go, shouting an incantation. The arrow wove through the air, with an unnatural zig-zagging path, searching for a scent in the air with its tip and then, finding it, zooming directly toward them.

Oravica pushed Delilah back away from the edge of the basket while Batelnut and Torrence snapped into action. Torrence blocked as much as she could with her shield while Batelnut, never taking her eyes off the route of the missile, climbed up onto the side of the basket. She wrapped a hand several times in one of the dangling bindings and then scaled up the front of the inflated vessel. The flaming arrow sliced toward them, and Delilah gasped as Batelnut threw herself out into mid-air and grabbed it from the sky, interrupting its course. As if in slow motion, the warrior grasped and redirected the projectile back down toward where it had come and then she plummeted out of view.

Delilah and the other Guard flew to the edge and looked over, the weight of Batel falling and the abruptness of their movements rocking the basket violently. The arrow, now perverted in its course, flamed off toward the evil centaur. The Beast turned tail, still burning them with his eyes over his backside. He retreated, yelling his furious, unsettling song, while clomping desperately away to outpace his own missile. The basket yanked back and forth and then Batelnut appeared, dangling with her one hand still wound on the end of the rope as she tried to get a firm hold to pull herself up. Delilah and the other women braced themselves and, with much effort, elevated the soldier, who collapsed on the floor of the vessel, unwinding the cord, and rubbing her wrist from where it had cut her flesh.

"That was quite heroic, Batel!" exclaimed Delilah, putting a hand on the tattooed shoulder of the Guard. The tattoo sizzled with energy.

"It was nothing, Your Majesty. If I could not at least grab an arrow from the sky to protect my monarch, I imagine you would have picked another Guard for this task."

"Yes, clearly you were chosen for a reason! You can go home now!" The four of them broke into laughter.

The next several hours were less eventful, yet Delilah was fascinated to watch the Whayer Wood from above. The fierce battle for life played out incessantly and the desperate howls of the dying wafted up. Watching the creatures in the woods below, looking tiny and in some ways inconsequential, reminded Delilah of being a young girl watching ants invade another colony. She had sat there for hours as the blood-red creatures devoured and demolished their black counterparts, leaving them broken with tiny legs and body segments crushed into the dirt. She had not interfered, though she had been rooting for the black ones: they had been minding their own business, occupied with harvesting tiny particles of pollen when they were invaded by the red army. In the forest below, Delilah watched frail creatures, who were merely trying to survive and stay out of danger, getting devoured by demons the likes of which she had never seen before. She had long been schooled in how the Gloom affected a body, unpredictably distorting its natural form and often making it monstrous and wicked. Some creatures were barely changed, or only sprouted an extra or deformed limb. Others acquired special powers without much change to their physical anatomy.

Forest animals were also transformed, with great horned owls turning into death-eating dactyls and deer becoming sleek fighting beasts or even flying pegasi. No two beings were affected the same, but many became fiends hunting weaker changelings in the Wood. Delilah's experience of seeing these effects of the Gloom had been limited to fisherfolk and pirates, and occasional visiting dignitaries who risked the danger and the sea journey in times of great importance. She communicated with regals in other lands, who often described how the Gloom had affected other parts of the world. Their tales were so farfetched they seemed invented or at least exaggerated. Now she saw that these bizarre stories must be true.

The tangled forest grew darker in places, and occasionally an encampment could be glimpsed through the dense overgrowth. Glowing cookfires were circled by what appeared to be small families or venturing parties. Some groups scurried about with the urgency of being hunted, while others appeared to be organizing hunting parties themselves. A pack of whayerwolves saw the airship floating above and congregated together to howl disapproval. It was a haunting melody that followed Delilah and echoed through her mind long after. "I will eat you," the song said, quite clearly: "I will devour you and suck on your bones."

Delilah shivered, the air above this part of the forest being cool and misty. The Guard were alert, watching the goings-on of the Wood with bright, intense eyes, calculating how they might conquer each beast they saw below. They whispered to one another, engaging in quiet discussions of the best way to decapitate a vampwhyr or parry with a troupe of undead dessicators or zhomboids. Finally, the Wood untangled, and they saw bright green clearings emerge among patches of shadowy woodland. These gave way to fields of wildflowers and hilly bluffs with trees in bloom, their scents wafting up into the air even to the height of the four travelers. There were still tangled patches of darkness and creatures lurking on the edges of the fragrant fields, yet there was more... air there. Less Gloom, Delilah realized. The fields spilled into magnificent gardens with massive willow trees, stone arches, and hedges cut to topiaries in fantastical shapes: grand unicorns and merfolk sat atop ponds with glittering fish and glorious fountains. They were entering Fallengrove.

Yet how would they alight? Delilah wondered by what mechanism they were expected to land. She looked around to see if there were gears or any buttons that she had neglected to notice in the basket, yet there were none. Again, she wished she had asked the Doktora more questions. The balloon was losing altitude now and the basket scraped along the top of a giant shoak tree, making a horrible scratching sound. There were so many trees in Fallengrove that if they kept sinking, they would be impaled on one thing or another. She looked to her Guard to see if they might have ideas and saw that they were talking amongst themselves, focused on an arched entryway coming up on the horizon. It looked to be a guard post with a flurry of activity. Centaurs! A whole mess of them, suited up in matching shiny blue armor with glistening weapons and huge, ornate longbows. After their experience with the evil centaur in the Wood, the sight of an army of them chilled Delilah's blood. Still, she felt compelled to reassure her soldiers, who had tensed and were preparing their own weapons. "They must be Xanfar's Guard. They are certainly expecting us," she said.

"Yes, then why do they look to be preparing to fight us?" asked Torrence. It was true. It seemed that the centaurs were organizing into formation and aiming their long bows in the direction of the craft. Before they could say more, the centaurs ran forward in a unified block, yelling an eerily rousing song reminiscent of the one they heard from the evil centaur. They stopped and aimed their bows at the airship. Arrows with long blue tails were whizzing past them. They were being fired upon! Delilah held on to Batel's arm to quell another bold attempt that might get the young woman impaled, and she and the Guard dropped to the bottom of the container to ready their weapons. Oravica began to load arrows into her crossbow.

"Wait," Delilah held out her arm to stop Oravica, and nodded upward. They looked up and saw that there were thick ropes across the top of the basket. Several blue cords were extended through one side, and out the other. They felt the basket lurch. It yanked again, and they could see the ropes churning and moving above. Another fierce yank, and the ship stopped its forward motion and stood stationary in the air. The synchronized yelling of the Centauri turned rhythmic and focused, like the songs of pirates hoisting sails. With each beat of the song, the basket was tugged, and pulled downward. "It is alright. They are simply bringing us down to land," Delilah said to the women, who had not stopped preparing their arms. "They mean us no harm."

"That is to be seen, Your Majesty. Let us not walk into a trap," said Oravica. "We will expect that they could be a threat, and if they are not, we will be pleasantly surprised." The others nodded. Delilah thought they were overreacting. Still, she knew she tended to trivialize risk at times, which is why she had a Council and army leadership to help her make important decisions. She sighed and took out her own blade, not wanting to seem naïve, despite feeling confident that they were not in any danger. The basket ground into the dirt with a jarring bump and the Centauri song came to an end. They heard scurrying and instructions shouted in a foreign tongue as the ropes were tied off. Carefully, the women began to raise themselves up, weapons in hand and loaded.

"Why, hello there, Your Majesty!" The voice came from behind and they spun around to see a huge, bearded face looking down at them. The centaur looked enormous and intimidating up close, yet had such a disarming smile, his reddish complexion giving him an undeniably friendly expression. "You will not need those weapons, friends. We are in the employ of Lord Xanfar. We mean you no harm, and no harm will come to you while you are in Fallengrove. We will see to that."

The Guard shuffled and stood up completely to look about, now with the other Centauri coming in closer to surround the basket. When they saw Delilah, they kneeled and bowed, each with one of their powerful legs extended and the tops of their heads down. "All hail to Queen Delilah! All hail to the Hope Queen!" Shouts of praise rang out, each voice resounding and a smile on every face. One of them walked up, looking golden all over, with a chiseled torso, which was glistening and muscular, extending into his equine lower half. His blond locks were tied back in a messy braid, and his blue eyes sparkled like sapphires. "May I?" he asked Batelnut, and she took both his hands, which dwarfed her huge ones, and climbed up to the top of the basket edge. He pulled and landed the soldier upon his back. Batel let out a little squeak as she alighted, looking confused about how she had gotten there. Holding tightly to her weapons, she looked intently around to monitor her queen in case she had to suddenly jump from the centaur and into battle to defend her charge.

Two more centaurs came up to assist the other soldiers. The ruddy one with the big smile who had spoken first held out his hand to Delilah. "I am Captain Ferrashi, Your Majesty," he said. "I lead this regiment. We know the risks you have taken to come here. Do not be alarmed. We will guard you with our lives as if you were our own queen." She took his hand, and he bowed his head slightly in deference before launching Delilah onto his own back.

"Wait! I have something I need to bring," Delilah said and jumped down and climbed back over the side of the basket to retrieve a leather-wrapped package.

"Do not worry about your bags, Your Majesty. We will have them brought to your chambers."

"I will hold on to this one," said Delilah, as she climbed up and stood on the edge of the basket and stepped nimbly onto Ferrashi's back, lowering herself to sit.

"As you wish, Your Majesty," said the Captain, then yelled to his troops. They fell into formation, the columns advancing through the great curved tunnel beneath the guard tower and through a winding road lined with orchards and gardens.

Delilah was dazzled, looking about at the heavily fruited trees and vegetables, plump and glowing on the vines. Small troll-like people in blue uniforms worked among them, pruning and weeding. "These gardens! How can they be so lush?" she exclaimed.

Ferrashi said: "Why that, Your Majesty, is a highly guarded Fallengrove secret!" and he let out a noisy flute of air from his rear-end. Delilah heard a "plop!" on the stone, and the regiment burst out in laughter. A woman with small horns ran up with a large dustpan and broom and scooped up the steaming manure, then disappeared back among the greenery. Delilah could not help laughing with them, and her Guard was swept up in the silliness and chuckled along, too.

"Oh, love is a sweet and dangerous fruit!
It tempts us to distraction.
It is useless to combat its lure
When it drives us into action."
-The Ghost Scribe

Chapter 4: The Secrets of Fallengrove

You could barely see the castle for all the vines. White flowers covered the mottled blue stones of the battlements and ran up the towers almost to the top. The stained-glass windows reflected late afternoon light like jellied candies, glimmering rainbow hues that made the entire building vibrate with life. "It is magnificent!" Delilah breathed, unable to contain her admiration.

"Yes, Your Majesty. Lord Xanfar's family built this estate three centuries ago and have been its caretakers since," explained Ferrashi. It has been in good paws…" he chuckled, "I mean hands." Delilah started at the joke, yet the centaur seemed to make it in good spirit, like all else. "I mean no disrespect to the Lord," Ferrashi assured her. "He is a good friend, and we are grateful for the work."

Footmen filed in a line, trumpeting to announce their arrival. Serfs opened enormous wooden doors and out walked a creature unlike any Delilah had ever seen. He was dressed in a pale blue velvet suit with large lace cuffs. A white silken scarf was tied neatly around his throat and tucked into his collar. His fashionable presence was not what was most striking, though: the man was almost entirely Beast. His sleeves fell over elegant paws with sharp moonbeam claws and his whole head was that of a whayerwolf. He had large, intelligent brown eyes and his scruff of forelock was brushed into a smooth wave upon his forehead, yet he was most certainly not human. Delilah had known this, of course, and yet it was still quite a shock to see the man she had conversed with for months, sending lengthy impassioned scrolls back and forth, there in full fur.

Xanfar bowed deeply: "Queen Delilah, it is such an honor to welcome you to my family's home."

Delilah gathered her wits and bowed her head in response to the well-dressed wolf. "And it is quite a home!" she exclaimed. A footman placed a small set of stairs to assist her from Ferrashi's wide back, then aided the other women down. "Let me introduce my Guard: Sergeant Oravica, and Officers Batelnut and Torrence."

"I am surprised the Council allowed you to come at all, much less with only three soldiers!"

"Well, Lord Xanfar, they sometimes forget that I am the queen, and then I must remind them. I adore my Council, yet many are stodgy quill-pushers." Oravica snorted and nodded her agreement. "Sergeant Oravica knows the dense politics of Hope too well," Delilah explained. "She is the sister of one of the esteemed Council Elders."

"You mean the *much* younger, half-sister of an Elder," corrected Oravica.

"Ah, Sergeant," said Xanfar, "it sounds that you, too, have dealt with the family drama of being a younger, different-thinking sibling! My older brother insisted that I take over the family's vineyards while he went off over the Agrathian Mountains to wander the world and study healing. He was called to medicine and then expected me to stay to do the droll work of wine production. I had other ideas and instead went searching for adventure myself! And look at me now, getting gray whiskers and managing the family vineyards after all!"

"Xanfar's family vineyards produce some of the finest wine on the continent," Delilah explained to Oravica. It is called *Fallen Vines,* and they export it... everywhere!"

"I have heard my wife speak of it!" exclaimed Oravica, impressed. "Well, I would not mind sampling some of that while I am here! Of course, I am not such a connoisseur as my wife."

"I will give you a case to take home to her," Xanfar smiled, his white teeth flashing.

"Thank you, My Lord! She will be over the moons to receive such a gift!"

"Let us get you inside!" He turned to a wolf dressed in butler's livery. "Darrow, please take our esteemed guests to their rooms."

Their "rooms" were more accurately an entire wing of the castle, with a sitting room, several enormous bed chambers, and even a small library. The Guardswomen were clearly uncomfortable with the luxury, scoping out security risks and assessing the safety of their arrangements. They discussed nighttime guard rotations and put an emergency plan in place in case they were attacked. "No one will bother us here," Delilah interjected as she laid out her things and hung her few spare garments in the voluminous dressing room. Then she flopped fully clothed upon an ornate wooden bed in the center of the room shaped like a temple with four thick columns carved to resemble tree trunks. The bed was easily four times the size of the one she slept on at home, and seemed more like a small house. Even thought it was enormous, it still only reached halfway to the vaulting ceiling. Delilah felt uneasy looking up at the silky fabric draped in cloudy peaks from the apex of the temple bed. She jumped up after no more than a moment. Xanfar had tried to assign staff to assist Delilah in dressing and managing her person and offered her round-the-clock attendants. "I am not that kind of queen," Delilah assured him when she refused the help. "Otherwise, why would I come with a bunch of soldiers instead of an entourage of courtiers?"

Over dinner, Xanfar began to lay out his thoughts for Delilah about the new technology he had uncovered. "It is old technology, really. The oldest there is, in fact. As I mentioned in my dispatches to you, Your Majesty, it is in the trees."

"Please, just call me Delilah."

"Of course," he smiled with a bashful glance down at his paws. "I am sorry if my manners are not very polished. We do not get many visitors here in Fallengrove."

"Your manners are better than most in my own court, I assure you, Lord Xanfar."

"Well, if I am to call you Delilah, then I insist you call me by my family name, which is Xan. I have not had the pleasure to hear my old pet name, nor have I had the company of family for so long."

"Can I ask what happened to them?"

"It is not very dramatic. My parents got old and died. My brother went off, as he had intended, to study healing. As the oldest, he was supposed to marry and take over the estate, yet he never returned. My sources say he died trying to test the effectiveness of a fungi broth for fighting the Scrounge. He tested it on himself. They say he stuck a tiny straw made of glass into his arm and pumped the broth through. Either it did not work or the medicine itself killed him. Either way, he died from the Scrounge as he was trying to find a way to cure it."

"That is so sad," Delilah said, putting her hand upon Xanfar's arm. It was odd to feel the lord's coarse fur beneath the fine fabric.

"Well, I did not much like him, if I am being honest. We never got along. To be truthful, he was a controlling prick. He was my brother, though. I loved him, if I did not like him."

"That is the way it is with brothers," she consoled.

"Yes, it seems to be. Was it not similar with your brother?" Delilah flinched. Xanfar continued, "Did not your brother launch a coup against your parents? That could not have been easy on you."

"No," Delilah said, "it was not." She could not say more.

"Well, let us depart from sad nonsense and return to the main objective of your journey here," Xanfar said, sensing the soreness of the wounds unearthed.

Delilah sighed a breath of relief, "Yes, please."

"I must introduce you to Aumenveill tomorrow."

"And who is that?"

"Why, I wrote to you about him! He is the oldest Andromeda tree on this side of the Whayer Wood! Just wait until you hear him talk!"

The rest of the evening was quiet. Delilah retired to her suite with Oravica taking lead of the watch. Batelnut and Torrence went off to explore, probably enjoying the rich food and unusual friends they had discovered in the kitchens. Most of the staff were touched by the Gloom in some way. This was the difference between living in a land like Hope that was protected by a magickal forcefield and a land like Fallengrove, where the Gloom was just a stone's throw away in the near Wood. Some of the staff had a tail, or patches of fur, or snake eyes over a scaly nose — all were enchanted in ways that seemed mostly non-threatening, like the fisherfolk that Delilah was used to. Some of the staff were more transformed, akin to their lord, in full black pelts with claws and fangs or with a completely glowing clear pallor where one could see veins pumping underneath translucent skin. It was hard to be at ease around an entire court of such folk, yet Delilah tried not to let it color her judgment of them. They were all dressed in ornate livery, and indeed, had more proper demeanor than those in her own court. It was impressive that they had kept up the formality even in their isolation, there between the Whayer Wood on one side and the great mountain range on the other side.

In the morning, Xanfar had five of his Centauri Guardsmen ready to accompany them. Delilah had heard her two younger soldiers coming in late and Oravica scolding them harshly for indulging too much with their new friends. Still, they were all three up and alert for duty, as always. Xanfar rode upon Captain Ferrashi, and Delilah was offered onto the back of a colossal centaur with a long beard streaked with red and silver strands and braided with glass beads. "Correll is one of our greatest warriors," Xanfar leaned over to whisper to Delilah. "He is the most skilled archer we have." Delilah noticed the weaponry loaded on the backs of the Centauri, as if they were going into battle rather than for a ride in the forest. It was odd to sit behind the broad shoulders of a man while also straddling his back, like riding double. Awkwardly, the riding partner was also the ride! It also made visibility difficult since the Centauri had such beefy torsos and were loaded up with weapons. One simply had to trust that they were being led in the right direction. Oravica seemed to sense this vulnerability and insisted upon walking beside her mount. Batelnut was again offered the mount of the golden steed. This time, Delilah saw Batel color deeply when the centaur reached back to pat the leather of the young officer's trousers to insure sure she was securely in place.

The orchards of Fallengrove were extensive. The party wound through narrow carriage trails pounded flat by centuries of hooves and harvest equipment. Trees, the likes of which Delilah never knew existed, lined the paths. She marveled at their contorted limbs and strands of clustered blossoms that drooped down like waterfalls. There were bushes with long, irregular fruit, grasses with triangular seed pods, and hedgerows filled with fragrant oversized blooms and giant thorns. It was like wandering through a living library of the world. Xanfar pointed out exotic species to Delilah and explained, "When my brother first set out in the world, he would send back a potted specimen every month or so from his travels," he said. "We planted them, not knowing anything about where he was or where they had come from. No personal letters attached: just root balls packed in wet sacks with a tiny note: 'Needs Sunlight' or 'Plant in Wet Place.' For a long time, I resented my brother for not sending reports of his travels," Xanfar confessed. "The trees seemed to be impersonal gifts, with no explanation or description of where he was and what he was experiencing. I did not realize that each of these trees is a living being with a history and a voice that can tell me more than any letter that my brother, Harvan, could have written. Now I know that these trees were uniquely personal to him." His voice caught and he turned his face away from Delilah. She tried to look the other direction to give Xanfar privacy while he gathered his emotions. "He was telling me a story," the wolf choked. "I was just not able to hear it. After he died, that is when my interest in botany and biophysics took hold. I studied endlessly and had some of the greatest scientists in the world take residency here to tutor me. I am still trying to understand Harvan's story."

They walked quietly for a while, with just the clopping of hooves, rustling of wind through leaves, and songbirds trilling ardent messages to one another. "I envy you, Xanfar," admitted Delilah. "I know your relationship with your brother was not easy. Still, at least you have the kindness of the trees he sent back to you, despite your differences. My own brother betrayed my parents, exactly as you suggested last night. He formed a renegade army of aelves to help assassinate them. Yet he also betrayed me! I have nothing to remember him by except the hole in my heart that he left by killing our parents. I could never even mourn him since he was a traitor and hurt me in the most profound way."

"Yes," Xanfar said, and reached out to touch Delilah's shoulder. He looked at her with softness in his liquid brown eyes. She would not have thought a wolfen face could hold such compassion. "You have been through so much, Delilah. I should be less bitter, given my own privilege."

Now it was Delilah's turn to swallow back tears. "I should not complain. I have been privileged, too. I was too young to know how to rule at fifteen when I became Queen. Still, it has been the greatest honor of my life to serve the people of Hope."

"And what a job you have done! The way you saved your queendom, perhaps even the world, from the Mungus?"

"Ah, well that was mostly Doktora Ilvana," Delilah brushed the compliment aside.

"Nonsense!" exclaimed Xanfar. "Ilvana told me all about how you determined it was the plants the goats were eating that made their milk protective against the Mungus. She sent us packages of the dried flower with the dosage to combat the illness. We had barely been touched by the Mungus when she sent it, although we were already hearing tales of other lands being ravaged. We were able to stamp it out quickly when it came with minimal losses because of your ingenuity."

"Well, she was right on the cusp of discovering it herself."

"Hmmfh," Xanfar smiled his toothy smile.

The orchards soon transitioned to heavily wooded forest. Below them, Delilah could see glimpses of the Gloom blanketing the Whayer Wood in dense plum-colored fog. They were high enough to escape its dangers, yet wisps of the smog seemed to reach up in vinelike tendrils that threatened to poison life on the mountainside above. The party turned onto a dark path that tunneled through the heart of the woodland. The sounds were muffled there, and even the heavy footfalls of the Centauri were softened by moss and debris. The air was filled with the rich humous of centuries of growth and decay.

"We have no forests like this in Hope!" Delilah looked around in wonder, dazzled by the delicate wings of small insects, fluttering in pinpoints of light filtering down through the overgrowth. The air hummed with shimmering rays of sunlight cascading from above. Delilah dismounted from her Centauri escort and walked ahead along the path of deep leaves edged in decomposing logs. The humming continued. At first, Delilah thought it might be a symphony of the tiny, winged creatures that flittered about, yet it was too deep and too… resounding. "What is that sound?" she finally asked Lord Xanfar.

"That," he responded, "is Aumenveill." He pointed ahead down the path.

Delilah now saw that the path led to what could only be described as an entity at the end of the trail. It was a tree, yes. Yet it was not like any tree Delilah had ever seen. For one thing, it was gigantic. It was as tall as her castle and reached as wide in all directions. Indeed, it seemed more wall than tree, with giant intertwining branches and a vast, gnarled trunk, marbled with verdant rainbows of lichen. Bumps and dark hollows were inhabited by nests of birds and other living things. Fuzzy squarrows darted in and out, chittering across the surface of the bark, disappearing and reappearing in other places, spiraling the trunk while scolding the others in high tinkling voices. Aside from its size, the other thing that distinguished this arboreal presence from other trees was the ever-present humming. Delilah now understood that the sound was not emanating from the forest life around the tree. It was a deep, primordial tone radiating from the tree itself. In fact, Delilah could feel the vibrations below her feet in the wild twisting root system that tangled out from the base, tumbling into the earth in every direction. Sections of roots submerged and emerged in other places, seeming to pulsate with the life force of Aumenveill.

"It is grander than I could imagine!" Delilah exclaimed.

"Yes," said Xanfar, "*he* is extraordinary in every way."

"He is," Delilah corrected herself.

"Would you like to talk to him?" Xanfar asked, leading Delilah by the arm, stepping carefully across the jumbled roots to sit upon a raised area. He slid off his leather boots and stretched his furry toes. Delilah tried not to look at his sharp, shiny toenails: though cleanly trimmed, still deadly.

"Yes, of course I would!" Delilah sat on a raised burl of grayish root across from Xanfar, trying to recall everything he had written to her about this enchanted being.

"You will need to remove your footwear, Your Highness," Xanfar said bashfully, pointing to Delilah's boots. Delilah pulled off her boots and lay them on the ground, embarrassed that her own toenails were not quite so manicured. "The bottoms of your feet must be flush with the earth so that the soles can send and receive thoughts to Aumenveill," Xanfar explained. Delilah shifted so that her feet were solidly on the ground with her toes burrowing into the mossy surface among the roots. It tickled! The startling sensation of tingling on Delilah's bare skin almost made her lift her feet away, yet she resisted. She forced herself to keep her feet still and felt warmth and vibration radiate up, winding around her ankles and massaging her calves, up her legs until her whole body felt as if it were buzzing with energy. It was completely external to her, yet she felt the force penetrating her face and head, felt the tingling even in her eyes, which began to water.

"Hello, child." Delilah heard the voice as if it were in her ears, yet she knew there was no sound.

"H- hello?" She spoke the word out loud, then looked to see Xanfar shake his head. He put a finger to his lips. She tried again, this time speaking the words in her mind only: "Greetings, Aumenveill."

"I have been waiting to meet you, Queen Delilah," said the tree. "Our friend, Lord

Xanfar, has told me great things, and I have been keeping an eye on you in other ways."

"I did not think trees had eyes." Delilah was trying to be lighthearted, yet she could sense the tree digesting this slowly, considerately. She could almost hear the wheels turning inside the heart of Aumenveill's trunk with thoughts running back and forth along his varied limbs like streaks of light.

The deliberate voice responded: "My dear, we do indeed have eyes everywhere, though not as you might imagine. In fact, trees and other forest beings watch and speak to one another much more than humans do. You do not see trees waging war on other trees, do you?"

"No, you do not," Delilah admitted.

"I have an important message to tell you, though, my dear, which is why I asked Xanfar to invite you here. I know you are the one who can spread this truth to all of humanity, and to the Beasts of the Gloom as well."

"I am listening."

"We are all connected, Delilah, all living things. When harm is done to one, it hurts us all."

"Yes, I would certainly agree with that. Tell that to the vampwhyrs, though! They are not all that concerned with the harm they do when they are sucking their victims' blood." Again, Delilah's attempt at humor fell flat.

"It is with great confidence that I impart this truth to you, Delilah. You must tell the world."

"Well, you seem to have… connections. With all due respect, why not tell the world yourself?"

"See how far you journeyed, the flight you took and the distance you traveled just to be here now to speak with me? What if that were not needed at all? What if you could speak to me, or any other being on our sacred planet, and perhaps even to the stars? I assure you, we are connected, myself and all the trees and fungi and spores, right down to the tiniest rootling and smallest algae, all the way through the vegetation in the sea and the roots and pollen right in your backyard orchard in Hope. Yet what good does it do if the humans do not listen? We scream for you to hear us, and it is futile. Until the humans learn to hear us, to hear the trees, all knowledge that could save them is beyond their grasp."

"Are you saying you can communicate with trees everywhere? Even in the orchards in Hope?"

"Oh yes, Delilah. I know them well. They try to talk to you always, try to send you messages in the petals that drift upon the wind and the apples that rot under your feet. I want you to learn how to hear them, as I hear them now. In fact, one of your chef's apprentices is there in the orchard today, in the sunlight, gathering thorn-plums. She has a lot on her mind, poor thing. The cook yelled at her this morning for letting a basket of garlic get damp and moldy. She is thinking she would have been better off raising sheep on the cliffs with her family."

"That is our Rusha, from your description."

"Yes, Rusha, sister of Rolly and daughter of Penniwhen and Argus."

"Yes!"

"I can see her, yet sadly, she does not know me. She does not hear me. Her mind is too occupied with her personal trials. Yet if she stopped for a moment, not only would her own suffering be relieved, she would hear the universal solutions that would help her to become a better chef, a better person, and it would help her avoid getting poked by thorns when she harvests plums."

Delilah tried to take in the significance of what Aumenveill was saying, yet she found the whole discussion elusive. "While it is impressive that you can know my dear Rusha in this way, I am not sure what you would like me to tell others about this."

"You have many enemies, do you not?"

"Argh, too many, I admit."

"What do they want from you?"

"Many things: vengeance for old injuries—real or imagined—treasure, territory, sometimes just blood if it happens to be an undead army."

"What if you could speak to them, hear their complaints, their innermost needs and desires, without ever engaging them in war?"

"It sounds like fantasy, Aumenveill. We are warriors, and the tribes around us are warriors. We are not good at negotiating. Problems are solved with swords. It is not my preference, yet it is the way of the world, and to be frank, the creatures of the Gloom only understand the might of steel. They are not interested in peace."

"And yet you avoided a war by offering a kindness to a pirate queen. Yes, I know that, too! You are the right one to deliver this message. I have been around a long time, Delilah, waiting for a time when one of your kind might hear me. I am older than you might imagine. I was here before the Gloom, and I believe I will be here long after the Gloom dissipates."

"Dissipates? Well, now that is a fantasy I would like to see."

"It is hard for you to believe, since all you have known is the Gloom. It may not happen in your lifetime. However, nothing is forever, dear child. Even the Gloom will someday vanish like the morning mist. Then the need to make peace will be even greater. Even the basest creatures have needs and desires, Delilah. When you are able to truly understand another soul, you can anticipate their greatest needs and avoid conflict."

"Some of these monsters have no souls, I believe. Have you spoken to the zhomboids or devourers? They are truly pure evil. They want flesh, nothing more."

"Have you ever been bitten by a flea, Delilah?"

"Of course."

"Does the flea have a soul?"

"I have not thought about it before. I would say it is a living thing, despite needing to be crushed."

"Some of the monsters transformed by the Gloom are just perversions of these types of natural creatures. The devourers want blood no more than a flea. Is a flea pure evil?"

"If you have ever had one in your bedroll, you would say it is!"

"I am not sure you are taking this seriously, my child."

"I am sorry, and I am trying to understand, Aumenveill. It is just that what you are saying goes against my training as a warrior. I am trained to destroy invaders and Beasts of the Gloom."

"It is a weakness of your kind, Delilah. You are all soldiers, even when you are not fighting battles. It makes you blind. You do not see the connections right in front of you. Are we not Linked right now?"

"Linked? Why, yes, we are connected now. I am hearing you."

"You hear what I am saying, yet we are not fully Linked as we should be and could be. When you learn to truly Link with another soul, you can learn all their knowledge, and all the knowledge of the other souls Linked with them. You learn the wisdom found in the root systems beneath you and between you, including all the tiniest beings, so tiny you cannot imagine. The smallest specks of lifeforms exist in billions along every fibrous strand of every tree and bush. It flows through the ground, feeding and communicating through the decomposition of millions of dying beings. You might find it hard to believe that those unbelievably small lives and deaths hold the secrets of the stars and the energy of the sun. They communicate with one another faster than light falls from the sky, in constant, pulsating rhythms, sending messages so quickly, that it is as if I am touching the plums in your orchard right now. Unthinkable quantities of these miniscule beings exist between here and your gardens in Hope, which is why we can talk to one another, how I can know what is happening there. When Rusha touches the plums, she sends all her thoughts and feelings into that tree in an instant, without even being aware. What secrets you could unlock if only you were able to hear these universal algorithms."

"I am sorry, Aumenveill. I am speaking with you now, yet I have spent a lot of time in orchards in my life, and I have never spoken to a tree before."

Delilah had not been aware that Xanfar had been listening, but he interjected then. "We are not trained to hear the Rithms—the algorithms of the universe. We can hear them now because Aumenveill is so very old and Linked, and some of the magic of the Gloom has reached him through his roots. It has made it easier for us to hear his thoughts. If you went home and tried to talk to your plum tree, you would not hear anything. You would need to find the oldest tree in your forest, the oldest tree in Hope to have any possibility of hearing the messages. We are just not trained yet to understand every forest and field, although there is life there! That is what the Doktora and I are trying to tap into. I can send messages to Doktora Ilvana because there is an ancient evergreen on the cliffs of Verily that assists us. That is how the Doktora and I planned to have the airship bring you here. Still, it takes practice, and I can only talk to Ilvana with Aumenveill's assistance. Someday, I hope to learn the secret of how to talk through the vines that grow right outside my window. Aumenveill assures me that the Rithms are in those, too, if we can just learn how to hear them."

"You can learn how to hear them, my child," Aumenveill said fondly. "You listen better than most of your kind." Xanfar colored beneath his furry face. Delilah did not think it was possible for a whayerwolf to blush.

On the walk back to the castle, Delilah fell behind. She watched her feet, listening to the sounds of the leaves beneath her boots, urgently seeking to hear what could be gleaned from their dry voices. Aumenveill had told her that even dead things held the secrets of the

Rithms and could communicate. It was not that the decaying plants could talk, he said, since life had left them. It was the tiniest beings, clusters of them in impossible numbers, that fed off the leaf's dying energy. He explained that incalculable multitudes of these invisible living things speak through the Links between them, conversing in universal algorithms… *Rithms*.

The others of their party had not been Linked as Xanfar and Delilah had been to Aumenveill, and so they had not heard the conversation with the elder tree. The Centauri and Delilah's Guard walked ahead, with Xanfar a bit behind them and Delilah taking up the rear. The queen walked as if in a trance, paying attention to the uneven pattern of rustling and snapping sounds as she tried to understand the magnitude of what lay beneath their feet and paws and hooves. Xanfar glanced back at Delilah anytime they went around a turn, giving her space for her deep thoughts, yet clearly eager to know what she was thinking.

"I wonder…" Delilah lifted her head from where she had been gazing at the ground, and as she did, an arrow shot across her neck, grazing it deeply. One of her hands flew to her throat, feeling the warmth of blood there, as the other ripped out her scimitar. A guttural battle cry poured spontaneously from her lungs. The Centauri and Sister Guard were in immediate action, Oravica instantly at Delilah's side, shielding her with her body. The Centauri had arrows strewn, scanning the forest for the attackers. A white glaze streamed between the trees at the perimeter. It took Delilah's mind a moment to register it as a figure moving extraordinarily fast. "Aelves!" she shouted, her battle senses fully engaged and comprehending that there were several of these blurry forms, shooting inhumanly behind the screen of shadowed foliage.

In moments, the forms were not just surrounding them—they were on top of them, long elegant limbs making arcs like dancers, sparkling light bouncing from their shimmering swords. Delilah tried not to be hypnotized by their graceful movements and focused instead on trying to keep track of how many there were and what weapons they held. The Crystal Aelves were white as snow and reportedly as hard and cold as the stone they resembled. Like statues come alive, Delilah watched an aelf with a silver braid of hair flying behind her jump on top of Captain Ferrashi's back, ready to slice his throat with a dagger. An arrow impaled the aelf through her back before she could complete her task and she fell off the Centaur, grasping the tip of the arrow that had come through her chest. Correll, living up to his reputation, wasted no time and had arrows flying in almost constant succession at the glistening shadow-light shapes around them. One after another Corell launched the arrows, yet as each one flew through exactly where the aelves should be, the space was empty, and the projectiles shot off into the forest.

"Demons!" Correll shouted and kept up his barrage in all directions, holding the aelves at bay if not killing any more. The other centaurs and Delilah's Guard were on alert, weapons drawn and circling with backs together. Delilah saw a glassy figure dip behind a boulder and she felt her legs begin to run toward it before she could even think. She lunged over the boulder and prepared to tackle the form at the other side, sword raised to slice through the pale invader. Somehow, the figure was gone as soon as Delilah reached the alternate side of the rock. She stood, looking around her, completely disoriented. A feeling overcame her, and she looked up, too late, to see the aelven warrior dropping from the trees above. Delilah barely had time to raise her sword to block the downward thrust of the creature's weapon, sharp and deceptively thin as a ribbon. It sliced through Delilah's scimitar as if it were butter, and she watched with horror as the curved end of her sword separated and fell upon the leaves below. As fast as everything was moving, Delilah was seeing in slow motion: the aelven warrior made a full arch of her weapon-arm, spinning it around to slice through Delilah. Patterns on the flexible silver leather armor of the aelf, raised white stitching in magickal symbols, danced over the woman's agile, muscular figure. It was a beautiful, hypnotic sight. For a moment, she almost gave in to the poetry of the woman's form making its deadly approach. Delilah's body moved automatically before her mind could process what was happening, and she mercifully spun out from the trajectory of the aelf's aim. She turned back to stab as hard as she could toward the warrior's torso with the broken end of her sword, but the aelf bent her body in an impossible sideways swirl and Delilah's joust met air. With nothing to catch her, Delilah and her broken weapon tumbled forward and she fell to the ground.

Delilah scrambled to her feet and found she had lost her attacker again. This time she looked above her first, yet nothing was hiding in the trees. Her comrades were engaged in their own battles with the other-worldly creatures bending and contorting, making inhuman shapes with their bodies. Batel and her golden Centaur were back-to-back, or rump-to-back more accurately, fighting off six or seven of the aelves. Batel swung her powerful fists and met air again and again in futile blows. It was hard to tell how many aelves there were in total, as they moved so frighteningly fast. Captain Ferrashi had received a nasty gash across his chest and Xanfar seemed to be guarding him, leaping and swiping with his dagger claws fully extended at the attacking horde. A few of his slices met flesh and streams of violet blood sprouted in fountains from the white skin of the aelves. Xanfar had some injuries himself. Delilah could see that some had gone through his furry, muscular frame to reveal white bones, yet these wounds were knitting themselves back together before her eyes. Oravica was clearly trying to make her way to defend her monarch, however each move forward was pushed back by an aelf flying in to chop at her with their strange, willowy swords. Correll was still sending out reams of arrows in all directions, and Delilah saw a few fallen aelves impaled with arrows and purple blood spilling from their wounds. Torrence had been able to slice a few as well, with her sword arm moving in competing speed.

Delilah took one more look about her, then began to leap over the boulder back into the fray. As she mounted the stone, she saw Oravica, still trying to work her way toward her. Their gaze met and Oravica's eyes grew wide. She opened her mouth to shout to her queen. Delilah tried to spin around and felt a cold arm slip around her shoulders and lock her into place. She tried to kick and twist, yet the arm held her steady. The aelf's blade came up to her chin, held there as the warrior yelled to her tribe in a language that sounded like music. The other aelves stopped and retreated from their engagements, looking to their leader who was holding Delilah with the sharp blade pressing against her skin. The aelf queen spoke, and Delilah concentrated deeply. It had been many years since she had studied Aelvish, however she was able to understand a few words: "*Let us eliminate these rodents to honor our King!*"

The aelven monarch was impassioned by her speech, her voice growing louder and more melodious like the rising crescendo of a song. She was holding a high note in the word for "traitor" when it was cut off in the middle and turned into a shriek of pain mixed with a growl. Delilah felt the blade on her neck clatter past her chest and she twisted out of the aelf's embrace to see the aelf queen flailing, fighting off a snarling, furry beast. Delilah had not seen Xanfar come from behind. Clearly, neither had the aelf queen. A few aelven soldiers flew to defend their ruler, and Xanfar, in the heat of full attack, flung each of the attackers away while holding the queen's neck in his jaws. The others had stopped in mid-battle when Delilah had been accosted, yet now resumed their assault. Suddenly, an eerie sound filled the woods, and all froze in mid-strike. The aelves stood on alert, listening to the note that was trumpeted through the trees, a sound that made Delilah's blood run cold, having heard it only once before in her life.

Like a flash, the aelves were gone, their ghostly shapes disappearing into the forest like drops of water evaporating in the sun. Xanfar had let up on his bite for a moment to listen to the haunting sound. The aelven queen took the opportunity to vanish from his grasp as well. Delilah and her comrades looked around for the fallen aelves and saw only the last of their moonlight bodies, purple blood, and discarded weapons turning to silvery dust among the leaves. All took stock and there were no life-threatening injuries: just deep slices from the ribbon-like swords and some scrapes and punctures from the aelven arrows. Despite their peaceful mission to see Aumenveill, Delilah was grateful that Oravica and Ferrashi had insisted upon full battle gear.

In addition to the laceration on his chest, Ferrashi had an arrow impaled in his shoulder, and Xanfar ran to him, wrenching the arrow free and taking a piece of silk from his pocket to press into the wound. Delilah looked with wonder at the wolf, who just moments ago was tearing into an aelf with claws and teeth fully engaged. Xanfar looked truly upset by the captain's injuries, tending to him like a mother. Xanfar had told Delilah that the centaurs were mercenaries, however, he had grown up with them in Fallengrove. The Centaurs had been employed by Xanfar's family long before he was born. The soldiers had no formal loyalty to the family, except as an employer. Still, they showed incredible bravery despite being a hired guard. They fulfilled their temporary duty, yet always stayed and renewed their contract, week after week, month after month, year after year. Xanfar had told her that Ferrashi's father had been a close friend of his own father, and he and Ferrashi had played together as children.

Xanfar's father had let him socialize with other races and those who had been altered by the Gloom. He was open-minded about Beasts, employing many of those who were only minimally affected. He knew his estate needed protection, living as they did on the edge of the Whayer Wood. You never knew when a giant rat with laser eyes might wander out to feed, so it was best to have a trained army in your employ. Delilah was grateful to them, too, as the group got themselves together to head back to the castle, this time, with Delilah in the middle. All Delilah could think was that she would surely have been dead if she had only had her three Sister Guard to defend her against the attacking aelves. Perhaps the Council had been right about bringing a heftier military attachment. Delilah's mind also turned to the eerie sound of the horn that had blasted through the forest. She had not heard that sound since the day her brother died. It had sounded right before he launched the attack that would end their parents' lives.

At dinner, Xanfar was pensive and barely spoke over their courses. Delilah had a lot to mull over as well, reviewing the unexpected battle with the aelves.

"It was an assassination attempt, you know," Xanfar said. Delilah looked up into the sincere face of the wolf. "They were coming straight for you."

"Yes, I realized that," Delilah said, not wanting to admit it out loud, although she had come to that conclusion.

"Why would the Crystal Aelves want you dead?" he asked.

"So many reasons, not the least of which that they hold me responsible for the death of my brother." It hurt her chest just to say those words.

"Really? What affinity do they have to your brother?"

"The deepest. Jarvis was entrenched with them from the time he was young. He was always fascinated by them. We learned Aelvish first from our tutors due to his infatuation. He studied them endlessly, read every book he could find on their culture and traditions, their powers. I think he wanted to be an aelf!" she laughed dryly. "He really did, I think. He started consorting with them despite our parents' disapproval. We had better relations with the aelves from Erithea, where my father originated, but the Crystal Aelves were enemies of ours for generations. They have always despised our family."

"And the Crystal Aelves are some of the most vicious of their race," Xanfar shook his head.

"Yes! Yet Jarvis worshipped them and began exchanging secret scrolls with them. Since the aelves are impervious to the Gloom, they can travel widely. They dispatched a group to see Jarvis a few months before the attempted coup. He was nineteen, so what could my parents do? They could not forbid him from socializing with other races, which would seem undiplomatic. So, they allowed the contact, despite warning him that the Crystal Aelves were dangerous and would try to use him to their advantage. He ignored their advice. They went so far as to forbid him to bring them into the castle, so he met them in taverns in Hope right in broad daylight. No one could dissuade him.

"There was a ritual on the cliffs. My parents were planning a sacred rite to secure Jarvis' place in the line of succession. It was supposed to be a private ceremony, yet Jarvis had spread the word and all of Hope was in attendance. He had plotted with the Aelves to kill our parents right there in front of everyone and take control. He would fill all the royal posts with his new allies and Hope would become an Aelven city, with the current populace pushed into servitude. At least, this was what I was told afterward. It all happened so fast on that day." Delilah gulped back the lump of emotion welling in her throat.

Xanfar reached out and took her hand in his paws. "You do not have to tell me about it if you do not wish," he said.

"No, Xan, I must tell you because it has affected you now. My history has followed me to your doorstep, so you deserve to know why you are being assaulted by Crystal Aelves in your own forest."

"I would be curious to know that, certainly. Still, it is so personal to you that I hope you will only share it if you are comfortable."

"It is uncomfortable business," Delilah said. "There is no way to soften it. My parents were murdered that day. The Aelves arrived at the edge of the crowd. They were there for backup and to witness the event to make sure Jarvis went through with the foul task. They were there, yet it was my brother's hand that killed our parents. They were walking to the cliff to perform the ritual. Suddenly, there was a sound. It was the same trumpeting sound we heard in the forest today. On that day, it was intended as a signal to Jarvis. He took out a knife and slit my father's throat from behind. Then he stabbed my mother in the chest. I will never forget the look of surprise and horror on her face as her son murdered her. Jarvis wasted no time. He pushed their bodies aside and mounted a rock at the cliff edge. He stood and began making a proclamation taking control of the monarchy. It was then that the Sister Guard attacked him. I do not think he anticipated that. I think he believed they would just let him take control, since he was the rightful heir. There are laws in place for those kinds of things, though, and the Guard were not going to let him get away with a coup, despite his lineage. They surrounded him. His back was to the cliff edge, and he had nowhere to go.

"He yelled something in Aelvish and then… he was gone. He dropped backwards over the cliff and into the sea below," Delilah paused. "The Aelves had their weapons drawn, yet when Jarvis yelled to them, they backed away. They scattered and vanished, like… well, you saw how fast they moved today. They disappeared. Before I knew it, the Mistress of the Guard was holding up my arm, yelling: 'Long live the Queen! Long live Queen Delilah.' I was in shock. I was just a kid and I had just lost my whole family and witnessed the vile betrayal by my brother."

"I can hardly imagine what that was like," Xanfar said softly, reaching for her hand. Delilah had a flash of Xanfar in battle, fierce and beastly. It was like another being entirely, sitting there with his forelock nicely combed, changed into a burgundy dinner jacket with cream lace trim brushing her wrist as he held her hands in his paws.

"It was like a knife to my heart. When Jarvis stabbed our parents, he stabbed me, too. I can never understand and never forgive what he did."

"And the thing he said, before he fell from the cliff? What was it?"

Delilah pulled one hand away to take a big swig of wine from the green glass goblet sitting in front of her. The wine looked black in the dim candlelight. She swirled it around the glass and watched the dark fluid drip down the sides. "I was not sure at first," she said. "I thought I imagined it. Then I checked with our Aelvish tutor, who had attended the ceremony. She confirmed it. He said: 'I will meet you on the other side, my Love!'"

"Hmmm. Strange. Why do you think the Aelves blame you for his death?"

"Well, it was my Guard who surrounded him, forcing him from the cliff. They were protecting the monarchy and protecting me. The Aelves thought they were taking over a Queendom, and instead, they got nothing and I was crowned. I am sure they resent me for it and want me dead. Perhaps they plan to take over Hope if I die, since I have no heir."

"What would they even want with Hope anyway?" he asked. "They have their own lands and people."

"Power. Expansion. Hope has a strategic advantage on the edge of the sea. Plus, they have always hated my family. My mother's great-grandmother, Queen Eshmerlain, defeated them on their own lands before the Gloom trapped our people in Hope. The Crystal Aelves had been waiting for vengeance for a long time. Perhaps they still are."

"It seems so. I will go back to talk to Aumenveill tomorrow to see if he knows anything," Xanfar said.

"Aumenveill! I had almost forgotten our miraculous time today! Nothing like a surprise attack by Aelves to distract one from a profound experience! I am so sorry to have put your Centauri Guard in such a compromised position."

"Nonsense! They loved it. They have not seen much action lately. Corell was practically exploding to show off his archery prowess! They are proud of their skills."

"As they should be."

"That reminds me. I should check on Ferrashi. His wounds were quite worrying," Xanfar rose from the table. "If you will excuse me, Your Majesty?"

"Of course."

Delilah finished her meal and retired to her quarters. As she went to close the heavily embroidered curtains, her eye was caught by movement across the courtyard below. She recognized Xanfar's form moving toward the stables. The huge door to the barn was open and light spilled out. She watched as a dark Centauri figure filled up the door, light spilling around the shape of his grand form. Xanfar approached and reached up to embrace the Centaur. It was quite a distance, and the shapes were muddled, yet Delilah could swear they kissed before retreating inside. She stood reflecting on what this meant, a small pit of loss in her stomach. Not a few minutes later, another figure approached scurrilously, looking around as if afraid of being caught. Delilah would recognize her Guard, Batelnut, anywhere, with her long limbs and self-conscious gate. Delilah could not tell the identity of the Centaur who came to the door to greet Batel, however she could only guess it was the Golden Steed who had turned her lanky guard into a bashful, blushing maiden earlier in the day. "Well," she thought, "we all cope with the aftermath of a good battle in different ways!" And with that, she lay on the giant behemoth of a bed and immediately fell to sleep.

The next day, Xanfar was missing from breakfast. Delilah spent the morning with her Guard close in tow, wandering the gardens. She wondered at the strange and unusual specimens among the more traditional planted rows of pink, yellow, red, and white Arliven roses and endless hobnail hedges planted in elegant patterns and shaped like all manner of creatures. One garden held what appeared to be a shrine to the mighty Centaur, with a round maze of low hedges, topiaries, and tumbled stone pathways leading to the center where a life-size Centaur was carved from swirled silver marble. The statue was in full glory, surrounded by a shallow pool of Jerushan copperfish with long, golden tails. Heart-shaped lotus leaves were scattered in clumps, flowers dancing on dainty stems atop them. The light, moonbeam faces of the blooms opened to the sky. Iridescent blue dragonflies swooped down to touch the pool, leaving tiny ringlets on the surface of the water. The pond was edged with wolfsbane, drooping toad lilies, and tall swooping grasses with pink fluffy heads that tilted over and reflected across the surface. It was clearly a monument to the Centauri people, honoring their long and important commitment to the family. Though the grand display was stunning, Delilah felt a bit of irritation that she could not quite reconcile.

She and the other women then hiked through the vineyard, which was also a delight. They sampled the dark purple, almost black grapes that made the Fallen Vines vintage so popular, as well as the light pink and pale green fruit that were in smaller quantities at the edges of the long and sweeping rows. They covered the whole expanse of the mountain's foothills and seemed to go on forever. The tiny people Delilah had seen on the way into Fallengrove worked the vines over carefully, almost lovingly, with small scissors, carrying sacks of discarded tendrils. They seemed content in their work, unrushed, some sitting on the ground as they worked, gently feeling through the vines to trim them and urge them into production. Honeybees swirled around, and Delilah and her Guard discovered a whole cluster of hives tucked under a grove of drooping willows, hidden behind the frilled silvery-green curtains of the trees. The funny little people with horns and tails, dressed in the blue livery of the estate, worked the hives, too. They cleaned up branches and harvested honey into tiny pots by moving slowly among the bees without disturbing them. A lady with a piggish nose and short spiky ears on top of her head among dun-colored hair came over and gave them some little wooden spoons of honey to sample. It was unlike any they had ever tasted, so fragrant and full of grapey flavor.

"I must ask Lord Xanfar if we can bring some of this home. I would love to try this in my special honey cake!" said Torrence, who was a novice baker, and always experimenting with new recipes.

The women returned to the castle and saw Xanfar approaching, riding a different centaur that Delilah did not recognize, with a few familiar faces in their entourage. Ferrashi was nowhere to be seen, perhaps still recovering from his wounds. Xanfar had a serious expression and jumped down, coming toward Delilah urgently. "Your Majesty, I must speak with you," he said, and led her away from the others. "I have spoken with Aumenveill… I am afraid it is quite shocking."

"What is it, Xan?"

"It is your brother… Jarvis is still alive!"

Delilah and Xanfar sat in one of the vast libraries in the castle, sipping strong cordials while Xanfar explained what he had learned from the great tree. Aumenveill had informed him that Jarvis had married the Aelven queen. Together, they had been gathering their armies for over a decade with the goal of invading Hope and taking it back. They saw Delilah's visit to Fallengrove as an opportunity to hasten the process by murdering Hope's queen so that Jarvis and Queen Nimevah could easily swoop in to claim the throne. Delilah was, indeed, in shock, unable to comprehend how her brother could have been alive this whole time. While she still hated him for what he did to their parents, her heart ached to know that her brother was still on this earth. They had been so close when she was a child. The terrible loss of their companionship was another tragedy piled onto the death of their parents and the stress of having to take on ruling the monarchy. Delilah had never expected

Queen Delilah and the Encroaching Gloom

that she might inherit the throne. It had been a given that Jarvis would take on that role because he was four years older. He had pranced around wearing their mother's crown from the time Delilah could remember. She had never even considered that she could become queen. A scenario where both her parents and Jarvis were gone was unthinkable to her and had probably been unthinkable to the rest of Hope, too. It was a strange twist of fate somehow orchestrated by her brother in his miscalculation that he could overthrow the whole system and take charge before his appointed time.

She had often wondered what Jarvis had planned for her in his scheme. Her advisors told her that he surely would have used her to form alliances with other races. That meant she probably would have been married off to a Hork king to forge good relations between Horks and Aelves, which was a historically troubled relationship. She might have escaped that fate if she were fortunate enough to be sent to a monastery. She had a hard time believing that Jarvis would be that cruel. Yet the brother she knew as a child was clearly a figment of her imagination, since the brother she knew would not have been capable of killing his own parents. Regardless, her life if Jarvis had succeeded would have been decided for her and it would most likely have been unpleasant. Now, as she dwelled on the knowledge that her brother was still living and plotting to have her killed, her mind was overcome with confusing thoughts and her heart twisted with overwhelming emotions.

"This must be a lot to absorb," said Xanfar. He poured Delilah another cordial and then another for himself.

They sat in silence for a few minutes, both staring into their respective glasses. "This has been quite a history on my family you have gotten while I have been your guest," Delilah finally said. "I am sure you were not expecting to learn so much."

"Well, I was hoping I would have the opportunity to get to know you better during your visit."

"You certainly got that," Delilah said. She was feeling a little tipsy. "And I was hoping to get to know you better, too. It has been exciting to have someone other than the Doktora and my stick-in-the-mud Council to talk to."

"Yes, I am a little starved for company around here, too," Xanfar admitted.

"Are you, though?" she found some courage to ask what she had been afraid to know. "It does seem that you have a special closeness with Ferrashi, at least?"

"Why yes, Ferrashi and I have long been friends. He is very dear to me," he shifted uncomfortably. "He is a soldier, though, through and through. He was raised by mercenaries, and he thinks only of battle and fighting. I adore him, yet he is not the deepest thinker," he chuckled.

"Still a better companion than no companion at all?" Delilah asked, knowing she was being a little intrusive.

"When the love of my life died, I never thought I would love again. I probably never will, at least not like that. Still, one gets lonely, and the comfort of the familiar is hard to resist."

"Your love dying… that is how you were… transformed?"

"In a roundabout way. We have always lived on the edge of the Gloom here in

Fallengrove, so we are no strangers to creatures that wander out of the forest. Truly, most of our staff are half-Beast at least. One reason we have such a fierce hired army is because of the dangers of living so close to the Wood. Hope, I have heard, has the benefit of a type of bubble? A force field that provides protection from the creatures of the Gloom?"

Delilah nodded. "The Vector."

"Well," Xanfar countered, "we have no such force field here. It is the Gloom and then it is Fallengrove. We have learned to live with that, with the risks, and with the diversity of species here. Most of the time it works out well. The unusual people who flee the forest and come to us mostly just want a peaceful life. They work hard, and just wish to not be eaten by fiends. Working our vineyard is a luxury compared to fighting for survival every day. We treat them well and they are well-compensated… and we do not eat them!

"Still," he continued, "it is not always so peaceful between species. Every few years there is an overflow of horrid beasts, one year it might be a plague of putrid zhomboids, another year the wampwhyrs may take control and seek blood. We beat them back, with the help of our Centauri Guard, and eventually they retreat into the forest. The year my love was taken, it was a horde of putridactyls. They are worse than dessicators and vampwhyrs: blood-sucking, undead flesh-eaters. Only they can fly, so even more horrifying. They started flying in and taking a sheep or cow here or there, which we could have tolerated. Then they started taking children.

"It is hard to grow up as the heir to an estate," Xanfar continued. "You never know when someone truly cares about you or just wants your fortune. I had dealt with that: the fortune-seekers. Some of them even came from other lands just to try to win my hand. I had royalty on other continents trying to set me up with a daughter who had a peculiarity of some kind, or nobles trying to marry at a distance to escape a local scandal. I had always politely declined, telling them I was not ready to settle down. The situation with my love was something different. I had been communicating with a duke from Erithea regarding the famine they were having. We were discussing alternate planting strategies that might help them cope with some of the drought. I was advising him on species of trees and vegetables that could withstand sand and almost no water. The duke had sent me a portrait of his cousin, Apple, who was in some trouble for sharing the family's secret caches of grain with the populace. The duke was ready to banish Apple, and was so frustrated that they were even discussing execution.

"I offered to be a safe refuge for Apple for a summer while things cooled down there, until the family forgot about the betrayal and perhaps the outlook for starvation would improve. I felt compassion for Apple's plight, surely, yet it was the portrait that got me. Those eyes! I had never seen such an intense and deeply passionate expression. They looked… well, like the eyes of someone who would share grain with the populace rather than let them starve. I knew I was in trouble even before Apple arrived." Xanfar sighed and poured himself and Delilah yet another cordial before continuing. "With Apple, I never worried that I was some prize to be caught, or that there were ulterior motives. Rather than coveting my wealth, Apple wanted to give it away. There was indignation that the kitchen staff only had one day off a week, and lectures about improving the quality of housing for the grape-pickers. Apple always pushed me to give more, be more generous with the people who relied on us and on whom we relied. 'You have so much,' I would always hear. 'Your wealth will only be improved if you take better care of those who live in servitude.' Apple was the one who got rid of picking quotas and convinced me that we should invest more in the quality of our product rather than quantity."

"Apple sounds like a righteous person with good priorities."

"Yes. I had never met anyone similar. I still have not to this day."

"So, what happened? Was it the putridactyls?"

"Indirectly, yes. Apple was outraged when they started taking the children and coordinated a hunting party. The idea was to go into the Whayer Wood and wipe them out before they could take any more. I was opposed and felt we just needed stronger resources at the edge of the wood. I even offered to hire additional guards, and double the Centauri numbers at the edge of the forest to keep the dactyls or other creatures from coming out. There were many who agreed with Apple that this was not enough, especially those who had lost children, yet the risks were clear: those who went into the Whayer Wood came out transformed. The Gloom would not leave anyone untouched. It was almost certain to permanently change those who entered. Maybe it was vanity, but I did not want to go, and I did not want Apple to go either. That portrait? Yes, I was in love with Apple's appearance, in addition to all the other amazing qualities. I did not want to risk having Apple changed and I feared that I would be revulsed if there were physical changes. I am sure my superficiality was part of why I opposed the raid.

"The hunting party returned and Apple was not with them. It had been successful, and they had wiped out the nests of most of the undead creatures. However, they said Apple had wanted to go further, kill more dactyls. They suspected that the Gloom was already taking hold, infecting the brain and making Apple more aggressive and vicious. They could not convince Apple to return with them. So, I went in searching. I wanted to find Apple and one way or the other, take my love out of the Whayer Wood, even if I had to do so forcefully.

"I was too late. The beast I found in the forest was not the Apple I knew. My love was gone, already permanently changed and dying. The Gloom affects some people that way. It burns right through them, makes them sick with fury and bloodlust, and then they fizzle out. That is how I found Apple, lying on the floor of the Whayer Wood, frothing at the mouth and wanting to kill. I could not bring back the dying beast I found. I wanted everyone to remember my love before the Gloom, so I stayed to dig a grave. Clearly, I stayed in the forest too long, since by the time I came out, I too, was transformed. Fortunately, it did not affect my brain or my personality, just my... physicality."

"So, you risked it all for love and then... Apple was just gone?"

"Yes."

"And you were permanently changed. Xan, that might be the saddest thing I have ever heard," Delilah hugged the wolf.

"Thank you, my friend," he said, and kissed Delilah on the forehead, more a human kiss, not the lick of a wolf.

She looked up at him wondering if there could be any spark there. She saw just sad eyes. Still, she had to ask: "And you have never felt that again? Or the desire to have that same kind of love?"

"There is no 'same kind of love' for me, I am afraid. Life can surprise you, yet I am aware that Apple was the one true love of my life. It was like a cosmic joke, to lose Apple and then to lose the body I was so proud of, the shape of the man I thought I was. I think Apple would have found that funny, too. Ferrashi accepts me for who I am. We were children together, and I never thought differently of him than the other children. Now I match him better," he laughed.

"Yes, I suppose you do. However, you probably still get those long-distance marriage proposals, even with your new look?"

Xanfar pulled open the drawer of a nearby desk, stuffed with scrolls and letters with elaborate wax seals. "I am still a catch, apparently, even with a tail!"

"Oh, I almost forgot!" Delilah pulled out the package she had brought on her journey and unwrapped it. It was a silver letter-opener fashioned with grapes made from purple gemstones hanging down with a foxlike creature that was jumping up to reach them. It depicted an old fable. Her father had sent this to her mother to open his letters before they were married. When Delilah had impulsively decided to bring it along to give to Xanfar, her mind had been filled with a different scenario in which she might present it to him. Now she felt ridiculous for having such thoughts and the gift seemed somehow garish and inappropriate.

"It is so beautiful. Too beautiful for an old wolf like me. I will cherish it, Delilah, and open every one of your letters and scrolls with it, as I hope there will be many more to come! Who knows, perhaps we will be able to speak through the vines and trees someday and have no more need for scrolls!" Xanfar placed the treasure carefully on his desk and excused himself for the evening.

Standing at the casement window again, Delilah watched as Xanfar walked across the courtyard toward the stable door, which opened to reveal Ferrashi's majestic form. Ferrashi looked up and saw Delilah in the window and leaned down to say something to Xanfar. The wolf turned around and gave a little wave to Delilah before going inside. Delilah raised her hand to wave back, but the wolf had already gone inside, and so she was waving to no one.

She lay down on the bed and looked at the folds of cloth and shimmering fabric hanging from the wooden canopy. She had hoped the cordials would have taken the edge off to fall into a numb sleep. Instead, her mind spun with thoughts of Jarvis and with the sad tale Xan had told her. There was a light knock on the door and Oravica entered. "Your Majesty, I am just checking on you. I see our host has gone… to bed."

"Yes, he has gone to find solace in the hulking frame of a Centauri stud, can you blame him?" Delilah laughed.

"Well, it is certainly working for Batel. She has gone there again! I am not sure how I keep letting her off the night watch. I must be a softie."

"Yes, well I am sure that Erigail would not agree."

"No, my wife would not consider me a softie, it is true. Maybe if I bring her back some of that wine!"

Queen Delilah and the Encroaching Gloom

"And Torrence? Where is our studious young Guard this evening?"

"In the kitchens, of course. Learning all manner of new recipes from the Fallengrove staff."

"So, it is just you? And what if my brother should send an army of aelves to attack the castle? Where would my faithful Guard be then?"

"One getting her jollies in the stable and one with her hand in the kitchen honey pot, I am afraid."

"Well, let us hope we do not get attacked…" Delilah sighed "…again."

"How are you doing, Your Grace? It must be quite a shock about your brother."

"A shock, yes. As if my whole life for the past fifteen years has been a lie. I do not even trust my own senses or our own intelligence. How could our spies, our allies, not know about this?"

"Well, there were whispers," Oravica admitted.

"Whispers?!" Delilah practically shouted.

"Rumors, Your Majesty. Nothing more. The Council felt it was not important to worry you with such untrustworthy reports."

"The Council decided!"

"Yes, you know my sister is very conservative. She voted to keep the information secret. She swore me to secrecy, however now you know, so…"

"I will stand before that Council and make them account to me! I am their queen! How could they keep something like this from me. Oravica… how could *you*?"

"Your Highness, please. You know I am honor-bound to the Council."

"What about to me? Am I not your first charge? It is bad enough to know that my own brother not only slaughtered my parents—hard enough to know that he is alive and trying to slaughter me! Yet, my own Guard? How could you know this and not tell me?" Delilah flopped back onto the bed. "There will be a reckoning when we return. I can assure you of that."

"I am sorry to disappoint you," Oravica said. Delilah put a beaded pillow over her face. "Your Majesty, is there anything I can get you? Anything I can do for you tonight?"

Delilah did not answer. She lay with her head practically smothered with the weight of the heavy pillow and wondered if she might just stop breathing. Then it would be all over: no more of the gnawing humiliation she felt by Xan's kind rejection, no more of the despair of twisting feelings toward her brother, no more dread of being attacked by a shiny, deadly, acrobatic army of aelves who had an enormous incentive to kill her. She heard something at the window and jumped up, tingling with alarm. Oravica had left the room to leave Delilah to her misery, so she was alone, yet she felt as if there were someone there in the room with her. The window was slightly open, and Delilah did not recall leaving it that way. She walked slowly toward the casement, feeling a breeze and a slight zap of energy in the fresh pooling air. Cautiously, she took her broken sword and pushed the window open a bit more, and air rushed in, tickling Delilah's hair and almost whispering in her ears. She was confused and scared. She thought for a moment to call for Oravica. Then, remembering her friend's disloyalty, she stopped and concluded: "As always, I must fend for myself."

"You are never alone, my child." The familiar voice came from the window, drifting in on the light wind, yet from nowhere at all.

Delilah ran to the window and pushed it open. There was only the vast night sky to greet her. "Aumenveill?" she asked.

"Yes, I am here, we are all here. We are Linked."

Delilah's eyes were drawn to the dancing tendrils and open white flowers on the vines that climbed the castle walls. "You are... here?"

"I am just one and there are countless others, zillions of life forms between you and I," the voice was everywhere and nowhere, as she recalled from her encounter with the tree spirit in the forest. "You can hear me, so you have mastered the art of listening! I know you are in pain, child. You are suffering. I can feel it all the way through the woods. I could feel it if you were alone in your chambers in Hope, would hear it echoing through the stones, and right through to my heart."

"So now trees have hearts as well as eyes everywhere?" She could not resist.

"Ah, Delilah," Aumenveill said slowly, "it is our heart that allows us to truly see. You are listening with your heart now, or you would not be able to hear me."

"So, the bugs, the tiny creatures, the... micro-beings that digest dead things... they all have hearts?"

"No, dear. They are *all* heart. They are too small to think or plan or know things, they just feel and communicate what they feel, connecting one to another. Of course, it is not a physical heart, not an organ that can fail. It is automatic. Thoughtless. What a relief it must be not to think, yes?"

"Yes, I can agree with that, as one who sometimes thinks more than is good for her."

"Do not worry about the aelves or your brother. You and Jarvis are connected, too."

"That clearly did not keep him from trying to kill me."

"And yet he failed. He failed because of the heart that connects you. It is all a misunderstanding, you see."

"A misunderstanding? What is a misunderstanding?"

"All of it: the murder of your parents; Jarvis' banishment to death; his reasons for wanting to kill you. It can all be worked out if you open your hearts to one another again, as you did when you were children."

"Those days are over, Aumenveill. I can never forgive him for his evil deeds. Alive or dead, I will not forgive his treachery."

"You are too caught up in punishment, in wanting others to pay for their actions. It makes you a good soldier, Delilah. Not a good ruler."

His criticism was like a slap to the face, yet rang with truth. "I am vengeful. It is true. That is my nature, though. I am not the forgiving type."

"You are hurt, as we get sometimes when we are injured. I have a slice in my bark that is hundreds of years old from a feckless young unicorn scratching his itchy new growth of a horn. I still smart from that old scar! I would be lying if I said I did not rejoice when that unicorn died of old age and went back into the forest earth. All is forgiven with the passage of time and death and decomposition and rebirth."

"Well, I may not be able to forgive this one until I, too, am decomposing on the forest floor."

"If you wish, Delilah. However, I hope that will not be necessary."

The airship lifted, and the Centauri Guard who held the tethered ends let loose the last ropes to swing below the basket. It was a slower takeoff, the bottom of the basket filled with several cases of wine, a few vats of honey, and several small trees with root balls packed in sacks. They were weighted down with their new bounty, and Delilah held the new scimitar that Xanfar had presented to replace her broken one. This one was made of iron, "better for fighting aelves," he said. Batel waved vigorously to the golden steed she had befriended, and Torrence waved to the kitchen staff who had taught her to make so many new culinary treats. Delilah waved to Xanfar, who rode Ferrashi alongside and under the departing balloon, waving up with a big, toothy smile.

Oravica watched her queen quietly as the others waved goodbye. Delilah looked at her and realized that Oravica had made no friends on their journey. The officer had devoted herself entirely to protecting Delilah and had not socialized. "Erigail will be pleased to have some of the Fallen Vines, I am sure, will she not, Sergeant?"

"Yes, Your Majesty," Oravica said. "I am sure she will be very pleased, indeed." Her formality struck Delilah and she knew she had hurt her. What else could the sergeant have done? She was sworn to hold Council secrets as part of the Oath of the Sister Guard. She had only done her duty. Delilah knew this and regretted lashing out at her. Delilah had so few true friends, having no family and only an army and council to surround her. She might be more careful with her words, she pledged, yet did not go further to apologize.

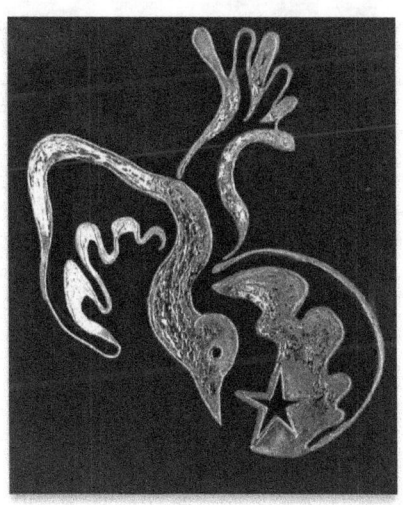

"Alas the world is moving fast,
As fast as the stars in their plight
Our journey here is brief indeed,
And lasts but a mid-summer's night."
-The Ghost Scribe

Chapter 5: The End of the Rope

Delilah sat upon a crate of wine at the bottom of the basket, so much on her mind she was barely aware of the others in her company. Oravica stood and watched the course of the craft and the activities of the Whayer Wood below, while the two cousins sat speaking in low voices with an occasional giggle and embarrassed glances in Delilah's direction. Delilah thought how strange it was to think you were going on a journey for one purpose and to have a completely different experience. She felt a pang of shame recalling giving Xanfar the letter opener and hoped it had not seemed as odd to him as she suspected it may have been.

"I can see Verily," Oravica announced.

The others stood to watch the tiny cliff-side observatory in the distance come closer. When they were approaching the hilly farms and small homesteads of the territory, they saw a crowd gathered at the place where they had originally launched. At first, it seemed that there must certainly be a way that they would alight upon the cliffs. However, it soon became apparent that they were moving at too great a speed and at too high elevation to have a successful landing. They went way above the heads of the crowd of burgundy-robed apprentices and saw Ilvana among them animatedly gesturing. They could hear the scientist yelling: "They did not follow my instructions!" Soon the aircraft floated well past the cliffs and out over the sea. Vivid waves far below made slow, mesmerizing designs. The Gloom overlayed the red ocean with its own spirals and irregular shapes. Sea sounds floated up, mismatched from the patterns below, as if delayed in their journey.

"Now what, Your Majesty?" asked Torrence.

"Well, I had not planned for this particular situation," Delilah said. "It seems there is not much we can do. We would not survive if we jumped, and this thing does not seem to be coming down anytime soon. I suppose we will have to wait for the air to subside and hope the basket will float upon the water until a boat comes along." The women began to inspect the basket, wondering if there was any chance the odd thing could be buoyant. It seemed unlikely.

"And we will have to hope we do not get affected by the Gloom upon the water as we are… if we must float for some time," Batelnut observed.

"Well, we have wine and honey, women of Hope! At least if we are going to turn Beast or sink to our deaths, we might as well enjoy our last moments," Delilah said, and opened a crate to pass around a bottle of wine. Even Oravica drank when the bottle went around, saying nothing and sternly watching the horizon.

Torrence nudged her cousin and said, "Maybe Batel will be lucky and the Gloom will turn her into a she-Centaur!" They laughed despite themselves, even with full knowledge that chances for survival were quite slim.

Batel, perhaps emboldened by their grave predicament, said: "What about you, Your Majesty? Would you not want to turn into a wolf, better to keep company with Lord Xanfar?"

"Ah, I am afraid that even if I were a she-wolf, I would still not be his type," she said. They all laughed even harder at this, having come to their own conclusions about their gracious host.

"There is something ahead!" Oravica had been studying the horizon and now pointed to a thin outline of a rounded shape in the distance. "It looks like an island!"

"We are still too high," Delilah said, trying to project if they would be able to land or would pass over the land mass.

"I think you are right," said Oravica, looking around and up into the hollow heart of the balloon. "Torrence, get your arrows ready," she said. The young soldier did as she was told and waited for orders. Oravica concentrated on watching and calculating. "Now!" she yelled, "shoot an arrow up into the fabric, toward the backside!"

"Are you sure we should…" Torrence hesitated.

"Now!" The senior officer shouted, and Torrence obeyed, shooting an arrow that pierced the thick hide. It left a small, barely noticeable, exit wound, with no obvious effect. "Again!" yelled Oravica. The next arrow had a similar result.

"No, this is not working," Batel said. She dug in her satchel and found a sharp knife. Putting it between her teeth, she jumped up on the side of the balloon and began to climb the corded netting on the outside. She scurried out of sight, and the others looked and, listening, watching, afraid to see the shape of Batel fall past them. They heard a sawing sound and then the tip of the blade and a big slice appeared on the inside of the inflated sack. A hissing sound began, and the ship began shuddering oddly, lurching a little with spurts of jumpy motion.

"Another one, Batel," called Oravica, and Batel's blade appeared a short distance from the first cut and made a parallel line. This time the double lips of the incisions seemed to sputter in for a moment. Then, ripping out in a giant gust of air, a gaping hole with jagged edges appeared where the wounds had weakened the fabric. It was blustering out like a child spitting out water, with the whole airship bouncing dangerously. The craft seemed to be going in the direction of the island, yet jerked violently, one way and then another. Then with a great shrieking sputter, the whole thing went into a spiraling corkscrew, frighteningly fast. Shrieks escaped their lips without their consent as they swirled madly, their bodies pressed against the outside of the basket. The most they could hope for would be a crash landing if they were fortunate enough to get close to the island. With the dizzying spiral, it was impossible to tell where they were heading.

In moments, a jarring impact occurred, and Delilah was dazed and disoriented, tossed out upon her side. She sat up: her shoulder was completely out of its socket and hung uselessly. She looked at the wreckage. Boards and ropes were strewn across the ground attached to the now deflated balloon. One crate was busted apart and most of the bottles inside had broken and were sitting in a pool of the burgundy wine. Batelnut had somehow held onto the rope net of the deflated balloon and Torrence had also tumbled out of the basket. The cousins were sitting up examining themselves, in stunned confusion. In moments, they found their senses and ran to their queen. "Your Highness, your arm!" exclaimed Torrence.

"Do not worry about me. Where is Oravica?" Delilah stood and surveyed the small island, which appeared to be made entirely of rock. It was rounded with many bumps and ridges, and covered in sea moss, crusted scales of seashells, and giant barnacles that made pools of water with sea life inside from the ocean waves. The Gloom was just below them, and there was almost no visibility in any direction. "Oravica!" Delilah yelled, feeling panic welling up inside her. Her loyal friend! Had she lost her after treating her so poorly? She called her name a few more times when they heard gasping and splashing over the opposite side of the rock. "Get some rope!" Delilah ordered. The officers grabbed the end of one of the cables and threw it over the edge.

"I have it! Pull me up!" They heard Oravica's breathless voice, barely audible below. Delilah was not much help with her lame arm, yet wound the end around her waist and leaned with her weight to pull the rope taught as the others did the harder work of pulling hand over hand. Soon a dripping Oravica was visible and then lying face down, safely upon the island. She rolled over and blinked at the sky for a few moments, not saying anything.

"Sergeant, are you okay?" asked Torrence, kneeling by her and putting her hand on her commanding officer's arm. Oravica looked at her as if she did not recognize her, then sat up and shook her head a few times.

"Yes. Yes, I am not hurt. Thank you." Oravica looked around for the first time, surveying the damage and the island and then her eyes fell upon her queen. "Your Majesty! Your arm needs assistance," Oravica stood up and wobbled a bit for a second, Torrence steadying her as she almost lost her balance. The sergeant squared herself, then moved straight for Delilah. Oravica was still sopping wet, and Delilah smelled the intense fishy saltiness as she came close and grabbed onto her arm with both hands. "Hold on to her!"

Oravica ordered the Guard, who each came to lay hands on Delilah.

"Really, this can wait, Orav….. Oooooowwwww!" she howled as the senior Guard twisted and thrust Delilah's shoulder back into its socket with a pop. "Oh, oh, oh my. Oh yes, that is better," said the queen. She then reached out and held Oravica by the shoulders, looking straight into her eyes. "Oravica, I need to tell you that…"

At that moment there was a roaring sound and something snakelike rose from the water. It had a beak and looked vaguely familiar. The mouth opened to hiss at them and Delilah recognized it. "Skilpada!" she yelled. "A sea tortoise!" They realized what should have been abundantly clear if they had not been so shaken by the crash: they were standing upon the creature's back. Its head lunged and snapped at the air in front of them. "Move back where it will not reach us!" Delilah commanded. They moved as far as the slope of the beast's shell would allow without slipping into the water and readied their weapons. "We need to kill it," she realized. "If it dives under, we are done for."

Torrence wasted no time and with a battle cry ran at the creature, which turned its head around awkwardly to reach and strike at the invaders on its back. Torrence advanced with no hesitation making a giant slicing motion with her sword, intending to cut the monster's head off. The creature yanked its head out of the way. It's toothy beak came back in one giant vicious movement, biting Torrence completely in half. The soldier barely made a sound as the two parts of her body dropped into either side of the sea. The turtle snapped its mouth and licked the blood.

"Nooooooooo!" Batel yelled standing with her arms wide and taught, then ran at her cousin's murderer. With one of her giant fists, Batel smacked up into the chin of the animal. Its head wobbled and fell, splashing down, then bobbed up to the surface of the water. The women ran to the edge. They could barely see the thing's head floating there. Only the vaguest glint of blood stained the surface of the water where Torrence's remains had begun to sink to their resting place at the bottom of the sea. "No," Batel said again, and stood there shaking her head. Oravica embraced her and the young Guard sobbed upon her shoulder.

Delilah came over and touched Batel's back. "She died honorably."

"She… she loved the sea," Batel said incredulously.

"I know," Oravica said, holding Batelnut and rocking her back and forth like a baby as the young woman convulsed with grief.

Delilah was still on alert and saw the tiniest movement in the head of the turtle. "Is it… still alive?" The monster's blood-red eyes began to blink. It attempted to lift its wobbly head, as if drunk. "We need a strategy. Retreat!" Delilah shouted, and the women ran to the far side of the turtle's shell. They began to discuss how to behead the thing and Oravica prepared a crossbow. The skilpada made a horrible roaring sound and began to regain its senses, snapping and hissing, thrashing around in the water. The women were tossed about, barely able to keep their footing as the beast spun and bit at them. Out of nowhere, there came a whistling sound followed by a huge explosion. The beast stopped thrashing. When the smoke cleared, they saw that its head had been blown completely off. Its neck dropped, unencumbered, into the water.

"What in the Gloom?" Delilah said, dumbfounded. They heard splashing, chanting, and singing, a pirate song, with a boat approaching at a fast pace. Terror sunk into Delilah's heart. Pirates were known to take no prisoners. They indiscriminately murdered anyone they encountered on the water. Perhaps they would take her for ransom, if they recognized her, however, they would likely slaughter the others. The boat's bow, with a snarling siren figurehead, came into view, with tall black masts arising from the mist. Delilah recognized the ship immediately. Jezschmel! This did not exactly mean that they were safe, however it certainly was the best of all possibilities.

The ship pulled up alongside the tortoise's floating carcass. Jezschmel's proud form emerged, her hands planted firmly on her hips and a great smile upon her face. "What is a nice queen like you doing in a place like this?" she asked, and her crew busted out laughing behind her.

"Clearly, I was sitting here waiting for a pirate queen like you to come along to rescue me," Delilah responded. Jezschmel leaped down and the two queens clasped arms and bowed their heads to one another. "Your timing is impeccable," Delilah observed.

"I have been meaning to kill that old bitch, Chaurlie, for years!" Jezschmel responded. "It is her hibernation season. You must have woken her. I am sure that did not go well."

"No, it did not. We lost one of our Guard," said Delilah.

"My condolences. I am sure she died bravely."

"She did."

"You do not seem surprised to see me," Delilah remarked.

"No, we were tracking your airship for the last hour or so. We saw when it accelerated and spun out of control. I was not positive it was you. Still, I could not think of anyone who might be crazy enough to be flying a balloon over the sea."

"Well, flying it over the ocean was not quite the plan," Delilah admitted. "We were returning from a journey and we… overshot."

"I see. Well, let us get you upon our ship to deliver you home. Have you brought us some lovely vintage? Why, is that Fallen Vines? How delightful!"

"Help yourself," Delilah said, and began handing up the remaining intact bottles to Jezschmel's crew. "We need to save one for my sergeant's wife," she said and handed a bottle to Oravica. "I am sure she will not mind sacrificing the rest to have her love safely home. Still, she will want a taste."

Oravica took the bottle from Delilah gratefully. "Yes, Erigail will be satisfied with just me and one bottle of Fallen Vines."

"Torrence will never be able to bake with her honey," Batel said, in a flat tone, as they lifted the remaining crates, battered trees in sacks, and their few small bags, and climbed aboard the ship on the wide plank that was extended down to allow them to embark. On board, the pirates bustled and got to sailing again, pointing the ship toward Hope.

"You did not bring your whole fleet?" Delilah asked Jezschmel.

"No, I assumed it was you and decided we did not need our whole brigade to rescue a few maidens in distress," Jezschmel winked at Oravica. "They would come at my command if I summoned them."

"How do you communicate between ships?" Delilah wondered.

"Old magick," said Jezschmel. "You probably would not understand. Our messages travel through the water."

"Is that so? I would like to hear more about that!" Delilah said.

Hope's entire army had met the ship with full artillery at the dock. However, they hastened to back down once they saw their queen intact and smiling. When the gangplank was lowered, Jezschmel surprised Delilah by coming up behind her saying, "Allow me, Your Majesty." The pirate scooped Delilah up as if she were nothing and confidently carried her down the gangplank. Delilah laughed at the thrill of the other queen's spontaneous gesture and felt a spark alight in her core.

Delilah stopped smiling when she saw Torrence's mother, who was a senior Guardswoman. She gathered herself and went to her directly to inform her about her daughter. The woman sobbed relentlessly, and Delilah consoled her the best she could. Batel, who had grown up in Torrence's house half the time, ran to her aunt and embraced her, both of them wailing and weeping in their grief.

Jezschmel did not stay long, however they were treated to a brief feast that Delilah's household staff brought to the docks for the returning adventurers, the pirate crew, and the Council of Elders, who wanted to know everything about the trip and what had gone wrong in the return flight. Delilah brushed them off and told them she would address them as a group the next day. Everyone was relieved to have their queen home safely. As expected, Oravica's wife, Erigail, was just happy she was safe, and pleased to receive even one bottle of the Fallen Vines. She worried, though, observing an irregular rash forming on Oravica's fingers and arms, most likely from falling into the ocean Gloom. Oravica minimized it by saying she probably just needed a long bath. The occasion was tainted by Torrence's loss, and Torrence's mother and Batel went home to share the news of her passing with the rest of the family. Delilah had some time to speak privately with Jezschmel, away from the others, and what she learned about conversing through the waves would rattle around in her brain for a long time to come.

⚻

Delilah stormed into the Council Meeting and let loose a barrage of insults at her advisors, who were already gathered there.

"Your Majesty, this abuse is outrageous!" The Council Elder who spoke was Doktora Ishlip, one of the oldest of the Council members who had been part of her parents' council. Jarvis and Delilah had called her "Fishlip" when they were children. When her parents had been killed, it was Doktora Ishlip who had mentored Delilah. The elder had encouraged the new queen to purge most of the Council by telling her that she suspected they were compromised and had, in fact, conspired to help Jarvis with the attack. Ishlip then helped Delilah install new members of the Council.

"Doktora, you will forgive me if I tell you that it is outrageous how many of you have known that Prince Jarvis was alive and yet did nothing to inform me of this," Delilah spoke slowly to keep her voice calm.

Fishlip sputtered and said: "It was of no great import to you, as we knew he was living in the Aelven territory of Raefenshire on the other side of the Whayer Wood. And I believe he is now 'King' Jarvis, as he is consort to the Crystal Aelven Queen and considered to rule at her side."

"And this was also information you kept from me? I am truly at a loss. Major Abbowhen: You are my highest-ranking officer. Explain to me how the Guard could keep this from me?"

The Major shifted in her seat to stand up and face the queen, looking markedly uncomfortable. "As the Doktora said, Your Majesty, it was not deemed to be fruitful intelligence. We certainly would have brought it to your attention if there were a threat."

"A threat!" Delilah was incredulous. "A threat like having the Aelven Queen and a team of assassins try to kill me in Fallengrove?"

"We advised you not to go there, Your Majesty, if you will recall," said Doktora Sinsarel, the monstrologist.

"Yes, because you were all so worried about the evil Lord Xanfar, who is as harmless as a pussycat, I might add, when he is not valiantly defending me against aelves! Lord Xanfar saved my life, no thanks to any of you. You may have done better to give me information about my brother being alive if you truly wanted to keep me safe."

"Your Majesty, our job is to protect you, so you must understand that we were protecting you from this information. It would have been nothing but a distraction to know that Prince Jarvis was alive. It has been fifteen years and he has not tried anything until now."

"Yes, however I should have been informed of the dangers. It is not just your job to protect me. It is also to inform me! Now I must wonder about what else I have not been informed."

Doktora Ishlip, looking offended, stood up and said, "Now, now, Your Majesty..."

"This Council is hereby dissolved," Delilah said. "You will depart from the castle immediately and will not return unless you are summoned." The council members looked around at one another, stunned, as if they did not understand. "You are permanently dismissed," Delilah said, and stormed out of the Meeting Hall. She heard rumblings behind her and turned to see Major Abbowhen following her. "Major, you are still a leader of my Guard. If you would like to maintain this position, you will make sure the Council departs immediately and then escort yourself out."

"Your Majesty, you can not intend to permanently disband the Council?"

"That is exactly what I intend," Delilah retorted, and swooped away. She walked briskly down the great hall to the center staircase and out a back door leading to the kitchen gardens and the orchards. Her heart was still pumping from the confrontation as she sat and removed her boots, placing her feet directly on the grass. If no one else was going to be honest with her, at least the trees would be, she thought. The Vector flickered at the edge of the Woods. Delilah noticed that there were places that the Gloom was seeping in, as if the enchanted sphere had small perforations. Small fingerlings of the Gloom were reaching in. Movement behind her had her on her feet instantly with the scimitar Xanfar had made for her held aloft in her hand.

"It is just me, Your Majesty," said the healer, Helanza, who was walking up with a bowl. Delilah had not seen her since she returned. "I tried to come to you last night. They told me you were sleeping and to let you rest."

"Yes, they all seem to think they know what is best for me," Delilah said, annoyance seething up anew.

"Please, drink this. You have been through a lot these last weeks. It will replenish you. It may also help with those," she pointed to Delilah's arm where Oravica had grasped her to pop her shoulder back in. Small iridescent ridges were rising in a band where Oravica's fingers had touched her skin. Delilah had not noticed the rash before. She took the bowl Helanza offered her and drank the thick fluid, fragrant with roots and a fresh, green taste that lingered in her mouth. She passed the empty bowl back. Helanza stood there holding the bowl, watching her. "You are too trusting, Your Majesty."

"How is that?" Delilah asked.

"If I wanted to poison you, I could have done it just then," Helanza said.

"Well, I should hope that you did not! You have been the Royal Healer since I was a child. I have never known you to poison anyone yet!"

"Of course, I did not poison you, yet it would be easy to do so. Some poison is ingested quickly, through a beverage or on an arrow in battle. Other poison is ingested slowly, over many years, in half-truths and outright lies. And sometimes it is those you trust most who are most likely to poison you."

"What are you trying to tell me, Helanza? I implore you to be direct."

"You know that I stay out of politics…"

"Yes, yes, it is your most redeeming quality," Delilah rushed her to get to the point.

"There are reasons to keep you in the dark about some things. Discovering one untruth unravels many others."

"Again, you are being quite obscure, Helanza. Tell me what you know."

"There are many who knew about Prince Jarvis being alive from the very beginning. His death was a fiction maintained to keep you feeling safe in your new role as queen and to dispel anyone who would question your right to inheritance."

"Yet if he is alive, he has a greater claim to inheritance than I do!" Delilah exclaimed, expressing the thing that had gnawed most deeply at her since she had learned of Jarvis' status.

"The attempted coup excluded him from the lines of succession," said Helanza. "Those are the laws. However, there are still some who would claim he could be installed as first in line, regardless of the coup. There are some who would say Jarvis' actions were justified because his own life was at stake."

"What do you mean, *his* life was at stake? He killed my parents!" Delilah exclaimed.

"That is true. Still, there are some that would say that your parents were trying to kill him first."

"Trying to kill him! That is absurd," Delilah shook her head.

"Perhaps. Perhaps I have said too much already. Just keep a watchful eye, Your Majesty. Things may not be as you have always assumed. Once a thread becomes loose, you must ask yourself if you want to pull that thread. Sometimes your whole world can unravel before your eyes."

Despite Helanza's potion, Delilah had a restless sleep. She awoke from her turbulent slumber to a soft petal floating down and tickling her nose. She batted it away and sat up, aware of a presence in the room and the air shimmering with an odd glow. She went to the window and suddenly felt herself float out of it upon an updraft of prickly air. The wind surrounded her like a crisp blanket, and sparkles of light filled her eyes. She floated down and hovered above the orchard garden, where she saw a gnarled old plum tree. She had never noticed it before, yet it looked somehow familiar. As she began to descend toward the tree, movement beyond it lifted up in a confusing swirl of Gloom-colored dust and a figure rose from behind the tree with arms outstretched. It was Jarvis! He was wearing an odd helmet made out of a skull and he was smiling. As Delilah drew nearer, though, she could see it was not a pleasant smile. It was a vicious snarl, like that of an angry beast. He opened his mouth and gray swirls came out and twisted toward Delilah like claws.

"I am coming for you, sister!" he said, his voice his own, yet deeper than she recalled and filled with loathing.

She awoke with her bed soaked in sweat and a plum blossom upon her pillow. She got up and found Olav to ask that Doktora Chastice be summoned to take her to the entrance to Verily.

"'Tis right in front of you," the old woman said, and Delilah walked into the passageway and removed her blindfold with one hand, holding a torch in the other.

"Thank you, Doktora," Delilah turned to say, yet only heard the brush falling down to cover the secret opening. After a vigorous walk through the dark mountain-tunnel, she came to the wooded vine-covered tunnel and extinguished the torch. The light above was fair enough to see by, yet she flinched with each close snorting and hooting of beasts on the other side of the tunnel walls. Delilah eagerly trotted through the last part of the passageway and tripped out into the glowing morning sunlight practically into the arms of the Doktora.

"Ilvana!" Delilah exclaimed, stunned to have the scientist standing before her in white robes and a dark burgundy sash.

"Your Majesty," Ilvana bowed her head in the smallest inclination of deference. "To what do I owe this unexpected honor?"

"Well not totally unexpected? You seem to be in exactly the right place at exactly the right time to receive me," observed Delilah.

"Hmmm, yes, well, I thought I saw a bunny in the garden eating my snap peas and came to investigate," the Doktora said. "Clearly you are no bunny."

"No, I am not. Have you injured yourself, Doktora?" Delilah asked, suddenly aware of a bandage wrapped around Ilvana's hand."

"'Tis nothing serious, Your Majesty. So, tell me: how may I help you? Or are you here to punish me for the failure of the airship? I swear I was explicit in my directions. I do not know how they made such a mess of the launch time."

"Oh, no, it was not your failure! You are not in control of the winds, after all."

"No, but any beast with half a brain should be able to predict them. I left too much to those on the Fallengrove side of the launch. I probably should have sent someone with you or gone with you myself," said the Doktora.

"Well, next time I take an inflated hide across the Whayer Wood, I will be sure to request that you accompany me," Delilah smiled.

"I have been meaning to go and meet Aumenveill in person, anyway. How is the old bark-brain?"

Delilah snickered, "Quite a character! I guess you get a little quirky after so many centuries rooted in the earth."

"Can you imagine? Being stuck in one place for so long? I would go completely batty!" the Doktora shook her head.

"Well, is it so different from our own fates: me stuck in Hope; you stuck in Verily?"

"Neither of us is stuck anywhere, Your Grace. One of the great advances of our species is that we always have a choice. Now trees, they do not get choices, so they must be content where they grow. However, it makes them very… creative. I suppose you were able to get a sense of the technology?"

"Talking through the root systems? Yes, I was. It has so much promise, yet I feel like we are ages away from being able to harness that. Unless you have old trees that can talk to one another."

"We do. We always do!" Doktora exclaimed and grabbed Delilah's arm. "Come with me." She practically dragged Delilah part of the way down the path then turned and walked ahead of her, without slowing down or waiting to see if the queen kept up. Delilah knew better than to ask any questions and dutifully followed the doctor. They wound up the side of the sea cliff. Bulbous clouds tinted pink from the dawn were punctuated by sea hawks and dactyls swooping and shouting to one another. The wind gusted up along the cliff face and blasted against them, and the salt air cleansed Delilah's mind. The sounds of the crashing waves below and cries of the flying creatures purified all the tangled thoughts of deception, her disturbing dream, and the weight she had been carrying since finding out about her brother and the Council's betrayal. She had always wished the castle had been built closer to the sea so that she could benefit daily from the cleansing air and rhythmic sounds of the waves.

"You have not met Kunnikah yet. You will quite enjoy her," Ilvana shouted over her shoulder, leading Delilah along the face of the crag, which was getting thinner and more treacherous.

They traversed a section that required that they hold on to the edge with both arms extended and crab-walk sideways on a narrow ledge to avoid falling to the rocks below. The path then opened to a large alcove of striped reddish rock. A weathered and gnarled cyfresian tree filled a shallow moon-shaped cave against the precipice. Its roots plunged directly into the rock and dark baked clay, with no earth or soil to speak of to support its life. Delilah felt the same vibration, tingling in her bones, and electricity dancing along the hairs on her skin, that she had felt in the presence of Aumenveill. She sat and began to remove her boots and then noticed Ilvana giving her a strange look. "What? Do I not need to remove these?" she asked.

Ilvana made a "tsk" sound and shook her head. "That Lord Xanfar. He is smart, for a wolf, yet he does not seem to understand some of the most basic principles of trans-dermal communication."

"Trans-dermal?"

"Yes, through the skin, Your Majesty. Our skin; their skin. Just place your palm upon her trunk, here," she took Delilah's hand and placed it upon a smooth part in the swirling reddish surface of the tree.

"Ooohh!" Delilah felt a zap in her palm and lifted it for a moment, then recovering, placed her palm again on the silky bark. This time she tolerated the vibration and felt her whole body come alive with a surge of energy.

"Your Majesty," a rich, slow, and deep female voice arose in Delilah's mind. "It is so kind of you to visit me. I have long wished to meet you."

"I… yes, well… I wish I had known you were here before. I am just discovering knowledge about the sentience of trees, unfortunately."

A measured and resonant chuckle bubbled from the tree's essence. "Humans are so amusing. Always thinking they have discovered things that have always been!"

"Yes, I understand how we might seem quite silly to ancient beings such as yourself," Delilah said.

"Yet, you know when to ask for help, dear. That is to your advantage," Delilah felt pure tenderness and gentle loving support from the tree, like a mother. The sensation was so foreign to her that tears welled up in her eyes. "It has been a long time since you accepted help," asserted the tree.

"I would not say that. I am helped every day. I am surrounded by people offering their assistance, more than I could ever need. It is the privilege of a queen to have so many who are eager to serve her."

"That is a different kind of help. You may let others make meals for you, defend you in battle, yet when was the last time you let someone nurture you, assist you in your innermost pain?" the tree's voice was so unctuous, her spirit so calm, that Delilah felt herself entranced.

"It is true. I have learned to rely only on myself to face the troubles of my life. I am so catered to, so cared for in my person, that I do not think I should burden anyone with my inner struggles. Anyone would be happy to trade boots with the queen, so I should not complain when life becomes complicated or difficulties present themselves. I should be able to handle that myself. A queen must be an island."

"Like your mother, Queen Zaryadne?"

"Well, my mother always had my father. Perhaps they were an island together."

"You were young when your parents passed, so it makes sense that you might not have known your mother's inner world. Did she ever confide in you?"

"In me? No! She was loving, kind to both me and to Jarvis. I would not say I ever knew her mind, though."

"No, I do not suppose you did," Kunnikah emitted an earthy sigh.

"Did you know my mother, Kunnikah?" Delilah suddenly wondered.

"Not directly. I know of her from the trees and living things surrounding her. She never spoke to me. She prayed to the Ancients, though, the spirits that are everywhere and in everything. She implored them to help her maintain the Vector to protect Hope, as her mother did before her."

"Too bad I did not seem to inherit any of her faith," Delilah commented.

"Well, that is to be seen, but no, your strengths are different. Your mother knew the Vector would not hold for much longer. That is why she tried to create safeguards to make sure it would keep. Unfortunately, it did not turn out as she hoped."

"Kunnikah, I have to ask you something: a healer of mine, Helanza, told me that my brother's life was at stake when he planned the coup. Do you know anything about that?"

"I do. Yet it is not information that will help you now, so I will not share it. You will find out when it is time, and you will hear it best from his own mouth, not from the bark of an old tree."

"My brother and I do not speak. In fact, I only learned he was still alive a few days ago. I would appreciate knowing. It could help me determine what to do next. I have fired my whole Council and I am very much alone now."

"As if this is a new thing. As you said, you have always been alone."

"Yes, I have."

"You will always have the counsel of the trees and you have others who can still advise you. You are right to spurn those who have kept secrets from you. Where there is one secret kept, there will always be many more."

"That is what concerns me," said Delilah.

Back at the observatory, Ilvana showed Delilah some of the new experiments she was conducting. "I was so humiliated by the airship failure," Ilvana confessed. "I never want that kind of fiasco again on my watch. Now I am working on a different kind of travel, one that does not depend on the winds or physical objects. I am trying to use the knowledge of the trees. They transmit thoughts and messages instantly across vast distances. If we can do that with messages, there is no reason we should not be able to do that with objects, too. Of course, I am only just beginning to understand how to transmit messages, so sending people might take a little longer."

"You are ambitious, Doktora! Tell me, have you had much success with the messages? I was able to hear Aumenveill from the vines outside my window at the castle in Fallengrove, perhaps because I was so close to him? Is that something that we can develop?"

"Yes, we can. The large trees across our world are all in communication. That is something that I have come to understand from speaking with Kunnikah and other Ancient Arboreals. There is a network of them, and they can speak to one another in a flash, directly to one chosen individual or they can send out warnings across the whole system, even across the planet in extreme emergencies. In between these networks live smaller pathways of younger trees and small living things. Their individual messages are not as strong, yet together they are powerful and are the secret to linking up the older trees. The smallest root fiber of a vine is at work. You might even say that they are more advanced than we are. Not being able to move, they found ways to talk to all around them. Also, they are so sophisticated, they can speak to anyone. Did you wonder how Aumenveill and Kunnikah were speaking our tongue and not Horkish or Drakonic? It is because the power in the trees translates a message instantly into a pattern the receiver can understand, whether they are a tree or an owl, a person or a pegasi."

"And how close do you think we are to being able to send messages anywhere in the world?" Delilah wanted to know.

"We are close. Still, if no one but me knows how to use it, it will not be worth much. Imagine having a device that would allow you to access any person in the world. If you do not know it is there or how to use it, then it would be worthless. Part of the challenge will be teaching others about the technology once we figure out how to employ it. Xanfar is working on putting together a list of contacts for all the scientists we know across the world. We may need to go personally to all of them. It would be helpful if we did not have to travel by airship!"

"This is fascinating, Doktora. Please keep me informed about your progress," Delilah said. "I must admit, I came here today for a specific reason."

"Of course you did," said the doctor.

"I have fired my entire Council of Advisors."

"Ha! Those old windbags. Well, good riddance. The only one that is worth her weight is that monstrologist."

"Yes, Doktora Sinsarel."

"She knows her Beasts."

"She does."

"Well, congratulations and good riddance, Your Majesty! You do not need their counsel. Do not expect them to go quietly, though. The most dangerous thing in the world is a person who has been spurned."

"I am still their queen!" Delilah said.

"Still, be careful. You must find people you trust to surround you, especially now that you have ousted the Council."

"That is what brings me here today, in fact," she said to the doctor. "I would like you to be an Advisor to me."

"As if I have not always been your advisor, Your Majesty. I have always been here to serve you and I will always do that. You can count on that."

"This would be in a more formal capacity, Doktora."

"I am not made for the Court, Your Majesty. I have not even left Verily in three years. I have no intention of sitting around in Great Halls, sipping cider and discussing battle strategies. I am not built for it. Besides, I know science, but I know nothing of the military," she said.

"That is exactly why I need your counsel. Sometimes those entrenched in combat mentality are not able to see the big picture. I fall prey to that kind of thinking myself, as Aumenveill pointed out to me. I think you see the big picture all the time. I need more of that."

"That is a great compliment. Yet what about the State/Science separation? Am I even allowed to advise you? I thought pure scientists were supposed to stay out of the politics of the State and vice versa."

"That was put in place before my parents' time. It is a tradition more than a law, made so that the waters would not become muddied. I have no Council to consult with, so I must judge for myself whether it would be a conflict, and I do not believe it would be. In fact, I think it is about time we had more science in government," Delilah said.

"Well, I would much rather consider you like I have all these years: as a friend and colleague, a partner purveyor of science." In an uncharacteristic gesture, the doctor put out her hand and touched Delilah's shoulder. She looked directly into her eyes. "You have a rare mind, My Queen. You must trust it now." She pulled her hand away and turned to piles of scrolls on her desk. "The answer is yes, though. I will always advise you if you ask me to. But please do not invite me to any royal functions!"

They laughed, and Delilah said, "I will respect your hermitage, my friend. I will only call upon you to come to Hope in dire circumstances. In the meantime, I will visit Verily often."

"You may not need to. As I said, we are very close, Your Majesty. We will harness the power of the growth beneath the earth… The Undernearth! Yes, that is what we shall call it. We will understand it soon, and you and I will transform history!"

"Well, you will anyway," Delilah laughed. "I may just retire and become a sheep farmer. I hear it can be quite rewarding."

"There will always be a hut and sheep pen for you here in Verily, if you decide that is your path," said the scientist.

⋈

Three days later, Delilah was summoned back to Verily.

"Which is your sword hand?" the Doktora asked her, in the confines of her clean laboratory. Delilah raised her right hand. "Give me the other one," Ilvana instructed. Delilah held out her left palm. "Do you trust me, Your Majesty?" the doctor asked.

"With my life," Delilah responded.

"Good. This may hurt a little. I will make it fast."

The Doktora took out a very small, extremely sharp knife and made five tiny slices in the shape of a star on Delilah's palm. Aaranon stood by to dab the blood with cotton dipped in strong hazel. With miniscule pliers, Ilvana took five tiny double terminated crystals and placed them under the flaps of skin. Delilah's eyes watered as the doctor took a needle and thread and made one stitch and knot in each of the five incisions and then rubbed a sparkling salve over the wounds. Delilah thought she heard the doctor mumble something in Aelvish.

"These threads can come out in a week. Your healer can remove them. I just had mine removed," Ilvana said and held up her right hand. Delilah saw there were five pink puckered spots on the doctor's hand. "Aaranon did mine. That is why they are so sloppy!" she whispered, looking over at the apprentice, who was cleaning tools and pretending not to hear. "I did not want to tell you when you were here last, since I was not sure yet. Xanfar did the same. With the crystals installed, we can talk through the vines anywhere. I would be able to call him now, just by going outside and touching the nearest tree. We wanted to test it ourselves before we shared the technology with you. We will be contacting other healers and scientists all over the world next."

"Astounding! So how do I use it?"

"Anytime you need me, go to the nearest tree. Place your hand upon the bark and think of me. My crystals will activate… tingle and glow a little. I will know you need me, and I will get to a tree to speak to you. You can do the same for Xanfar. We hope that soon we will be able to contact people in any queendom across the world."

Testing it in the days that followed, Delilah found it was easy to summon the image of Ilvana or Xanfar and within a few minutes, they would respond. Once she felt her own crystals tingle while she was up in the tower and had to run all the way down and out to the back of the castle to answer Ilvana's summon. It was even possible to connect the three of them at the same time! They simply created a plan to connect at a certain time, and the three could talk together. While Delilah sometimes felt nostalgic for the long trek through the tunnel or sending scrolls back and forth anytime they wanted to report something to each other, now the three were in contact almost every day. They could even Link in Aumenveill and Kunnikah to discuss some key aspect of the ancient technology they had tapped. In this way, Delilah suddenly had the advisors she had been missing in the Council. She was able to hear how the science was advancing and discuss strategies to get the word out to more people at key points across the globe. For the first time in ages, Delilah felt that she had friends.

She asked Helanza if she would want the crystals installed. "For what?" the herbalist asked, sounding insulted. "As if any good healer does not already talk through trees. We have been doing this for centuries." Despite this assertion, there were many clerics, healers, and scientists from other lands who were eager to have the means for communication. The procedure was simple, and it was easy to get used to the tiny bumps under the skin of the palm to assist trans-dermal connection. They experimented with smaller and smaller trees and found they could talk if they had only grass to lay their hands upon. Anything that was alive could be used to make the connection. Even if there were no visible living things, sometimes just laying a hand on the dry earth was enough. As Aumenveill had told her, there are always infinitely small things living upon the dead things in the earth, and the multitudes of these, apparently, were strong enough to connect minds across great divides.

Delilah had become so distracted by her new pastime and the important work they were doing that she was barely aware of other goings on in the castle. One day Oravica stopped her in the hall as she was running outside to speak with Xanfar, who was summoning her.

"Your Majesty, I must speak with you," Oravica said.

"Can it wait, Oravica? I am occupied at the moment."

"No, I am afraid it will not. There are… military concerns." Oravica explained that although many on the Council had simply gone about their lives, some were holding a grudge. Those connected to the Guard were duty-bound to protect Delilah. Although insulted by being booted from the Council, the Senior Guard knew they had other channels to address her and so their access was still intact. Others were ousted completely from the inner royal circle and some of these were making concerning statements that had come to the attention of the Guard. Of particular note were troubling remarks by the infamous Fishlip.

"Doktora Ishlip is very powerful in the old circles. She feels herself entitled to her position on the Council and is rousing others to feel that they have been slighted."

. "What could she possibly do?" Delilah wondered out loud.

"Do not underestimate her influence, Your Grace. Recall that she was in the inner circles of your parents' reign. She is well-connected. There are many who would follow her."

"Follow her to *what*?" Delilah asked, not seeing any cause for concern.

"There are whispers. Come to the barracks this evening. Please, Your Majesty. The Guard will address you there."

That evening, Delilah strolled out by lamplight to meet her Guard. Her mind was preoccupied by recent news of connections through the Undernearth being made as far away as Oceanika, with the technology even capable of crossing the seas. Ilvana hypothesized that it traveled by speaking not only through ocean vegetation, but the invisible life existing in even the smallest drop of seawater. This confirmed tales of talking through water Jezschmel had revealed to Delilah. It was an exciting advancement. As Delilah crossed one of the main courtyards to get to the barracks, a small movement caught her eye. She thought it might be someone else heading to the assembly, yet when she turned to see who had joined her on the path, there was no one there. Delilah's senses were heightened, and though she walked along as if nothing were afoot, her mind was on high alert to every movement as her hand went to her weapon.

She required it within moments as a person dressed entirely in black emerged from the darkness and launched at Delilah's legs, trying to drop her. Delilah quickly saw they were trained in Qi-Kai, as their movements were fast and smooth, like dancing. Delilah had been trained as a girl, however, had gotten out of the daily discipline. Though she jumped to avoid the sweep, it caught painfully on her calf. Fists and kicks were flying in her direction like a cyclone, and Delilah struggled to sense where the next blow would be. She was kicked painfully in the stomach and flew backwards, tumbling to the ground. Leaping back to her feet, Delilah held her scimitar aloft and slashed down at the flash of black that bulleted toward her. She felt the weapon meet air and stumbled forward. She turned to see the attacker's body twist in the air in a movement she recognized as a flying backward dagger. Delilah twisted her face away just in time to feel only the barest glance of the attacker's foot make contact with her chin.

The figure landed facing the other direction. While Delilah had a momentary advantage, she reached down to hook under her opponent's leg and lifted up to drop them over her back to the ground. She followed the momentum of the figure's fall backwards and landed a fierce elbow blow as hard as she could to their face. She heard groans of pain that were markedly female. Shouting at the end of the yard caught Delilah's attention and she saw Guardswomen pouring out of the barracks. They had been alerted to the scuffle. Delilah turned back toward her opponent, who landed a punch on Delilah's cheekbone that made her roll away in pain. They both struggled to stand and Delilah saw the attacker reach down into her boot and come up with a glistening knife. She barreled at Delilah, trying to get in close enough to stab her. Delilah used the movement of the woman's attack to put her own blade between them. Despite not being able to see her target precisely, she heard a gasp. She knew she had penetrated by the slippery feel of her blade.

"Your Majesty! Are you alright?" The Sister Guard who came running held weapons and torches aloft, ready to battle an intruder who was no longer there. Delilah looked to see where she had gone and caught just the bare outline of a figure going over the far wall, clearly injured and holding her side while still mounting an admirable ascent over the barrier.

"I am fine. Send someone after her," she gasped, catching her breath as she pointed her bloody sword toward the wall. Several Guard were dispatched while others looked over Delilah and fussed at the marks on her face and calf. "I said, I am fine!" Delilah asserted impatiently and strode toward the barracks where the Guard were assembled in the meeting hall.

After some shuffling and explanations, and apologies to Delilah for not seeing the skirmish earlier, the Guard settled in for a serious address from the leadership. The Guardswomen who had chased the assailant came back and reported that they had lost her beyond the wall.

"We will find out who it was," Major Abbowhen asserted. "In fact, we already know who must have coordinated it. Your Majesty, we have reason to believe that Doktora Ishlip and other members of the Council are angry about their banishment from the royal inner circle. They are staging a coup."

"A coup!" Delilah was indignant. "And just who do they propose to replace me?"

"That is not clear yet, Your Majesty," Abbowhen admitted.

"Doktora Ishlip was the only member of the Council that I retained after the coup that took my parents' lives. She was responsible for selecting many of the current Council members."

"Exactly. Our intelligence suggests that Ishlip may have been planning this for a very long time, waiting for a chance to put her own people into power."

"Into power? As if being a member of the Elder Council is not a position of power? What more could she want?"

"We believe that the Doktora has not been pleased with her fading advantage with you. When you were a new queen, she was able to shape and persuade you," said the Major. That is no longer the case. As you are aware, Your Highness, you very much have your own mind. Doktora Ishlip knows her influence over you is waning. She is unhappy with that and being expelled from the Council has only exacerbated her grudge."

"If anyone should have the grudge, it is I," said Delilah. "The Doktora and the rest of the Council have deceived me for years, from what I understand. And let us not forget that my own military left me out of critical information." Delilah stood chest to chest with the Major and looked her directly in the eyes. "I should really strip you of your rank, Major, for keeping sensitive information about threats to our Queendom for so long." Delilah had never been one for public reprimands, however she believed this occasion warranted one.

The Major lowered her eyes. "Your Majesty, I put myself at your mercy. If you no longer trust me to lead our Guard, I will humbly retreat and give up the rank. I would only remind you that I have been at the helm since Colonel Massama took ill five years ago. I have been successfully leading our defense. Our Sisters know me and support me."

Delilah saw subtle nods of agreement in the assembly. "That is true, Major, although I do not appreciate you using your troops to hold you up. A woman should be able to stand on her own merit without the endorsement of underlings. Still, I am cognizant of your excellent service. Clearly you have the loyalty of the Guard. In fact, it is exactly because of your strong leadership that I have decided not to replace you." She noticed sighs of relief among the gathered soldiers and could see that many had been worried she would use this venue to dismiss their beloved officer. "I trust that this will be the last time you withhold information from me?" The Major nodded sternly. "Now," Delilah continued, "we have much more pressing items to discuss. Major, is there any other information you have gathered about this potential coup?"

The Major shifted and coughed, adjusting to being forgiven. "There are concerns that Ishlip may be coordinating with… outside forces."

"What outside forces?" Delilah demanded.

"We are trying to determine that, Your Majesty."

"Please do, and quickly. To that end, I have an announcement about new technology that could help us. Our Chief Scientist, Doktora Ilvana, and Lord Xanfar have worked together and have made an astounding scientific discovery. You may recall old stories about mystics and healers talking through trees over long distances. Like many of you probably did, I always dismissed these as myths and fantasies. Doktora Ilvana has found the technology to make this form of communication a reality. It has the potential to transform our whole planet, the way we wage wars, and our entire survival. As you know, when the Mungus took hold, we were on our own to fight it. Others across the globe were on their own as well. When we found the solution, we had to send it… by ship, by messenger bird, by pages on horseback… to assist other lands to fight the pestilence. If we had accessed this technology then, we could have sent information about the cure immediately to our contacts on other continents. We could have saved millions sooner."

Delilah held up her left hand with the five pink puckered scars in the shape of a star. "These are Tharovian crystals, installed in my own hand by the Doktora." She heard gasps and whispering. "With these, I can speak to others who have these same devices implanted in them, far away, across oceans and mountains. I can speak to Lord Xanfar all the way in Fallengrove, or a shaman we just recruited in Sabsinthe, or our new connections in Oceanika. It is called *transdermal* communication. We place our palms upon a tree or living thing and our thoughts are sent to the person we hold in our mind. It is made possible by something Doktora Ilvana calls the *Undernearth*. It is ancient and has been evolving for eons, these connections between infinitesimally small life forms underneath the earth. It is… simply magnificent, the most elegant technology we have ever uncovered. It will truly change our world." Cheers went up among some utterances of astonishment and disbelief. "Major Abbowhen, I would like you to be the first of our Guard to try the technology. It is your decision, so you will need to feel comfortable and agree to this modification. Either way, you should decide which officers should be offered the procedure."

The rest of the gathering devolved into dozens of separate conversations, discussions of the possible applications, and Guardspeople coming up to see and ask permission to touch the crystals under the skin of Delilah's hand. As they ran their fingers over the scars, Delilah could not help thinking that her own mother would never have let her Guard touch her like this. No one who was not attending to the queen's personal needs was ever allowed to touch Queen Zaryadne. Even Delilah had rarely been allowed to touch her own mother. Still, she and her mother were very different types of queens. Before long, a banquet was laid out and tankards of cider were brought in. The soldiers feasted and talked through the night. Delilah took her leave early, although Oravica insisted upon having soldiers walk her back to the castle. She had only just laid down upon her bed when her crystals began to tingle. She had ordered ivies planted on the outside of the castle so that they would eventually cover the walls, like at the castle in Fallengrove, yet as of now, she had no access to plants. She dressed quickly and ran down the back stairway and out to the nearest bay tree in the kitchen garden.

"Your Majesty, can you hear me?" It was Xanfar.

"Yes, I am here, Xan. What is it?"

"I have some disturbing news. Are you ready?"

"I was born ready," she replied.

"The Crystal Aelves are amassing their army on the far side of the Whayer Wood. They are staging an attack."

"An attack on what?" she asked, already knowing the answer.

"An attack on Hope. They are looking to overthrow you for the Crown and put Prince Jarvis in your place."

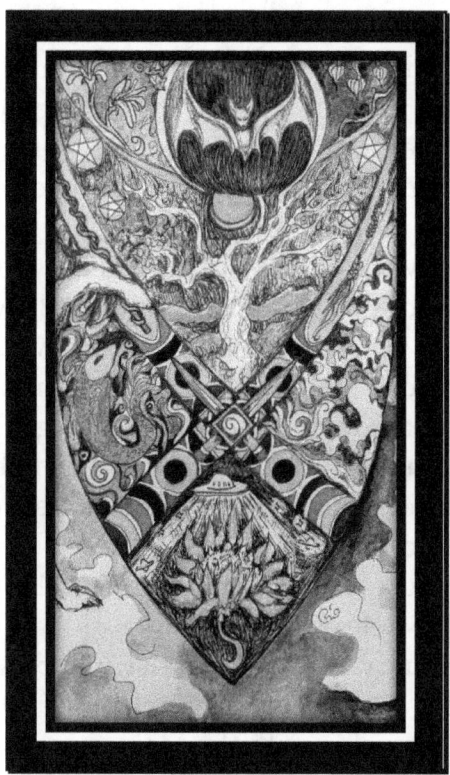

*"A ship will go to any port
When a storm is upon the sea,
Yet what will be the price
of the tavern for the night
When the port is of the enemy?"*
-The Ghost Scribe

Chapter 6: The Aelven Shield

The truth about the matter was that Delilah itched for battle. She yearned for her enemy's blood in her eyes and the sounds of clashing metal all around her. That was something she could understand. Tumultuous feelings and waves of emotion, like the ones she had been pummeled with over the last several weeks, made her feel powerless and out of control. No one had taught her how to sort through distress, yet she had trained her whole life to be a warrior. She was ready to fight the Crystal Aelves the next day if she had to. However, Delilah quickly learned that heading to war with their current resources would likely mean the slaughter of her army. They were simply outnumbered.

"How could it be 100,000?" Delilah asked Major Abbowhen. The senior officer had gone to Verily to have the Tharovian crystals installed and had begun communicating with military leaders in other lands.

"That is what I am told," said the Major.

"I did not even know there were 100,000 aelves on the whole planet, much less in one place!"

"I must admit, neither did I. You can see the dilemma. We have only a small fraction of that in our Sister Guard. Even if we compelled every able-bodied person in Hope to fight alongside us, we would still be massacred. We were not a large queendom before the Mungus, which cut us down even further. It would be butchery," Abbowhen shook her head, looking despondent.

"And I have seen the way the aelves fight," Delilah agreed. "Even our most trained soldiers would be hard pressed to survive a one-on-one battle with an aelven warrior. I could not expect our regular citizens to go up against them. If we wait too long and the aelves come to Hope, everyone will be forced to defend their own homes. Still, I am not willing to ask them to go to a foreign land to lay down their lives willingly against such miserable odds. Each of our soldiers would be outnumbered by five, if we are being realistic."

"If we pulled our healthy older Guardspeople from retirement, we could probably get it down to one against four," said the Major.

"Still, I could barely hold my own against one aelven fighter," Delilah admitted. "Against four, I would surely be defeated."

"And you are more vicious in battle than most," Abbowhen smiled.

"Oh yes, remember those darn mountain trolls?" Delilah mused, recalling past encounters she had fought side-by-side with the Major.

"We have seen action, that is for sure. Those trolls had such giant..."

"Heads!" Delilah finished, and they laughed. "Very hard to chop off, much as I tried."

"Well, we made do. The aelves are another situation entirely, though."

"What do you recommend, Major?"

"First of all, we need reinforcements. We must strengthen our numbers in any way we can. Secondly, we are going to need to travel to Raefenshire. We must bring the fight to them so as not to jeopardize the lives of the innocent in Hope."

"How can we do that?" asked Delilah. "Their lands are on the other side of the Whayer Wood. It was hard enough getting a few of us over the Wood to get to Fallengrove."

"We could go by ship."

"We have no fleet that could transport all of the Guard."

"What of your… friend? The Pirate Queen? Would she transport us? And could they be compelled to join us in the fight, perhaps for a price?"

"Mercenaries! It would be a shame if we had to resort to that, yet that might be necessary. In fact, Lord Xanfar has a small army of Centaurs that might be hired. They do very well against the aelves, from my experience. And being impervious to the Gloom, they could travel right through the forest without fear."

Over the next several days, both Abbowhen and Delilah reached out through the Undernearth, putting out the word to find anyone who might have a grudge with the aelves or could be employed to fight. Delilah tried to send scrolls to Jezschmel through fisherfolk heading out to sea in alternate directions and got no response. In desperation, she sent out a message using her crystals, holding the image of Jezschmel in her mind and hoping for the best. She knew it was not likely the technology had reached her yet, and still was aware that the pirates found other ways to talk across the sea.

"Eh? Who is this?" The crusty voice that popped into Delilah's mind was not the Pirate Queen's silky tone.

"Um, this is Queen Delilah of Hope. Who is this?"

"Argh, should have known the Maggot Queen would bother me while we are in hot pursuit of a whaylderbeast."

"Admiral, is that you?" Delilah recalled the shrunken form and creepy neck gills of Admiral Razzle-Eye, who had infiltrated her castle not so long ago.

"Who else would it be?"

"Well, I was trying to reach Queen Jezschmel. I have important business to discuss with her and she has not responded to my scrolls."

"She has not had the time to respond to your love letters, Your Ugliness, because as I mentioned, we are QUITE BUSY chasing a pod of whaylderbeasts! Unlike you, we pirates are not so fortunate to have our food delivered to us on silver trenchers! No, we must hunt for our supper. No one will get meat for our bellies and fat for our lanterns if we do not do it ourselves."

"Well, I am surprised to hear your voice. Does that mean you have had the Tharovian crystals installed in your palm?"

"Crystals? What are you talking about? Any self-respecting pirate can speak across the waves. Crystals! You truly are a lazy bunch. Not able to even send your own messages without the help of crystals…" her voice trailed off and then Delilah heard shouting and Razzle-Eye yelling frantic directions to her crew. She must have taken her palm from whatever she had touched to make the connection, if that is indeed how she had picked up on Delilah's urgent plea, because suddenly there was just dead air.

"Admiral? Admiral Razzle-Eye?" Delilah's heart sank as she realized the Admiral was not there any longer. She sighed and laid her hand in her lap facing up, staring at the star-shaped scars. When they started to buzz and blink, Delilah quickly laid her hand against the tree again.

"Is that my delicate Queen Delilah?" a deep, honied voice asked.

"Jezschmel!" Delilah was ecstatic.

"What is it, Your Majesty? Are you stuck on another tortoise?"

"Nice one. I suppose I will be forever in your debt."

"I am confident you will find a way to make it up to me."

"Do not tally the score just yet. I am afraid I have another favor to ask you," Delilah said.

"I will see what I can do, however you must know that I have queens in virtually every land who need my assistance. It is quite tiring, always sailing here and there to do the bidding of one pretty queen or another."

"I am sure your services are widely required. Are you familiar with the Crystal Aelves of Raefenshire?"

"Of course. Those nasty creatures are worse than any undead Beast,"

"I need your help waging a war," Delilah said.

Oravica and Delilah were taking a walk in the orchard behind the castle to discuss battle strategies. "You will be pleased to know we found the assassin," Oravica announced.

"Really? Well done! Who is she?"

"It was Raphibia, the granddaughter of Doktora Ishlip."

"She sent her own granddaughter on that kind of mission? She must be serious. Where is Raphibia now?"

"In the dungeon, Your Majesty."

"The dungeon! We have not had a guest there since I was a child."

"Well, we have nowhere else to keep her securely," Oravica explained.

"How was she found?"

"Her injuries betrayed her. She went to a cleric and told them she had fallen upon a sharp fence. Helanza is well-connected in the Healers' Guild, so she was alerted immediately. She brought the information to the Guard."

"Helanza! Thank goodness for her. I want to speak to the traitor. I will go there directly."

"Your Majesty, I wish to discuss something with you first," Oravica said hesitantly.

"Well, go ahead."

"With our current situation, we could afford some more… variety in the Guard."

"Variety?"

"Yes. There are many who think we should recruit more men."

"We have men in the Sister Guard already!" Delilah asserted.

"Yes, a few here or there. It is just that we could use the numbers. It has always been the tradition for the women of Hope to defend Hope. Perhaps it is time we allowed for more openness in our ranks. For instance, we do not have any male senior officers. There are many loyal male citizens in Hope who would be happy to serve in our army."

Delilah shook her head. "Too risky. Men are impulsive and guided by their emotions. They belong in the trades."

"Our Sister Guard *is* a trade for many families. Why not capitalize on that? Just about every Guardswoman has a brother or cousin eager to be enlisted. I have polled our troops. We could double our numbers if every Guard recruited just one strong and healthy male relative."

"But the training! We have no time to train up such an army of… children."

"Leave that to me and the other officers. We could do it in a matter of weeks."

"I am not sure we have weeks. What about the weaponry? How will we arm them?"

"I have already looked into that," Oravica said. "I spoke to the Smiths' Guild. The smiths had nothing else to do during the Time of Great Isolation so they stockpiled a large surplus of weapons. They are awaiting our order. We could have the additional arsenal completed in just one week."

"Well, we are in desperate times, indeed," Delilah shook her head.

Oravica insisted on escorting Delilah to the dungeon, where guards had been appointed to keep watch over the captured assassin. The dungeon was a dark, cavernous place under the castle that had scared Delilah when she was a child. Her parents had a handful of prisoners, usually people who were accused of plotting treason, or captives from other lands used for strategic bargaining. There was one old man, Gravenwell, who was locked up for practicing illegal sorcery. When she had found the courage to sneak down there on a dare from Jarvis, the old man had told her stories. She had returned countless times to hear his tales, so she had a soft spot for him. Despite being so old, he was the only inhabitant of the dungeon still alive when Delilah's parents had been killed. Delilah took mercy on him, against Doktora Ishlip's advice, and let him go to return to his family and live out the remainder of his days. She wondered now what became of him.

Raphibia was housed in the cell that had been Gravenwell's, one of the few with a small window high above. The chamber was barely lit by this and the torches in the corridor, yet Delilah could see that the girl was in an extraordinary amount of pain from her wounds.

"Good day, Raphibia," Delilah addressed her.

"Your Majesty," the girl stood on wobbly feet from her cot and lowered her head to bow.

"I would think there would be many other places you would like to be today."

"Yes, Your Majesty."

"Perhaps you might consider that the next time you try to assassinate your queen."

"There has been a terrible mistake, Your Majesty. I have done no such thing."

"Please, Raphibia. Let us not play games. I know it was you. I inflicted those wounds on you myself." The girl's whole body deflated, and she sat back on the cot as if she had lost all will to fight for herself. "Now," continued Delilah, "I just need to understand why." Raphibia was silent. "Do you have a grudge against me? A complaint about how I am ruling?"

"No, Your Majesty!" she practically shouted.

"Then why would you try to kill me?"

"I am not at liberty to say."

"Well then, let me be more direct. Why would you risk your own life at the behest of your grandmother?"

The girl would not meet Delilah's eyes. "My Grandmother did not ask me to do this. She is innocent."

"I doubt that greatly. Still, if not her, then who compelled you to do this?"

"I took it upon myself."

"Yet you say you have no grudge upon me!"

"It is not my own grudge. I did it for my family. They did not ask me to do so, though, so please do not punish them."

"Then enlighten me as to how you came to this decision."

"I overheard my grandmother talking to my mother. She was telling her that since the Council of Elders was dissolved, we have been shut out of the inner circle of Hope and that we would never recover so long as you are queen."

"And did she propose an alternative?"

"No, but she said if you were no longer alive that she would be able to gather support for our family to become part of the inner circle again, maybe even higher ranked than before. She was not conspiring, Your Majesty. She was just talking, expressing her discontent. She had no plan and did not ask me to get involved. I was fearful for my family's future, so I acted without anyone knowing. I did not intend to ever disclose what I had done."

"So, your plan was to sneak out during the night, murder your queen, and then go quietly back to bed?"

"Something like that."

"It was a brave plan, if not well thought out," Delilah admitted. "You do know the punishment for treason?"

"Yes, Your Majesty. It is death."

"Well, let it come swiftly to cut short your suffering and poor judgment," Delilah said, turning to walk away with the girl's sobs at her back.

"She was not exactly contrite about it," Oravica observed, when they got back into the sunlight.

"No, it was as if she expected understanding. She is very young," Delilah said.

"Do you believe her that Ishlip had nothing to do with it?" Oravica wondered.

"No. I think fish-brain was behind the whole thing. She is not beyond sacrificing her own kin."

"Shall I schedule the execution?"

"That would be the wise thing to do. However, I have other ideas. Send Helanza to attend her wounds. Let us see what information she can glean from her. And... Oravica- Make sure there are at least three Guard present. Raphibia is practiced in Qi-Kai. The last thing we need is for her to harm my healer or attempt an escape."

"Yes, Your Majesty."

Later that day, Delilah was alerted to the presence of Doktora Ishlip and her daughter at the castle gates. They came to petition for an audience with Delilah and mercy for Raphibia. Delilah told her Guard to turn them away. Oravica had already informed Delilah that they had round-the-clock eyes on Ishlip and spies deployed, trying to determine the old Council member's next move. Oravica had Guard following Delilah everywhere now. She had insisted on taking no more chances, as the risks were too high. Delilah hated having the small attachment of Guardswomen following her. Now, three or four guards trailed after her everywhere. She felt stifled when she wanted to speak to Ilvana or Xanfar privately, even though the soldiers stood a distance away while she conversed. Delilah had always valued her freedom more than anything. She would almost rather have the risk of being killed than the constant intrusion. Oravica's orders came directly from Major Abbowhen that the queen could no longer be left alone.

As she returned to the castle after a conversation with Ilvana, she saw her old Guardsman Olavfin coming toward her with a scroll. Olavfin was trained in the Guard, however he had spent most of his life of service taking care of her daily needs and being her intermediary to the rest of the world. "Is it not funny that a scroll is starting to seem old-fashioned, Olav?" she asked him, as she broke the wax seal. She unrolled the parchment to reveal a letter from an ally in Beduran. It was bad news: They could not afford any troops to send since they were currently entrenched in a war against a vicious band of ogreds. As Ilvana and Xanfar were promoting the use of the Tharovian crystals far and wide, Delilah had sent out requests across the globe to anyone who might help them in their plight against the Crystal Aelves. "Another 'no' from our allies. If we are not able to depend upon them in times of war, what good is it to have allies?" she asked.

"Everyone has their own struggles, Your Majesty. Unfortunately, our war is not their war."

"True. Olav, may I ask you something?"

"Anything."

"How was it for you when you enlisted in the Guard? You were one of the only men to serve then. Was it hard for you?"

"Oh, well, I got a lot of teasing, for sure. I had to try twice as hard as the other recruits to prove myself, yet the Guardswomen accepted me. No one was cruel. Still, I did not always feel I was used to my full potential."

"No?" she asked. "How so?"

"I was given less risky tasks, assigned work in the kitchen, attending to wounds. I was the last to be sent out when there was an invader."

"I see," she said.

"Please do not misunderstand me, Your Majesty. It has been the honor of my life to serve you so closely, keeping you safe and attending to your needs. It is just that I sometimes think if I had been a woman, I would have been taken more seriously in the Sister Guard."

"I have been told we need more men in our ranks, Olav, especially now when we are so desperate for soldiers. What do you think about that?"

"The men of Hope would give their lives for you, Your Majesty, same as any of your most devoted Guardswomen."

"Yes, I believe you are right."

As Olavfin brought her meal in the evening, she thought of all the times she had barely even thought of him as part of her Guard. While he was responsible for keeping her safe, he was also her personal attendant, making sure she ate and received communications, and got where she needed to go on time. To be truthful, she had treated him as more of a servant than as a soldier. Yet she had also seen him fight, when necessary, and he was as capable as any of her other Sister Guard. She trusted him with her life every day.

The next day, Delilah sought out Major Abbowhen and told her to start recruiting and training the willing men of Hope. When she returned from the barracks, she found Olav and told him that he needed to go and see the Major.

"Is everything alright, Your Majesty?"

"Yes, my friend. Everything is fine. I want to thank you for your years of service, Olavfin."

"That sounds foreboding. Am I being retired?"

"No, just the opposite. You are being promoted. You will be responsible for training the new recruits and leading them in battle against the Crystal Aelves. You have spent enough time in this old pile of stones taking care of me, Olav. It is time to use your talents as they were intended."

"But who will care for you, Your Majesty?"

"Anyone can bring me soup, Olav, though not anyone will know how to anticipate my needs like you have, time and again. I have benefited greatly from your companionship and constancy over the years. It would be selfish for me to keep you here just because you know how I like my tea."

"I will not let you down, Your Majesty."

"No, you will not."

"We know Doktora Ishlip's plan," Oravica said, as she walked with Delilah to see the new recruits being trained. Several Sister Guard followed, as always now, a few paces behind.

"What is it, Sergeant?" Delilah asked. Things were still a little stilted with Oravica and Delilah had not yet found a way to mend the divide.

"We intercepted communications. She was directly conspiring with the Crystal Aelves and Prince Jarvis. She promised to rally support to have him anointed as King of Hope once you were killed. In exchange for carrying out your assassination, she would be given the title of Royal Advisor with rooms in the castle for her and her family. This could have been the plan all along. She may have been conspiring with Prince Jarvis from the beginning. It is possible that Doktora Ishlip could have even been directly behind the coup so many years ago. When things went differently than she expected, she switched her plan to groom you until the time when Jarvis might return."

"What is to be done? We must not let her continue these treasonous acts," Delilah said.

"They have already captured her and her daughter and put them in the dungeon, just to be safe."

"Good! Let her try to conspire from there. It will not stop the advance of the aelves, yet it will cut off their source of inside information. What of the support she was expecting? Who in Hope should we be worrying about now?"

"That is what we are looking into. Helanza is concocting a truth potion to assist in getting more information from Doktora Ishlip," Oravica said.

"Fishlip! I never should have trusted her! Why did I give her so much power after my parents died?"

"You were young, Your Majesty. And alone. She was a comfort to you in your grief, I am sure."

"She was. I had no one left and she was as much of a parent as I had to rely on for guidance. I can see now how she manipulated me, though. I feel so foolish! She had me purge anyone who might stand against her! Whole families wiped out. It was a bloody time, and I was on the wrong side of it."

"You were barely more than a child."

"I should have been more prepared. In truth, my whole life should have been preparation: all the training I was given, the lessons. I feel like my mother may have known this would happen, and she gave me the tools to lead. I did not take it seriously because I did not expect to ever have to rule. That was Jarvis' role. I never expected to be Queen of Hope."

"There is no point berating yourself for things you cannot undo, Your Grace," Oravica put her hand on Delilah's arm, in a gesture of tenderness that was like the way things used to be between them. "You still have the scales!" Oravica noticed. The rash had melded into a band of silvery raised scalelike bumps in a circlet around Delilah's bicep. It was exactly where Oravica had grasped her to push her shoulder back into its socket after they fell from the balloon. Oravica's own fingers and hands were also covered with the scaley pattern. It did not seem to interfere with anything, although it was a noticeable irregularity. "I am so sorry that I seem to have infected you, Your Grace."

"Nonsense! You fixed my arm and had no idea the sea water was tainted. I have not seen any effects from the scales other than reminding me of the day poor Torrence died. Oravica, I want to apologize for the way I treated you in Fallengrove." Delilah forced the words from her mouth while she had the courage.

"Your Majesty, I am here to serve you, not only as your Guard, but as your friend. I would never keep anything from you that I thought would hurt you. I truly thought the rumors about your brother were fantastical tales that would only upset you. I never would have kept them from you if I thought there were any credence to them."

"I know. I should have realized you, of all people, would not keep secrets from me."

"I never would. I swore to protect you with my life, and I will do that."

"From now on when I see the scales upon my arm, I will remember your loyalty. I will never doubt it again," Delilah pledged.

The castle compound was filled to the brim with new recruits and abuzz with training exercises. As Oravica had proposed, everyone seemed to have at least one male member of their family who wanted to fight to defend Hope. Men had always been accepted into the Sister Guard, if they pursued service. Still, it was unusual, and they had never been explicitly recruited. It was a strong tradition of womanhood in Hope that the Guard was dominated by women. Those who had husbands were proud to leave childrearing to them while they engaged in the most esteemed profession in Hope: defending the monarchy. It was a common sight to see a man carrying a baby on his back while cutting wood or men working together in smithing or another trade while children played nearby, with wives gone on a long shift at the castle. Mothers who were part of the Guard encouraged their daughters to enlist when they came of age. It was a family tradition passed down from the maternal line.

Now, walking through the swaths of new male soldiers practicing coordinated sword exercises or hand-to-hand combat in the yard, Delilah saw the sense of the plan just in sheer numbers. She still had doubts about whether men could control their passions enough to follow orders in the heat of battle. She kept these thoughts to herself, as she did not want to undermine the project. She walked the ranks, offering encouraging words and praise for the strength and commitment of the new recruits. Seeing Olavfin, head held high as he commanded his troops, put a knot of shame in her stomach for not realizing before that his aspirations in life did not consist entirely of waiting on her person. It was all new and uncomfortable. Even so, Delilah knew in that moment as she watched Olav fulfilling his potential that it was the right path to follow. There was no going back. Men were now being fully embedded in the Sister Guard and it had doubled their strength.

The courtyard was so busy that she barely felt her crystals tingling. She walked away from the activity to a quiet part of the grounds by a large shoak tree. Her detail followed her at a respectful distance.

"Xan! How goes it in Fallengrove, my friend?" she said upon hearing the gruffly whayerwolf voice speak his greeting in her mind.

"Very well, Your Majesty. The Centauri army is ready to deploy at your command. A few will stay back to protect Fallengrove, of course, but the greater part of the battalion is at your ready. I will travel with them."

"Wonderful! I know they will be well-led with you at the helm. We will compensate them handsomely. I have had all these piles of treasure sitting around for so long wondering what purpose they could ever serve. Now we finally have a use for our wealth!"

"I have a feeling the centaurs would do it even if they were not paid. There is little to entertain warriors in Fallengrove."

Delilah laughed, "Well, we will certainly give them some action."

"There is something else, Delilah, something… exciting."

"What is it?"

"I sent crystals and a diagram for the procedure to my connection in Erithea so they can start to access the Undernearth. He followed the directions, and I was able to speak to him this morning. Have you heard of the Aelven Shield, Your Majesty?"

"Yes, of course. It is the pact between the races of aelves."

"It has never been broken. All aelves will align with all other aelves in times of war."

"I had not considered that more aelves may join their army! Please, Xan, do not tell me there are more than just the Crystal Aelves to contend with. Even with the new recruits and the mercenaries, we will still be outnumbered by the Crystal Aelves."

"No, it is strange, yet compelling news: the Duke of Erithea has told me that he has been in communication with the leader of the Usiku tribe of warriors."

"The Dusk Aelves!" Delilah exclaimed. They were a reclusive, nocturnal race that were renowned for their powers of sorcery and deadly warcraft. One rarely saw a Dusk Aelf. If they did, they would not be likely to live to tell the tale.

"The Usiku have a long-standing animosity for the Crystal Aelves. They see them as inferior, living beneath the earth like rodents. Still, they have always maintained the Pact," Xanfar explained.

"Has that changed?"

"It may have. Last year, the Usiku high priestess asked the Crystal Aelf queen—Nimevah—for assistance when they had an infestation of giant sandworms that were infected with the Mungus. Aelves are immune to the Mungus, it seems."

"I did not know that!" exclaimed Delilah.

"It is true. The sandworms, though, who are normally quite reclusive, turned particularly aggressive when they became ill. The Dusk Aelves were in a terrible predicament and reached out for advice. Being ground-dwellers, the Crystal Aelves have developed special magick to control giant worms. The Usiku implored them to share their expertise, yet Queen Nimevah refused to help them. The Usiku high priestess felt this was in violation of the Aelven Shield and has publicly withdrawn from their pact."

"Well, that is interesting. Still, withdrawing from the pact does not assure that they would support us."

"I do not know, but aelves are not really the forgiving type. A grudge like that might compel them to join forces with us."

"How can we find out?"

"I am already brokering that proposition now."

"Is there anything that might convince them?"

"We can ask."

As it happened, the Usiku did want something. Tucked away in the corner of Delilah's treasury was a tattooed onyx skull. Delilah was not even aware of it. Yet Xan was able to describe it so she could locate it in the caches. Xanfar informed her that it was not made of gemstone: it was an ancestral ceremonial object made from the actual skull of an Usiku high priestess. While aelves generally turned to dust upon their death, this ancient aelf priestess had prepared for her passing and had self-immolated in order to immortalize her skull to pass her power on to her descendants. The crystallized skull contained enchantments and other mystical properties known only to the shamans and holy people who inherited the sacred object. Delilah's father, King Yuli, had come from the desert lands. His great-grandfather had captured this skull in a battle with the Usiku, according to the tribe's historians. It was passed down to Delilah's father and came with him as part of his dowry when he was married to Delilah's mother, Zaryadne. It was the first Delilah had even heard of this sacred object. She promised to return it to the Usiku for their support in battle with the Crystal Aelves. She sent this message through Xan and the Duke of Erithea. They awaited the Usiku response. It was hopeful that perhaps they would have the advantage of aelf-against-aelf. The Usiku were powerful sorcerers, and would be frightening in battle. They were perhaps even more advanced than the Crystal Aelves.

As she awaited this response and oversaw the training of the new Guard, Delilah became more anxious each day. It was not like the aelves to assemble for battle and then fail to act. They would have the advantage if they chose to attack Hope. Delilah could not understand why they were not on the move already. Still, their sources consistently informed them that the 100,000-strong army was still intact on the border of the far side of the Whayer Wood. The Crystal Aelves could easily traverse the Wood, so it was unclear why they would delay. Delilah pressured Major Abbowhen to speed up the training and stayed in contact with Jezschmel. The pirate queen assured Delilah that they could convene their fleet to transport the Sister Guard to Raefenshire as soon as they were summoned. Still, Delilah knew it would be foolhardy to launch an assault without the necessary reinforcements. Securing the Usiku support would improve her confidence to initiate such an attack.

Delilah had commissioned an earth sorceress to invoke a charm to make the vines on the castle walls grow faster so that she could contact the others from her bower at any time. The vines were now right outside her window, so she no longer had to rush out to the gardens when her crystals activated. The green tendrils waved around the opening to her casement, white night blossoms filling her room with their perfume. When Ilvana's alert came in the middle of the night, Delilah had only to fumble to the window and grasp some leaves to hear her.

"They are here, Your Majesty!" Ilvana's frantic voice came through to Delilah.

"Who? Where?" Delilah asked, trying to shake the cobwebs of sleep away to make sense of the Doktora's words.

"The Crystal Aelves! They are here! They are attacking Verily!"

"When warfare haunts the minds of the pure
Not a single one can truly be sure
How the sordid story will end
When death becomes the enemy
and the enemy becomes a friend."
-The Ghost Scribe

Chapter 7: Assault on Verily

Delilah sent word to gather the cavalry for battle. The logistics of getting troops to Verily had never come up before, being that the small coastal region was so isolated and had no real advantage for conquest. What could the aelves possibly want with Verily? Delilah had no time to reflect on this question, despite its prevalence in her mind. What was even stranger was Delilah's brief conversation with Ilvana. "In Verily, we are prepared for this type of invasion," Ilvana had said, to Delilah's confoundment. Delilah knew the Doktora's acolytes were trained in meditation and hand-combat arts and were probably in peak physical condition from their daily exercises and traversing the hilly cliffsides. Still, she could not see how a bunch of monks could fight off an attack of aelves.

When she alerted Xan of the situation, the whayerwolf chuckled and said, "Do not underestimate the good doctor! She is more resourceful than you know!" It irritated Delilah that Xanfar was so flippant about the crisis. She was reassured when he confirmed he would be immediately deploying the Centauri army as backup. The centaurs would not arrive for at least a day even if they ran at top speed through the Whayer Wood, but it was better than nothing. The pragmatics of getting the Sister Guard to Verily became the most pressing challenge. Despite the urgency of the situation, Doktora Chastice, who was charged with maintaining the secrecy of the entrance to Verily, would not budge on maintaining the sanctity of the clandestine entrance to the tunnel. It must remain concealed, she insisted. Therefore, it became quite an ordeal to transport soldiers in volume to the entrance, although the elder agreed to have several Guard at a time blindfolded and led on horseback. They then had to wait inside the tunnel entrance for the rest of the troops to arrive, since it would not make sense to send the defense through the tunnel piecemeal. By the time a few hundred Guard on horseback were convened inside the secret entrance, several hours had passed and the tunnel was crowded and filled with wall-to-wall horse manure underfoot and restless animals snorting and chomping.

When the troops were gathered in the tunnel, Major Abbowhen gave a short address reminding the Guard of the trickiness of elves. They commenced with riding as quickly as they could, although they could only ride two-by-two, and in places, only one rider at a time could pass. Those soldiers who had never been close to the Whayer Wood were spooked by the hooting, hissing, and howling they heard through the vines on the other side of the tunnel. Their horses jumped and their footing faltered when they were startled by the more vicious noises. Delilah's mind was still occupied by how and why the Crystal Aelves had targeted Verily. Before leaving, she had contacted Jezschmel. Like the Centauri, her reinforcements were at least a day away. To calm herself, Delilah left her horse tethered in a wider area and walked back among the troops, encouraging them as they passed, and thanking them for their bravery. At the tail end was Olavfin and fifty of his most promising recruits. Delilah had deployed them as an afterthought, sensing that there would be no time like the present to test their mettle.

As the small army approached the entrance to Verily, they began to hear the clashes of battle. There were other confusing sounds: a tearing, like a giant piece of fabric ripping, and the whizzing and crashes of projectiles. The plan was to quickly assess the situation and deploy segments of the Guard where they were needed. Abbowhen and Delilah exited first and the troops began to gather in rows behind them as they looked around to see that the aelves were ascending the mountainside toward the observatory. The invaders were being fought back by spinning, twirling figures with long poles, some shooting white balls of energy from their palms to blast the attackers back. These, Delilah realized, were Ilvana's acolytes, burgundy robes separated in the middle and bound with cris-crossing gold cords to create pant legs from their typically flowing garments. Their bodies were spinning so fast that they approached the velocity of the aelves. Delilah was surprised to see that they were well-matched. Ilvana practiced a strict regime of physical and mental training for the monks. Despite the doctor's assertion that she was not interested in military strategy, Delilah saw that Ilvana had trained up a sophisticated army.

"They busted through the Vector!" Major Abbowhen said, pointing to an area at the base of the mountain. The Ancients who had formed the Vector around Hope had extended the enchantment through the secret tunnel into Verily, protecting it from penetration from the Whayer Wood and the Gloom. Just as it was in Hope, the Vector formed a duplicate, smaller bubble around the mountainside town and cliffs of Verily. Aelves were still pouring in. The small area of perforation in the Vector had irregular edges that sizzled and popped with lightning flashes of energy.

Pow! The impact of a large missile smashed into the cliffside and a few of the ascending aelves were blown apart, purple blood spilling on the rocks. Delilah traced the course and saw several ballista catapults set up along the periphery of the cliffs. They were womaned by Ilvana's monks and being loaded up with boulders and hot coals by teams of three muscular devotees each. This was how, Delilah saw, they had been keeping the aelves from overwhelming the area. Indeed, there were spots of purple blood and fallen aelves dotting the entire bottom of the mountain. Still, aelves were pouring in through the hole torn in the fabric of the Vector.

"Why are they here?" Delilah asked Abbowhen, not really expecting a response. The aelves could have just as easily launched an attack on Hope, which would have made more sense. More missiles flew and picked off clusters of the beautiful forms of the aelves, sending elegant white body parts in all directions accompanied by arcs of violet blood. The Verily army was holding its own. Atop the mountain, Delilah saw Ilvana, standing out in her white robe, which was also transformed into a military jumpsuit, with burgundy lacing cords matching the robes of the monks. Ilvana usually kept her hair in a braid, yet today it was loose and flowing all around her.

She was high above them and the gust of ocean winds and sounds of battle created a clamor. Even so, Ilvana spoke and her voice was amplified across the cliffs and could be heard by all: "Women of Science: Attack!" she commanded, and another stream of acolytes descended to fight the aelves who had escaped obliteration and were still climbing, gingerly dancing over the stones. Delilah resented the Crystal Aelves' pretty, almost casual movements as they invaded her sister settlement, assaulting *her* people.

"Attack!" Delilah yelled.

"Attack!" Abbowhen echoed, and directed half of the troops along the side road to where the aelves were entering through the hole in the Vector. The other half was sent up the road to the observatory to defend it. Delilah did not understand most of what Ilvana did inside her laboratories, however, she knew that they could not let the aelves destroy the scientist's important work. The Guard who got to the tear in the Vector began hacking and chopping at the aelves as they entered, handily dropping many of them. A few aelves launched through and Delilah saw several of her good women sliced apart by sharp, willowy swords. A giant whoosh of air burst through the perforation, and something flew above the city and hung in the air. It was an aelf, yet one whose form and dress was different from the others. They wore silver, flowing robes that hung down and billowed out in the air beneath them, seeming to hold them aloft.

"A sorcerer!" Delilah said to Abbowhen, who was still guiding troops to their battle locations.

"That is not any sorcerer, Your Majesty," said the Major. "That is a Necromancer!"

"How can you tell?" asked Delilah.

"Look there on their robes: those marks in black, the spiral with the cross over it. They control the dead!"

Delilah watched in horror as the necromancer shot bolts of zinging energy from their palms, in spiraling waves toward the broken aelves that littered the hillside. Typically, bodies of aelves turned into dust within several minutes of dying and many of them had already become powder on the cliffside. However, the sorcerer was working to get to the other fallen aelves before that happened. The aelves' dismembered body parts began to move and stitch with threads of black and blue light, sewing the grisly pieces together. In some cases, the parts were clearly on the wrong body, or stitched on backwards, or with a leg in the place where an arm should be. Regardless, the horrific creatures that were pieced together began to move with life again, although awkward and slower than the aelves in life. The creatures moved disjointedly on reversed limbs, yet with purpose to kill, picking up fallen swords along the way.

"They are making zhomboids!" Abbowhen shouted. "Undead aelves! Just what we need."

The Guard who reached the zhomboid aelves began to hack at their irregular forms. In almost comic movements, the zhomboids again lost their attached parts. Yet those who were separated from portions of their body simply lay there until their limbs rolled back and re-stitched themselves together. Then they rose to fight again. The necromancer floated in the air, shouting incantations as they looked down. Multiple streams of spiraling energy radiating from their palms to find their marks below. Dead aelves were being re-assembled and undead aelves were fighting the Verily monks and Delilah's guard. Delilah jumped in and began chopping at the animated dead side-by-side with her soldiers. It was hardly challenging, yet took a lot of effort to smash them down. The zhomboids were not terribly effective, and still they were a horrifying distraction. They got in the way, coming at the soldiers again and again as the Guard also had to fight off the living. As the re-animated aelves fell, Delilah realized with horror that the necromancer was also re-animating their dead Guardmembers and putting them to the awful task of turning against their own.

Abbowhen ran up. "Your Majesty, we have another problem," she said, and pointed with her sword to the entrance. In addition to the aelves that continued to pour in, creatures of the Whayer Wood had come to investigate the hole in the Vector. A few were entering. First a whayerwolf poked its furry nose around, sniffing and huffing. It let out a blood curdling howl, then launched itself at a nearby Guard, tearing out her throat and chest and sat feasting atop her. Next a vampdactyl swooped in and attacked one of the Crystal Aelves who was preparing to launch up the cliffside. It was holding onto her with its clawed wings, trying to attach itself to her neck to suck out her purple blood. The aelf sliced the vampdactyl in half, right through its body and leathery wings, then reached into her garments and pulled out a small vial. She dropped a few flakes of sparkling dust on the creature and it dissolved instantly.

"Well, at least the Beasts do not just target us," Delilah said, and ran up to assist a Guardswoman who was fighting off a small round furball the size of a bladderball with a dozen mouths and sharp teeth. It had attached itself to her leg, growling and gnawing, and would not let go. Delilah kicked the thing hard. It rolled over to an aelf and promptly went chomping after her legs instead. The aelf, in one graceful movement, leapt into the air and stomped down on the furball with a great crunch. The thing yelped and howled as it died, a broken pile of flat fur. As more creatures ventured in and indiscriminately began attacking both human Guard and aelves, the battle became even more chaotic.

"Look there! What are they doing?" Abbowhen was pointing at the Necromancer, and Delilah saw that the streams of light they had been sending to the undead aelves had ceased and the creatures had begun fighting and rebuilding themselves on their own. Now, the magician was focusing rays of spiraling light onto the ballista. The machines began to emit a green glow and the monks operating them were bolted away, falling back upon the rocks. The catapults turned their aim. Delilah, aghast at what she was seeing, watched as large rocks floated up and were set into the leather pouches. They were launched, not at the aelves, but at her own Guard and at the army of monks gathered atop the peak! Boulders were hurled in multiple directions at once. Delilah heard the long, piercing shriek of a horse. The sound of the dying animal burrowed into her brain and reverberated through her body as if in her very bones. Another stone struck a cluster of monks. Splattered guts and intestines spilled out across the ground in a creeping crimson stain.

A stone crashed through the colored glass ceiling of the observatory. Ilvana looked up with utter rage upon her face. The Doktora gathered herself up and ran at full speed toward the edge of the cliff and leaped off into the air. Delilah was stunned to see that the scientist, rather than plummeting to the earth, floated at full speed on a gust of sizzling energy and zoomed directly toward the Necromancer, her legs pumping the air as if she were running on solid ground. The aelven mancer was distracted, still sending energy to operate the equipment below, and did not see Ilvana hurtling forward. Ilvana lept sideways with a Qi-Kai move called a bone dagger, stabbing fiercely with both legs into the mancer's middle. The aelf flew backwards through the air. The billowing robes that had appeared to hold them up faltered and the Necromancer fell to the earth below, lying in a crumpled heap.

A low rumbling came from the tear in the Vector. Above the din of clashing swords and crashing missiles, it was hardly noticeable at first. It grew like a pounding stampede until all who were not in the throes of deadly engagement turned to see the cause of the noise. A jumble of giant arms and legs came through the passageway and a half dozen strange creatures stood blinking in the light. They held an assortment of spiked clubs, maces, flails, and morning stars. Their weapons were only outdone by their strange bodies: they were almost twice the size of a human, covered in rough fur, with bulbous heads, beasts' snouts, and pointed ears. Their necks were made from many rings of hairless translucent fat connecting their horrid, hairy faces to their oversized, muscular bodies.

"What are they?" Delilah asked Olavfin. She had ridden up to help him with the incoming horde.

"Grub-bears," he answered. "Horkish, fierce, with very small brains. An incredibly dangerous race who live only to kill."

Though the creatures walked on two legs, they suddenly dropped to the ground and lumbered out in all directions, awkwardly holding their weapons as they ran on all fours into the fray. They stood and began indiscriminately swinging their clubs and the chains of their flails to smack into anything and everyone around. An aelven soldier, with an annoyed look, turned and took a long swing with her thin sword to cut a grub-bear's head fully off its fat-ringed neck, as if it were barely a nuisance. The beast fell, greasy oil and blood pouring from the hole atop its shoulders. The aelf turned back to attack one of Delilah's Guard with the same nonchalance. The aelves already had an advantage with their gymnastic abilities and impossibly sharp weapons, so the creatures were a mere distraction to them. Delilah quickly saw the monsters could pose a serious threat to the Guard's slim holding.

"We must wipe out those grubs!" Delilah yelled to Olavfin, her blood pumping with the thrill of a clear target. Delilah kicked her mount into a run while Olavfin called to his troops and followed her at full speed. The new Guard were vicious, ready to prove their worth and their thirst for battle. The grub-bears were taken off-guard by the cavalry's incoming assault. Still, the beasts fought with an unmatched quest for blood, swinging weapons with frightening power. One of the monsters whirled its awful flail, the knobby ball on the end of the chain striking a Guard from his horse. The soldier did not rise from his fall. Seeing their comrade unseated, the Guard let out resounding battle yells and plummeted forward, slashing and hacking at the beasts. Delilah exalted in the moment and heard her own voice screaming along with her Guard; her body moved of its own volition with pent up rage and frustration as she sliced one grub-bear after another. In just a few minutes, the creatures lay dead around them, in oily pools of their disgusting juices, faces even more ugly in death. An irritation on her palm got her attention and she saw that in the heat of the battle, one of her crystals had gotten dislodged. There was just a loose flap of skin where the stone was missing. She began to look around for the crystal on the ground when a moan behind her drew her attention. A young Guardsman had fallen from his mount, his stomach and leg punctured with large gashes. He was bleeding out fast. Delilah jumped from her horse and went to comfort the young man, whose terrified eyes showed he understood the seriousness of the wounds.

"Your Majesty, please stand aside." The voice sounded familiar, and when Delilah turned, she was face to face with Aaranon, Ilvana's slight apprentice. He kneeled next to the fallen soldier and said something quietly to him. The young man nodded, and Aaranon, with his tiny frame, scooped up the soldier as if he were a baby and held him crosswise over his shoulder. Aaranon nodded to Delilah. Then, as if he were carrying no more than a sack of gourds, Aaranon leaped up the cliff, practically hopping from one boulder to another to avoid the clashes between Guard and the Crystal Aelves. He disappeared with his cargo into the observatory.

Delilah shook her head and turned to Olavfin, who seemed similarly bemused. "Well, we are not done yet," Olav said, gesturing to the living and undead aelves who were still climbing the cliffside, making progress toward the peak. The Guard and monks were losing ground. The Necromancer had fully recovered from the doktora's fierce attack and was again floating above the battle, re-animating fallen aelves. There were truly no losses on the aelven side because all of their dead were still fighting for them, and re-animated Guard were also recruited to their task. Bodies of dead Guard were becoming more common upon the rocks and these, too, were being transformed into the aelves' undead army. Delilah picked up a fallen man's crossbow and shot off a series of missiles toward the necromancer, grunting her fury. Though the shots should have been clear, each one missed, bending away from the mancer. With each failure, Delilah's anger bubbled more violently.

"There is a shield around the cretin," Olavfin said, trying to reassure his monarch.

Before Delilah could respond, a deep and terrible roar erupted. The gash in the Vector rippled, edges flapping like a tent opening. A bumpy pink snout came through the entrance and snuffed around, with steaming nostrils shooting hot air that sizzled the grasses around the entrance.

"Oh no," Delilah said.

Olav stood rigidly and grasped his weapons. "Could it be… a Fire Drake?" he asked, barely whispering to Delilah.

"I am afraid so," Delilah said. She immediately began revisiting her lessons with her tutors about the Drakonis species, their habits, tendencies, and weaknesses in battle, which were unfortunately few.

The tearing they heard then was so frightening that all stopped in mid-battle to turn to the sound. It was like fabric ripping, yet amplified and terrible. Claws came through the invisible barrier in the sky and tore giant slits into the Vector. The drakeon haphazardly smacked away any remaining shreds of the barrier and stumbled through. Drunkenly, the beast looked around, head weaving and bobbing. Something was wrong with it. Delilah looked closely at the reddish-orange scales of the monster and saw irregular bumps and boils all over its body. Its scales were splitting and patches were welling up on the creature's face and limbs. Its front talons had dripping raised welts that made the whole paw swollen. It had lost a few of its nails and there were oozing holes where its claws had been.

"It is sick," Delilah said in amazement. "Olav… I think it has the Mungus!"

The creature let out a howl that was filled with rage and pain. It spurted fire at the side of the cliff, frying several aelves and singeing a few Guard at the top. The Guard dropped their weapons and shields, which had become red with heat, running to find water for their swelling burns. The drake took a few steps, and then, unstable and wavering, began to fall.

"Look out!" Delilah yelled, and Guard scattered and moved back, out of the way of the gigantic creature. Its shadow filled the sky as it came down in an enormous thundering wave. The living aelves were too quick to be crushed, however their undead counterparts were slow and uncoordinated, so a good number were squashed beneath the creature's body. Delilah was relieved to see no Guard were harmed. "The Drake is dying!" she said, astounded to see the titan lying in a heap, sending out smoke and ashes from its diseased snout. Leaking wheals covered its nostrils and were bubbling with sizzling flesh from the drakeon's own flames.

"I did not realize that drakes could be affected by the Mungus!" Olavfin said.

"Neither did I," Delilah admitted. "It must have smelled the blood and followed it here. Poor thing. It is surely suffering."

It was true: the sick drakeon barely had enough vitality to lift its head. Tremors and chills wracked its body. Chanting from above drew their attention. The aelven necromancer was floating above the fray. The mancer zeroed in on the massive beast and began to send rays of energy down to the fallen creature. Spiraling coils wound down and began to surround the dying drake.

"He is not even dead yet!" Delilah yelled up at the mancer, infuriated. The sorcerer barely glanced at her and continued chanting. They were intent on the target, seeming unphased that the drakeon was not yet dead. Beams of power were focused on the writhing beast as it entered its death throes. "That cretin is going to turn the firedrake into a zhomboid as soon as it dies!" Delilah shouted to Olavfin. "We will not win against such a foe, even a re-animated one. We have to stop them!"

Olavfin called to the archers in his unit, who had been stationed along the road up to the peak trying to pick off aelves when they could, despite their limited range to the peaks of the cliff. He ordered them to get up as high as they could and begin their assault on the magician. This quickly was revealed as a fool's errand since the arrows simply bounced off the invisible forcefield around the mancer. Meanwhile, Delilah ran to the nearest tree, an old twisted batelnut, bark smoothed by the sea winds. She placed her crystal-hand on its surface, hoping that it would still work with the missing stone. She had not seen Ilvana in a while, as the scientist had retreated to defend the observatory and the laboratory. "Answer me, Ilvana! Ilvana: I need you!"

"This is not the best time," Delilah heard the response, along with the doctor's winded breath as she seemed to be amidst a duel. "I had to grab on to a potted fern just to answer you and it is impeding my defense!"

"Sorry! Listen to me closely: this is incredibly urgent. I need as much of the Aelves' Blessing as you can find. I need a dragon-sized dose."

"Seems like an odd time to commit yourself to saving the dragons, Your Majesty."

"Just do it. You will understand soon."

Delilah ran to the beast, who was clearly in its last moments. He huffed small streams of black soot from his singed nose, golden eyes rolling back in his head. Radiating shafts of light pulsed around him, encouraging him to give over to death. In a moment of inspiration, Delilah placed her left hand on a patch of the dragon's scales that was not affected by the Mungus. She concentrated as hard as she could amidst the battle sounds that still raged on the cliff. "I am here, Great Drake. We are going to help you," she thought the words in her mind, sending her energy into her remaining crystals.

She was surprised to hear a response, a faint and deep voice rolling back at her in her mind. "Hello, Little Sister. I am dreadfully sorry, I am not myself today," she heard.

"How could you be yourself as you fight this horrid disease?" Delilah spoke silently. "Listen to me, friend. The sorcerer above is trying to finish you, to do the bidding of the aelves and destroy us in your undeath."

"I am not in the business of harming aelves or humans. I have just been so… ill"

"Yes, I know, Your Greatness," Delilah said. "I need you to hang on for a little bit. Do not give in to death! I am trying to save you."

At that moment, Aaranon appeared next to her with a large sack. Despite his burgundy robes, Delilah could see that his front was still covered with the blood of the Guard he had hauled up the mountain. Some of it had gotten on the sack. "You asked for this, Your Majesty?"

"Aaranon, you have made yourself quite useful today," Delilah said, grabbing the sack and untying the cord. She put her hand back on the drakeon's scales for a moment to tell him: "I need you to swallow this," and then dumped the contents of the sack into the monster's mouth. His tongue lolled out, and Delilah watched as his eyes closed and he lay still. "No!" she shouted. She put her hand on him and said: "Swallow it! Do not give in!" There was no response. The beast lay motionless. The mancer's chants grew louder and zaps and swirls of sparks burst into flame around the dragon. Delilah jumped back to avoid getting fried. In disbelief, she watched as the dragon's body lifted from the ground, surrounded by the sorcerer's crackling magick. The fire drake's giant body floated up and then spun in the air, first slowly, rotating in slow motion, and then speeding up rapidly into a dizzying blur. The drakeon's wings opened and he caught on the air, his head drooping down, lifeless, onto his armored chest. Suddenly, his eyes opened and were no longer gold, but fire-red and angry. He roared and his whole body trembled, as if shaking off death. "We are in trouble," Delilah said to Olavfin, who was standing nearby.

"We have been in trouble all day," Olavfin responded. "Get to the ballista!" he ordered the troops nearby, taking advantage of the fact that the necromancer had neglected the cannons to focus on the grand new weapon.

"A zhomboid drakeon! We are going to need more than a few ballistae," Delilah shook her head.

"It is the best we can do," Olav replied.

The drakeon flapped his wings and the blisters along its arms oozed and dripped, creating a waterfall of sickness splashing onto the rocks below. Pain contorted the dragon's face, and Delilah saw him look directly at her. He roared and rolled his neck, the way a horse will do when it has been mortally injured. Then he flapped his wings again and flew up to hover beside the floating necromancer. The sorcerer looked quite pleased and laughed, glowing with triumph at having captured this magnificent giant. The drake roared again and blew out a stream of fire, scorching the whole face of the cliff, the blast knocking back anyone in range. The beast dipped then, flying circles around the sorcerer, as the magician laughed and sent spirals of energy out to surround its body. In one great backflip, the drakeon swooped back around, zoomed in, and promptly swallowed up the necromancer in a giant gulp.

"Great Goddesses!" Olav stood, dumbfounded. "Hold your fire!" He shouted to the troops who were beginning to load the ballista, ready to shoot the fire drake.

The drakeon looped and flew in great, round circles around the cliffside. "He is smiling!" Delilah shouted. The beast looked as if it were laughing, remnants of a piece of the necromancer's cloak that had gotten stuck on his teeth hanging from his great jaws. Delilah watched in wonder with each swoop as the boils and pustules that covered the drake's scales closed and healed up, disappearing as if they had never been there. "It worked! The Aelves' Blessing worked!" she yelled. The beast alighted carefully atop the observatory, where the ballista had left a shattered hole in the glass. He balanced there and looked down at the armies strewn across the landscape.

In Aelvish, the great creature began to speak, his voice resounding across the cliffs and valleys: "I am not one to harm aelves or humans without cause," he said, as Delilah struggled to hear and translate his words. She repeated these quietly to Olav and Aaranon, who were still close by. "And yet you have harmed me, my Aelven siblings! I will not forgive you! To use me as your undead weapon is unforgivable. I am not an object to be played with and manipulated! I am Nhyddogg, descended from the Great Serpent, the holy mother Woshana! How dare you try to possess me!! You will leave this country now and go back to your burrowing worm holes or you will all pay the price, you disgusting vermin!" With this he roared and began to shoot fire directly at groups of aelves who had made it to the summit and were preparing to attack.

Everything froze for a moment, as if time stood still. Then, in a synchronized movement that looked like a piece of sheer fabric being pulled over cushions and through a ring, the aelves swarmed across the face of the cliff and vanished through the opening in the Vector, disappearing as if they had never been there at all. Nyhddogg flew in circles around the peak of the cliff, dipping and plummeting in free falls, the last of his scabs falling from his wounds. A dazzling bluish light covered him, healing his body and making it shimmer from within, as if lightning was contained inside his golden-red scales. He landed with a resounding thunder next to Delilah, his wings creating a powerful wind that made hair and loose clothing fly sideways on all nearby.

"I knew and loved your mother, Queen Zaryadne," he said, in Drakonic, which Delilah had fortunately studied enough to comprehend. "She was a friend to me, and so you are as my Little Sister."

"Your Holiness, the Great Nhyddogg," Delilah said and bowed low, now understanding who this magickal beast was from her lessons. He had helped the Ancients to create the Vector that protected Hope and Verily, first from invaders, and now from the Gloom.

"I owe you my life, My Queen," the grand serpent said, and bowed low in response. "Those nasty aelves roused me from my slumber under the Hematite Mountain. That awful charlatan summoned me and possessed me. Then they infected me with that dreadful disease and made me come through the Whayer Wood. I have not been awakened in 20 years! And to think, those tricksters tried to use me to wage war! That is not what the Mighty Serpents were created for. We are peacemakers! We are fearsome so that we can prevent war, not destroy!"

"I am sorry that you were used so poorly," Delilah said, putting her hand out to touch the scales of the creature. Her crystals hummed and a light inside the dragon's armored skin sparkled.

He answered in his mind: "How did you know you could speak to me?" he asked, silently.

"I did not know!" Delilah insisted, speaking in her mind. "I just felt that you might be the same as any tree or ancient stone made from things living and dying over centuries."

"As I am," Nhyddogg said, and laughed a deep and thunderous guffaw. "And if it were not for you, I would likely have become dust and stone and returned to the earth to greet my ancestors."

"It must not be your time," Delilah said.

"No, and it is not your time either, Little Sister!" he flew up into the air, doing a series of somersaults and tumbles, looking admiringly down at his own whole and shining body, which was now unmarred. In a moment, he shot through the tear in the Vector and towered like a glowing tree of fire on the other side. "I call upon the Ancients! I call upon my own Holy Mother," he rumbled the words aloud in Drakonic. A dizzying gust of air swirled around him, like a radiant dust storm. He held out his massive paw, claws grown back and healed from their decayed openings to make perfect new pearly scythes. He spread his palm wide within the hole where the Vector had torn apart. The ripped and vibrating edges melded together, weaving itself in front of the creature. The giant serpent's image was obscured as the Vector repaired and became a seamless barrier once again.

All was quiet, and the only sound was the gushing air from the sea and a few distant sea birds calling to one another. "Huzzah!!!" The cry rang out from the top of the cliff. The shouts and screams of conquest echoed down and rippled through the Guard who were still standing.

"Huzzah!" Yelled Delilah, holding her scimitar high.

The cleanup from the battle had been grisly and almost worse than the fight itself. Delilah and Doktora Ilvana sat to rest and drink tea in the doctor's library. Most of the troops had been sent home through the tunnel along with the injured and dead. The ones with wounds too grave to move them had been set up in a wing of the observatory to be nursed until they either died or were healthy enough to be transported. Aaranon was put in charge of directing the healers there to tend to those who were in the poorest condition.

"Aaranon was extraordinary today," Delilah remarked, once the acolyte left the room. He had come in to give a report to Ilvana and the queen about the status of the ill and dying. Ilvana was busily sewing a replacement crystal into Delilah's palm. The doctor tied a knot and cut the end of the thread.

"Yes, there is a reason I keep him so close to me," Ilvana admitted. "You want the one who can save your life nearest to your person at all times."

The thought of Olavfin flashed through Delilah's mind, and she felt a pang of loss at having given up his daily company and protection. Yet today, he had proven his worth on the battlefield. "The unit of men that we trained performed well."

"Of course they did. Men are just as capable as women in battle. Much of the world fights with men in their ranks. It is only in Hope and a few isolated countries that the soldiers are mostly women. Would you believe that in some places, they only allow men into their armies?"

"That is certainly hard to believe! It seemed like such a huge change to train men to fight in our Guard."

"Doing something different than the way it has been done before always feels uncomfortable at first. And then, quite quickly, it seems to be the most natural thing in the world."

"Kind of like how I have been thinking of all of you here in Verily as the brainy scientists and squash farmers and now suddenly I see you as a critical part of Hope's defense?"

"Yes, like that," the scientist smiled.

"Ilvana, what was all the nonsense about you not having any interest in military strategy? What I saw from your acolytes and the residents of Verily today shows that you are leading one of the most highly trained armies I have ever seen!"

"Yes, but that does not mean I have any interest in military strategy. We prepare for war because we are vulnerable here in Verily. As you have seen, if we are attacked here without the reinforcement of the Hope Guard, we need to be able to defend ourselves. Your parents understood that, so they always supported our efforts here. There has been a long tradition in Hope that the most promising and bright people are sent to be trained in Verily. Doktora Chastice has been responsible for selecting these candidates. Before her, it was her mother, and soon it will be her daughter."

"How could I not know this?" Delilah wondered.

"Few do. It is a secret society. An extremely intelligent girl who shows promise in the sciences and natural world may be selected to be sent to grow up here in Verily. Often it is a lifetime commitment. Those who come here usually stay to raise families and farm here in Verily after they complete their apprenticeship. Few are chosen to begin with, so our population remains stable. All who live here have undergone extensive disciplinary training in physical combat, meditation, sciences, and farming. We perform full-scale drills at the quarter moons, preparing for the kind of invasion we had today. We grow only the best in Verily!"

"From what I saw today, I concur. Also, what was it with you floating on a cloud of energy? After all of this time, how could I not know that you were a sorceress?"

"Sorceress! Do not be silly. All you saw was completely scientific, I assure you. What we do not understand appears to be magick."

"Well, you will need to explain the science behind that to me some other time. For now, my friend, while you can no longer claim that you are inexperienced in war, can you tell me what you think the aelves were trying to accomplish here? Why attack Verily instead of Hope?"

"Because it is isolated. The aelves mistakenly assumed that meant that we would not be protected and would be easily conquered. From here, the aelves could position themselves to launch a full-scale invasion of Hope more easily than attacking directly."

"Their armies are so vast. Nothing like the small fraction we saw today. They sent only a tiny portion of their numbers compared to their full resources. Did they truly think that it would be so easy?"

"I think they were relying on their secret weapon, the Great Firedrake Nhyddogg. They summoned him and infected him with the Mungus so they could turn him undead and control him. They also had greater assurance in that snuff-magician than perhaps they should have."

"They miscalculated," Delilah said.

"Aelves are characteristically over-confident. It is possibly their greatest weakness. They believe they are invulnerable. Aelves consider themselves to be smarter, stronger, and better than any other race. Clearly, they make extremely formidable foes. Their arrogance can make them blind to potential failure, though. We can use that to our advantage."

"How?"

"Well, if you were a conceited aelf, how would you interpret your defeat today?"

"As that belligerent drakeon messing everything up?" Delilah guessed.

"Exactly. They will not have learned a lesson from this, placing the blame elsewhere and assuming their own superiority. They will go into the next battle the same way."

"And they will assume that we are weak and unprepared. They will go straight for Hope next time."

"We must not wait for that, Your Majesty. We are not able to afford to even give them a day. We need to act tomorrow… no, today!" Doktora Ilvana stood and looked as if she were ready to go fight more aelves that very second.

"We are awaiting the Centauri Army. They should be here soon. And I am waiting to hear back from Queen Jezschmel."

Delilah's crystals began to tingle and light up, and Ilvana pointed to a potted tree in the middle of her study. "That is why I had it moved in here," Ilvana explained. Delilah grasped the slender trunk and heard Jezschmel's smooth voice in her mind.

"I was just thinking about you!" Delilah exclaimed.

"Of course you were," responded the slick pirate queen.

Jezschmel confirmed that the fleet could get to Hope by daybreak to transport the Guard to Raefenshire, home of the Crystal Aelves. After their conversation, Delilah and Ilvana continued their plan. "Wait a second! I have a question," Delilah was distracted by something that nagged at her. "That tree," she pointed to the potted tree in the middle of the room, branches reaching up to the glass ceiling above. "How is it that we can communicate through that, when its roots are not connected to the Undernearth? And how is it exactly that we can communicate over the water, to Jezschmel? This has been troubling me."

"Well, as we like to say in Science, the simplest explanation is often the correct one. The Undernearth—the *Nearth*—is not just underground. It is in the air and water, and probably even in the stars. It is greater than we have room in our primitive minds to imagine," she said.

Delilah did not answer as she pondered this. She almost did not see Aaranon come in. "Your Majesty; Doktora," the apprentice made sure he had their attention. "We have just received word: Lord Xanfar and the Centauri Army are on their way. They are bringing reinforcements. Almost the entire Usiku Tribe is with them. The Dusk Aelves have aligned with us against the Crystal Aelves!"

"Why must the young grow old and die
Or perish in youth at war?
It seems like a terrible waste of time
To live and then vanish once more."
-The Ghost Scribe

Chapter 8: Of Water and Wood

Delilah watched Jezschmel's strong back as the pirate heaved ropes to turn the black sails. The sight of those dark sails had once struck terror in Delilah's heart. Now they brought comfort. The odd-shaped collection of fish creatures that made up Jezschmel's crew had come to seem like any other folks from Hope, despite the occasional gills or scales. The pirates nodded at Oravica, apprising the scales covering her fingers and lower arms, as if she were one of them. Oravica had accompanied Delilah on this ship. The sergeant was readying her unit with exercises on the deck. Some of the Sister Guard looked green and uncomfortable. A few ran to the edges to empty their stomachs into the pitching sea. The fleet contained over 100 ships in all, and the Guard were packed in, with weapons and horses below. Delilah had not realized that Jezschmel had such a large fleet at her disposal. From what the pirate queen had told her this was not even all of it. There were several other fleets of ships that were currently engaged in "search and capture" missions in other territories.

"Someone must do it," Jezschmel asserted. "If I do not take control of the sea, another bitch will." There were apparently three other major bands of pirates that wandered the oceans, along with some fringe sects with only one or two ships. Delilah had no contact with other pirates, being that Jezschmel's band had taken over and defended that territory in the ocean surrounding Hope over so many decades—perhaps even centuries.

"Just how old are you?" Delilah asked Jezschmel, as they leaned against the railing.

"Old enough to know better and young enough to try anyway," Jezschmel said, and pinched Delilah's cheek. "Now, let us talk payment," the pirate said, true to her nature. They had agreed on an initial installment of gemstones and gold for the transport, however had not settled on a price for participating in the upcoming battle against the aelves.

"Mercenaries do not come cheap, Your Majesty. As you know, our army is vicious and cut-throat; the best you can hire. We would love to hack apart some snobby aelves — for the right price."

"Would you not want to do it just because of our special… alliance?" Delilah asked.

"Your Majesty, pirates do not do anything for free, not even for those with whom we have… special affinity. And even for one who has such a beautiful new pirate tattoo," she joked. She ran her fingers over the band of scales that had appeared on Delilah's arm after Oravica had grasped her there with the ocean Gloom still on her hands.

"That is a shame. I thought we had more of an understanding," Delilah said, playing at being insulted.

"Who was it who rescued you from the giant sea turtle? Why yes, it was I! Queen Jezschmel. How soon you forget."

"Yes, that was very… charitable of you," Delilah smirked.

"I promise you, my dear, the next time you fall from a balloon into the ocean, I will be happy to rescue you again, free of charge. However, a full-scale deployment of pirates in battle is another matter."

"Of course," Delilah agreed. "One would want compensation for such an endeavor. We are grateful for your assistance, Queen Jezschmel, and I have no qualms about paying for it. I do enjoy teasing you, though!"

Jezschmel grabbed Delilah around the waist and pulled her close, looking deep into her eyes. "At some point," the pirate said, her voice low, "I do hope you will stop teasing me, My Queen."

Oravica cleared her throat nearby and Jezschmel released her grasp on Delilah. Delilah stuttered, "Yes, Sergeant? What is it?"

"We should continue discussing our strategy, Your Majesty."

"Yes, of course," Delilah said, turning slightly away to hide the flush across her cheeks.

Jezschmel showed Delilah how easy it was to communicate across the waves. As Ilvana had speculated, the energy that was under the ground was also in the water. It was even in the air, if you knew how to access it. This was ancient knowledge that many tribes, like the pirates, had utilized for centuries, without the use of crystals or other artificial scrying methods. Delilah was a little envious that it had taken so long for them to come upon this knowledge when it seemed to be common practice for some of the less "civilized" groups. Jezschmel had a special connection to her own ship: it was made from the wood of a giant Sesquayah tree. When Jezschmel had overthrown her sisters to rule over the pirate nation, she had searched the world to find the perfect tree for her primary vessel. Jezschmel had gotten permission from the tree, as it was dying, to use its flesh for this purpose. Because of this agreement, the tree's spirit had lived on in the boat. Jezschmel's bond with it was so intimate, Delilah was almost jealous. The pirate queen would often stroke the ship like a lover as she talked. She would laugh as if sharing a private joke with the vessel, her fingers tickling the surface of the railings, worn smooth with time and salty air.

"You call it 'the Nearth' yet we just call it 'Linking,'" the pirate explained. "We just find a channel and send our message through until we Link with the one with whom we wish to speak."

"Yes, Aumenveill calls it a Link, too. And how do you find a channel?" Delilah asked.

"It is just there; it is everywhere. As soon as you send out your thoughts, if you trust that it will find its way, it will travel where you want it to go."

"So, I did not need these?" Delilah asked, holding out her palm with the raised scars. The skin around the replacement crystal was still pink where the new stitch had been removed.

"I do not know," said Jezschmel, tracing the bumps on Delilah's hand with a calloused finger. "They are kind of cute!"

The plan was for the ships to dock in Far Arroway, a trading port south of Raefenshire. It was one of the few ports that could accommodate such a large fleet. The Dusk Aelves had joined Xanfar and the Centauri army in Fallengrove. They would travel through the Whayer Wood to meet up with them in the mountains above the High Emerald Plains. Delilah hoped it would be enough. From there, they would lead their assault. The Crystal Aelves had an elaborate system of tunnels and caves beneath the ground and stayed almost exclusively underground. Living without sunlight was said to contribute to their pale color. However, it was also rumored that they had captured starlight, and so their underground universe was illuminated by the power of the stars. The Crystal Aelves had left their underground home to amass on the High Emerald Plains on the border of the Whayer Wood. They were camped there by the tens of thousands, sleeping under the stars. It was not clear what they were waiting for. After their failed assault on Verily, perhaps they were adapting their strategy.

"Is my brother with them?" Delilah wondered, when discussing the plan with Major Abbowhen.

"Yes," she said. "According to our sources, he and the aelven queen are there with their troops."

"I do not look forward to facing him in battle," Delilah said.

"You will not be the first queen to have to fight her own brother," Abbowhen reminded her.

"Yes, there does seem to be historical precedent. As my old friend, Gravenwell, used to say: 'One's own family is the most likely to kill them.'"

The pirates became listless as they approached Far Arroway. Jezschmel explained that they liked to get into mischief there when they happened to be traveling through. It was a city of traders, thieves, mercenaries for hire, and hustlers of all stripes. If someone was looking for a rare item, they might be able to find it—stolen, of course—in Far Arroway. If someone had treasure to sell, regardless of how they came by it, they could hawk it without fear in the lawless city. There was some form of loose governance, yet it was sloppy and corrupt. Jezschmel assured Delilah that for the right price, she could buy herself a small army attachment there. However, the pirate queen disappointed Delilah when she told her that she had decided not to accompany them on to Raefenshire to participate in the battle. "We must get back to pirating," Jezschmel said. "This little ferrying journey has taken us from our regular occupation of pillaging and plundering." Delilah tried to tempt Jezschmel by offering to pay even more. Still, the pirate declined, saying they needed to get back to open water. "We will come back to transport your army — what is left of it — when you return to Hope."

They entered the port at night, slipping into the harbor. All hundred ships were aloft of each other, moving in unison, the waves masking all sound. A giant explosion to their starboard side broke the synchrony of the movement, a fiery plume of water bursting from the waves. Another blast came on the other side of them, and this one took with it one of the fleet, splinters of wood and a shower of debris raining down upon Jezschmel's ship. The pirate yelled a stream of curses that was interrupted by another explosion. Yet another ship was destroyed, and sank, those aboard screaming and scattered to the waves to be lost to the sea.

"What is going on?" Oravica asked, running up to them. "Who is attacking us?"

"I am guessing the Crystal Aelves got to Far Arroway first," Jezschmel said, between shouting directions to her crew to avoid flaming flotsam on the water.

"They are here?" Delilah asked in disbelief. None of their communications had indicated that the aelven army had moved from the plains.

"Not likely," Jezschmel said. "They came here just long enough to buy some help. Your Majesty, I am sorry to say that it seems the mercenaries you wanted to hire have already been employed by the aelves. Clearly, they seek to diminish your numbers right here in Far Arroway before you even make it to Raefenshire."

They ducked instinctively as another detonation erupted from far behind them and a third ship sunk, pieces of debris floating on the waves to tell of its destruction. Delilah's heart sank with the loss as she tried to calculate the numbers of Guard on board each ship. "Can we not fire back?" Delilah asked.

Jezschmel shook her head, nodding to the vast coast and dark city. "Where? We have no idea where our enemies are hidden. They are not firing at us: we are triggering some kind of underwater devices. They could have been laid for us days ago. We will dock and see what we find. You should steel yourself for an assault once we disembark."

"We? Does that mean you are coming with us?" Delilah asked hopefully.

"Oh yes, the pirates will be coming. Now it is personal. No one sinks the ships of Queen Jezschmel without paying for it directly."

Despite the losses, they continued slowly approaching to dock the huge fleet. Those versed in such things were able to carefully disarm a few remaining traps. They were all on high alert and expecting another discharge at any time. None came, however, and they were able to peaceably disembark. They took stock of their casualties, determining which ships and comrades had been lost as they prepared to cross the city. They would be meeting Xan and the Centauri and Usiku armies on the far side, where the city turned to mountainous farmland before stretching out into the High Emerald Plains that abutted the woods and mountains of Raefenshire. It was getting to be daylight, and the shapes in the city took form to look like recognizable things instead of nebulous looming threats. Delilah sent most of the troops on the road ahead with Major Abbowhen to make camp beyond the city. There, they would meet up with the other columns to launch their attack. Delilah sent word through the ranks to be wary of assaults from regular citizens, since it still was not clear who was in the employ of the Crystal Aelves.

Jezschmel sent her fleet back out to sea with the minimal amount of womanpower to crew them, directing them to stay just off the coast and return at her command. She sent some of her pirate crew ahead with the soldiers and kept her most trusted posse with her to accompany Delilah as they began to work their way toward the Rogue's Guild in the center of commerce. Seeing the pirate queen's trusted inner circle filled Delilah with appreciation for the hard life of the pirates. On land, the pirates stood out with the bizarre malformations they acquired from a lifetime spent with the Gloom washing over the sea: eyes with no irises or double eyelids, extra rows of sharp teeth, some tentacles, webbed fingers, an occasional fin, and lots of patches of iridescent scales. A thin waif-like girl that looked no more than 15 could barely be seen if she turned sideways due to her body being almost completely see-through. She had tiny translucent bones below her watery flesh that made her almost invisible at the right angle. Most of the women were tattooed and had scars or other dramatic injuries. One very large woman had a garish scar across most of her face that looked like her head had been cleaved almost in two in the past. Behind her two stocky legs she had a tail that looked like that of a mermaid. Her iridescent tail swished from side to side as she walked, in graceful contrast to the thundering power of her large thighs. It was going to be hard to remain low-key with this group, Delilah thought.

Far Arroway was a mishmash of uneven streets with irregular buildings tipping in every direction, defying gravity. It was as if the city had been built in a hurry a long time ago and had been neglected since. The result was a montage of leaning structures that were sometimes propped up by beams to keep them from falling. Damaged parts of buildings looked as though someone had patched them up, meaning to come back to repair them correctly later, and just never did. There were mismatched wood panels nailed haphazardly over holes and punctures in the rotting wood that looked to have been caused by fists and brawls. A ditch filled with foul waste ran in front of the structures. Scrappy boards were laid down to cross the sewage. There were rats everywhere: unhealthy-looking deformed and bumpy critters. Delilah watched one with a lump the size of a second rat on top of its shoulder scurrying irregularly up a buttressing post that was barely holding up a building. The creature ascended, balancing precariously under the weight of the tumor, in jeopardy of falling into the drainage ditch. The creature turned to glare directly at Delilah before scrambling over the edge of the roof, noisily dislodging loose tiles.

"This way," Jezschmel said, leading Delilah and the entourage down an alley that looked about to fall in upon itself. The queens walked in sync, their strides matching each other perfectly. Delilah could not help the thrill she felt hearing their boots fall upon the stone in unison. She glanced over at the pirate's face: high cheekbones and smoothed, leathery skin. It was a face that was sea-worn yet youthful and even-toned, aside from some noticeable scars. Jezschmel's dark hair was embedded with occasional shells and beads that clinked together. One would think she was slightly older than Delilah only due to her utter confidence. She had the composure of a mature woman, yet it was impossible to tell Jezschmel's true age.

The city was waking up. A few shouts rang out from the first hawkers to hit the streets selling wares. There was the sound of a chamber pot being emptied into the ditch from a second-floor window, a flung dish clattering, someone yelling at someone else to get their lazy britches out of bed to start the fire, and dogs barking in scattered chains echoing between the tilted houses. People stopped to look at the group walking through the narrow alley, a troupe of about 50 women—fish-gilled pirates and Sister Guard—who had stayed to accompany Delilah and Jezschmel. At the end of the alley, a large drunkard staggered out and stood, hulking in the passageway. He looked up through long greasy hair that covered his face and leered at them.

"Make way!" Jezschmel ordered and stopped several strides from the man, waiting for him to comprehend that there was an army that needed to get through and he was blocking the way.

"I do not think so, darlin'," he said through blackened and broken teeth, standing up to his full height. Dozens of men in leather armor and an assortment of weapons folded in behind him. Standing upright, he looked less like a drunk and more like the fighter he was. "I do not think we will 'make way' for the likes of you," he spat.

Jezschmel glanced over at Delilah and sent her an intense look. Without any hesitation, the pirate drew out her sword and ran forward to stab the man through the chest before anyone had a moment to think. He collapsed, mortally wounded. "Anyone else want to block our way?" she asked. The group of men stepped back a few paces, then with aggressive yells, pulled their own weapons and flew over their fallen leader to attack the women. Delilah and Jezschmel, practically in lock step, took down the first half dozen attackers with their practiced swords, menacing the men to fall back and out of their reach. They heard sounds behind them and realized they were also being attacked from the other end of the alley. The Guard and pirates to the rear were already engaged with thieves and rascals of all sorts. They were trapped.

"Where did they all come from?" Delilah asked between swipes.

"Your aelven friends must have hired them. We got here too late," Jezschmel said, punctuating her last words while stepping in to lop the head off of a scraggly looking ranger.

"Well, this confirms the source of the explosives in the port," Delilah said.

"Thank you for reminding me," Jezschmel said, and ravaged another foolish man who tried to take her on. She stepped on top of his body and held her bloody sword aloft, yelling a guttural war cry, then ran up over bodies, climbing on top of the chests and shoulders and heads of the men, hacking down at them below her. She used her opponents as a ladder to jump up and grasp above her to climb up onto a balcony. Delilah was invigorated by watching Jezschmel in action and followed her lead, climbing over the living wall and ascending to the balcony on the alternate side of the alleyway, across from the one on which the pirate stood. From that height, the queens saw that three magicians had entered the alleyway behind the fighters. They were young and looked as if they had just put on their robes for the first time that morning. Nervously, they chanted magical words and sent dim sizzles of sparks like dampened firecrackers from the ends of their wands. "Now this is just sad," said Jezschmel. "I almost feel sorry for them." A cable had been run from one balcony to the other and garments were hung to dry. Without further discussion, Jezschmel leaped from the balcony and grabbed the cable, swinging her strong legs. The magicians became louder and louder in their chants, shaking their tiny wands toward the pirate queen, who swung back and forth, building up speed. She let go and launched toward the young wizards, kicking one in the head and one in the chest, taking them both down. Neither got up. The third turned around and fled from the alleyway, taking his little sputtering wand with him. "Are you glad you did not hire them?" Jezschmel called up to Delilah, who was still on the balcony above.

"Jezschmel, watch out!" Delilah yelled. A brute of an ogred on a chain was approaching the pirate queen. A man held the end of the ogred's leash: the owner of the beast was dressed in exotic black furs, holding a long black whip that glowed with blue light. He was snapping the whip in the air at the monster to drive him forward. The ogred had one good eye: the other was sewed shut with ugly, uneven stitches of black thread. The monster grabbed Jezschmel completely around her arms in a deathly bear hug. Jezschmel struggled and tried to move her arms to hack her sword at his legs, but the creature had immobilized her. She kicked his shins and tried to squirm free, yet the ogred just hugged her tighter and tighter. Delilah felt utterly helpless as she watched Jezschmel lose her breath as the grip held her without release. "Oh, no, I will not let this happen," Delilah said and leapt out into the air to grab the clothesline. Apparently, the line could only hold one queen for the day: the railings on the far side broke loose from their place on the balcony and Delilah tumbled down to the ground below, the wind knocked from her.

She got up and held her scimitar aloft, trying to determine how best to approach the oaf, who was snarling as he snuffed the life from the pirate queen. Before she could do anything, a streak of blue hair streamed by and a shriek like none she had ever heard filled the air. The horrid high-pitched sound came from one of Jezschmel's crew: her First Mate, Eluviel. The pirate, sounding her awful siren, leaped on top of the ogred. Her jaw seemed to detach as her mouth opened larger than her own head, with sharp, jagged teeth closing down like a hunting trap upon the ogred's neck and shoulders, just below where his metal collar sat. The beast howled in pain and dropped Jezschmel, who fell with a thunk to the stones. Eluviel did not release the ogred's shoulder, even as he swiped and swatted at her with his log-sized arms. Her light body tossed around in the air, yet her mouth stayed clamped upon the ogred's nape, which was bleeding profusely.

A sharp "snap" shocked the air. Eluviel's face, which had just been attached to the ogred, was suddenly a splatter of red and black, as the illuminated whip of the beast's master obliterated her head. She dropped to the ground, her face almost touching Jezschmel's, but unrecognizable. There was just a mash of blood and bone where Eluviel's skull had broken free from the skin. The ogred sat down, holding his bleeding neck and weeping like a babe. His owner, intolerant of such nonsense, immediately turned the whip to crack upon the beast for which it was intended. The ogred wiped snot from his dripping nose and stood up, ready to fight again. This time he had Delilah in his sights. Despite causing her friend's injury,

Delilah suddenly felt compassion for this overgrown child: his sad, weepy sewn-up eye, wounded shoulder, and bare, claw-toed feet seemed like those of a grotesque toddler. Although he came lumbering at her, Delilah ducked around him and instead, swiped her scimitar at the owner. The beastmaster had one hand on the chain holding his charge and the other wielding the glowing whip. She struck and he struck at the same time, and as she reached her mark, she chopped him down across his chest and practically severed his arm from its socket. She felt the bite of the whip wrapping around to her leg, making a deep searing cut through her leather leggings above her boot. The slice in the leather filled with blood and sizzled with heat. She winced with pain. The man looked at her with horror, holding his arm and chest together with his other hand for just a moment before falling back, his life's blood spent upon the stone alley floor. Rats scurried from the shadows to lap at the blood, climbing over the fallen to find exposed skin to chew.

Delilah grabbed the chain that the man had been holding and turned to the ogred, who looked at her with puzzlement. He reached his arms out, almost on impulse, for his master, then dropped his hands. She held the chain up, showing the creature that she held the end of it where the man with the black furs had held it before. He looked at her and tilted his head, then looked down where the whip had fallen upon the stones. "We will not be needing that," Delilah said and kicked the whip aside. The ogred breathed out a shuddered sigh of relief. Delilah reached out her crystal hand. The ogred backed away, but Delilah came forward and wrapped her palm around the ogred's meaty wrist. She concentrated, as best she could among the fighting that was still going on around them at either end of the alley. "I am sorry you were imprisoned," Delilah said. "I am not here to replace your master. I am here to set you free. If you come with me, I have healers who can look at your hurt eye. They might be able to help you. They can at least fix your shoulder."

She was about to release his arm when she heard the creature's response, clear as day, in her mind: "Thank you, Lady. I come with you. Nobody nice to me in long time. Me Ook," he pointed to his chest.

"Ook," Delilah said out loud.

"Ook," said the ogred, and smiled an awkward, crooked smile, his face clearly unused to such movement.

Delilah reached down and felt inside the man in black's coat until she found the key to the ogred's collar, which had a big lock in the back holding it in place. She unlatched it and the heavy loop of metal clanked to the ground. Ook rubbed his neck, which was red and raw from the metal cutting into his skin. Delilah reached down and picked up the whip. She wrapped it in a loop and held it out to the ogred, who cowered. She held it until he tentatively reached his monstrous hand to take it from her. She gestured that he should tie it to his own belt and stepped in to help him loop it there. Then she touched the beast's arm again: "Ook, I need you to carry my friend now, if you can," Delilah said, and pointed to Jezschmel, who was still sprawled out, her head at an odd angle, limbs askance. Ook immediately reached down and threw the pirate queen up over his good shoulder and looked to Delilah for guidance. "This way," Delilah said, and they started to go in the direction they had come down the alleyway. They quickly stopped, since more and more rogues had crowded in to attack them. There were bodies everywhere and only a few dozen of the pirates and Guard were left, about half at that end, and half behind them, fighting the first group that had revealed itself at the far end of the alley. More of their women were falling by the minute.

It was not that the fighters were particularly skilled; in a one-on-one duel, any of the women would have easily bested them. However, it was not one-on-one, but dozens-on-one. The sheer volume of the mercenaries was overwhelming them. They could not go in either direction safely. Delilah looked up at the alley balconies: there was the one which had fallen apart when she had hung from it, and no other real escape route in that direction. Unless Ook could climb? She pointed up to the balconies above, and Ook followed her finger. "Hummphff," Ook said, nodding his head, and quickly reached up with his bad arm to pull himself up to the one porch above that was still intact, all the while cradling Jezschmel. Once he laid the unconscious pirate safely down on the platform, he reached his apelike arms down and pulled Delilah up next to them. Delilah looked down to the fighting and knew that she was leaving their people to their deaths, yet she could not see any other way.

They were fighting valiantly, the few who were left, yet there was little hope they would prevail. Delilah was awash with guilt, knowing that if Jezschmel were awake she would never flee while her pirates were under attack. She would fight to the death to protect them. Yet what was Delilah willing to do? She could jump down and sacrifice herself, yet what would it prove to give her life for her comrades if there was no one left to defend her homeland? What would become of Hope? Surely, Jarvis and the Crystal Aelves would defeat them if there were no Queen of Hope to rally and fight for. At that moment, and for the first time in Delilah's not so very long life, she wished that she had married young. If she had at least had the foresight to become impregnated, she could now have a daughter who could take her place if something happened to her. As it were, she had almost no romantic history and had not even come close to partnering or having a child with someone. She had been married to Hope at the age of fifteen. The city had been her one love, the one driving force in her life. She was the only one who could save it.

At that moment, she knew what to do. She had no plants or trees or anything vaguely alive on the veranda, yet she looked down at her hand and concentrated with all she had on her crystals. She sent out a beacon with her mind, imagining it radiating out from her, calling upon her allies, anyone who could come to their aid. The whole alley and unstable buildings seemed to be shaking with the fighting from below reverberating, so she could not really tell if her crystals were tingling. However, almost immediately she heard a soft "thump... thump" from above on the rooftop. She looked up and was shocked by what she saw: two dark faces peered over the edge of the roof, looked at her, then surveyed the fighting below. In perfect unison, the two forms jumped down, landing like dancers on one foot, and spun to join the fighting in opposite directions. Perhaps "join" the fighting is too simplistic for what they actually did. The two Dusk Aelves, for Delilah quickly ascertained that was what they were, twirled and leaped into the battle on either side of the alley, willowy swords in hand, drawing fancy squiggles in the air with their weapons that created streams of blood in artful spiraling sprays.

Another "thump... thump" on the rooftop across from them, and Delilah saw two more crouching aelves with long staves. These two looked at her and nodded, then jumped into the air, floating down from the roof as if on gusts of air. Their staves were quickly employed in dramatic leaps and swirls that resulted in cutting hired mercenaries completely in two, as if the dark poles were not made from wood, but some other material that could sear through skin and bone. Another two aelves alighted across from them. Delilah could not see where they were coming from: it was as if they were emerging from the sky itself. Each of these two had dart guns and they began assaulting the enemy, hitting them with small, feathered missiles that dropped their targets within a second of hitting skin. Within moments, the new arrivals had wiped out most of the troublesome mercs, who continued to flow in until they realized they were being massacred. Then, those who were left turned and fled for their very lives.

All was almost quiet for a moment, as the remaining pirates and Guard acknowledged and thanked their rescuers. The Usiku just nodded and put their hands together, as if in prayer, in response to the praise. Loud blasts interrupted this exchange, and three oddly dressed rangers with muskets came barreling into the alley. They wore fur caps with animal tails hanging down the back, with full leather gear and moccasins. They were like a strange woodland family that had stumbled out of the forest. The rangers held up their muskets and began shooting indiscriminately at the gathered pirates, Guard, and Dusk Aelves. One of the Guard and an Usiku was struck right away, the wound in the aelf's stomach ejecting a fountain of turquoise blue blood. She fell back and turned almost instantly to indigo smoke. Her partner ran to where the dust was disappearing and beat the ground where her mate had been demolished.

The rangers laughed and began to fire again, yet were stopped in mid-launch by projectiles, pointed silver stars, suddenly sprouting from their faces. Delilah had not seen the two new aelves that had dropped in from above, however when she looked up, there they were. The Usiku masters rained a stream of pointed stars down on the gunmen, their hands a blur as they tossed the tiny deadly weapons with pristine accuracy. Quickly, the threat was no more and the gunmen lay dead, covered in sharp silver nibs. One pirate ran up and kicked the attackers, spitting her rage. Others began to look through the dead, trying to see if any of the fallen in the alley were still alive and had a chance of being saved. The Usiku leaped up to join Delilah on the large balcony. Ook seemed spooked by the aelves. He blocked Delilah with his body until she put her hand on him to tell him it was okay, and that these were their friends. All seven of the surviving aelves stood before her. One of the first that had arrived came up to Delilah and held up his hand. To her amazement, upon the dark palm, Delilah could see five glowing dots in the same shape and pattern as the crystals on her hand. Her own crystals buzzed, and she said "Thank you, friend," in her mind, with as much feeling as she could muster.

A groaning from the pirate queen drew their attention. Jezschmel moved her head for the first time since collapsing. The aelf who was still mourning her slaughtered partner turned her attention to Jezschmel. She got up and went to kneel next to her. The aelf put her hand on Jezschmel's head and Delilah could see a glow of energy spilling across the pirate's temples. In moments, the pirate queen sat up, shook her head, and looked around at the midnight-dark aelves and the ogred that had previously attacked her standing protectively at Delilah's shoulder like a pet.

"What did I miss?" asked the pirate.

Those who had gone ahead had set up camp on the mountainous farmland on the outskirts of Far Arroway. It was a sprawling green hillside with endless wildflowers. Large shade trees were mixed among a patchwork of fields filled with nodding purple amaranth and tall rainbow corn. It was expansive compared to the small homesteads in Hope. Delilah was impressed by the openness of it, the way the wind blew over and rustled the delicate grasses and grains, and how it smelled of earth and goodness, its elevation high above any remnants of Gloom. The armies had set up some cookfires and small makeshift tents to keep out the sun as they rested. Delilah was reunited with Xan and hugged the wolf long and hard. She greeted the Centaurs, too, who hailed her with great enthusiasm.

The Dusk Aelves were assembled there, keeping their distance from the others, and instead mingling among their own kind. They engaged in silent rituals: sweeping things that did not require sweeping, sprinkling water in circles, and stoking small fires in the broad daylight with no clear purpose. Pairs of them stood with their foreheads touching one another's for hours at a time in some type of communion without language. Delilah noticed quickly that the Dusk Aelves clustered in sets of two. A few were off on their own, yet most of them could be seen in couples, holding hands, walking together, touching foreheads, or just sitting facing one another, locked in silent eye contact. They seemed to have little interest in the humans and other creatures with whom they had allied. They were part of the convened army, yet separated in their own community within the larger brigade.

The aelf who had lost her partner in the alleyway and had healed Jezschmel had not left the pirate queen's side. The slight woman stood silently next to Jezschmel. The sea queen did not seem to mind having her in such proximity, despite occasionally sending her questioning looks or even asking outright, "Can I help you, Madame?" The aelf just stood and looked directly at her, without saying anything, not wavering at all in her gaze until Jezschmel sighed and went back to conversing or planning strategy with the other pirates or Guard.

"What is going on with that?" Delilah asked Xan pointedly, referring to Jezschmel's silent aelf shadow.

"The Usiku mate for life," Xan explained. "If one of the pair dies, the survivor either self-immolates, or bonds quickly with another."

"Do you mean that this aelf has replaced the bond to her dead partner with one to Queen Jezschmel? Does Jezschmel know?" She almost laughed to think of the pirate queen as life partner to an aelf.

"She is starting to suspect," Xan replied, pointing out that Jezschmel had relaxed into the company and was standing closer to the aelf than she had previously.

"Can that really be binding without Jezschmel's consent?" Delilah wondered.

"Oh no, it would not happen without her consent," Xan said.

"I thought aelves look down on the other races," Delilah protested, feeling a little childish to be poking holes in Xan's assessment of the situation.

"They do, usually, however they are far from home. All the aelves who want partners in their tribe probably have them already. She may select a partner that is not typical rather than go on alone. Is it so unthinkable that an aelf might be attracted to Jezschmel?"

"It is unthinkable that anyone would *not* be attracted to Jezschmel," Delilah admitted. The pirate queen's charisma was legendary and undeniable once one had met her.

"I would have to agree with you there. She is not my usual type, yet even I find her charms appealing," the wolf chuckled.

Delilah elbowed the wolf and they chuckled. It felt good to joke after the day she had. Delilah was also surprised to find that she felt a bit relieved. Her connection to Jezschmel had been powerful and alluring, yet it was also overwhelming. She could not imagine their attraction as anything but tempting trouble. It was probably for the best if the pirate's heart were attached to another. It made things simpler for Delilah. Still, it was a loss. She reflected back for a moment on the strange regrets she had, in the midst of the battle, where she had qualms about not procreating. It was the first maternal yearning she had ever had, and had come at such a strange time. She looked at Xan and was ashamed that she had once held romantic fantasies that they might partner, before she really knew him.

"Ook" said the ogred, coming up to her. She had almost forgotten all about her new protégé.

"Hello, Ook," she said. She had stationed him near the cookfires to get something to eat when they had arrived, and now he had sought her out. He blinked at her with his one good eye. She looked at him, wondering what he might want, and almost reached for him with her crystal hand to ask. Then she remembered she had promised to try to heal him. "Come with me," she said. She walked him over to where the healers were gathered. Helanza was leading up a lesson on the herbs of the High Emerald Plains. Delilah had been so relieved when she found out that her healer was not on one of the sunken ships. She felt guilty that she would favor some over others, yet she had known Helanza since she was a child. "Sorry to interrupt, Helanza. This is Ook," Delilah said. "I was wondering if you might take a look at his eye… ooh, and his neck too while you are at it," she noticed the puncture marks and bruises left by the pirate's bite starting to ooze a yellow gunk.

"Making friends, Your Majesty?" Helanza asked, eyes twinkling.

"Yes, you could say that."

Major Abbowhen was holding a meeting of the high-ranking officers of the Guard, Centaurs, and Usiku under a large tree. Delilah walked up to get a sense of the strategy. It was about a half-day's march to where the Crystal Aelves were camped and it was still unclear how they might take them by surprise. "We have already sent scouts out, Your Majesty, and we are using the Nearth to contact anyone in the area who will talk to us. Nothing seems to have changed," said Abbowhen. "The Crystal Aelves are still there, and oddly enough, they seem to be waiting for something. We do not have any information that explains what they might be planning. It is as if they are waiting for us to come to them."

"Then we shall go to them," Delilah said.

"Your Majesty," a voice came from next to the tree. It was soft, with an unusual accent.

It was coming from a Dusk Aelf who had been kneeling there. He now stood. "The Usiku know the Khattu well—the Crystal Aelves, as you call them—and we are certain they would not just be sitting in wait for an attack."

"And you are?" she asked, walking up to him.

"Your Majesty, this is King Kejanu the leader of the Usiku tribe," Abbowhen interjected. Delilah nodded her head toward the king. He bowed his head without dropping his eyes from hers.

"King Kejanu, can you please tell us what you think the Crystal Aelves might be planning? If not waiting for us, what might be their tactic?"

"We believe that they have something valuable in their possession, something that they would not want to abandon," he spoke pointedly, and Delilah got the sense that there were ten words not spoken for every word he chose.

"And what could that be?" she asked, a bit impatiently.

"Perhaps a sacred object, or a holy entity, something they would not want to leave unprotected."

"An entity?"

"It could be an ancestor spirit. One that gives power to the tribe," he said simply, as if this explained it all.

"A spirit? And they would not want to leave the territory unprotected because it could be stolen?"

"Stolen or conquered, to be used against them."

"Can that happen? Could someone conquer their ancestor's spirit to gain mastery over them?"

"Oh yes. That has happened many times to our people. In fact, one of your ancestors conquered our tribe many years ago. It weakened us for many generations. It is why we wanted the onyx skull back."

"Ah yes, the skull. And has the skull been returned to you?" she looked to Abbowhen, who shifted nervously. "We did bring it with us," Delilah assured.

"Umm… Your Majesty. Unfortunately, the skull was on one of the ships that was sunk in the harbor," Abbowhen said sheepishly.

"Oh no! Is this true?" Delilah quickly tried to calculate what this could mean for the Usiku commitment. "King Kejanu, we had promised the skull to you, and now it seems we are not able to give you what you had requested. I must ask if this changes your willingness to assist us against the… Khattu?"

"We came to help you in Far Arroway, did we not?"

"Yes, however you may not have realized then that we had lost the skull that was meant to repay you," she reasoned.

"We knew it already."

"And you helped us anyway?"

"It was not your fault that the skull was lost. Your intention was to deliver it to us. While we mourn for its loss, we do not hold you accountable and we will still honor our pact with you."

"I am humbled by your integrity, Your Majesty." Delilah said. She could not help thinking that he was a better leader than she was, to be so intent upon his commitment that he would follow through despite having no clear advantage in doing so.

"We are not so free from our own agenda," the aelf said, playing with a gold hoop that hung from his earlobe. "In fact, we have a very clear motive to assist you, and that is because the Crystal Aelves betrayed us not too long ago. You may have heard? Our tribe was suffering from a giant sandworm infestation. Normally these creatures are docile and stay deep underground. However, they became infected by the dread Mungus. They turned aggressive and came to the surface. They attacked our people. They killed many, at least 200 of our tribe in just a few weeks." The assembly was alert and hung on every softspoken word, leaning in to hear him. "We asked the Khattu for their help. They are experienced with such creatures, having tamed the wild earthworms of the plains. They refused to assist us. They would not even send advice or share magickal spells to combat the creatures. For aelven tribes not to assist one another, especially in a time of crisis, is the same as a crime in our culture. Our Pact is the basis for our whole civilization. It is why we have thrived in this world as other races have perished. Our unity is our strength. To deny us was to go against our whole way of being. It is punishable by death."

The aelf's speech moved the assembly, and many made sounds of agreement or understanding. Those who had not heard the history had wondered why the Usiku were here and why they would go against another aelven tribe. This made it clear to all, and confirmed their trust in this foreign race to assist them in battle. Many stirred and mumbled, and they almost missed his additional words: "I know how to best them," said King Kejanu, gaining their attention once again.

"Please," said Delilah. "We would be most grateful for your counsel."

"We must find their sacred shrine, capture and conquer their ancestral object. Once we have that in our possession, they will be weakened. Many of their powers will be diminished or destroyed. It will allow us to have a fair chance to defeat them with the simple mechanics of war. It is not a guarantee, yet it is the best option we have."

"And just how can we do that?" Delilah wondered. She suspected it sounded simpler than it was.

"We are meditating now," Kejanu said. "Our tribe members are communicating with the Spirits of the Plains. The spirits of the dust, wind, grasses, wildflowers, and the fire spirits are not aligned with any sect. They are neutral. We are gaining insights as we speak."

Appreciating that the Usiku's ceremonies had a purpose made them seem more mystical than when she first observed the rites. There was so much she did not know about them. She again realized how her education had been full of enormous holes. She only knew a bit about that part of the world because her father came from the lands near Erithea. She had not studied much about the desert races since they did not adjoin Hope and had little risk of invading. Therefore, it had not been a priority to learn their ways. She had barely been aware of their existence before hearing about them from Xan. She thought now how sheltered and naïve she had been, living in Hope, learning Drakonic and Cypher, practicing cubic glyphs and Sarphonian script, and researching whayerwolves and other monsters of the Whayer Wood. She had tunnel vision, seeing only a small portion of her sequestered world.

The group disbanded after some time, and she wandered away with Xan. "They are so interesting," Delilah confided in the wolf.

"Yes, terribly interesting. And terribly deadly."

"Do you not trust them?" She asked, suddenly wondering if she had missed something.

"I trust them, yes. Still, I would not want to be on the other end of their rage. Can you imagine how upset they must be for aelf to turn against aelf?" he asked. They walked for a while, edging the camp.

"Xan, I must confide in you: before the Usiku came and saved us in Far Arroway, I had the strangest thought. I wished I had put more energy into having an heir in case something happened to me."

"That is not so strange, Your Majesty. You are, in fact, approaching middle age."

"Thanks for reminding me," she said. "No, I mean that it was strange that I had never thought of it before. I always figured I would have plenty of time for partnering and having children in the future. What if I do not? What if I die on the battlefield? What will become of Hope?"

"I do not know the answer to that, Delilah. I only know that you must not die. We must not let you die and you must go on to have lots of warrior babies to defend Hope when you leave this world."

"But what if I never find the right partner?" she asked, bashful that she sounded like a forlorn juvenile.

"I am not sure how much your mother told you of these things, Your Majesty, but you do not need to have a partner to have a child."

They laughed. "I feel like I might need to get on that track soon," Delilah said. "Even if we win this battle, what about the next one? Suddenly I have realized that although I have devoted my whole adult life to protecting Hope, I have not done the one thing that will protect Hope's future."

"I am sure you can find a chap or two who can help you with that," said Xan.

"And what about you, Xan? Lord Xanfar of Fallengrove. What will happen to your estate when you pass from this world?"

"Have you not heard, Majesty? Whayerwolves are immortal."

Delilah was asleep in her bedroll when she heard the whispering. She sat straight up in the dark. The distant stars above were the only light. No moon was visible, and a wet mist clung close to the ground making it hard to see. She heard her name, spoken softly, and tried to tell the direction from which it came. She heard it again and saw a dark form coming out of the mist. She grabbed her sword, which was right by her side, yet when the shape came close, she saw it was King Kejanu. He came toward her and knelt by her, without saying a word. He reached out his hand, pushed her hair back, and stroked the side of her face, looking deeply into her eyes. "Delilah," he said again.

"Queen Delilah!"

It was bright daylight and Delilah jumped to a standing position from where she had been sleeping. How had she slept so late and what was that dream? It felt so real. She shook the sleepy dust from her eyes and looked toward where her name had been called. It was Abbowhen, running toward her, looking excited. "What is it?" Delilah asked the Major.

"They have found it! They intercepted the communications of the Crystal Aelves and know where they have hidden the source of their ancestral power. It is under the Crystal Mountain in a deep underground cavern. A giant dog-beast with three heads guards it."

"Well, that is… good news?" Delilah asked, unsure if it was.

"Yes, well at least we know where to find it. Getting it may be another story. We must engage the aelves and draw their attention away while a squad goes in to capture the skull."

"What is proposed?"

"King Kejanu has suggested that the Usiku should go first to attack the Crystal Aelves. The Dusk Aelves are the best matched and the Crystal Aelves—the Khattu—will not be expecting them. It will keep them distracted."

"Yes, that sounds right, and is very generous of them."

"Lord Xanfar and the Centaurs will go in from the other side, hopefully surprising them by coming out of the Whayer Wood, followed by the Sister Guard and Queen Jezschmel and her pirates from the opposite direction. If we send in a succession of troops and surround them, we can keep battering them from all sides with waves of new forces."

"Yes, I like it," Delilah said. "And who will go to the Crystal Mountain while they are engaged?"

"We are putting together an expert crew. Oravica will lead the mission."

"I will lead it," Delilah asserted.

"Your Majesty, that is much too dangerous," Abbowhen shook her head.

"Well, I think I should be able to handle one three-headed monster!"

"Yes, if that is all it is, however it would be unlikely for them not to guard it better, given how important it is to them. There could be any manner of guards and enchantments in place to prevent its loss."

"Sounds like fun!" Delilah asserted.

She went to see who Oravica had chosen for her squad. If she was going to be eaten by a three-headed beast, she was happy to have her friend beside her. She had barely seen Oravica since they got to the camp, so she sought her out. The sergeant and Batelnut were lingering near the Centauri camp. Batel was embroiled in a giggling conversation with her old flame, the golden steed, Sethran, and Oravica was discussing weaponry with Captain Ferrashi.

"Ah yes, Queen Delilah, we were just discussing equipment the team going into the Crystal Mountain might need," Ferrashi said.

"Do you think we will require more than our usual weapons, Sergeant?" Delilah asked Oravica.

"We know not what beasts lie in wait. There will certainly be aelven guard, so we will need weapons of iron. Captain Ferrashi was saying that we can use a few of the centaurs' light compound bows in case there are enemies that must be picked off at a distance."

"What about undead creatures? What might we need to fight them that we do not already have in our arsenal?" Delilah asked.

"Helanza gave me powders that can be used to de-combust some monsters," Oravica said. "We will distribute those among our Guard."

"Do you think you might want to bring an Usiku or two?" Ferrashi asked, looking over at the Dusk Aelves, many still in ceremony, sitting with foreheads together or turning slowly alone while looking up at the sky. Some lay curled up together in pairs, sleeping. Delilah recalled that they were traditionally nocturnal, so functioning in a camp that was up all day was probably an adjustment. "They understand what to look for and will clearly have the greatest advantage with the Crystal Aelves, if there are any stationed in the caverns of the mountain." Ferrashi said.

"I do not know that they can spare any," Delilah said. "They will have their hands full going in to catch the Khattu off-guard. It might not be fair to ask them to send any with us on this mission. They are already doing us a huge service by deploying first and will take the greatest losses." She wondered for a moment what would happen to all the paired aelves who might lose partners in battle.

"Still, it will not hurt to ask," Oravica said. "Your Majesty, would you like to join me to go speak to their King?"

"Certainly," said Delilah, a tangle of butterflies suddenly trapped in her ribcage.

They approached King Kejanu, who was kneeling in the dirt, tracing a spiral around a leaf, around and around in larger and larger circles. He looked up, and his direct gaze shocked Delilah into reliving her dream.

"King Kejanu," Oravica started, bowing respectfully. He nodded at her then bowed his head to Delilah. "We were hoping to speak to you about the plan. Queen Delilah will be leading the mission to the Crystal Mountain to find and capture the sacred skull relic of the Khattu. I will be accompanying her with a small battalion. We expect there will be aelven guards to protect their sacred treasure. Would it make sense, in your opinion, to send some of your warriors along with us?"

"Yes, I will accompany you," he said without pausing, as if he knew the question was coming.

"You?" Oravica questioned. "I thought you would be leading the charge on the Crystal Aelves?"

"Yes, I will do that, too," he said.

"I apologize, King Kejanu. I know your kind are extraordinarily fast compared to humans, yet I am not sure how you can be in both places at once."

"I will lead the charge on the Emerald Plains. It is important that I greet their Queen on the battlefield to show that we have disintegrated our Pact. I have a message for her from our High Priestess, who remained behind to guard our lands in the desert. We will initiate the battle, then I will slip away with a group of our solo warriors to come to your aid."

"Your... solo warriors?" Delilah asked.

"Yes, we have two types of warriors: duo warriors, who fight in pairs as life partners, and solo warriors, who have no partner and fight alone. The duo warriors have an advantage against the Khattu, who are each fighting by themselves. Our pairs have trained and fought together for most of their lives, so they will have the most leverage when fighting the Khattu. The Usiku are already stronger warriors than the Khattu. In pairs, even more deadly."

"And so, you and your solo warriors will come to our aid once the battle is in motion?"

"Yes, if I am not killed first," he said. "If I am dead, I will not be able to assist you," he said dryly.

"Well, let us hope that does not happen," Delilah said.

"Out of curiosity, Your Majesty," interjected Oravica, "your single warriors—are they alone by choice? Do they not have partners because they have not found them or because they do not want them?"

"Most solitary warriors are just built that way. They are self-sufficient even as children. Others are designed to be in pairs and have not yet found their mate. That is the case for me. I am created to have a partner," he said, piercing Delilah with an incisive look. "I have just not been bound to her yet." She trembled and looked down, feeling the hairs on her arms stand on end.

Back at the camp, Delilah engaged in small talk with some of the officers. They were discussing the unique abilities of aelves and how they have exceptionally long lives, so long as they are not killed. The topic of aelf reproduction was broached, including the fact that a female aelf might live hundreds of years, yet only produce one child, and sometimes none at all.

"What of a cross between an aelf and human child?" Delilah wondered out loud. "Would it have a normal lifespan, or long like an aelf?"

"Of that, I am not sure, Your Majesty," said one Guard, who seemed to know the most about the subject. "We all know that it is possible for humans and aelves to interbreed. A half-aelf has some of each race's qualities. They are so rare, though, it would be hard to study them. They might take more after one parent than another," she speculated, "in lifespan as well as in other qualities. I am not sure it could be predicted."

"What of the Ghost Scribe?" another young Guard asked. "Some say he had an aelf parent, which is why he lived so long. He may still be living, indeed, and not a ghost at all."

"Ah, the Ghost Scribe," Delilah recalled. "I have not heard from him in a long time."

"Yet he still sends scrolls every few years into the lands of Hope from the netherworld or wherever he is hiding, whether he is a ghost or living a long life with aelven blood," said the Guard.

"I heard the Ghost Scribe is actually a litch—an undead wizard!" piped in another Guard.

"Litch, aelf, or ghost, I would like to see him," said Delilah. "Perhaps if we triumph, he will write a ballad about our battle with the Crystal Aelves."

"I am certain he will, Your Grace."

Ook was following Delilah around the camp. Helanza had started to heal his eye, which was still droopy and wept a constant clear fluid, with dark red holes circling it from whatever horrid surgeon had sewn it shut. The healer had also treated and bandaged the creature's shoulder. Ook reminded Delilah of an overgrown puppy, the way he traced her every step and looked as if all he wanted was her approval. She gave him tasks, like carrying wood for the cookfires, yet he always returned, waiting for another command. He understood most of what was told to him, she found, yet could generate only the most guttural words in response. Mostly, he just did what she asked, sporadically flinching as if she might strike him. Delilah felt sorry for the life he must have led at the tail end of the whip by the man in black fur, who most likely could have controlled him without ever having to use force or cruelty. Ook kept the glowing whip that had previously kept him captive tied onto his belt.

When she went to check in with Jezschmel, the pirate queen looked the ogred up and down. "I am not sure I trust that one off the leash," she said, clearly recalling the crushing hug that had rendered her helpless in Far Arroway. Jezschmel still had her own shadow, the petite dark aelf that had bonded to her. Jezschmel barely seemed to notice her aelf partner, who stood at her elbow, sometimes even with her hand on the pirate's arm. It was as if she had always been there at her side. Jezschmel had adapted to the turn of events as if it were only natural. "When are we getting this party going?" Jezschmel asked, urgency in her voice. "I am eager to get back to the sea." Delilah noticed another new streak of silver in Jezschmel's hair. It seemed they appeared every time the pirate queen spent too long on land, as it was the ocean that gifted her with long life. Delilah wondered what it was costing her to accompany them on this mission.

"We will depart tomorrow morning and be in positions by midday. King Kejanu says that bright sunlight is the worst for the Crystal Aelves. They are used to being underground with filtered starlight, so they do not do well in daylight. I imagine the Usiku do not, either, being night-dwellers, however, this is the plan they feel is the best." She looked at the Usiku woman. "What of… your new friend?" Delilah asked. "Will she return to your ship with you after the battle?" she asked, genuinely curious how this relationship could be negotiated.

"Ah, my little queen," laughed the pirate. "Jealousy does not suit you! You could have come to live on my ship with me long ago if you would just have cast away all of this 'Queen of Hope' business. Too bad you missed your chance!"

Delilah laughed and said: "I will be sour for a few years and then I will forgive you."

"In the meantime, my pirates and I intend to save the lives of all you silly humans, and maybe even an Usiku or two." With that she stroked the chin of the aelf, who looked up at her adoringly. "I will be blasting those crystal snobs all over the place until the ground is littered with their snooty, fluffy aelf powder," Jezschmel continued, venom in her voice.

"Well, we will definitely need your passion for battle," Delilah said. Then in a serious moment that was atypical from their usual banter: "Thank you, my friend. We owe you."

"Yes, you do. We will work it out later. It is nothing gold and gemstones will not settle."

"My treasury will be open to you, Queen Jezschmel. It does us no good sitting and gathering dust."

"And who will be your companion on your mission, My Queen, other than your…

pet?"

"Oh, I do not believe Ook will be coming with me. We have selected a squad."

"Ook!" Ook said vehemently, clearly understanding he was being overlooked.

"Yes, Ook, I know you want to come."

"Ook!" he said again, puffing out his chest and holding a hand on his whip. Delilah looked into his sincere face and realized this creature would die defending her, if needed.

"Okay, Ook. I would be honored to have you at my side."

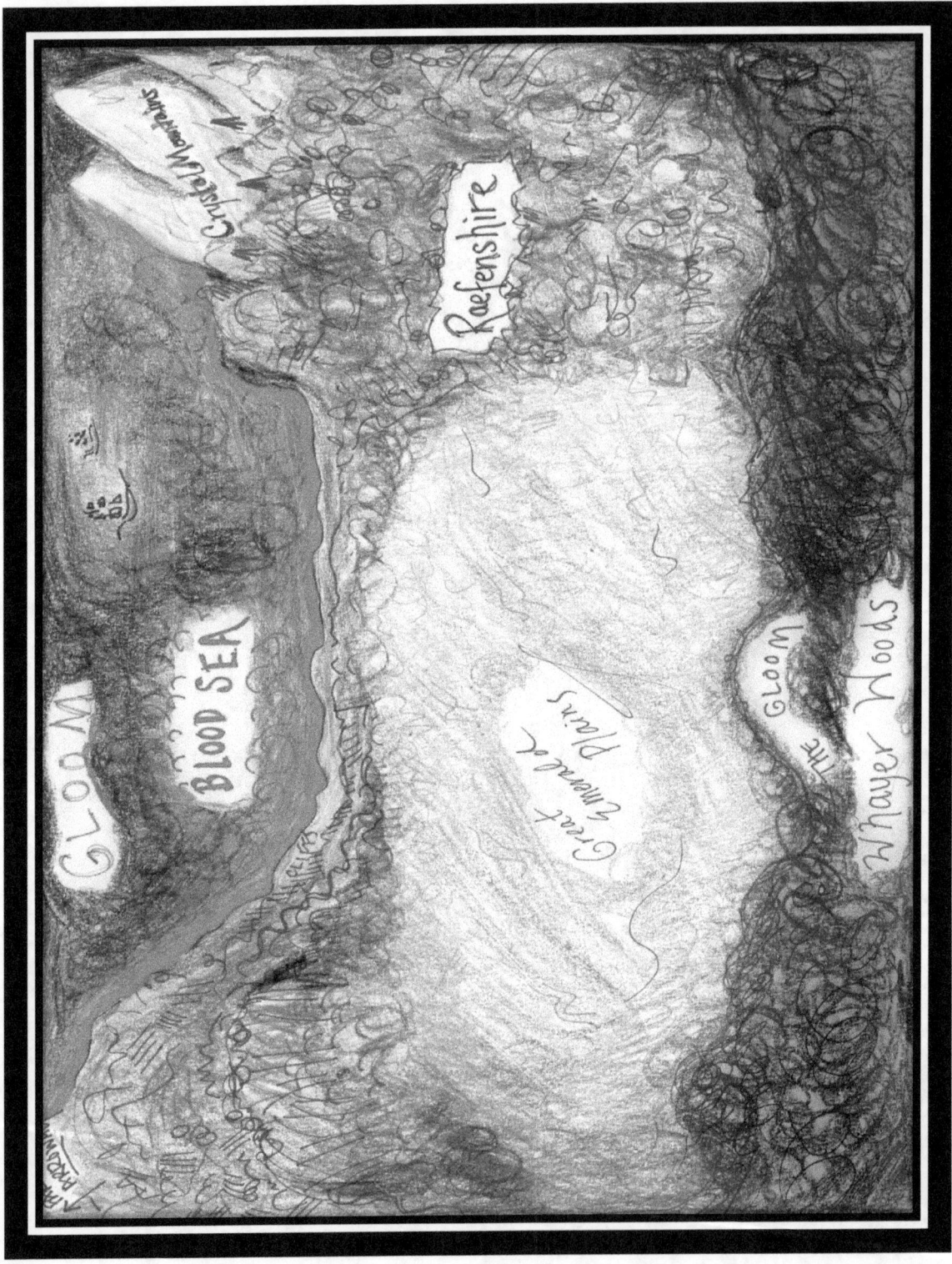

"Oh, once there was a Warrior Queen
Who fought fair aelves on the prairie green
With centaurs, whayerwolves, and a pirate queen
And dark-as-night aelves on the prairie green."
-The Ghost Scribe

Chapter 9: A Fateful Day

Delilah held a flat round stone in her hand that had been delivered by Belk that morning. The kind satyr had run all the way from Verily through the Whayer Woods to deliver it to Delilah. She did not think it would work, however when the crystals in her hand were activated, she could see an image appear. Doktora Ilvana's face now gleamed up from the smooth surface of the stone. "I told you it would work, Your Majesty," the doctor said, her voice ringing with triumph.

"This is incredible, Doktora!" Delilah said. "It is wondrous to see your face as if you were here with us!"

"This is not a tool for socializing," Ilvana scolded. "It is a weapon for war. You can contact other members of your party while you are separated to see how the battle is going."

"Do they need to have a stone on the other side for me to be able to see them?"

"No—the stone will naturally tap into the Nearth to Link you. You will be able to see them."

"This will be invaluable for the battle, Doktora. Today we are going to war."

"Yes, I know. I am Linked to all the squadron leaders, too, Your Majesty."

"Of course you are, how silly of me," Delilah said.

"You have a lot on your mind, I am sure," said Ilvana. Delilah did not realize how much she had missed the doctor. They had become close since sharing the crystal technology and speaking every day through it, especially after fighting the Battle of Verily together. The scientist had insisted upon staying behind with her monks, who were monitoring key areas in Hope to launch defenses, if needed. It was unlikely that the fighting would land in their backyard at this point. Still, they did not want to leave the territory undefended. After seeing how Ilvana had directed her forces through battle, Delilah now knew she could be trusted to defend Hope while she and most of the Sister Guard were away, if it came to that. Delilah had left minimal forces at home to defend the castle since she needed all of her military resources for this war. The Doktora was also continuing her work on her inventions, such as the scrying tool, and was still invested in finding a method for transporting objects and people through the Nearth.

"I do have a lot on my mind," Delilah agreed. "Doktora, have you known many half-aelves?"

"Of course! There have been many in Hope's history."

"Truly? I have not heard of any," Delilah said, mystified.

"They are rare. The aelves tend not to breed with humans to keep their bloodlines pure. Still, sometimes love has a way of breaking through this tradition. The offspring do not always appear to be aelven, which helps to keep their heritage secret. If they take more after a human parent, you might not even know they had any aelf blood. They could have just one pointed ear or an aelven power, like seeing in the dark. You would not necessarily know they were part-aelf just by looking at them. If they take mostly after their aelf parent, you might mistake them for any other aelf."

"I had no idea. I have not the time now, yet I would like to hear more about this when I return," Delilah said.

"Yes, I think you would be very interested to hear about the half-aelves who have lived right under your nose," said Ilvana.

Despite Delilah being more than a little intrigued, she knew she needed to focus on the day. She said goodbye to her friend and slipped the thin stone into her satchel. She went to find Xan, who was making last-minute arrangements with the Centauri army, to be sure all were equipped and knew the order of deployment on the battlefield. They would be leaving within the hour to march through the Whayer Wood to the area on the edge of the plains where the Crystal Aelves were camped. The area was buzzing with activity, except for the Usiku. By dawn, the Dusk Aelves had gathered along the ridge facing the rising sun. There they had sat, hands on knees, looking toward the sun and barely moving, like onyx statues. They were preparing in their own way.

Delilah felt uncomfortable disturbing them except she had a few details to discuss with King Kejanu. Timidly, she went to the front of the mass of still and silent figures to speak to him. "Your Majesty," she said, leaning down to whisper to him. His eyes, which had been focused on the sun, snapped to hers and she almost jumped back. "I am sorry to disturb you. I was hoping we could go over a few things." The dark aelf rose silently and gestured to a place a distance away under a cluster of trees. There, he stood expectantly, waiting for her to start speaking. Delilah found his whole manner unnerving: his quiet seriousness, his intensity, not to mention how the remnants of her dream lingered in her mind. "I was hoping we could discuss how we will know when to head toward the Crystal

Queen Delilah and the Encroaching Gloom

Mountain. Is there a way for us to communicate with you while you are in battle so you can locate us when the time to join has come?"

"We will be able to locate you," he said assuredly.

"Oh, I see," she said. "I mean to say, I have this scrying stone and I have used it to see our Chief Scientist back home. I was planning to use it to communicate with Lord Xanfar and Major Abbowhen so that we know how the battle is going and if we need to change strategies."

The king looked at the stone as if it were a useless trinket. "You may use that, if you wish. You can send messages to me with or without it, whichever you please."

"Do you mean that you are able to hear my thoughts regardless?" she asked, suddenly flushed. Had he realized she had been thinking about him, wondering what their half-aelf child would look like and if it would live an extraordinarily long life with which to rule Hope?

"I can only hear the thoughts you want me to hear," he said. Delilah tried not to betray her relief. He continued: "If you need to reach me, you can send your thoughts to me and I will respond. That is, I will respond if I am alive. If I am dead, I will not be likely to respond." For a moment, Delilah saw just the tiniest corner of his mouth twitch up and she realized that he had made a joke.

She chuckled awkwardly and said, "No, nor will I, if I am dead."

"Do not worry, My Queen," he said. Then he did something that took her completely by surprise: he held out his palm and reached out to touch her on her bare skin, right over her heart. She almost pulled away, yet froze, holding her breath as she felt the warmth of his hand on her chest. "I will be with you through the battle." He dropped his hand and turned, walking briskly away. Delilah stood there, trembling, watching his dark form recede toward his companions. She had not heard Oravica coming up behind her and practically jumped when the sergeant appeared at her elbow.

"Well, he is an interesting one, is he not?" she said, looking over at Delilah. "Your Majesty, are you quite well? You look a little flushed."

"What, oh, yes…" Delilah started to respond and then saw that Oravica was smirking at her, clearly teasing her over her intimate exchange with the king. "Come along, Sergeant," Delilah said. "We have a lot of blood to spill today."

On the far side of the Tharovian Mountains lay the wide and verdant plains, just high enough in elevation to escape the Gloom. Spilling down into the dark valley to the east, the Whayer Wood fringed the plains, steeped in the purplish glow of the Gloom. To the north lay the rocky and forested slopes of Raefenshire, the territory of the Crystal Aelves. Irregular jags and bluffs assembled and scrambled up to blend into the cliffs of the Crystal Mountain, which lay in the northernmost territory of the aelven lands. Delilah, who had spent her life in the relatively small confines of Hope, gasped when she poked her head above the protected cliffside and saw the expanse of green plains surrounded by mountains. It was like a beautiful offering bowl, open to the sky. She squinted to see the camp of the Crystal Aelves, which was so far below it was barely visible. Jezschmel was at her elbow and handed her a viewing scope. The glass amplified the image of the tiny ant-like figures until she could see faces, even the expressions of individual aelves.

The aelves seemed quite relaxed, many involved in playing music alone on oddly shaped instruments, writing on long scrolls, or meditating. Some were practicing hand-to-hand combat, their moves like a silent dance from so far away. Could they still not realize that enemy armies were approaching? Could they truly not be expecting an ambush? Their casual demeanor made it seem as though they had gotten used to camping under the stars in this cluster, by the tens of thousands, just living out in the open, awaiting… what? Their assault on Verily had not been as successful as they had hoped, and so what was their next move? Perhaps it did not matter now, because the plan of Delilah and her allies was in motion. King Kejanu had already departed with his army and Delilah wondered when they would be able to see them from this vantage point. His forces were nowhere near the size of the Crystal Aelves, so the element of surprise was essential. It would be critical for the other forces—the Centauri, Sister Guard, and Pirates—to be in place to swarm in once they had launched the power of their first attack.

The Usiku were surrounding the Crystal Aelves, Delilah knew, with some platoons creeping down the slopes hiding behind the shadows of the jagged stone faces. Others had snuck down through the Whayer Wood, and would attack from that side. Still others had gone to the edge of Raefenshire and would be attacking from the North. Yet another segment would be coming from the ocean side toward the West, where little stood between the plains and the sea. Together, the Usiku troops would form a ring around the Crystal Aelves and, en masse, close in and attack them from all sides. Delilah watched closely, since she knew she would not have much time once the aelves were engaged in battle to sneak around the far side toward the west and the ocean to get into the protection of the forest that led up to the Crystal Mountain.

She felt a hulking presence behind her. "Ook?" the rough voice asked.

"Yes, Ook, you are coming with me."

"You are taking your life into your hands bringing that one along," Jezschmel said, still untrusting of the beastly creature.

"Ook is harmless to me," said Delilah, "yet I am hoping he will not be harmless to my opponents. I want him to give them the ol' Pirate Queen strangle!" she joked, and Jezschmel cracked a smile.

Jezschmel's shadow aelf was there and smiled as the pirate smiled, looking up at her as if she were a goddess. Perhaps she was, thought Delilah and felt a stab of remorse at losing the attention of the charismatic queen. Should she have tried harder? She shook the thought from her head, knowing she needed to concentrate. Just then she saw a dark ring slowly and silently forming around the aelves on the plains. Although they were in broad daylight, the flickering vagueness and smooth motion of their shapes could fool you into thinking you were just seeing sunspots for a moment. Delilah tensed and nudged Jezschmel, who was seeing it, too. "It is happening," said the pirate.

Delilah put the viewing glass to her eye again and saw that the Crystal Aelves did not seem to notice they were being surrounded. They continued in their benign activities as if they were at a picnic enjoying the brightness of the day. They were not exactly the playful type, yet a few threw bundles of fabric to one another in a game designed to waste time in leisure. All of a sudden, the entire assemblage of aelves stood up completely still. Those who were sitting or relaxing upon the earth jumped to their feet. They all stood silently, their pointy ears quivering. Delilah watched and saw the moment they realized that they were surrounded, grasping for weapons, jumping to the perimeter where the Usiku were overcoming the edges like a giant dark wave. And like a wave, Delilah saw the moment the Usiku overcame the Crystal Aelves with their surprise assault, saw the splashing purple fountains of blood from the pale, elegant creatures. There was a roar that reached her ears of both the Usiku emitting their war cry and the Crystal Aelves issuing their own melodic scream of defensive vengeance.

Jezschmel grabbed the glass from Delilah so she could see, and Delilah looked out again, seeing almost no detail in the giant conglomeration of war unfolding, just the pale shiny bodies spanning an enormous area in a circle on the green plain, and then the dark forms of the Usiku closing in around them, spraying violet blood as they squeezed in. Delilah was entranced by this thing, which did not seem like a battle at all, but a moving painting in the vast valley below. Ook grabbed her elbow: he remembered the plan when she had not. Oravica was nearby, and ten of her best soldiers were ready to follow Delilah down a hidden trail toward the ocean to shield them from the activity of the battle. They were on the move, Delilah and her special unit of treasure hunters, the most talented and agile Oravica could muster of the Guard. Batelnut was there and nodded to the queen when she caught her eye. Delilah raised her scimitar to her in acknowledgment.

The path down was steep and footing was tricky, so they went single-file. Delilah's blood was pumping and she listened thirstily for clashes and clangs which rang out from the field below. They could not see, their view being blocked by the rocky bluffs, yet the sounds of fighting and dying reached them over the rocks as if bouncing off the clouds and raining back down upon them. Delilah was unnerved. Nothing felt right. It seemed too easy to surround them. With thunderous recognition, Delilah realized that the entire layout had been—could only be—a trap. She stopped in her tracks to pull the smooth scrying stone from her satchel and held it with her crystal hand, concentrating on contacting King Kejanu. Within moments, the stone blurred and revealed a roiling scene, dark aelves tumbling over light with maddening speed.

"May I help you, Your Majesty?" the king's calm voice reached her mind, despite the rapid movements he was clearly engaged in. She saw him slice the throat of a Crystal Aelf priestess and her purple blood squirted as if it would splash Delilah in the face.

"It is a trap, King Kejanu. It is too easy. I just know it. They have been waiting for us to come to them because they had something planned, something that could only happen on that field if we came to them."

"We are winning thus far," said the monarch, slicing into another pale warrior. From what Delilah observed, it seemed true. The Dusk Aelves had the clear advantage of skill, despite the greater numbers of Crystal Aelves. Indeed, Delilah watched a pair of Usiku handily chop a Crystal Aelf into pieces by one going up and the other going down, the middle part of their enemy falling to the ground among severed chunks of torso and leg.

"Perhaps I was wrong, Your Majesty. I felt for a moment that we might be making a mistake going to them, that there must be some reason they were luring us to this battlefield," Delilah said, feeling foolish for bothering the king in such a dire situation. "I am sorry to interfere," she said.

"We are besting them at the moment, so I will get back to that," said Kejanu.

Delilah slipped the scrying stone away and continued her walk down the path amongst her party, her intuition still gnawing at her. She was so distracted that she almost lost her footing and felt Ook's strong arm under hers, catching her. They reached the bottom of the hill, where stone turned into clay. Approaching an area with patches of green and dried grasses, they heard the rumbling. It was so deep and loud that Delilah was certain it was an earthquake. The low hills and grassy knolls provided cover, so she and the others who were the first down fell to the earth and belly crawled until they could peek over the hilly mounds to see far off into the edges of the fray. There was chaos there, as the Dusk Aelves had fallen back somewhat upon hearing the thundering noise. Dust was kicking up and rocks and earth were popping from the vibrations below. Then they heard the shrieks: awful, horrendous sounds that chilled Delilah's blood with their unnatural pitch.

The ground erupted and a tube of pinkish-white flesh poured out into the air, arching up, and then diving back into the earth, shrieking all the while. Another one, or perhaps the same, exploded the ground a distance away, and the creature jumped and dove back down, shooting out clouds of dust and leaving dark holes with piles of earth behind.

"Megalostrangi!" Oravica exclaimed, her eyes wide with fear.

"What in the Nearth?" Delilah sputtered. More of the snakelike monsters broke the surface of the ground.

"They are giant sandworms! They have a terrible temper. Mostly they stay well below the surface," the sergeant explained.

"They are enchanted," said Batel, pointing. Sorcerers sat astride the worm-beasts, riding them as if they were horses as they dove under the earth and back up. The riders were chanting and pointing, shouting directions to the beasts. One monster stayed atop the surface long enough to fully extend its long body across the grassy terrain. It had no eyes, just one terrifying round mouth in the middle of its face with rows and rows of razor-sharp teeth. It struck out and grabbed a Dusk Aelf by chomping half his body, his partner below stabbing at the creature with a long spear as it chomped down and ate the rest of the warrior. His partner screamed and ran at the beast, stabbing and yelling. The worm sniffed around, its phallic, droopy face turning this way and that before it snapped out to gobble the woman whole.

There were at least a dozen of them, diving and jumping, like dolphins in the waves, often returning down into the dirt with a mouthful of Usiku. They knew their targets and were unstoppable when they zeroed in on their prey. The Megalostrangi were not coordinated. Instead, each one was directed by the sorcerer on its back, who drove the mount toward the densest areas where Usiku were congregated, plowing through them, sending rivers of turquoise blood spilling out in all directions on the earth. Dust from the deceased Usiku mixed with the red clay and made a muddy cloud under which streams of iridescent blue blood rolled in rivulets over the baked earth. It was a massacre.

Delilah used all her energy, placing her palm on the ground to contact Xan, Jezschmel, and Abbowhen to tell them what was going on. They were aware—watching the destruction from the distance of the Whayer Wood and above on the ridge. Abbowhen had brought her troops around to the far side and was ready to deploy into the battle from the north, in the direction of Raefenshire. They had them surrounded, yet no one wanted to give the order to jump into the death trap they saw unfolding. Jezschmel broke the stagnated terror that had befallen them all: "Pirate bitches! Let us get some worm meat!" she yelled, and Delilah saw the fishy entourage jumping into the fight to slash at Crystal Aelves. A tall, gilled pirate jumped on the back of a Megalostrangus when it passed and tackled the sorcerer. She was successful in knocking him off of his mount, yet when the aelf stood up, he took out a wand and zapped the pirate into dust in one flick of his wrist. He looked around and called his mount back, yet the beast was now loose and terrorizing everyone: Crystal Aelves, pirates, and Usiku alike, since it had no one to tell it what to do any longer. It lashed out, indiscriminately biting and gobbling anything it could reach.

"We have to unmount the sorcerers," Delilah sent her message out to her friends. "It is the only way to disarm the worms," although as she said this, she realized this just sent the beasts into a random feeding frenzy.

Seeing the pirates deploy, Xan launched the attack with the Centauri army. The whayerwolf went to work slicing worms into pink and red ribbons of gore that left hunks of flesh in piles. The dismounted aelves were powerfully armed with magick. Still the Centaur's hooves trampled them into broken piles on the hard earth. Delilah watched as an aelven magician rose from a flattened pile to stand again and hover in place. The centaur who had crushed her down went at her again, hooves flying. The aelf priestess grew to an alarming height and seemed to sprout two extra arms that stopped the front legs of the centaur while her other two arms reached out to grasp the warrior's throat, ripping the vocal cords out from his neck. Tangles of veins and spurting blood sprouted from the warrior as he collapsed backwards, his life spent instantly. Delilah could not look away as the priestess turned toward her next target.

"Your Majesty!" Abbowhen yelled, drawing her attention. "You must go to the Crystal Mountain. Do not forget your mission. You cannot help us here by watching our demise. Find the sacred object! It might be our only hope!"

Delilah knew the Major was right and gestured for her group to follow her as she retreated carefully, still trying not to be noticed. The action on the field was so intense, it was unlikely that anyone had time to watch the perimeters where Delilah and her small party ran. They bulleted through the brush, leaping over hills and mounds of tumbleweed. Soon, the grass grew greener and the air was less arid. The cool shade of the Raefenshire Wood reached out to embrace them as they left the sounds of death and dying muted behind flanks of green growth. They ran through the forested hills and Delilah could not help being entranced by the mossy outcrops, the ancient shoaks, and tangled berry bushes, lush with fruit. The smell of ripeness was in the air, and the whole area was infused with the perfume of old growth and juicy berries. They scanned the area as they ran, still aware that they could be ambushed by the Crystal Aelves on their own territory. Instead, the land seemed vacant, as if it had been empty and uninhabited for a long time. Could the aelves have truly all gone to the field and left their homeland unguarded? It seemed unlikely, yet Delilah hoped they were as alone as they seemed.

King Kejanu had told her that the entrance to the caverns in the Crystal Mountain was hidden behind three elder echobark trees that were woven together. She recognized the dark peeling skin of the trees and marveled at their three intricate conjoined limbs. It was not simply braided: each tree had overlain each other, growing together for so long that the bark of each one had melded into the others. The three trees were really now one entity. Kejanu said that it was important to get the trees' permission before entering. As her Guard watched the perimeter for danger, Delilah walked up and placed her crystal palm upon the tree in the middle of the heart where all three joined.

"Queen Delilah, how remarkable! We have been speaking with the elder trees in Hope about you!" It was a blended voice, like three distinct voices that had mixed to speak together in perfect synchronicity.

"Greetings, Honorable Elders," Delilah said. "May I ask your names?"

"We are She-Sha-La," said the triple voice. "We each had our own name long ago, yet we might as well forget those times, since we now grow and think as one."

"I bring greetings from the Queendom of Hope," said Delilah. "I wish to ask your blessing to enter the Crystal Mountain."

"Yes, of course that is why you are here," said the trees in unison. "Yet we do not condone violence and war, and we know that war is what brings you."

"Hope is a peaceful queendom, I assure you. We are defending ourselves, since the Crystal Aelves invaded our lands and intend to do so again. If it were not for that, I would still be back enjoying mead by the fireplace at my castle!"

"Yes, and still there is a part of you that is built for war. You are a Warrior Queen, as much as you desire peace."

"You are right, She-Sha-La," Delilah admitted. "I must confess that I have trained my whole life to defend Hope. There is a part of me that revels in the glory, in my ability to defend my homeland from invaders."

"Did you know that trees are warriors, too, Child? We may not move as quickly as you: we grow over eons, yet we can bend and send our energy to grow away from a threat. Even if we sacrifice ourselves, we protect our children and neighbors. We share our strength with other trees in the network below the soil. When we are attacked, nearby trees send food and nourishment, they produce healing juices to help mend our wounds, like good human neighbors share in times of trouble. And if we should die, we send a giant rush of the entirety of our life's energy to the trees around us. In that way, we are the best warriors. We fight by defending each other and by sharing our entire beings with those nearby."

"I am amazed by the superiority of your species," Delilah said. "I only lately have come to know of the sophistication of trees and the complex lives and relationships you have. I feel like quite a fool for what I did not know until only recently."

"You are barely as old as a new mayfly, little queen. There is still much you do not

Queen Delilah and the Encroaching Gloom

know about the world."

"You are right," said Delilah. "Now as much as I am enjoying our conversation, I have to ask you again for permission to pass into the caverns, as we are in the midst of a dire battle."

"Ahhh, humans—aelves—silly creatures, always in the midst of a dire battle," She-Sha-La sighed. "Yes, you may pass."

"Can you tell us anything of what lies beyond? Are there aelves in the caves, do you know?"

"Yes, there are aelves, and monsters, too. Many beasts lie hidden in the recesses, and many ancient ghosts as well. The most dangerous are the angry ghosts, spirits who did not die well. They are still upset about the betrayals and injustices that ended their lives."

"Can you advise us how to approach them?" she asked.

"Angry spirits are the same as angry living creatures. They all want to be acknowledged. They want you to understand their suffering."

"Thank you, Great She-Sha-La. You honor us with your friendship."

With that, the great trees creaked and moved their tangled trunk aside to reveal a cave beyond. Oravica and the others approached with lit torches and entered the black space. It was only dark for a moment, because soon they saw small lanterns containing burning embers of starlight tucked into recesses in the cave walls. The surfaces were smooth and crystalline, like melted glass. It became evident how the mountain got its name. Delilah would have been reassured if it were completely dark, yet seeing the evidence of someone keeping the place lit announced that it was inhabited and therefore dangerous. Still, it did seem to be empty. Silence filled the caverns and only the soft echoes of their careful footsteps were detectable. All else seemed still and undisturbed. Oravica reached her arm out and touched Delilah's shoulder in a quiet gesture to tell the queen that she thought she should go first. Despite not wanting to give up the lead, Delilah fell back and let Oravica, Batel, and another guardswoman pass ahead to ascertain the safety of the cave. Delilah now was next to Ook, who had been absorbed into the center of the group among the other soldiers.

The narrow tunnel twisted and turned, sloping downward in dizzying curves. Delilah soon lost track of which direction they were facing. Eventually the way opened up and became wider. Irregular pillars of stone broke up the space and pathways led off in different directions so it became confusing which way to follow. The main path continued to plummet along down into the depths of the cave and appeared to lead into the heart of the mountain, so intuitively it appeared to be the correct way to continue. Delilah glanced at the many dark and starlit passages spidering away from the main route and wondered if perhaps they were making a mistake. "Do you think this could be the wrong way?" she whispered.

Ook sniffed the air and said gruffly: "Ell—fees," pointing down one of the side pathways.

"Are there aelves that way, Ook?" Delilah asked, and he nodded. That decided it, and they kept going down the main channel of the cave. "Let us not go where there are aelves, Ook. You must help us." He nodded again, and Delilah saw the advantage of bringing the ogred along with them. For the next few minutes, every once in a while, Ook would tap

Delilah or grab her sleeve and point down a passageway and the party would be sure to go on an alternate route. Since they had no idea where they were headed, going any way that was away from aelves seemed as good a strategy as any. The caverns had an unusual odor, stale with the absence of air. The torchlight created lifelike shadows on the irregular rock formations, making them look like goblin faces with long hanging noses and sharp teeth. They had been trekking for almost an hour when they began to hear noises: dripping, an occasional splash, and wind whooshing, making low moans on its journey through the cave. "I liked it better when it was quiet," Delilah said, the eerie sounds giving her chills.

"No ell-fees" Ook said, shaking his head to assure them that while the sounds were creepy, at least there were no aelves about.

The passage sloped down and around again, then opened up into an enormous grotto filled with water. Dripping iridescent stalactites hung from the ceiling like clear moss with crystal stalagmite spires rising up to greet them. It was breathtaking! The light from the embedded starlights sparkled over everything, making the water and walls glisten and radiate with rippling light. It was a bit dizzying, and Delilah slowed to get her bearings as the movement of the water and gyrating kaleidoscopic spectrum shifted around them. It was hard to focus on the far side of the pool with all the moving light, yet Delilah could make out what seemed to be another lit passageway on the other side. "We should go there," she said pointing, and saw that a way across had been laid out for them in circular round disks in an alternating pattern, presumably for one to walk across to get to the other side.

"There are likely to be traps, Your Majesty," said Oravica. "We will go first."

"I will go first," said Batel, who looked like she was itching out of her skin to do something. Only waiting for the barest nod from her senior officer, the young soldier took a running leap and hopped lightly from one stone to the other, barely touching each one, to land on the other side. She turned and grinned at the others. Her new friend, Hammerly, an eager guard who had finished her training and had shown enough promise that she had been recruited into Oravica's special platoon, looked to the sergeant, who nodded again. Hammerly jumped, a bit slower, and went from one stone to the second, hesitating on one foot. She looked for a moment as if she were doing Qi-Kai, with one knee raised and her hands out at angles for balance. She was about to jump to the next platform when the stone she had landed on began to tremble. It vibrated and then started to wobble down to become submerged under the water. Hammerly lost her balance and fell with a splash. She stood up, with an embarrassed laugh, and raised her dripping arms to look back at the party when her expression suddenly changed. Pure horror fell over her face as her outstretched arms dissolved in front of her. Her mouth opened in what was certain to be a blood curdling scream when a blast came out of nowhere. Hammerly's face exploded with an arrow protruding from it. The soldier fell into the pool, each part of her body dissolving as it touched the liquid, which was certainly not water as it had first appeared.

Delilah turned quickly toward the source of the arrow to see that one of the Sister Guard had stepped up from the rear and had her bow outstretched. Sensing the urgency of keeping the dying girl quiet so as not to alert the aelves of their presence, her fellow guardswoman had acted quickly to stifle Hammerly's scream. Delilah bowed her head to the archer to show her that she had done the right thing. The woman was trembling, her shoulders quivering as she looked away to hide her face from the queen, tears beginning to erupt from her eyes. Delilah walked forward to the front of the group and, with no hesitation, jumped on the remaining stones quickly, barely letting her feet touch the pedestals. When she reached where Batel was standing, still staring at the place where her fellow soldier had dissolved into the pool, Delilah turned to face the others. "You must not hesitate," she asserted. "Any extra pressure on the stone will make it collapse."

Oravica went next and the others jumped over one at a time, despite there being a heightened sense of anxiety, with most of them sure they would meet the same fate as Hammerly. Ook was last, eyeing the stones with nervous appraisal. Delilah quickly realized that the giant oaf would never have the dexterity to accomplish the task of dancing lightly across the steps. "Ook, wait a minute!" Delilah called to him. "I need you to stay here and guard our escape route," she said. The monster looked a little relieved and puffed himself up, putting his hand on his belt where the glowing blue whip was tied in a loop. "If anyone comes this way to do us harm, I want you to destroy them!" Delilah called.

"Ook!" Ook said, and turned his back to them, already on alert.

The far side of the cavern opened to another tunnel, even more glassine than the rest of the mountain. The walls were almost see-through, and star-lights installed inside made strange distortions. Several times, Delilah thought she saw someone ahead and realized it was her own reflection submerged in layers of crystal stone. The illusion was startling at times, and unnerving. Delilah felt that the stones must be playing with her mind, because she sometimes thought she saw others from her past as well, a flash of her mother's face, or Jarvis. These vanished each time she stepped forward, yet left her with the feeling that she was being tested or watched. Her paranoia increased and she looked around, trying to grasp the images that seemed to evade her, teasing the corners of her eyes.

Suddenly Batel, who was in the front, stopped short and looked at the wall ahead. The path had curved to the left, however Batel was looking directly into the wall at her own wavy likeness in the crystalline wall. "I did not mean to do it," she said. Oravica, who was right behind her, looked at her questioningly. "I am so sorry, Torrence," Batel said, looking at her own image, shaking her head. "It was all my fault."

"Batelnut," Oravica said sternly, "what is going on?"

"Can you not see her?" Batel asked, turning around with eyes wide and pointing to the wall in front of her. "It is Torrence! My cousin! My best and truest friend!" she said. "She is right there and she is very upset with me for letting her die. It was my fault. Do you not hear her telling me that?" Oravica looked at Delilah, then pulled her aside.

"I think there is sorcery here," Oravica confided in the queen. "It is not like Batel to be so disoriented."

"I agree. She is not fit for duty, though. We must send her back."

"Yes, and yet she may not be safe to go alone," Oravica worried.

"Send the archer, the one who shot Hammerly," Delilah said. She had heard the woman sniffling and trying to stifle her tears for most of their journey since the pool. Oravica gave instructions to the archer to care for Batel and take her back by the pool where Ook was waiting. The woman led her away, though Batel kept turning back and looking at the empty wall, muttering to herself that it was all her fault.

"Sisters of the Guard," Delilah said. "Be on alert. These walls may hold enchantments that twist reality. We must defend ourselves against magick playing with our minds." The others nodded their understanding and they carried on. Only minutes later, though, another guardswoman began hallucinating spiders covering the walls and crumpled in terror on the floor of the path, covering her head and whimpering. Yet another started laughing hysterically and pointing at the ceiling, "Those little people are looking down at us!" she said, giggling as if she were a child. "They are making faces at me!" She began sticking out her tongue and making faces back at the imaginary people in the ceiling. Sighing, Oravica assigned another soldier to escort the two impaired women back and away from the magick in the crystal walls.

This left Delilah and Oravica with only four Sister Guard to assist them. None of them seemed as affected as the others. Still, the power of the stones played with the edges of their minds and made them agitated and alert, feeling things tickling their neck or hearing words spoken right next to their ears. It left them in a state of hypervigilance that sizzled electrically through their veins, yet they knew it was spellcraft trapped in the translucent stone. When Delilah saw the image of Jarvis between icy layers of the wall, this time she knew she was imagining it. Or was she? After what seemed like hours of pushing through their own mental barriers to keep their senses about them, they came to what could only be described as a temple at the heart of the mountain. It was a large circular room with a high ceiling, covered in carvings and embellishments on the walls and floors. Cryptic symbols glowed with the blue light of the stars trapped in undulating patterns and glyphs.

As much as they had felt the power in the passageway leading to the sacred chapel, here it was even more present, humming and vibrating with energy that was almost intolerable. In the center of the temple was a low altar, laid with a blue cloth, a small silver bowl, and a few other objects. Delilah began to walk toward the center of the room, but Oravica held her arm out to block the queen. "Wait," said the Sergeant. "There are likely to be traps here, too." Delilah felt silly for not being more cautious and realized the incessant humming and throbbing of energy was wearing down her focus. They looked along the walls and ceilings, trying to get some sense of how to approach the temple. Delilah wished that King Kejanu could advise her. He would probably know exactly where the relic would be hidden and what dangers might lurk. She thought of bringing out the stone to see what might be going on in the battle and instead just lay her hand against the crystal wall, thinking of Kejanu's face.

"You are there, My Queen," the king's voice was low and calm despite screams and clashing all around him, as if she were hearing through his astute pointy ears.

"I think so," Delilah said. "We are in a crystal chamber: a ceremonial space. There is an altar in the center."

"The relic would not be near the altar. It would be hidden in a room on the north side. That is the direction of the ancestors."

"Are there likely to be traps here?"

"Yes."

"Any advice on how to avoid those?"

"Do not trigger them."

"Yes, that would be my first option."

"When one's eyes are closed, that is the best way to see the world."

"Meaning?" Delilah tried to quash her impatience.

"I must go, Your Majesty. We are in a desperate situation."

"Yes, of course. How goes the battle?" Delilah waited a few moments, then realized King Kejanu was gone. She looked at Oravica, who realized she had been in communication with the king and was waiting for her to relay any messages. "He says we should close our eyes to avoid the traps. The relic should be on the north side."

"North would be that direction, Your Majesty," Oravica pointed to the far side of the room.

Delilah's eyes were beginning to swim from the blue symbols and dizzying resonance in the chamber. "I am going to try something, Oravica. Please stand guard and let me know if it does not seem right," Delilah said. She stood up tall, holding her scimitar in front of her, and closed her eyes. After just a moment, the buzzing around her ceased. The dizzying vibrations of the starlight stones and magickal writing were quieted once her eyelids were closed. The sounds that had been humming in her ears disappeared, and she could finally think clearly again. She reached out with her weapon and took a careful step. Nothing happened, and so she took another step. She continued this for a few more small steps. Then she reached a foot out and felt a sharp vibration and pulled it back quickly. Testing her foot in another direction, there was no reaction, so she stepped that way. She continued, with eyes closed, testing the air and ground around her, sometimes feeling a sizzling of energy that let her know that she was in danger and should change course.

"You are at the far wall!" Oravica finally let her know. Relieved, Delilah opened her eyes for a moment and the flood of thrumming and pulsating energy filled her mind and confused her vision again. She quickly shut her eyes and instead reached out her hands to feel the walls. "It seems there may be a button," Oravica instructed her. "It is in the middle of a spiral." Delilah felt the wall until she felt rows of concentric rings. She followed her fingers across these, slowly, making sure she did not sense any disturbances, and came to what she felt must be the center of the spiral. Inside was a small raised button that was shaped like a five-pointed leaf. She put pressure on this, yet did not feel any give to the raised shape. It was familiar, this shape. Delilah recalled Kejanu tracing rings around a leaf in the sand. It was that, but there was more to it. "Your palm!" coached Oravica from her position across the room. "It looks like the shape of the crystals!"

Delilah raised her left hand and placed the whole surface of it over the button. She felt the crystals tingle and pop. With a distinct "click" the star-shaped button flattened smoothly into the stone around it. Delilah heard a rumbling and could not help but open her eyes to see the wall dissolving. It was evaporating like smoke, as if it had never been a solid thing, and fizzled away to reveal a vast opening. A room was revealed, opaque with darkness. "Toss me a torch," Delilah instructed, and a guard slid a lit torch over the smooth crystal floor to reach the queen. In doing so, it must have triggered a trap, because four needle sharp blades of clear stone projected out from four alternate points on the walls and clattered against the far sides of the room. Had it been a person who had touched the trigger on the floor, they would have been impaled from all four directions.

Delilah breathed a sigh of relief and stepped into the room, holding the torch up. She recognized it immediately as a throne room. However, it had the feeling of a shrine to the dead instead of an honorarium to a living ruler. It was decorated with a frieze of a painted battle scene: Crystal Aelves fighting human warriors who wore fur clothing and carried wooden shields and spears. Without the blue glowing lights and strange symbols, Delilah's mind was clearer here. She could see treasure surrounding the throne, goblets and offerings to the dead. The throne itself was carved right out of the stone of the mountain, glowing with refractory light from the torch. Seated on it was a statue made of a darker stone, its form oblique and relaxed into the seat, as if it had been placed there a long time ago and had blended into the mountain. Atop the statue's head, Delilah now saw, was something shiny and sparkling. It was a crown… no, it was a skull! Placed carefully atop the head of the figure was a helmet made from the relic she was looking for—she was sure of it!

Eager now, Delilah walked slowly toward the statue. She knew there could be, must be, more traps to protect this ancient treasure, the source of the Crystal Aelves' power. She walked close to the throne and then, knowing now that she could see better with her eyes closed, set the torch carefully on the stone floor. Facing the effigy, she closed her eyes and reached her hands up toward the skull. She felt no zinging in the air, no tingling sense of danger. Her fingers made contact, touching the cool, smooth shape of the relic. She slowly closed her hands on it and prepared to remove it, still waiting to see if there were any warnings that she should not proceed. With no such indicators, she opened her eyes and found, to her alarm, that she was looking at a pair of eyes just inches from her own. It was not a statue, she suddenly realized. It was a human face, a dark face in shadow, with wide and angry eyes staring back into her own.

Delilah jumped back and lost her footing, falling onto the hard floor. In the light of the discarded torch, she saw the figure rise. It raised its hands wide, as if gathering power, and a deep rumbling erupted from the belly of the mountain. In flashes, Delilah heard Oravica shouting to the other soldiers. She heard them running toward her, felt the cavern vibrate with projectiles launched from all sides of the walls, down from the ceiling, and up from the floor. Delilah twisted around to see the others and watched them dive between crystal shards. Oravica tumbled into an acrobatic roll and missed being hit. The sergeant was still low to the ground, crouching, one knee bent, frozen between jumping forward to assist Delilah and trying to make sure she did not trigger more of the deadly missiles. Delilah turned back to the statue, its face becoming more visible in the light. A sneer—a familiar sneer—danced across its lips. Its mouth opened, and out came the word, hissing as if it were a curse: "Ssssisster!"

"Jarvis!" she yelled out, unable to hold back her brother's name once it became clear that it was he who stood before her. She sensed movement and turned to see Oravica charging forward, ready to protect Delilah from her brother. Time slowed and Oravica met her eyes as she ran. Delilah watched as glassy spears shot from all directions, impaling the soldier. The sergeant fell to her knees and her head slumped onto her chest, the shards holding her up as blood pooled from her wounds onto the floor. The other guards had followed Oravica's lead, and only now Delilah heard the shrieks of the other women, saw them injured and crawling, smelled their blood wafting in drafts from voluminous wounds. She turned away from the sight to meet her brother's eyes. He was smiling now, a terrible, cruel smile, mocking the torment she felt to see her comrades die.

The whole temple was vibrating, shaking with the explosion of the projectiles from the walls. It seemed now that the whole cave was percolating, violently bubbling. Loud rumbling tore through and echoed within the chambers like thunderclaps. Stones and big chunks of the ceiling began to fall from above, tumbling around Delilah. She tucked in her body to avoid them, yet kept her eyes on Jarvis who had begun to step toward her. More massive shaking tossed Delilah into the air and back down, crunching her body as she landed. She looked up, but it was too late as a large boulder came down upon her head. The crack of the impact was a flash of shocking pain before all went black.

♓

Delilah woke up with one thought: "But there was no three-headed dog!" Her head hurt and her vision was fuzzy. With painful clarity, she recalled her friend's death and her brother's appearance in the tomb. It dawned on her that the intention all along had been for Jarvis to capture her. The information they had been fed was crafted to lure her to come into the Crystal Mountain with only a small number of guards. She had walked right into the snare. She was in a small cell, unbound, yet clearly a prisoner. She recalled the moment when she saw Jarvis's eyes upon hers and shuddered. She had not been that close to her brother in over 15 years and had thought him dead for most of that time. He felt like a ghost to her, and an unfriendly one at that. What was it that She-Sha-La had said about angry ghosts? It was important for them to feel heard and understood. Delilah felt annoyed now that the tree had not warned her that she was walking into a trap. Still, she knew that it was not in the nature of trees to understand the threats and feuds between mortals.

"Ly-la?" she heard. It was the unmistakable voice of Ook.

"Ook, is that you?" she asked, running to the bars and frantically trying to figure out where the echoing voice came from in this honeycomb.

"Ook," said Ook, and Delilah saw at the end of the passageway a large arm waving out from a cell.

"Is anyone with you?"

"We are here, too, Your Majesty," she heard Batel's voice. "It is me, Batel, and the others who had to leave the crystal cavern from the… hallucinations. There are five of us and Ook. We were captured back at the grotto. I do not know why they did not kill us."

She heard a clang at the end of the hallway and boots echoing through the chambers. She backed away from the cell door as the visitor drew near. The filtered starlight bounced off the crystal walls here, as it was everywhere beneath the mountain, yet Jarvis' face was cast in the shadow of the skull helmet he still wore upon his head. He stood, arms crossed, observing her through the bars of the cell.

"Nice of you to come and visit me, little sister," he said, with a twist of his mouth. Delilah felt tongue tied. She could not find words to respond. "You have come all this way, tried to steal our ancestor's skull, and then have nothing to say for yourself?" he asked.

"I only learned recently that you were not dead, Jarvis, when you tried to have me killed in Fallengrove. Then I found out you wanted to take Hope from me. You want to steal my city. Why should I not try to steal your relic?" she asked.

"Hope is *mine*!" he roared. "Rightfully mine. You have already stolen that from me!" he said, spitting his fury.

"It would have been yours, Jarvis, yet you threw it all away when you murdered our parents! You would have had Hope to yourself in a few years. You could not even wait for it, so you… slaughtered them!" She had held this anger at him for half of her life, without any outlet to express it.

Jarvis shook his head and sneered: "You know that is rubbish! Our parents were planning to sacrifice me before the whole realm! My own sister would have watched them throw me from the cliff!"

"What are you talking about, Jarvis? It was a ceremony to announce your inheritance of the throne as their chosen heir!"

"Please sister, do not pretend that you believe the story they concocted to get me to come willingly. They intended to murder *me* that day, and I only stopped them by killing them first!"

"Jarvis, that does not make sense. Why would they want to kill you? You were their son, their successor, the one they placed the future of Hope upon! Did the Crystal Aelves tell you that our parents—our own mother and father—were going to try to kill you?" Delilah asked, trying to figure out where he could have gotten these strange ideas. She could only assume it was due to the aelves' deception.

"Yes, thankfully. They opened my eyes to what was happening in time for me to take action. You must have known about it, Delilah. Our parents wanted me out of the way and they wanted you to take over as the heir. I am sure you knew all about their plan!"

"I knew no such thing and can only think that the aelves have deceived you this whole time. They got you to kill our dear parents so that they could try to take over Hope. They fooled you, Jarvis!"

"I have proof. You can ask Helanza. She knows all about what really happened on that day."

"Helanza?" Delilah asked incredulously. "What does she know?"

"She knows that they were trying to kill me—to sacrifice me—to save the Vector," he said.

"The Vector?" Delilah asked, more confused than ever.

"It was failing. The ancestors knew it would not last. When they placed the enchantment on it, they designed it so that it could be restored to full power with the blood sacrifice of the monarch's firstborn."

"The Vector was not restored. It is still failing," Delilah said.

"Yes, because I was not killed. The sacrifice was not complete." Jarvis looked at her for a moment, and a perplexed expression overtook him. "Do you truly claim not to have known any of this?"

"No! Jarvis, no! It is so terrible and so unthinkable to me that our mother and father would sacrifice you, even if they thought they could save the Vector. You must be mistaken."

"They may not have wanted it, but it was the only way to save Hope," Jarvis said. "In that, I understood their intention. Yet I will never forgive them for trying to carry out such a heartless deed against me, their son. If the aelves had not warned me, I would surely have died."

"You became dead anyway," Delilah said. "At least to me. And I have hated you for 15 years because you murdered our parents!"

"And I have been hating you for conspiring with them," he said, a twinge of sadness creeping into his tone. "And even if that part was not true, it does not change that Hope is rightfully mine and I intend to take it back."

"Unfortunately, the law does not see it that way. It was as an act of treason that you murdered the queen and king. Even if it were revealed that you were, indeed, defending yourself, they would never accept you as their ruler now. You ran away with the aelves, Jarvis, and became their king. You have conspired against us, killing your own people—here and in Verily—the people you say you want to lead. You have not acted like a king of Hope," she said.

"And yet I am the rightful king. And if I am not accepted willingly, I will make them accept me with force."

"To what end? To forcefully rule and make Hope an aelven city, with your true people enslaved?"

"The aelves have been loyal to me! They are my true people!" he yelled. "And they have the magickal abilities to restore the Vector. I will not need to savagely kill my firstborn! I will be saving you from that fate, Delilah. The only way you can save Hope as its queen is to have a child and sacrifice it. I thought you knew this and that is why you have come to middle age without procreating."

"I came to… middle age… without procreating because I have been too busy caring for Hope!" she said, flustered. "I had no knowledge of the Vector's enchantment or why it has been failing. I have only been concerned with protecting my city for the past fifteen years. I would have gladly stepped aside to see you crowned if it had come naturally. Instead, our parents were dead, and for all I knew, you were dead, too. I did what needed to be done."

"And will you do what needs to be done now to save your city? Will you be willing to have a child and then sacrifice it?" he asked.

"I do not believe that can be the only way to heal the Vector," Delilah said. "If the aelves can fix it, someone else can," she said, her thoughts going immediately to Doktora Ilvana.

"Sadly for you, sister, you will not have the option to try. We are butchering your pathetic patchwork army as we speak. Now there is no one left to come for you. The rest of your armies are retreating. After their defeat, I will announce that the Hope Queen is dead. You have no successors. Once you are executed, they will have to accept me as their leader."

For not the first time in the last few days, Delilah wished she had accepted one of the many marriage proposals she had received in her first years as queen and had become a mother in her young teen years. She would now have a child that would be almost of age to take over as monarch if she expired. She tried to think of some way to reach this man, who somehow still looked like the older brother she had admired and played with when she was a child. Yet she could see that the Jarvis she knew was no longer there. In a flash, Delilah realized that she did not know for certain what happened to the rest of her Guard, though Oravica's grisly death played clearly in her mind. "Jarvis," she said. "Can you please tell me the fate of the other soldiers who were with me?

"They are all dead," Jarvis said. "As you will be soon." He turned and stomped out of the dungeon.

She grabbed the bars on her cell and stood there, her body beginning to wrack with sobs. The threat on her own life was immaterial to her. All she could think of was Oravica and the others and how she had failed them. She banged her hand on the iron gate and banged it again.

Batel's voice called out quietly: "What the Aelven King—your brother—said is true of the others. The rest of our squad were lost, Your Majesty."

Delilah shook off her grief. "I must contact our officers and see how the battle is faring. Jarvis said we are being slaughtered. I just hope it is not true. Hang in my friends. If there is anyone left out there, they will rescue us, one way or another," Delilah said, wishing she could deliver on the false confidence in her voice. She went to the far side of the cell. Her satchel and weapons had been removed however she still had the stones in her palm. She placed her hand on the clear stone wall and thought with all of her intention, calling to Abbowhen, to Kejanu, to Xanfar. She waited and heard no response. She sent out her strongest, most heartfelt messages and still received nothing back. In desperation, she pulled up Doktora Ilvana in her mind.

"Your Majesty! Where are you?" Ilvana's voice was filled with distress.

"I am imprisoned in the Crystal Mountain," Delilah said. "No one is answering me. I fear it has been total annihilation," she said, gulping back a wrenching cry that almost escaped along with her words.

"I fear it, too. The messages I have received have been very troubling. I have seen only glimpses and it is most terrifying. I am afraid for everyone."

"Jarvis plans to kill me and take over Hope! He believes that once our armies are beaten back and I am pronounced dead, the populace of Hope will have to concede. He plans to take control… with the Crystal Aelves! Ilvana—I do not know how, but we need to stop him!" again she fought to control the deep moan that wanted to escape her throat. She only held it in by clenching her whole body to suppress it.

"I have a plan," said Ilvana.

"Please tell me," Delilah gasped, hoping the brilliant doctor had some miracle up her robe sleeves.

"I fear our communication is compromised," she said. "They must have known our strategies all along to have entrapped you. I do not trust the confidentiality of our messages.

Just hang in there, Your Grace. We will put something in motion… something unexpected!"

Then the doctor was gone. Delilah tried again to reach Xanfar and the others, again hearing nothing at all in response. Kejanu's haunting words telling her that he would not respond if he were dead floated through her mind. Delilah tried to contemplate the possibility that all of her troops and allies were dead: the Guard, the Usiku, the Centaurs, the Pirates… the Pirates! Delilah put all of her energy into summoning Jezschmel.

"You will forgive me for setting sail, Your Majesty," the pirate queen's silky voice entered her mind.

"You have retreated?" Delilah asked, dumbfounded.

"Not just my crew. All of our allied troops were squashed. Anyone who still had soldiers standing fled after the first night. And where are you? Was your quest successful?"

"I am afraid not," said Delilah, careful not to tell her that she was captured. It would not be fair to ask them to return on her behalf. "Jezschmel, what happened?" asked Delilah. "How were we so gravely defeated?" She was afraid to know the details and the losses, yet had to ask.

"The Megalostrongi were just the beginning," started Jezschmel. "They caused so much bloodshed with their awful mouths and beastly, squirming bodies. Yet the Crystal Aelves were worse. By the time the Centauri, Sister Guard, and my sea warriors entered the battlefield, the Usiku were all but demolished. It is true that they are better fighters than the Crystal Aelves, and should have held their own. If they were evenly matched, I have no doubt the Usiku would have prevailed. The worms were a catastrophe from the outset and that was not even the worst of it. Delilah- the forces of the Crystal Aelves were double what we saw above ground. They were like vermin, swarming, coming up through the tunnels made by the worms, more than we imagined in our greatest estimations.

"We tried to come to the Usiku's rescue. We truly did," said Jezschmel, her voice relaying her genuine remorse. "We gave it everything we had. The losses were terrible. Most of the Centauri were wiped out, and I am ashamed to say that many of my own dear crew were lost to the land. I could not even collect them to bury them at sea as they would have wished. Abbowhen called the order to retreat. I saw Lord Xanfar riding a Centaur right into the center of the battle as we were departing. He was overtaken by a wave of aelves. I doubt he could have survived."

"And King Kejanu? What of him?"

"I do not know. All I can say is that it did not look good for any of the Usiku. Their numbers were devastated if they were not completely wiped out. I would guess he did not survive."

"And what of your Usiku friend, Jezschmel? Where is she now?"

"Why, she is right here with me, Your Majesty, as she was through the whole battle. She did not leave me for an instant. She is an excellent fighter, and saved my life more than once on the field. I am afraid you no longer have a chance with me. My heart has been won by another."

"I missed my opportunity," said Delilah, almost smiling despite the morbid news of their losses. "Yet I am glad you have the company. I am sorry for your lost crew."

"Yes," said Jezschmel, with a sharp intake of breath that sounded like a swallowed wail, "many of those women have been with me for… a very long time," she said. "Delilah, I regret that I could not do more."

"You did plenty, Jezschmel. You will be paid, as we had agreed. You may go to Hope and ask for what you are owed, even if I am not there. You will be compensated handsomely, although I realize no amount of gold will make your casualties less painful."

"I did not do it for the treasure, Delilah. Please do not tell anyone, though. I have a reputation to uphold. I do not need anyone thinking that the Queen of the Pirates has gotten sentimental."

"I would never reveal that you are anything but a fierce Sea Warrior," Delilah promised.

"Until we meet again, My Queen," said Jezschmel.

"Until then, My Queen," replied Delilah.

Delilah did not realize how thirsty she was until a strange dwarf-like woman brought a small bucket of water with a ladle and a bowl of mash. The servant brought similar accoutrements for the other prisoners at the end of the passageway and Delilah heard grateful mutterings. Delilah drank well, then tasted the mash, which had the flavor of orange blossoms and honey. "Decadent for prisoners," she thought. It was not until she finished the last spoonful that it occurred to her that the food could be poisoned. She wondered if she should try to make herself throw up, yet at that moment she was overcome with drowsiness and had to lie down on the slate bench.

"Queen Delilah!" she heard Batel's voice from the end of the hall. "Do not eat the mash, Your Majesty. We think it is drugged!"

"Too late," she could barely get the words out before falling into a deep pit of deathlike slumber.

Her body felt paralyzed as she drifted into a swirling, dreamlike trance. She tried to open her eyes and she thought she saw Oravica walk by outside her cell, her limbs stiff and her face rigid. Delilah tried to sit up, tried to yell to her friend, and could not move her body. She could not even open her eyes, so she could not have seen Oravica, could she? She tried to think logically in the midst of the blur of her confused mind.

"Delilah."

She heard the voice from far away and tried again to sit up but her limbs were like stone. Her eyelids were still too heavy to open.

"Delilah, I am with you." Although she could still not open her eyelids, it was as if she could see through them into the dim light in the cell. A form appeared, floating above her and she saw it was Kejanu! He looked at her with deep fondness in his expression and put out his hand. She felt the weight of his palm on her chest, on her skin, and felt her heart beating madly under it. Then, he vanished.

In a moment, the vision of Kejanu was replaced by Jarvis. Not an adult Jarvis, the traitor who married the queen of the Crystal Aelves. No, it was Jarvis as a boy, a young adolescent, not even a man yet. She heard her own 8-year-old voice ask him: "How will I know if you are really you, Jarvis?"

"What do you mean, little sis?" he asked.

"Well, what if a fiend takes over your body and you look like you, except you have really turned Beast?"

The young Jarvis smiled at her and reached over to yank her braid. "Silly, he said. I will always be me. No one can take over my body. If you are worried about it, though, we can make up a secret password, one that no one else will know. That way, if I am ever possessed by a demon pretending to be me, you can ask me for the secret password. If it is not really me, they will not know the secret words, and you can run to tell Mother and the Guard."

"What should the secret password be?" she asked.

He looked about the room. "How about 'purple unicorn'? No one would think of that."

"Yes, it is like GooGoo, the purple unicorn that Helanza made for me, filled with herbs to help me sleep."

"Exactly."

"No fiend would know that," Delilah said, and hugged her big brother.

Except now as she held him, he vanished in smoke, filling the cell with pungent blue smog that filled her nose and choked her. She felt the tendrils of it turn into snakelike appendages and twist around her throat, tentacled fumes covered her face and mouth until she could not breathe at all. She sat up and her visions dissolved like water pouring out through the corners of the chamber. She was gasping for breath, trying to stay sitting, yet the weight of her throbbing head pulled her back down to lie upon the stone and sucked her into a vacant black hole of sleep.

When Delilah finally awoke, she was filled with a desperate thirst and her stomach growled with fierce emptiness. Day and night looked the same underground with the starlight lamps dimly lighting the honeycomb passages of the prison. It was impossible to tell what time of day it was, or even how many days had passed. She saw that someone had re-filled the wooden bucket and she stumbled to kneel by it, slurping ladles full of the tepid water. There was also a heel of bread, which was so hard she could barely chip off pieces with her teeth to let it soften in her mouth, in between more sips of water. It briefly occurred to her to be wary of the food, given the mash which had clearly been drugged, yet she barely could make herself consider not eating. She was too hungry.

After a bit, she called out to her friends: "Batel, are you there?"

"Yes, Your Majesty, we are here. Simmie is still sleeping, though. I think the drug affected her the most. I fear she will not wake."

"I am sure they will be sending help for us soon," Delilah said, not even sure anymore who "they" could be. Who was even left? What she needed was an escape plan that did not rely on anyone else, just in case there was no one else. Feeling slightly sated from the bread and water, Delilah's mind was much clearer. She began running through everything she could recall from the very beginning of the battle when the Usiku had gone out on the field to attack. She replayed the arrival of the Megalostrongi worm beasts, her small platoon's journey through Raefenshire, and their hardships in the Crystal Mountain. She forced herself to revisit every piece of information she had stored, every tiny detail she could recall, even the shards impaling Oravica and the dark blood that pooled on the floor in the swirling starlight. She tried to find a piece to grab on to, some way that she could escape and get her surviving posse out of there.

There was something nagging at the back of her mind that she just could not bring to the forefront. It was something that had seemed inconsequential, yet Delilah had the strong feeling it would be the secret to their freedom. Her mind wandered to the old man, Gravenwell, in the dungeon. She recalled one time he told her that the mind sometimes goes "down the garden path." In those times, it is easy to take the wrong turn and get lost. The more you tried to get back on the trail, the more lost you became. "The best thing you can do," he had said, "is stop trying to find your way and just think of something completely different. The path you had lost will emerge before you as soon as you concentrate elsewhere!" Delilah thought it was worth a try, so she brought Kejanu to mind. It was an easy thing to focus on, when all else seemed so bleak: a small comfort. She recalled how he had put his hand on her chest in real life, and then again in her drugged dream. Feeling a wave of romantic longing, she imagined the two of them lying under the stars. They were out in the desert, the night sky a huge bowl of twinkling crystal chips. Light flickered from these astral bodies, curving out into endless space. The two of them were entwined, surrounded, rocked, and embraced by the sparkling darkness.

An electrical charge shot through her. "Starlight!" she thought. The thing that was ubiquitous in the Crystal Mountain was the starlight! It was present everywhere so you could almost forget that it was there, tiny fragments of light from the stars captured and used to illuminate the darkness. Yet they were not true pieces of stars, it was starlight that was trapped within small crystal shards. If they had trapped the light of the stars, would it be possible to trap other types of energy? As a plan began to formulate, Delilah reviewed her resources: Batel and the other women were trained soldiers and Ook was a type of weapon on his own. She could not rely on anyone else being alive to come to their rescue. They would have to save themselves.

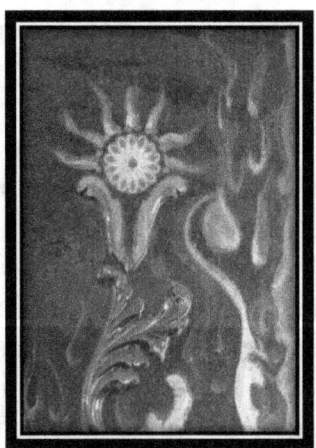

"Let no one say that fate is sealed
Even when times are bleak;
The world finds a way to turn topside down
Even as we speak."
-The Ghost Scribe

Chapter 10: Topside Down

Delilah woke on what she assumed was her third day of captivity. After eating the drugged food, she could not be confident if it were three or ten days. She had been wary of food since then, yet the small crusts of bread and water she had been provided since the mash had seemed untainted. She expected that at any moment, Jarvis would come to kill her, as that was what he had said he intended. She wondered if he might just poison her food. What was he waiting for and why drug her in the meantime? Nothing made sense.

Delilah had slept little the previous night, or what she assumed was night, as day and night looked exactly the same in the underground prison. Once she had gotten an inkling of how she hoped to save them, she could not sleep. Ideas tumbled around in her mind, yet she could not get her full strategy in order. There were such limited opportunities to impact anything. The only time anyone came or went was when the tiny servants brought in crumbs of food or refilled buckets of water. The buckets were replaced through small doors in the bars of the cells that opened just wide enough to allow the vessels to be slid in or out. This way, the jailers could avoid opening the whole door and a possible escape. At least they gave them plenty of water, because the small portions of hard bread would not sustain anyone for long. It made one eager for mash, even if it happened to be drugged.

Occasionally, the sound of roaring and rattling of chains could be heard from the other side of the main door to the prison. Delilah watched carefully, and saw something big and furry through the door when the dwarven people brought in replenishment. Perhaps it was the three-headed dog monster after all. When the entry door was going to be opened, there was the sound of a great chain being cranked. Delilah was able to infer that the beast's chain was cinched when people came in or out. After they exited, she would hear the unraveling of the chain again. Whatever was out there needed to be able to reach the door to prevent others from coming and going, yet needed to be restrained when someone had to enter. This suggested to Delilah that the creature was not tame, and would attack anything it could. This was good news, in a way. It meant that it would eat her imprisoners, too, if it could reach them, although she had no grudge against the little people who brought the food. In some ways, they seemed like prisoners, too. They were solemn, never spoke, and barely raised their eyes from what they were doing. She felt badly for them.

"Thank you," Delilah said to one older dwarf with silver braids when she brought the next pail. The woman looked as if Delilah had slapped her. "What is that beast out there? Is it a Cerberus?" Delilah asked, ignoring the terrified look of the servant from being spoken to. The woman shook her head and rushed on with her work.

"They will not speak to us either, Your Majesty," Batel called from down at the end of the passage.

Delilah was a little jealous of the group that was in the large holding cell. They were together, which might be comforting, even if there was no privacy. She heard them talking in low voices, reassuring each other, and telling stories to Ook. The ogred loved to hear tales of great battles and faerie folk, and got upset when there was not a happy ending. Delilah thought it must be nice to have the company and distraction of others in such a harrowing situation. Having someone to share ideas with would be helpful. Delilah did not have access to any of her regular confidants. Still recovering from the fogginess of the drug, she questioned the soundness of her own ideas. It made her feel lonelier that the sad little people would not even talk to her.

"Do you think you might be able to bring me a writing implement?" She asked the same woman next time she went by. "Just a piece of charcoal would be fine," she said, "and any old thing to mark upon, even if it is the rattiest old scroll." She got no answer again, and the woman rushed out even faster. Delilah sighed and laid back on the stone bench to rest her mind. She was pushing too hard and her mind was getting stuck on "the garden path" again. She closed her eyes, and when she woke much later, all was quiet. She had not intended to sleep, just rest her mind a bit, yet she felt she had dozed for quite a long time. There was something over by the bars. When she went to look, she saw a small rolled bundle. Inside, she found a hard, sharpened piece of charcoal and a long strip of parchment paper. It warmed Delilah's heart that the woman had risked endangering herself to fulfill this request. She promised herself that if she got out of there, she would find out if the dwarves were indeed captives of the aelves and try to help them.

Before she could put her new tools to use, she heard a loud scuffle in the hallway, and the chain of the beast being wound. "Make way for the King!" The door was thrown open and she heard distinctive boots on the stone.

"Sister," said Jarvis, his characteristic sneer upon his face and the skull helmet still upon his head. "How are you enjoying your stay?"

Queen Delilah and the Encroaching Gloom

"We are quite settled here," Delilah replied. "I am not sure why you felt the need to drug us when we clearly cannot leave."

"We needed to make sure you did not try to alert anyone to attempt a rescue. Now that all your soldiers and allies are vanquished, there is no one left to come to your aid."

"What is our secret password, Jarvis?" she asked.

"Wh-what?" he stuttered.

"Our secret password. What is it?"

"I do not have time for childish games, Delilah. I came here to tell you that we have conquered your troops. Any survivors have retreated. Soon, we will be marching upon Hope, where I will take the crown. I will bring you and execute you there for all to see so there is no question about your death." He stood there, hands upon his hips, waiting for her reaction.

"Jarvis, what is our password?" she asked again.

"Aarrghhh, you are still an infant, not fit to be a queen!" he said, then turned and stomped away.

Their interaction gave Delilah the conviction to do what she needed to do next. She had noticed small, spidery threads going through the crystal stone that made up the walls, floors, and ceilings. They looked like fractures at first, however Delilah realized that they were roots! The minuscule threads and fibrous strands in the walls came from the trees above. The Nearth was all around her. While she knew that the aelves were probably monitoring messages sent through the Nearth, she did not think they could monitor all energy sent through it. She had spent much of her time the previous evening trying to recall her mother's lessons about summoning the energy of the Ancients and how to cast a simple enchantment. Now, she put her recollections to practice. With the charcoal, she wrote the word "HOPE" on the parchment. She sat on the floor, placed her crystal hand on the stone above a tangle of roots, and stared at the word until her eyes began to blur. She allowed the meaning of that word to fill her mind and heart. An intense sensation of love flowed over her: she pictured Hope's people and all who had come to her aid in her mind until she felt her whole being filled with meaning and purpose. Tapping into the energy around her, she felt deep and sincere tenderness flowing out and the nourishment of the Nearth flowing back into her.

"This is what it feels like to be a tree," she thought. Time slowed and all she could see around her were the roots in the walls sparkling in her peripheral vision as the word "HOPE" grew and shifted, like water off of hot stone. Time stood still in the middle of the mountain, yet intention and and meaning flowed from her hands into the spidery filaments of roots, which glittered and twinkled. From the corner of her eye, she saw that the starlight lamps embedded in the walls were pulsing, together, like a heartbeat, along with hers and in sync with the power flowing through the Nearth. Delilah sent all the caring and passion she had ever felt in her whole life flooding out through her body. It rippled like a tidal wave, building and bulging. It rushed through the trees' veins, echoing in the dancing tempo of the starlight lamps. She felt an enormous pulsing of her life's energy, Linked and in perfect synchronicity with the dazzling lights. Waves pushed out a beacon that radiated into the sky. She could not see it, yet she knew that the force of her love, her message of total devotion to Hope was being broadcasted out across the Nearth in a perfect, glorious sonnet.

As Delilah felt connected to all the world in that moment, she could pick up the heartbeats, the spirits, and the connections to all those she cared for, near and far. She felt the funny, heartfelt loyalty of Ook and the courageous fire of Batel. She held Xanfar in her mind's eye and felt him in her heart, as she felt Ilvana and Jezschmel. The rhythm became louder and more intense with every moment, building into an all-encompassing crescendo. Just when she felt she could not contain any more, the floor beneath her started to crack. The roots were growing! Vines shattered through the surface of the floor and immediately sprouted translucent lime green leaves and phosphorescent curlicues. The glowing roots grew larger and twisted around the bars of her cell. In an instant, a limb burst through the side of the wall, breaking the bars from their attachment to the stone. The metal clattered to the floor and she heard the doors on the other cells bursting apart. Excited yelling came from the end of the hall, and in moments, Ook, Batel, and the four other Sister Guard were standing before her.

Ook reached down to where Delilah was sitting: "Ly-la!" he said, and she took his hand as he pulled her to her feet. The group ran down the hall to the door of the prison and stopped when they saw that it had busted apart like the others. Instead of a clear passageway, they found themselves face-to-face with a massive dog face with a long, slobbery tongue and sharp white teeth. A moment later, a second dog head appeared next to the first, then a third next to the second. All three heads were growling, gnashing their maws together, smacking their lips and drooling. The beast was still tethered to its chain, yet blocking the whole passageway. Chambers were shifting and rumbling as illuminated chartreuse roots splintered the walls. Vines grew at unthinkable speed to cover the floors. Ook reached into his belt and pulled out the blue glowing whip!

"Ook! How did you hold on to that?" Delilah asked.

"Ook ate," he said, pointing to his mouth. Delilah looked at Batel, who nodded, with a somewhat disgusted look on her face.

"Does that mean you… expelled it?" Delilah asked in astonishment.

"He threw it up, fortunately," Batel explained. "After he ate the drugged mash. It upset his stomach, probably with that darn whip burning a hole in it, so he retched it out. We helped him clean it off," she reassured the queen.

"Well, better than it coming out the other end," Delilah reasoned.

Batel and the other Guard, including the fast-thinking archer, looked alert and in peak condition considering that they had been impaired by magickal crystal enchantments, imprisoned, drugged, and then fed nothing but crusts of bread and water for several days. This was the benefit of having strong, young women in your service, Delilah thought. Ook had a big toothy smile on his face as he proudly held his whip. The walls and floors continued to throb and vibrate, rippling with the energy of spurling vines fracturing through the walls and unfurling into lush green handfuls of sparkling fresh leaves. The three-headed dog monster yanked and yearned on the chain, which creaked along with the rest of the uprooted structure of the caverns. It seemed the chain would bust at any moment. Delilah brought her team in for a huddle to quickly concoct a plan.

"I never thought I would get to fight a Cerberus!" said Batel, with excitement. A true soldier, Delilah thought, thirsting for battle.

"Ook, you will have to do as much damage with that whip as possible," Delilah said. "We will not have much time, since that chain is about to break. Batel, you grab as much of that chain as you can with your big, beautiful hands and do your best to strangle at least one of the heads. And you, archer… What is your name?" she asked the young woman who had destroyed one of her own to save the rest of them.

"Fallon, Your Majesty," she replied.

"Fallon, you will go around the back of the thing and see if there are any projectiles you can launch at it—anything in the hall that you can find, even if it is just fallen shards of stone. The rest of you, do your best to keep its eyes on you—move fast, distract it, keep it watching you so the others can do their jobs." Delilah knew it was a shabby plan, yet it was the best they could do.

The team went into action immediately: Ook ran up and began lashing at the beast with his whip. It did some minor damage, yet the thing was quick to pull its heads back and got only a few searing black lashes across its fur. Delilah led the group of three soldiers, running up in front of it, waving their arms, yelling and jumping to get its attention while throwing fallen stones in its direction. This worked for a moment, and Batel was able to swoop in and grab a lead of chain, catapulting herself in a tumble back over its body to make a loop around one of its necks, pulling it taught from the other side. It hardly had an impact, since having the chain wound around it did little except toss Batel around. As inhumanly strong as she was, she did not weigh enough to keep the chain taut, and so she just got bounced about, holding on as best she could. Meanwhile, Fallon had snuck behind the monster, as planned, however there was little on the far side of the cavern to use against the creature. She found a broomstick and broke off the bristled end to at least have something to poke at it. It was barely better than nothing, looking like a puny toothpick next to the colossal dog monster.

The Cerberus was getting more and more frenzied in its actions, lurching toward Delilah and the soldiers who were taunting it. In a horrifying grinding sound, the chain burst free from the wall and the monster launched forward, grabbing the soldier next to Delilah in its great mouth. It held her down and shook his head, blood splattering across the crystal walls. The woman screamed in agony as she was ripped apart. Tempted into a blood-rage, the other two heads of the beast began fighting with the one that held the bloody soldier. This led to a brawl between the three heads as they ripped the woman to shreds, each trying to get a mouthful of flesh and crunching bone while defending against the other heads.

Ook used the opportunity to get in close and unleash the whip. The end wrapped perfectly around one of the dog's necks, and when Ook yanked back, the skin and bone of the monster sizzled away to nothing in its embrace. The loosed head thumped to the ground, leaving a bloody white stump of spine exposed. The creature's other heads howled in pain, distracted from their feast. They trained their sights on Ook. The beast was no longer chained, so it leapt forward, knocking Ook back to slide dozens of feet across the floor. He landed, still holding the whip and mercifully out of the immediate reach of the creature. The dog sat back on its haunches and wailed, licking at the founts of blood gushing from the exposed neck. Fallon took that moment to run full-force at the beast and thrust the end of the broomstick as hard as she could into one of its eyes. The stick protruded from the skull of the monster as it roared in rage, shaking its head to dislodge the wood pike.

Delilah, sensing a power she had never felt before, laid her crystal hand upon the walls of the cave and called out to She-Sha-La to help her. She felt a vital force coursing through her, her mind and body throbbing with the Link to the Nearth. Green spindly vines began growing at lightning speed to wind up around the body of the beast. The injured monster struggled against the twisting creepers rising up to restrain it, leaves vibrating with the momentum of the Nearth. Hundreds of tendrils spiraled and wove together, denser and more binding every moment, until the creature was covered in a verdant shroud. In minutes, there was just a wriggling pile of twisting vines where the Cerberus had been. The soldiers gasped and grasped their knees to catch their breath, surprised to have defeated the beast. Ook walked up and kicked the pile of green growth.

"Bad dog!" he said.

"It does not know any better," Delilah said. "You were kept chained once, too," she reminded the ogred.

Ook looked sideways at the pile of leaves as the soldiers turned their attention to the spot on the floor that had been their friend. "Simmie!" Fallon cried and fell to her knees in front of the bloody smear. As the others were distracted, Ook surreptitiously knelt to pull apart the vines to unveil a snout of the creature. Warm mist huffed from the beast's nostrils. Ook turned back and stood blocking what he had done.

The soldier's body had been almost totally consumed, with stringy bits of intestine strewn about. Fallon reached down to dip her forefinger in the blood. She wiped it on her cheek. Batel and the others did the same, a small mark to remember their friend. Ook leaned down and marked his cheek, too, and a big tear ran through it, creating a rivulet in the red smear. Delilah did not know the young woman enough to mourn her, yet marked her own cheek to honor their comrade before they proceeded down the passageway formerly blocked by the beast. Spidery roots and limbs were now protruding from the walls. The stones still creaked and shifted with the network of living vines that grew more robust by the moment.

Delilah worried that the halls might grow ensnared to the point of being impassable if they waited much longer, and so she picked up her pace, leading the way. She ran, boots pounding, looking to Ook now and again to see if he smelled the presence of aelves. He did not seem triggered, so they kept along. The passage rose up, and Delilah instinctively felt this could only be the way out, ignoring side trails that were smaller or led down from the main path. She was passing one such narrow trail when her body physically stopped in its tracks. Ook, who was behind her, bumped her quite roughly and then caught her before she fell over. The pile up of soldiers looked at her questioningly. She tried to continue, thinking it a leftover remnant of being drugged, yet she could not make her body move forward. It was as if she were stuck in a spider's web and could not escape the invisible threads.

Compulsion took over and she walked back a few paces to where a small alley ran off to the right. It was dim in there, with few starlights. She had to duck her head and walk slightly hunched over to fit in to the opening of the path, which widened once one was through the narrow entry. As she was pulled in, compelled to go forward, she saw a dark spot in the crystal wall ahead. It was a person-sized being in full shadow implanted into a curved indentation in the wall of the crystal. The light refracted and she could barely see. As she walked forward, recognition flooded her. It was Kejanu! He was immobilized, crystallized like an insect in amber. His features, with eyes closed, appeared wavy and distorted, yet it was him, there was no doubt. He was trapped inside a thick layer of the transparent wall, submerged as if underwater. Delilah could not tell if he was alive or if he was frozen in death within the crystal. She placed her hand where his heart would be, though there was at least a foot of stone between them, and could feel nothing.

"Ly-la," she heard Ook's voice behind her and turned as he gently pushed her to the side and away from the wall. The ogred took out his whip, which he had neatly tucked away again in his trousers, and motioned the others to step back. Delilah tensed as Ook let loose the whip, cracking the stone to one side of Kejanu's motionless body. She braced for the next sizzling swoosh of the whip, and Ook made a giant crack in the other side. He continued, handling the whip with surprising grace, like a sculptor. Ook's large awkward frame suddenly seemed elegant as he moved in dancelike motions, shaping and carving around Kejanu's form. Soon, he had formed a rough arch, searing the crystal into a curved shape, like a doorway. The ogred stepped in and put his big fingers into the crevices on each side. He grunted loudly, and with enormous effort, pulled the arch away from the wall. Ook threw the stone slab clattering to one side. Kejanu's form, which had been rigid and frozen, melted like ice, sliding to the floor. Delilah ran to the Dusk Aelf and felt his face and body, which were as cold as the stone around him. She tried to listen for a heartbeat and did not hear any, nor did she feel a pulse. She listened for even the faintest breath and did not hear that, either.

Ook put out his arm to gently nudge Delilah out of the way. The ogred picked up the aelf like a doll and put him over his shoulder. "Ell-fees" he said, and they knew their time was running short. The group ran, Ook in the lead carrying Kejanu, with Delilah and the others behind him. Ook had to kneel and walk on his knees carrying the aelf to get through the small opening and back to the main passageway. They proceeded swiftly up the incline to where they hoped the way out lay ahead. A few times Ook indicated that he smelled the aelves nearby, yet what could they do? The walls and floors were growing thick with twisting roots, thicker by the minute and tripping them up. They really could only go up and out, even if it led to where the Crystal Aelves were gathered to slaughter them. After a few minutes, they saw daylight at the end of the tunnel, and the triple twisted torso of She-Sha-La blocking the way.

"She-Sha-La!" Delilah yelled: "I beg of you, let us pass!"

"As you wish, children of war," said the triple voice, and nudged her entwined bodies to the side to let in harsh white light that burned their eyes.

The party stumbled out, blinking in the sunlight, unable to gather the shapes and scenery around them. Their eyes, adjusted to the starlight environment, rebelled by creating giant white spots that blinded their field of vision. As their eyes adapted, it seemed for a moment that they were standing in an orchard, as the trunks of trees seemed to be surrounding them, yet Delilah could recall no orchard there. As her eyes began to focus, she saw that they were not trees, but aelves, standing completely still, by the thousands, surrounding them, spread out and yet so dense that they saw no end to the bodies of the countless army.

"Ell-fees," said Ook, pointing out at the forest of still, crystalline figures.

"Yes, Ook, we can see," Delilah said.

All was silent among the quiet, endless field of aelves. The only sound was the mountain, still shifting and breaking apart with roots and swelling vines. Loose piles of rocks tumbled down, making way for the living vegetation that was taking over the stone. Delilah and the others saw no way to pass. They just stood, the small group of them, with the lifeless form of Kejanu still cradled on the ogred's shoulder. They had harrowed the escape from the confines of the prison, fighting the Cerberus, freeing Kejanu, escaping the overgrown tunnels of the mountain, and now it seemed it was all for naught. They were surrounded nonetheless. No better than when they were in their cells, and worse for losing one of their own in the struggle. Delilah looked around, trying to see if there was anything that could possibly be a sign that this was not the end for them. She saw only seas of pale faces with no true expressions: impassive, unfeeling, inhuman faces.

In that moment, she was filled with loathing for the Crystal Aelves, hated their whole race, for what they had done to Jarvis, and to Oravica, and Kejanu, and for annihilating her people and allies. She saw nothing of beauty in them, despite their graceful forms and pretty features. They were pure monsters. If Delilah was on her own at that moment, she probably would have run toward the aelves and taken out any she could before submitting to annihilation herself. Yet she was not alone. She owed her life to her Guard and Ook. She could not jeopardize them any further than this cursed mission had harmed them already. After her violent impulse passed, Delilah was overwhelmed by the uncontrollable urge to sit down in the dirt: to just give up, surrender, and take whatever was coming to her. She felt a tingling in her palm, then, and heard a clear voice in her head. It was Ilvana's voice saying, "Look up, Your Majesty!"

Startled, Delilah raised her eyes to the sky and saw a large bird on the horizon. It was not a bird, though, the realization overcame her. It was a drakeon! A reddish orange form was flying toward them at incredible speed. She recognized the shape of Nhyddogg as he came closer and swooped and circled above. Someone was riding on his back, and Delilah knew in the depths of her soul that it was Ilvana. The Crystal Aelves looked up, almost disinterestedly, as if a fire drake flying above them was not an unusual occurrence. They seemed completely unthreatened by the giant creature. This was to their detriment, though, because as the beast circled and his path grew lower to the ground, he blew out a tidal wave of fire onto the field of aelves, sizzling them back to make a clear path around Delilah and her friends. Tufts of purple smoke wafted up from where the closest aelves had been disintegrated by Nhyddogg's flames. The aelves in the next rows ran toward the drakeon, and he neatly fried those, too, before landing with a whoosh of his great wings. The aelves seemed to see the logic in staying back, since it became clear that coming closer would result in their immediate demise.

"Great Firedrake, Nhyddogg!" Delilah called to him as he landed. "We are so grateful for you, Honorable Drakeon!"

"Little Sister," said the drake, bowing his head in greeting. Delilah bowed back.

Ilvana called: "Let us do away with the formalities! We have trade winds to catch! Climb up. There is room for all."

Ook handed Kejanu up to Ilvana, who looked alarmed by the motionless form of the Dusk Aelf. The ogred then helped the others up into the framed box that was attached to Nhyddogg's back, and climbed aboard himself. Swarms of the Crystal Aelves began to rush forward, realizing that this was their last chance to prevent the prisoners from escaping, but Nhyddogg handily zapped any that came close before alighting to the sky. The quick rush of air made Delilah lightheaded as they rose high above the bands of aelves, who looked like tiny white dolls. Instead of leaving, though, Nhyddogg circled around, observing the mountain's curious destruction. Giant limbs were now erupting from the peaks, as if an enormous tree was about to break free from beneath its destabilized mound. A thundering crash shook the heavens. Waves of sound and air buckled the sky around them as they watched the mountain implode and collapse upon itself. Great ripples of air tossed the drakeon about as he teetered to keep his balance while watching the spectacle.

The Crystal Mountain was demolished, a pile of broken glassy stone among the writhing roots and massive vines. It was both thrilling and terrifying to see the monumental devastation. Delilah was shamed by the rush she felt in being partially responsible for this geological event. An enormous tree spurled forth, with glorious twisting branches reaching out toward the sky, tossing stone in all directions. A cluster of movement at the base of the pile of rubble caught Delilah's eye, and she saw forms scattering. They were different from the pale aelves, with colorful clothing and smaller, wider frames. It was the dwarves! A small contingent of them had escaped the collapsing mount. The tiny folks were milling around and huddling together.

"Nhyddogg! Can we go and help those small people? I believe they are captives of the Crystal Aelves, too."

"Ahh, the queen has a bleeding heart!" said the beast, but turned to angle down toward the forms of the dwarves. The aelves began firing a rain of arrows at the drakeon as he landed. He blocked his riders with an armored wing and a few of the arrows stuck in between his scales.

Delilah called to the dwarves, who looked at her and then looked fearfully around at the aelves. "Come on! We are rescuing you! Come with us!"

Without waiting, Ook jumped down and began tossing dwarves up upon the drake's back. The tiny people seemed horrified to let the ogred touch them, yet froze with fear as the projectiles fell all around them. One of the younger dwarven men backed away, shaking his head. As he retreated, he was impaled by an arrow and died instantly. A woman, perhaps his mother, ran up to him and held his head in her lap. She was knocked completely back by another arrow. The rest of the small group cooperated with Ook and allowed him to launch them up to the back of the drakeon, and Ook then began to haul himself up. An arrow caught the ogred on his free arm and his sinews were laid bare, blood running in a torrent down his arm as the gaping raw ridge of skin on his shoulder flapped loosely. He pulled himself up the rest of the way with just the strength of his good arm, the others assisting him. Ilvana quickly bound his arm with the sash from her robe as Nhyddogg again took to the sky.

It was quite crowded in the open riding box now, with an ogred, an unconscious aelf, several humans, and nine dwarves with horrified wide eyes, all crammed together with no consideration for personal space. Delilah breathed a sigh of relief as they outpaced the projectiles of the aelves, and rubbed Ook's big head reassuringly. "Do not worry, my friend, we will get you all healed up, like we have done before. You have been a real hero today, Ook."

Despite his injury, Ook glowed with Delilah's praise. The fire drake barreled at full speed now, rushing away from the collapsed mountain and the aelves. Delilah looked back, and was alarmed to see a white plume of smoke coming from the center of the fallen peak. There was something flying up from the roots of the Great Tree. A creature rose from the base of the rubble! Delilah tried to focus on what the thing could be, and then realized that it was pursuing them!

"We are not alone!" she shouted, and Ilvana looked where Delilha pointed out the white fluttering shape.

"Oh no! That is another drake!" Ilvana said. Nhyddogg pulled up fast and spun around, clearly not believing another drakeon could be in the air. Yet it was: a smaller, daintier creature, though a drake nonetheless. Nhyddogg had essentially stopped, hovering in the air as he watched the new creature approach, still perhaps not believing that another of his kind was chasing them.

"It is not a Fire Drake… she is a Crystal Drake!" he exclaimed. As it drew nearer, they could see the translucent shine to its scales. Its body was almost clear, like moonstone, with opaque white bones visible underneath the misty form.

"Well, that would make sense," Delilah said. "Nhyddogg, not to criticize, but perhaps it is not the time to make her acquaintance?"

"That puny thing? I have nothing to fear from the little runt. She is barely born!"

"Still, Great Drake, you have quite a load at the moment. Will you please prioritize our escape?"

"It has a rider!" Ilvana noticed, and they could see that it was true: a standing form rode upon the creature's back, holding reins to control its flight.

"Oh no, no, no, no, no," Delilah chanted, as if her imagination had conjured up her brother riding on the back of the glistening drakeon and denying it firmly could make it go away.

"Is that… Jarvis?" Ilvana yelled, letting Delilah know she was not imagining that her brother was coming after her on drakeon-back.

The white drake drew closer until it was undeniable that Delilah's brother, still wearing the skull helmet and grimacing menacingly, rode astride her. The crystal drake dove in and sank her teeth and claws at Nhyddogg's left flank, leaving a deep tear in the scales. The red drakeon practically laughed as he pulled his body out of her reach, "Now that is a lot of spirit for such a little one!" he exclaimed. He began to go into a posture of defense, yet the jumping around tossed his passengers against the walls of the carriage box. Many of them, especially the dwarves, shrieked madly at the jostling. "Yes, I can see how having refugees onboard might impede a battle," he said, and despite seeming uninclined to retreat, Nhyddogg put on a burst of speed and headed over the plains and toward the dark edges of the Whayer Wood. The white drakeon also put on speed and was able to continue at a constant close distance from them.

As they approached the edge of the Wood, Delilah questioned Ilvana: "Please tell me you brought some weapons?" The doctor reached into a case and took out a large compound bow.

"Thank goodness," Delilah said and began stringing it with multiple missiles.

"Your Highness, may I do it?" Fallon asked her, and Delilah realized the archer had a much better chance of hitting her target.

"Please," she said, and handed the weapon to Fallon, who quickly strung the barbs and with rapid succession, sent them hurtling at the dragon in pursuit. A few bounced off the creature's scales and then one knocked into the rider, hitting him squarely in the chest. Delilah watched for the second time in her life as her brother fell, free from the bounds of the earth, tumbling through the air.

Perhaps the shock and horror of it unbalanced Delilah, because suddenly she lost her footing and leaned back against the hatch of the box. It became unlatched and then she, too, was falling! Out through the air she plummeted, tumbling toward the earth. With all her strength, she sent energy into her crystals and shouted as vehemently as she could to Ilvana: "Return to Hope!"

A crashing of trees rushed up to batter her body as she fell, and then, all went dark with her impact upon the hard earth.

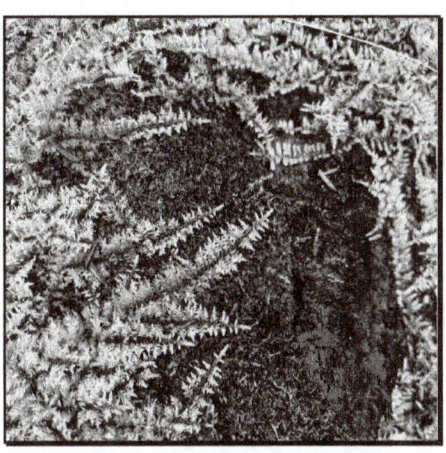

"Beasts of the Air and Beasts of the Wood
None can say which ones are good
Bad ones seem kind when one's vision is bleary
And those who seem evil may be only weary."
-The Ghost Scribe

Chapter 11: The Gloomy Woods

If Delilah had ever wanted to see what would happen to a human who went into the Whayer Wood, she now had her chance. By pure luck, a patch of giant fireswamp cabbage had broken her fall from Nhyddogg. In addition to creating a kind of pillow to catch her, the plant's strong odor had the benefit of masking her human smell so that she was not immediately devoured by the beasts that lurked about the swamp. Delilah was relieved that her party had not pursued her, since that would have only endangered them further. The others should be mercifully safe by now, she thought, back in Hope. Shreds of Gloom snaked through the forest. She had always assumed that the Whayer Wood was wall-to-wall Gloom. Instead, it seemed that the Gloom floated through in long strips and clumps that could be avoided, with some inconvenience. Perhaps other sections were more saturated with Gloom than here, as Delilah had always been under the impression that just minutes in the Wood could turn a person Beast.

Delilah was not Beast, at least not that she could tell. She seemed her normal self, if a bit banged up from her fall and reeking of stagnant water. As it was, she frequently had to duck and cover when a monstrous creature flew overhead or trampled nearby through the dense growth. There was a good deal of growling and howling. Unrecognizable creatures lumbered or floated along looking for something to eat. Although she had washed off most of the blood from her scrapes, she still had to hide when they came close to avoid being sensed. Two ugly trollves sauntered by, sniffing the air. They walked upright with bald, knobby legs and full chests of wolf hair, with snubby, piglike snouts and hairy pointed ears. Delilah took refuge in a snaking briar patch with curious blossoms that turned their heads to look at her.

"There is human nearby, Harley, I can smell it!" the larger trollf said to his friend.

"You are always imagining human meat, Herk. That is your stomach making you smell things that are not there."

"It is grumbling," Herk admitted, rubbing his fat, furry stomach. "Hey, remember those tasty morsels we had roasted with honey that time?"

"That was a decade ago, Herk. There have not been humans in this part of the Wood in a long time."

"Yes, I am probably so hungry I am hallucinating human meat again. Let us go eat some zhomboids then, I guess, Harley. At least they are easy to catch."

"Yeck, zhomboids are disgusting. They taste like rotten chalk," Harley spat.

"Do you have any better ideas?"

"Nope, another night of zhomboid souffle it is, Herk. Desperate times, my friend."

The monsters departed along the path and Delilah came out from hiding. She tried to estimate which direction Hope was by how the sun was traveling across the sky. It was so dark and murky in the wood that the sun barely reached the forest floor, making it impossible to navigate. She considered using her crystals and then rejected that idea. Since the aelves had been spying on their communications, she suspected that sending out an alert would result in her being promptly tracked down and killed. It hit her like a thunderbolt that Jarvis could be nearby, perhaps mortally injured. He had been shot in the chest and had fallen right before she had. Despite trying to kill her on that damned baby crystal drakeon, when Jarvis fell, all Delilah could think was that it was her big brother who was falling and she did not want him to die. Jarvis had found ways to harness the aelven magick, so maybe he could be restored from his injuries, Delilah reasoned. He might be living and hunting her still or could be lying dead in a bush.

She wondered if she should try to find his body. It would guide her decisions if she found that he had not survived the arrow and the fall. She began to look among the undergrowth, trying to estimate how far back Jarvis had fallen. She picked up a long stick and lifted creepers and poked inside piles of tangled ivies. The vines moved of their own volition, recoiling when she prodded them. Rays of light filtered down in jagged rays, sparkling on the scaly fungi of the trees. The branches creaked and seemed to shift and move more than they should. Delilah felt eyes upon her and looked up to see a spider the size of a dog pull itself back into a funnel-shaped web. Two shrieking howells flew down, with one big eye in each of their round heads, emitting haunting calls. The spider jumped out and grabbed one of the howells, spinning it up quickly in silk and pulling it back into its cave. The other howell screamed and dove at the spider a few times before retreating to the tree canopy, its hooting call turning into a wail of grief as it continued to chastise the spider from above.

Delilah heard water then and realized how thirsty she was. It had been a long time since she had anything to drink back when she was imprisoned in the Crystal Mountain. She had known enough not to drink from the putrid swamp, yet this water seemed to be coming from a fresh source. She followed the sound and saw a rippling, clear brook, light dazzling the surface in pinwheel currents. Was everything here tainted by the Gloom? Delilah was so thirsty and the water looked so clean that she stooped and cupped her hands to drink mouthful after mouthful. Once she started, it was hard to stop, but finally she was sated. Sitting back on her heels, gulping for breaths of air, she again sensed being watched. Perhaps it was just the ever-moving trees, yet she turned slowly toward the path leading back into the wood.

In the dappled pinpoints of sunlight spilling from above, Delilah saw the most dazzling sight: a glorious specimen of a unicorn stood, a luminous glow emanating from its vigorous body. The creature was a rich, florid shade of dark magenta. A purple unicorn! Delilah's heart thrummed loudly in her chest. The beast bowed to Delilah and its glistening mane fell down over one eye. As it bowed, it looked up at her through its forelock in a familiar, almost playful way. It rose and pawed the ground, beckoning to her. As Delilah stood, her head swam and she almost lost her balance. She walked slowly toward the animal and saw that in the center of its chest was a puncture wound where violet blood had coagulated.

As she walked near, her legs gave way beneath her and she slumped to the ground. The unicorn drew close to her and nudged her face with a concerned nuzzle. Delilah was not sure what was happening to her body. Her limbs were unable to move. She felt herself being lifted although nobody except the beast was there. An invisible power levitated her up to seat her upon the unicorn's back. Though she had lost control of her body, she was fastened upright there by some unseen force. The unicorn took off and then it was running with Delilah through the treetops as if the trees were intangible and the forest was just a projection of light. Delilah and the creature were like phantoms, flying through the sky, no physical things interfering with their flight. Even when they encountered monsters of the Wood, they passed through those, too, and the Beasts did not even seem to sense their presence. It felt like hours that they leaped through the Wood. The mesmerizing pattern of dark tree limbs made cool impressions on Delilah's feverish skin. They passed through them as though they did not exist. Were the trees not real or had she turned into a ghost? Delilah could not help wondering if perhaps she had not survived the fall after all and was now trapped in the spirit world. She gave in to the odd sensations and fell into a dreamlike trance.

Delilah only became alert when she recognized the lights of Hope and the form of her castle through the dusky trees at the end of the Whayer Wood. She tried to call out, but her voice was paralyzed like the rest of her body. Instead of breaking through the last barrier to the fields and orchards behind her castle, the unicorn circled widely around and did not pass into Hope. Instead, it kept going, back into the dense wood. Delilah tried again to yell to the unicorn to take her home, but could produce no sound. She was being taken somewhere, and it was not Hope. The ground got steeper and they began to ascend a mountain. From Delilah's sense of their location, she thought it might be the Peak of Yonderlot across the ocean inlet from Hope. Yonderlot was not accessible to Hope, far away across the enclosed circle of sea in the bay under the cliffs and cut off entirely by the intervening Whayer Wood and the Gloom. There was only speculation about who lived in the archaic stone tower at the crest of the cliffs. A constant light burned in the watchtower, yet no one knew what type of folk lived there. It was above the Gloom, so there could easily be humans trapped on that mountain top, isolated from the rest of the world.

Delilah was surprised that suddenly the dark stone of the tower rose before them. It was fully night now and the only light was from the burning embers in the citadel above. She felt herself being lifted and set upon the stone. Her body flopped, as she still had no mastery over her muscles. The unicorn bent its head and snuffed into her face, tickling her. She felt a sharp nip and realized that the creature had bit her ear! Her eyes filled with tears from the wincing cut, and she tried unsuccessfully to open her mouth to yell at the beast. It just nuzzled her and trotted away. Delilah lay helpless, unable to move. Her body felt as if it had sunk down to become part of the mountainside in front of the towering keep. She had no choice but to submit to the feeling of being nothing but stone. In the moment that she turned her will over to the mountain, the night passed in an instant. She found herself inside on a comfortable cot of hay and warm blankets, having no idea how she had gotten there.

Delilah felt as if she had not slept at all, yet was completely rested. Her body was weak, though. Still, she could sit up. She stretched her limbs to test that all were in working order. As she did, the door opened, and an elderly man came in with a tray. He came toward her and Delilah could not believe when she recognized his face. It was the old man from the dungeon whom she had released so many years ago after her parents died and she took over as Queen.

"Gravenwell!" The name erupted from her lips as she recognized the old storyteller.

"Queen Delilah, my esteemed guest. How you have grown since you were first crowned Queen!"

"Yes, I could not stay a young girl forever. I have recently been informed that I am 'middle aged' now," she said. The old man cackled with riotous laughter. She recalled that his laugh was what she liked most about it him. It was so boisterous: the guards used to yell at him to shut his trap or they would shut it for him. "I am glad to see you, my friend," Delilah said. "Yet puzzled why I am here. Did you meet the unicorn that brought me?"

"'Twas no unicorn that brought you, Your Majesty," said Gravenwell. "'Twere only an aelf."

"An aelf!" Delilah shouted. "I was brought here on the back of a purple unicorn, I swear it!"

Gravenwell shook his head and chuckled in a much more subdued fashion. "I would not like to argue with a queen," he said, "but it was no one except an aelf who carried you here and left you on my stoop. You were quite disoriented, so you may have dreamed of a unicorn. I believe you have had some injury," he said gesturing to her torn clothes and dried blood that had dripped from her ear.

"Yes, I fell from a drakeon and then the unicorn bit me," she said, realizing how crazy it sounded as the words came out of her mouth. Now the man laughed again raucously, and took a wet rag from his tray, offering it to her to wipe the blood from her face and neck. As she put the used rag back onto the tray, she saw it was streaked with purple blood. "You see! Look at the blood! That is no normal human blood! It was the unicorn! He must have poisoned me!"

"Well, I do not know about that," said Gravenwell, "however, you have had quite a trip. The aelf who brought you seemed concerned for your welfare. He told me to keep you safe and not to let you use your 'crystals.' Not sure what that meant, so I am just passing along the message."

"These," she said, and held up her hand.

"Oh my!" said Gravenwell, and reached out. "May I?" he asked. She nodded. He felt the stones beneath her palm. "A new fad for the nobility?" he said with a wink. "Well, this certainly explains a lot."

"Does it?" she asked.

"Why, yes," he said. "I have been picking up all kinds of odd fragments of conversations, battle plans, strategies, even personal conversations of a... romantic nature."

"You say you have 'picked them up'?" Delilah asked.

"Yes, from the Beacon. The crystal in the tower. It is made from Lavandite: it refracts the light and keeps the glow of the sun trapped through the night. It radiates moonlight all day long. Do more people have these?" he asked, gesturing to her crystals.

"Yes, we have been sending plans for their installation throughout the lands and over the great seas. There are people on the other side of the world we can contact if we wish," she said, filled with a sense of pride at Doktora Ilvana's invention.

"My, my," he said. "It used to be I would just hear conversations from the healers and pirates. Occasionally, I could hear aelves or magickal creatures. In the last few moons, the chatter has increased tenfold. I sometimes lose track of all the conversations. It has kept me entertained, though!"

"Did you hear about the attack on Verily? Or the fights in Far Arroway and Raefenshire?" she asked, wondering just how much was out there and who else could have access to all the communications that had been traveling through the root systems and waves.

"I heard some," he said. "It gave me a lot to ponder, and quite a lot to write about."

"Oh, you are a writer?" Delilah asked.

"Why, yes, I thought you knew," he said, looking sideways at her.

"How would I know?"

"I have sent scrolls to Hope every season or so since I left. I only signed them with a "G" because of my... tenuous freedom."

"The Ghost Scrolls!" Delilah said.

"I am hardly a ghost," he objected.

"No, that is what they call them in Hope! They call them the Ghost Scrolls, and you the Ghost Scribe! I swear, I am not sure why I never made the connection."

"I thought you would recognize my style of storytelling, being that I told you so many tales when you were a little girl."

"I apologize, Gravenwell. I probably should have. I was quite distracted for my first years ruling Hope after my parents died. There are many things I might have pondered more closely."

"Silly of me to assume you would remember the stories of an old fool," Gravenwell said.

"Oh, I do remember your stories! I just never connected them to the scrolls that became known as authored by the Ghost Scribe. How is it that you came to live here in Yonderlot?"

"When you freed me, I was at a loss. I had been captive for so long, yet I had nowhere to go. My family in Hope had played a foul role in my incarceration, and I had outlived them all by the time I was freed. I knew you took a risk releasing me from my imprisonment. There were those, like Doktora Ishlip, who would have seen me killed rather than freed. I knew I needed to leave Hope, so I wandered down to the docks. There was a tiny row boat docked there and I stole it. I felt bad for taking it, but had nothing to give in return. After rowing across the bay and around the cliffs, there was a place that looked like I could climb. You may have noticed that I am not as young as I once was. It took me two weeks to scale the far cliff: making just a little progress each day, eating grubs and grass and the roots of trees that clung to the rocks, drinking dew and rainwater until I reached the top.

"At the top of the cliff, a small dwarven woman stood up from where she was sitting, as if she had been waiting for me. She handed me a key without speaking, then went back down the cliff from the direction I had come. There I was with a key in my hand. My starving belly led me to venture to see what the mountaintop held. The light that burned in the tower could be seen from Hope, so it made sense there might be people and food. However, although the key unlocked the tower, the whole place was empty. There were scrolls with some instructions for keeping the Lavandite shiny and reflecting light. There also were directions to the mountain brook to fish and suggestions for growing and keeping vegetables, advice for how to store food for the winter and how to keep the seeds of the plants to grow the next year. There was a plentiful garden. And then there was a decree instructing me to stay here to hand over the key to the next Keeper."

"The next Keeper?"

"Yes, the next Keeper of the Tower. I am not to leave until the next Keeper arrives, the edict stated. So now, My Queen, I must ask you: Are you the next Keeper?"

"Me?" Delilah laughed, and Gravenwell looked a bit bashful.

"I thought it was unlikely, yet here you are," he said.

"I have no idea why. For all I know it is because I am the next Keeper! Still, Gravenwell, I have to tell you that even if that were my fate, I would defy my fate to go back to Hope to save my realm."

"You did not strike me as the tower-keeping type," he sighed.

"Are you so eager to leave?" Delilah asked. "Where would you go?"

"I might try to find my mother's people in the heartlands, on the other side of the Whayer Wood."

"Are they even still there? Have you been in touch with them?"

"My mother, who came from the Sapphire Aelves, left my father due to his cruelty when I was young. She went back to her people in Winnawater. It was my father and his brother—my uncle—who betrayed me. They died soon after working with Doktora Ishlip to frame me for aelvencraft. That was how I wound up in the dungeon."

Queen Delilah and the Encroaching Gloom

"You are part aelven?" Delilah exclaimed.

"Why, yes. This is why my father hated me. I reminded him of my mother. Now I have outlived all on my father's side! An old aelven joke goes like this: 'How do you win a fight with a human?'"

"How?"

"Just wait!" Gravenwell cracked up, giggling hysterically.

"So how old are you?" Delilah asked. "You had already been in the dungeon for half a century when I met you, if I recall."

"I am a spry 120. Or no… it is 121 now, I think," he said and cackled again.

"You must have been around before the Gloom!" Delilah exclaimed.

"Quite. I was a young man when the Gloom fell upon the earth. There was widespread panic. Everyone was trying to explain it, trying to understand its impact and how it would affect humans and other species, estimating how long it would last. Some said it would dissipate in a year, just a passing fog. Clearly that was a foolish guess. My mother was involved in the creation of the Vector. She helped your great grandparents channel the Ancients and create the bubble," Gravenwell said.

"I did not know that there was aelven assistance in that. Do you know about the blood-curse on the Vector that requires the sacrifice of a royal firstborn?"

"I had heard that. I thought it was unusual for the Ancients to have such a bloodthirst. Still, those who needed the protection were happy to agree to anything that would save Hope from the Gloom at that point. As it happened, it was not their generation that was affected anyway, so they did not have to pay the price."

"So why did your family turn on you?" Delilah asked. "Your father and uncle?"

"They resented me. My father had to care for me when my mother fled. She would have taken me with her, except he and my uncle told her that they would hunt me down and kill me rather than let me be raised by aelves. Not that he wanted me, you see. It was only to hurt my mother. I learned a small amount of aelven lore from her in secret while I was very young. Before she left. Then I only had what I could learn from the other secret half-aelves of Hope. There were about a dozen of us, and none could be open about our lineage. Still, we recognized each other and found solace in our shared heritage. We traded knowledge and history. We learned of the obscure magickal traits that arise when humans breed with aelves. Half-aelves may have characteristics of either race or something completely unique. One of the half-aelf women in our secret group turned into a frog each moon when she experienced her menses. If we could not find her, we knew she was in the pond for a few days."

"And what about you?" Delilah asked. "Do you have special traits?"

"Longevity. That is one, although my body became aged since I was just half a century old. Living a long time is not all it is cracked up to be if you do not maintain your youthful appearance and stamina! I also can communicate with most flying creatures: birds, raptors, drakeons. I can call them. Usually, they will do as I ask. It is how I have gotten the scrolls to Hope all these years. A group of dabbydactyls live on the cliffside. They carry my scrolls to Hope and drop them down on the grounds of the castle so that they would find their way to you."

"They have, by way of the Guard and the populace," Delilah said. "It is a favorite pastime of the Hope masses, reading and interpreting the verses, trying to make sense of the poetic lines, guessing about what might be prophetic. You are quite a popular character in Hope, despite no one knowing who you are, including me!"

"Well, it gives me comfort that they have provided some entertainment, at the very least," said the old man.

"I am still not clear, though: your father resented you. Yet what led to him betraying you so many years later?" she asked.

"I was in love with a woman, one of the half-aelves—not the lunar frog, just so you know. She was an herbalist and had many talents. Her aelven skill allowed her to detect plants for healing. My father and uncle accused her of aelvencraft. When I defended her, they accused me as well. It was about this time that my father was trying to keep me from inheriting his property. He had several other children with subsequent wives, all who left him because of his abuse, mind you, yet he favored those human children. He wanted me out of the way so that when he was gone, they would inherit his land. He could not stand the thought of a half-aelf taking over his smithing shop, though it should have gone to me as the eldest. He and my uncle conspired to tell stories about how I was enchanting the metal in the shop, making it stay hot for days after smithing so that it would burn its owners. He convinced Doktora Ishlip, one of the more conservative members of the Council, to take up the cause against me. I was imprisoned with no trial and no one to stand witness for me. I was a loose end that my father and uncle tied up so that my siblings and cousins would get their property."

"How tragic. All those years in the dungeon for nothing?"

"The ironic thing was that Doktora Ishlip had her own secrets. As much as she was publicly against aelves, she was secretly conspiring with them to overthrow the Hope monarchy. I was able to learn of this from my half-aelf brethren who would send me tiny scrolls of parchment in the dungeon by way of birds I enchanted. The Doktora was working against her own queen—your mother! I knew of this treachery when I was finally freed and was aware that Ishlip would see me as a threat because I was connected to the aelven world and would learn of her traitorous connections. This is why I was so eager to leave Hope when you released me. I knew if I stayed around, Ishlip would have found a way to have me murdered. I may have an exceedingly long life, yet I am not immune to an executioner's blade."

"And your mother and her people—are they still living?"

"Yes, I have heard her name picked up in the Lavandite crystal, and hear that she still lives in Winnawater. I have an aelven sister and even my 300-year-old grandmother still lives! This is why I would like to leave the tower at some point. I can leave anytime I want. I can walk unharmed through the Whayer Wood, same as any full aelf. Yet I was given this duty and I do have time that other mortals are not given. I felt that I should at least stay until the next Keeper arrives. That is why I was hoping it was you, Majesty."

"I am sorry to disappoint you. I can tell you that once I get back to Hope and my

Queen Delilah and the Encroaching Gloom

Queendom is restored, I will try to send a replacement for you," she said.

"No need. I am sure the right person will be called here, as I was," he said, with a somewhat despondent tone.

"Regardless, I am afraid I will need to leave this place soon to return to Hope, although it has been delightful to see you once again and learn the identity of the famous Ghost Scribe!"

"I am not sure that it is wise to go, Your Majesty. The aelf who carried you here decided this place was safer for you than Hope for a purpose. He was very clear about not using your crystals. You may be in danger if your location is picked up."

"The aelf who brought me… did you know him? Was he familiar to you at all?" she asked.

"I do not know him, yet he was familiar in some way. Perhaps his voice. I found it strange that his knife had a spot of purple blood on it. He was wiping it on a cloth when I came out and found you on the stone."

"Could he have cut my ear?" Delilah asked, reflexively feeling for the dried blood on her ear, however there did not seem to be anything there. She realized that as they were talking it had lost its tenderness.

"Let me see it again," said Gravenwell, and leaned in close. He almost jumped back when his face got near Delilah's head. "The cut is gone! Your ear is… it has changed, Your Majesty."

"Changed how?" Delilah asked, jumping up and feeling for her ear, which felt strangely shaped.

Gravenwell ran to his desk and brought back a small round mirror. When Delilah held it up, she was astonished to see that her ear had grown a noticeable peak at the top. It was an aelven ear that she saw! "What in the moons?" she exclaimed.

"You have been marked, Your Majesty," Gravenwell shook his head.

"What does that mean? Marked how? Marked for what?" She was panicking.

"You belong to the aelves now. You are not fully human anymore."

"What? How can that be? By a simple cut to my ear?"

"It was an aelven blade which has cut you, and most likely an aelven royal who marked you as his property, either slave or kin."

"Well, there is a big difference between slave and kin. It would be helpful to know which it is!"

"Agreed. I will listen to the Lavandite tonight and see what I can gather. We should seek more information before you venture out in the world. There is no safe path from here. The cliff to the sea would not bring you any guarantees, since you would not be able to get across the bay without a boat."

"If only I could summon my pirate friend," Delilah thought aloud.

"Hmmm, yes and the other way is through the Whayer Wood, which would not be the wisest. Otherwise, you might travel by drakeon if there is one nearby that I might enchant. However, there is no guarantee that it would not gobble you up as soon as it was far enough away from my influence. Perhaps we can call upon a passing pagasi."

"I will rest and think on this, but I will leave tomorrow, Gravenwell, one way or another," she said with confidence.

"I will do what I can to help you tonight. As you rest, I will gather information from the Lavandite to give me a clue as to what the journey might have in store for you and if it is even safe to return to Hope."

"Whether it is safe or not, I need to return to my realm," Delilah said. She was awash, suddenly, with all the losses that they had experienced, realizing she could not even begin to know the extent of those losses. She had no idea what she would be returning to and if it would even resemble the Hope she had left.

※

The morning came quickly. Delilah and Gravenwell had dined on smoked fish wrapped in cabbage from his garden. It was a surprisingly savory meal, especially after being deprived of real food for some time. Afterward, she had fallen right to sleep on the comfortable straw-filled bed and had slept soundly through the night. She awoke at first light and went outside to see the dew on the grasses and slugs feasting on the compost heap. She walked to the cliff edge and looked out over the bay to Hope. It was too far to see any people or movement. She just saw her home, her castle in the distance with smoke rising from the chimneys. Someone was keeping the fires burning, at least.

Gravenwell came up beside her and looked with her toward the city. It was his city, too, Delilah realized, for even longer than it had been hers. "Do you miss it?" she asked him.

Gravenwell sighed. "I had some wonderful friends there and a wonderful love. Much of it was painful, though."

"Would you go back? No one there could harm you now. You might be vindicated to know that Doktora Ishlip is now imprisoned in the dungeon you once inhabited, accused of plotting against the Crown. At least, she was a prisoner when I left."

"There is nothing left for me in Hope," Gravenwell said, sorrow in his tone. "I want to see my mother and family before I die."

"Yes, I understand that."

"I will fulfill my duty as the Keeper and then head to Winnawater."

"Gravenwell, what is it that the Keeper does? Why are you needed here at all?"

"Honestly, I am not sure. The crystal would go on shining, capturing light without me. The garden would fail, yet that does not implore me to stay. I have always felt that when one accepts a duty, they should complete it. I will honor my duty, even if I do not fully understand why it is needed."

"And now, friend, I must fulfill my duty," Delilah said.

Gravenwell packed her a small sack of leftover fish and vegetables. He had written a few obscure things on a scroll that he had learned from the Lavandite by sitting with it overnight. Glancing over the words, none of it seemed to make much sense, but Delilah thanked the scribe and kissed his papery cheek.

"Be careful in the Wood," Gravenwell said, handing her a staff made out of bonewood, the closest thing he had to a weapon in the tower. "Just remember, things may not be as they seem. Be wary of anything that looks too good to be true. Also, Queen Delilah, you may have some strange effects of being marked," he pointed to her now pointed ear. "It may have given you different senses than you had before, so use that to your advantage."

"Thank you, Gravenwell. I hope you will send me scrolls from Winnawater. I would love to hear of your reunion with your mother."

"Perhaps I will speak to you through your crystals!" Gravenwell said. "Farewell, dear girl!" He waved as she walked down the hill and toward the dark forest.

At the edge, Delilah looked back. The sun was in her eyes, yet it almost looked as if the man had birds sitting on his shoulders. She turned to scan the edge of the forest, Gloom trapped among branches and rolling over brambles, concealing the view beyond the first row of trees. Delilah's ear felt prickly, and she reached up to touch it. The odd sensation of the pointed tip sent a chill over her. Her body had changed against her will. It was unsettling, like the scales she had gotten from Oravica that still glittered on her bicep. Oravica— Thinking of her pierced Delilah's heart. She could not afford to think about her friend now, since she needed all of her faculties to face the forest. Without any further delay, Delilah stepped into the shade and felt the coolness of the landscape overtake her. A few steps in and Delilah sensed things in ways she never had before. The plants and ferns and rocks breathed and shuddered with living energy. Delilah could see an aura around the vegetation, the rich glow of life that radiated sentience.

It would be a long journey through the broad forest to Hope. If all went well, it should take a day or two. If things did not go well… then it could be longer still. Delilah tried not to think of how things could go wrong, instead focusing on the vibrating life around her. It was shimmering—the woods—with a gleaming radiance. Although the Gloom might turn animals and humans into Beasts, it seemed that it turned the flora into almost another species that breathed, watched, and listened. The trees and vines seemed as though they were observing her, rooting for her. She felt aligned with the vegetation, at least, and believed that if she continued to connect with the sensations she was feeling, that the plants would guide her safely through the Wood. This illusion was short-lived, as it turned out, since the plants did not warn her that a pair of trollves was coming; she did not see them until they were almost upon her.

"Human!!" one of the horrid beasts yelled. They ran after her in hot pursuit, their pig-like snouts turned up and nasty mouths spilling saliva at the sight of her. The creatures trampled over the shrubbery toward her and she bolted into the forest, finding she had speed in her legs that she had not possessed before. She lost the monsters far behind, ran down an embankment and then launched up into a tree. Delilah had always climbed trees, yet now she could ascend one with barely any effort, the branches reaching out to grasp her hands and help her up to the very top. There she was camouflaged in the overstory while the two awful fiends stalked below, sniffing the air and looking around to track her.

"Herk, you fool! We finally get near a human and you lose her! If you were not so fat from eating all those caterpishes we would have caught it!"

"Me? You are the one who is so slow you might as well be a giant landsnail, Harley."

"Landsnails," Harley said, licking his chops. "Now, those are not so bad."

"No, they are not. A little chewy, but nothing a little froggle butter will not help,"

Herk said wistfully.

"Landsnails with froggle butter. Now that sounds like a decent meal."

"Yes, it does. I know where we can find them, too: in the patch of flaming swamp cabbage by the pond. Froggles will be right there, too. Our own little café, sitting next to the pond, eating landsnails dipped in froggle butter. How does that sound, Harley old buddy?"

"I am still mad at you for making us miss out on roasting up a human, Herk!"

"Sorry, Harley. Another day, I know we will get lucky."

"Even if we never find another human to eat, Herk, you will still be my best friend."

"Aww, Harley," said the rounder trollf, and they walked off into the forest with arms about each other.

Delilah waited several minutes before descending to the forest floor. There, she decided to test out her new speed and began running through the Wood at top notch. Amazed, she ran as if her legs could sense every stump and log as she leapt over obstacles and wove in and out of the forest to avoid the Gloom. Her body innately sensed the topography of the forest, as if she were just an extension of it. She knew she should save her strength in case she got attacked, yet she was exhilarated by her new capacity, and justified it by thinking she could probably get back to Hope twice as quickly if she ran the whole way. She did not tire as easily either, so she could go for long bursts at a time, only stopping to rest for a few moments to eat some of the food Gravenwell had packed for her, or taking a swig out of a flask of water. After her experience drinking from the stream, she figured she was safer if she could avoid eating or drinking anything native to the Wood.

At times, Delilah hid in the dense wooded growth or climbed trees to avoid Beasts. In the treetops, she saw a herd of Pegasi being chased by some sort of wormlike flying reptile. She watched a giant plant below open its leaves to swallow a long-fanged deer in a single gulp. The toothed deer tried to bite its way out of where it was wrapped inside the foliage, but the plant persevered and soon the form of the animal stopped struggling. As dusk fell, the filtered light gave the forest a spooky feel as the dense vegetation held bruised purple shadows that turned to shades of gray and black. Delilah was surprised that she could still see at night. Dim outlines of living things appeared to her highlighted in a pale milky glow. Her hearing was enhanced, too, so that she could pick up movement and avoid approaching creatures. Finally, she had to sleep, so she climbed a tree and found a fur-lined nest that appeared abandoned. It was a tight fit inside the nest, yet so soft and comforting. She was able to curl up in it and pass into dreamless slumber for a few hours.

She awoke with fur in her mouth. She tried to yell, but a muff of hair smothered her. Something was wound very tight around her, constricting her, pushing any air she had left in her lungs out through her mouth and nostrils without letting any back in. She saw ebony black eyes with white diamond centers blink at her. Snake eyes! Yet the beast that had her in its grips was coated not in scales, but in a full fleece of fur. Knowing nothing else to do and not being able to breathe or speak, Delilah glared directly into the creature's eyes. She stared past its soulless orbs to its strange reptilian-mammalian brain and saw embedded there a memory of it nursing its young: pink wriggling, hairless worms hanging onto countless breasts along the fur-snake's long torso, there in that very nest! Another image flashed of monkraptors, hanging down to snatch up the snake babies and flying away, grasping them in their teeth and claws and she felt the terror and loss in the snake's heart. "I am sorry about your babies," Delilah thought to the snake-Beast. A surprised look passed over the snake's formerly impassive face. It blinked a few times and then released Delilah to slither down the tree.

Delilah gasped in deep shuddering breaths, realizing how close she had come to death. She sat a moment to recalibrate, and then quickly climbed down, not wanting to see what might happen if the snake returned. Dawn had barely touched the deep Wood. Dark blue shapes blended together, disguising the landscape, and pale blue patches of sky peeked through from the place far above the trees. Delilah ate the small remains of her food from Gravenwell. She had propped her staff at the base of the tree, and picked it up before running through the forest again. She must be almost there, she thought. It must not be too much further. Before she realized what was happening, she smelled something fishy, then ran smack into the two trollves she had encountered before.

"Well, looky what we have here, Harley!" the plump trollf said to his friend, grabbing Delilah's arm.

"Why, Herk, you were right! You really did smell the human again this time!" said the other trollf, grabbing Delilah's other arm. Delilah struggled to get away, but the foul creatures had a strong grip on her. Herk leaned in to take a big, deep, whiff with his snout and sighed a rapturous sound from his flabby lips.

"It will be a good day, Harley, my friend! How will we prepare it? Oh, I wish we had some honey. I love me some honeyed human!"

"I think I saw a bee hive a-ways back," Harley said and as he turned to gesture behind them, Delilah pulled her arm from his grasp and smacked him upside the head with the staff. "Ow!" said Harley, holding his face. "I am going to enjoy eating you, human!" he said menacingly, coming toward her with arms outstretched. Herk had let go of her other arm when his friend got smashed, and he resumed coming at her now, also with arms out like a zhomboid. Delilah swung the staff, faster than she could recall being able to do in the past, smacking one, and then the other. She spun swiftly and repeated the motions, hitting one upside the head and whacking the other with the opposite end of the hard bonewood pole. Both monsters fell, stunned, to the ground, rubbing their heads, not sure how their meal had turned on them. Herk bolted up to lunge at Delilah.

"I will just eat it raw!" he yelled.

"Save me some!" Harley said, also rising.

Herk and Harley stopped mid-assault when howling filled the wood. The sounds came closer, from every direction, and the trollves looked fearfully around, spinning to see where it was coming from. Shapes began to emerge all around them from behind the trees, slowly, purposefully, stalking closer, surrounding them. "Whayerwolves!" Herk said, and Delilah could see it was true: a pack of at least 15 of the canid Beasts were coming in, closer, circling them and letting out an occasional yip, howl, or growl, from snarling jaws.

"Harley," said Herk. "I think we forgot that thing we were supposed to do."

"That thing? Oh yes! That thing we were doing. We should have been there already, right?" Harley asked.

"Yes, in fact, I think we are late. Terribly late. An awful shame we have to leave."

"Yes, a shame!" Herk said, and began to run with Harley following close behind, pushing through the whayerwolves, who backed away, but let them out of the circle. Delilah hoped some of them might chase after the trollves, but they just turned back to her, and continued moving in closer.

With synchronized timing, the wolves went from putting one careful paw after another, slowly on the ground, to leaping, in unison, toward her. Delilah raised her staff and batted several of them away with new inhuman speed, but they kept coming at her. One beast might fall, but another was always behind it to jump at her, again and again. They closed in so that she barely had room to swing. She felt the claws of one pull her legs out from under her. She fell and felt needle sharp jaws clamping down upon her shoulder and another set furiously ripping into her thigh. A pile of claws, teeth, and fur battered her down into the ground. It was surely the end, she thought. Delilah flailed the best she could, knowing she was overpowered and had no more fighting chance. When she heard even deeper snarls and growls above her, she thought the Beasts on top were fighting their way through the pile to devour her. However, she then felt teeth release from her leg and the weight of the pile being thrown off her. Wolves were tossed through the air in dizzying chaos, landing with whimpers. Some got up and ran off. Others did not get up at all.

Delilah saw the back of an enormous whayerwolf, larger than the others. It had disrupted the feasting frenzy, probably to devour her itself. The wolf breathed heavily in and out from the effort of casting off so many of its brethren before turning to face her. Delilah recoiled, expecting to be fully consumed by the monster. Instead, she recognized a familiar face. It was Xanfar! He wore a black velvet suit with a blue silk handkerchief tucked into his breast pocket. Brushing some clumps of wolf fur off his suit, he took out the cloth to wipe sweat from his brow before smiling a full, wolfy smile at his friend.

"Xanfar! I thought you were dead!" Delilah said, trying to get up, but falling back on the ground, her wounds gushing blood.

"I told you, Your Majesty. Whayerwolves are immortal. Now let us get you cleaned up. You are needed in Hope."

Delilah was reclined on a pallet that was hoisted on the shoulders of four whayerwolves. Xanfar walked along beside her as the wolf-creatures, so similar to him yet vastly different, labored to hold Delilah aloft. Delilah had tried to walk, but her wounds were too impairing. She had been amazed that after conquering the canid foes, Xanfar had then demanded in a wolfen language that the ones who were still alive assist him in taking the queen back to Hope. For some reason, they complied!

"How did you find me?" Delilah asked Xanfar.

"I smelled you," Xanfar said, smiling over at her.

"I have not been bathing regularly since I departed for Far Arroway, so I would imagine I smell quite ripe," she said.

"No, you smell fine, Delilah. You smell like… you. And yet you also smell like… an aelf." He looked at her quizzically. Delilah absentmindedly reached up to touch her ear, which was still pointed at the tip, but the gesture brought Xanfar's attention to it. "What in the Gloom is that?" he asked.

Delilah described in detail what had happened from the time they had gone into the Crystal Mountain to when she had fallen from Nhyddogg into the Whayer Wood. She relayed her strange trip through the forest that ended at the tower in Yonderlot.

"You must not drink the water in the Whayer Wood," Xanfar scolded. "It will drive humans to madness. You got off lightly that it only put you into a dream state."

"It may have just been a dream, but it was very convincing that I was flying on the back of a purple unicorn," she said.

"And yet, Gravenwell seemed to think it was an aelf who brought you to Yonderlot? What do you make of that?"

"It was Jarvis, I am sure of it. I just do not know why Gravenwell thought Jarvis was an aelf. Unless he has been so changed in his time among them? Gravenwell is part-aelf, so I would think he would know."

"Did Gravenwell know your brother?" Xanfar asked.

"Why, yes, of course. Wait… no, he did not. Gravenwell was imprisoned our whole childhood. When I went to visit him in the dungeon, I went on my own. So, no, I do not think they ever met. Gravenwell said that my ear shows that I was marked as belonging to the aelves, either as kin or as property. What if Jarvis had been marked also? Perhaps this is why Gravenwell thought him to be an aelf?"

"Yes, or perhaps he was already an aelf, or half-aelf anyway," Xanfar said.

"That is impossible. Neither of our parents were aelven."

"Well, your mother was not," Xanfar said.

"Not our father, either," Delilah insisted.

"*Your* father was not aelven, anyway."

"What are you saying?"

"That you may not have the same father. It would not be unheard of. Maybe Jarvis had an aelven father. That would explain his affinity toward the aelves and their acceptance of him."

"I do not believe my mother could have had a child with another man when my father raised us both, loving us both the same. He claimed Jarvis as his heir." She paused. "Still, I have found it curious that the queen of the Crystal Aelves would want to partner with a human. I thought she must have married him for his connection to Hope."

"If Jarvis had a different father, perhaps your father did not know. It would not be the first time this has happened. In fact, history is loaded with children of secret parentage, especially royalty."

"This is all too much for me to even ponder now, Xanfar. My healer, Helanza, will know if this is even a possibility. She was in my mother's service before me, and was her closest confidante. Helanza may be able to shed some light on this when we return… if she is still alive! Is she?" she was afraid to ask yet saw the wolf nod his confirmation. "Now please tell me, Xan, what happened on the battlefield? I was told you and Captain Ferrashi were seen being overpowered by the Crystal Aelves. That is why I thought you had perished."

"I almost did. I may be immortal, but I am not entirely impervious to weapons and sorcery. Captain Ferrashi was unfortunately… lost," he gulped and turned his face away.

"Xanfar, I am so sorry," Delilah said and reached out to touch his arm.

"It is the way of the world. I am not new to this kind of loss," he said, and drew in a shuddering breath.

"Still, it does not take the sting away. I know how special Ferrashi was to you, and how much you meant to him."

"Yes. He followed me to his death."

"What of the other Centauri? Did any survive? I understand it was a massacre," Delilah said. She really did not want to hear about the casualties. Still, being the one who had compelled them all to war, she felt like she had no right to be protected from the truth.

"Almost all were lost. A handful survived by retreating when Abbowhen called the troops off the battlefield. Many of the Centauri would not retreat, despite being ordered to do so. I am ashamed to say that they were taking my lead. I refused to retreat, and so many stayed by my side to fight. I was the death of them," Xanfar said.

"No, Xanfar, *I* was the death of them," Delilah insisted. "It was *my* battle, my war. None of you would have been involved if I had not asked for your help."

"Yes, but I have always been their patron. They followed me."

"And how was it that you survived?" asked Delilah.

"Funny thing about Megalostrongi worms," Xanfar said, "the creatures leave gashing holes everywhere after they break the surface of the earth. As we were being swarmed by the Crystal Aelves, I happened to get knocked back into one such tunnel. It was deep and winding. I cracked my head and lost consciousness. When I awoke, I had quite a hard time finding my way back up. I had to claw my way to the surface. Had I not these," he showed his fierce claws, "I likely never would have made it back. When I finally reached the surface, everyone had gone and the place was littered with corpses. Any of the aelven dead had disintegrated, so there were spots of purple and shiny blue powder in between volumes of blood. It may have been the worst moment of my life when I saw the devastation. The evidence of our failure in sheer numbers was… horrifying."

"I am sorry, Xanfar. It was my failure. I was the one who led you all there, and it was under my leadership that our losses were so great."

"Yes and no. War is war. The Crystal Aelves deceived us in ways we could not have anticipated. They were more cunning, more prepared, and more numerous than we could have imagined. It also turns out they had been spying on us and misleading us with bad information for some time. Plus, you really had no choice, Delilah. If we had not gone to them, they would have come to Hope. Then most of the city would have been wiped out and they would have taken control of the castle, probably killing you in the process."

"Yes, I know what you say is true. I felt I had no choice when I planned to go to war and built alliances to help us. I knew there would be casualties. I just did not think…" Delilah tried to complete her thoughts, and instead broke down quietly weeping. She placed an arm over her eyes to try to disguise her loss of composure.

"Queens do not cry!" Delilah imagined her mother's voice scolding her and felt even more ashamed, not just of her failed war, but for not being stronger. Xanfar gave her space and fell back to talk to some of the other wolves. Their strange low growly language sounded exotic to Delilah's ear. Focusing on what they could be talking about, Delilah calmed herself and pulled her feelings together. She rolled them up tightly into a tiny ball and shoved them deep down inside herself somewhere, knowing that she would have plenty of time to grieve her lost allies in the days to come.

While traveling with the whayerwolves, no other Beasts bothered them. They occasionally encountered some roaming zhomboids or odd misshapen creatures of the Wood, yet these beings gave them a wide berth. Delilah wondered if being in the Gloom would affect her, yet intuitively sensed that her new aelven marking gave her some protection. While listening to the low rumbling snarl-talk of the wolves, and feeling the rocking of her cot, she could forget the pain of her wounds. She was lulled into a peaceful trance. In this half-wakeful state, Delilah felt both sleepy and strangely alert to the trees and wildlife around her. Through partially closed eyes, she saw the trees leaning down to check on her, felt their cool breath blowing over her skin, relieving her agitation. She had the sense that even the Gloom was a benevolent presence, turning things to their true form rather than distorting them from their natural state. "Perhaps we have it all wrong," she thought.

"Alas, we are quick to call another foe
Although we may not ever know
The truth of their birth or how they were sired
And what their heart most deeply desires."
-The Ghost Scribe

Chapter 12: Return to Hope

Delilah awoke when her cot was laid down at the edge of the Whayer Wood. She heard hushed growls from the wolves speaking to Xanfar before they disappeared into the dark shadows of the forest. Dusk was falling upon the orchards and fields. Xanfar reached out to help Delilah to her feet, but her injured leg would not hold her weight. She almost fell before the whayerwolf caught her and scooped her up in his velvety arms. "I was hoping to give you a dignified entrance back to your queendom," Xan said, "but it looks like I will have to deliver you this way."

"Better to be carried home alive than to die upon a battlefield. I am ashamed to be alive when so many perished in my name."

"Such is the fate of queens," Xanfar said. "A heavy burden to carry."

"Now I am the burden to carry," Delilah said.

Shouts rang out and lanterns were held up as the two were spotted coming across the fields. Guards ran to take Delilah from Xanfar's arms. They propped her between them, examining her injuries, and sped her toward the castle. She was rushed to Helanza's quarters downstairs by the kitchens to attend to her wounds. The healer did not seem at all surprised to see Delilah. Bowls of poultices were at the ready as Delilah was laid on a cot. Helanza began to dab and wipe, picking odd whayerwolf hairs out of punctures in Delilah's skin. The healer painted thick layers of powdered herbs in the bloody gouges, and wound her limbs with clean bandages.

One of the dwarven women they had rescued was crushing aromatic plants in a bowl.

Nikki Peone Pison & Niko Peone

She looked up at Delilah to meet her eyes, then bowed her head in greeting.

"I am glad to see our liberated friend from Raefenshire has found a place here," Delilah said. "And I am relieved to see you, Helanza."

The healer did not look at Delilah, simply nodded and kept working. Abbowhen arrived and ran to Delilah's side. "Your Majesty! We are so grateful you have returned!" she said.

"I wish I could have sent back all of the soldiers we lost instead," Delilah said.

"They died bravely, as our soldiers have always done," Abbowhen said.

"Have we taken full stock of our casualties?" Delilah asked, afraid to know.

Abbowhen sighed. "We lost one in three of our army," she said. "Our numbers are profoundly diminished; it is truly devastating. Everyone in Hope is grieving."

"How awful!" Delilah cried.

"It would have been worse if we had persevered any longer. I called the order to retreat when I saw how futile it was. The Usiku, pirates, and Centauri fared even worse than we did."

"I heard. Are there any Usiku left?" Delilah asked. She wanted to inquire about Kejanu, but worried it was in poor taste.

"A few. They have stayed here with us in Hope. They are like ghosts, wandering the grounds. They truly have no community to return to. The surviving Centaurs have stayed also, as well as Lord Xanfar, but of course you know that."

"Yes, he found me in the Wood and brought me back. Where did he get off to?"

"Probably back to his temporary quarters. When he sensed you in the forest yesterday, he told me he was going after you and refused to take reinforcements. It would have done no good to send anyone with him and he knew it. Our Guard would have been compromised by the Gloom. Most are in poor shape anyway. We have been awaiting Lord Xanfar's return, hoping he was right and could bring you safely home by himself," the major said, looking at her fondly.

"I need military updates. Have there been signs of invasion? Any indication the aelves will attack here next?"

"Actually, they were here, Your Majesty, when we returned," Abbowhen said with apprehension, as if she was not sure how much she should tell Delilah at that moment.

"What?" Delilah said, bolting up. She had not seen any sign of aelves or a battle upon her brief return to the castle, but perhaps she had missed something.

"Jarvis and Queen Nimevah were here and had taken the castle," Abbowhen said. Delilah felt her heart racing, needing to know the story and if and how they were safe. "Lie back, please, Majesty," Abbowhen pleaded. "There is no need to be alarmed now. The threat has passed."

"But how?" Delilah demanded. Helanza came over and gently urged her back onto the pillow, laying a cool rag soaked in herbs across her forehead.

"The Crystal Aelves had taken the castle by the time we returned," The major explained. "It took us several days to retreat by ship. First, we had to go back to Far Arroway and wait for the pirates to transport us. When we finally made land in Hope, we were greeted by city folk who told us the aelves had come from under the ground and had taken over the castle. We could not believe it, yet they had burrowed all the way from Raefenshire on their devil worms! Hope was not heavily defended. As you know, the Guard who stayed back were posted on the perimeters of the city and the castle compound. The enemy was just suddenly there: a castle full of aelves! They let us through the gates and into the castle. I was called into the throne room, along with the other high-ranking officers.

"Your brother and Queen Nimevah were on the thrones," Abbowhen continued. "Jarvis was sitting in your throne and the queen was in the one that has been empty all these years. Jarvis told me that you were dead and that the aelves were claiming Hope for their own. Of course, I objected. He would not let me speak and simply told me that he was the rightful monarch and that Hope would be an aelven city, as it had been intended all along. He sent me away and told me to convene the Guard the following dawn so that he and Nimevah could inspect the troops.

"In the morning, we lined up and waited. We thought it best to do as they directed, since we did not want to incite them to terrorize the rest of Hope. We stood for a long time and when no one came out from the castle, we sent a messenger in. They had disappeared, Your Grace, as if they had never been here at all! The hole at the bottom of the castle where they had entered through the dungeon was plugged up with solid, impenetrable crystal. There was no sign of the aelves. I have no explanation for it. They were here and gained the upper hand and then they were simply gone."

"How bizarre!" Delilah exclaimed, turning the information over in her head, trying to make sense of it. It was gravely unsettling to know that the Crystal Aelves had been there and had easily occupied Hope. They presumably could do so again at any moment. Despite their current absence, the fact that they had come and chose to leave was almost more distressing than if she had found them still in charge. At least that would be understandable.

"That was about a week ago," Abbowhen said, "and we have lived on-edge since then with the assumption that they could return at any moment. Still, we have been busy accounting for the dead and grieving our lost sisters. We had to begin to put our military back together. With so many holes amongst our ranks, it has been a task for the remaining officers to work together to promote those who were valiant in battle and create new squads. You will be pleased to hear that Batelnut is now a sergeant. She has taken over for... Oravica." Abbowhen seemed reluctant to name the departed woman.

"Yes... Oravica. That was a good choice to replace her with Batelnut, Major. Batel was invaluable to our mission at Crystal Mountain, regardless of the outcome. How is Oravica's wife, Erigail?"

"As would be expected, Your Majesty. Unfortunately, she has much company in her grief. Many have lost spouses, daughters, mothers, sons. There is a community of mourners here in Hope, going through their losses together."

"It would have been more if you had not called the retreat, Major. It was a hard call, yet it was the right one."

"If you had seen the bloodshed... I have no doubt it would have been your call, as well, Majesty."

"And how are our prisoners? Doktora Ishlip and her family members. We must decide what to do about them."

"That… has been decided for us. Yet another strange action on the part of the aelves: the prisoners were killed—all three of them—with throats slit open in that unnerving surgical fashion, unmistakably by aelven swords. They must have done it on their way out through the dungeon. It was a confusing choice. If they were allies, why not take them?"

"While I am not able to say I regret that outcome, it is a puzzle," Delilah said. She had been dreading having to implement the punishment allotted to traitors, which was always death. After so much death, it was a relief that it had been strangely handled for them. "Well, one less thing for us to do," Delilah said.

"Yes, it saves us the trouble," Abbowhen agreed. "We have enough on our conscience."

When the major left, Delilah's mind turned to Oravica. She was overpowered with the realization that she would never be able to talk to her again, to confide in her. She had the distinct sensation of a knife penetrating her heart, could almost feel the shaft protruding from her breastbone. Second to Oravica, in the past she would have gone to Olavfin. No one had told her that Olav had been harmed in Raefenshire, so she assumed he had come back safely. She tried to stand up, however the motion made her dizzy with pain and she fell back upon her bed.

"Can I help you, Your Majesty? Shall I get Helanza for you?" It was a new Guard she did not recognize, a young woman with a long black braid.

"No, thank you. I just thought I could walk for a moment, but I was mistaken," Delilah said.

"We can carry you to your chambers, if you wish, Your Majesty" the young woman said. The earnestness of this young soldier nearly broke Delilah's heart. After all they had gone through, they still loved their queen.

"No, thank you. I will rest here. Can you please get a message to Sergeant Olavfin that I would like to speak to him when he has a moment?"

"Of course, Your Grace."

Helanza came in then and held a bowl of strong-smelling liquid to her mouth. "Drink," she said. Delilah did as she was told, and within minutes, she dozed off.

It was dark when she awoke. The same Guard was at the door. She told Delilah that Olav had come by while she slept and that Helanza had sent him away. Delilah tried to rise, and this time was able to do so with considerable pain in her leg. A large crutch was leaning nearby and Delilah reached for it and hobbled to the door. "Where has Lord Xanfar been staying?" she asked the Guard, who told her how to find the chambers he had taken.

When Delilah knocked at the door, she was surprised to see it opened by an Usiku man. Seeing Delilah, he bowed and motioned for her to come in. Xanfar entered from an adjoining room. "Queen Delilah, I would like you to meet Lord Calliwe," he said. "You are looking much better! You were half-devoured by whayerwolves only two days ago, Your Majesty," he smiled his wolfish grin.

"I would have been more than half-devoured if it were not for you," she said. "Lord

Calliwe, it is an honor to meet you. I regret having pulled your… friend away from your side to rescue me."

"Lord Xanfar is my soul's match. I would have gone with him, yet he insisted on going alone. He is not yet used to being partnered. I, on the other hand, have been partnered for most of my life, so I am not used to being left alone. We each must get used to doing things a little differently now."

"Your soul's match?" Delilah said, looking at Xanfar, who did not object and yet somehow had not informed her of this development on their journey back through the Wood. "I am sorry, Lord Calliwe, does this mean that you lost your mate in the battle at Raefenshire?"

"Yes, Rawelle was lost on the first day of the battle. I fought on, though broken-hearted. When the troops retreated, I went with the others into the Wood. It is there that I met Xan… Lord Xanfar, who had lost his love in battle, too. We had much to console one another about, and our attachment grew from there."

"It is true, Your Majesty. By the time we traveled with the others to Hope, we were very much bonded," Xan said.

"And will you return to Fallengrove with Xanfar?" Delilah wondered out loud how this arrangement would play out.

"Only a few Usiku tribespeople survived the battle. We are only a handful compared to what we once were. There is but a small contingent of Usiku high priestesses and holy people who stayed in the desert in Erithea. There is almost no Usiku nation to return to. Many of us lost our mates and have re-bonded with new partners. I imagine the Usiku tribe will never fully return to their homeland in the desert. We came here together for a noble cause. It was fate that we were diminished in such a way that our tribe will now be dispersed among others. There is a part of me that wishes it were not so, and yet, I have found my love," he said, reaching out to stroke the fur on Xanfar's nape. "I do not wish it any other way. When Xanfar returns to Fallengrove, I shall go with him. My life is with him now."

"And what of your King?" Delilah asked. "He was with us when we escaped from Crystal Mountain, although he was in a compromised condition. I was hopeful that our healers could revive him. Did they?"

"No, I am afraid not," Calliwe said. Delilah's heart hit the floor. "He is still unconscious," the aelf clarified, and Delilah took a shuddering breath. "It is a sleep like death and yet the healers say he is still alive and may awaken in time." Relief washed over Delilah. Calliwe continued, "It is like hibernation, they say, when the organs and blood slow down so much that they are barely perceptible. King Kejanu is still in there, though, slumbering. Hopefully, he will awaken soon."

"What happens if he awakens and wishes to return to the desert? Will the tribe follow him then?" Delilah wanted to know.

"King Kejanu will do what is best for the tribe. I do not believe he will order them to follow him to the desert if they have chosen partners here. He values the sacred union between souls too greatly to separate partners. It is part of our culture and how we are designed. It is unimaginable that he would ask us to betray that."

"I would like to see him," Delilah said.

"I thought you might," Xanfar said.

As they walked to the lazarette, which was only down the hall from where Deliliah herself had been recovering earlier, Delilah asked Xanfar about his newfound love. As cagey as he had been about the topic in the past, he now seemed to have no misgivings about his partnership. He admitted it was an adjustment to have someone following him everywhere, as Calliwe was inclined. Still, there was something comforting about being wanted so completely, he said. Even on this brief walk down the hall, Calliwe had prepared to come along until Xanfar kissed him and said, "I will return in just a moment, my love."

Delilah was skeptical that Xanfar could feel the same about Calliwe as the aelf clearly felt about him. Xanfar did not dispute or dispel her curiosity about it, and simply said that he had fallen in love with Calliwe in a way he had never felt in his long and loyal friendship with Captain Ferrashi. "I did not think I could truly love again after Apple. When I met Calliwe in the forest and we bonded so quickly, at some point, I thought: 'Why fight it? So that I can die alone?' I just gave in to the tide of emotions and let myself have feelings for him. I was still crushed about Ferrashi, just as Calliwe was mourning his love, Rawelle. It was something different that did not erase our attachment to those who died. It instead just became what it is: love between two beings."

"I am happy for you, Xan. It is just a little surprising. I was accustomed to thinking of you as an eternal bachelor."

"You are just jealous that you could not win this big hairy prize first," he said, gesturing down at himself in all his wolfiness. If she had been more stable on her feet, she probably would have jabbed him. After walking through the castle for what seemed like ages, they finally got to the door. Xanfar warned, "This might be upsetting."

Delilah did not expect her heart to jump upon seeing Kejanu lying upon the cot, still as marble. He truly looked dead, as when he had been freed from the tomb within the Crystal Mountain. Delilah walked over and reached out her hand to feel his skin. It was cool, like that of a cadaver. Although he was probably not aware of her touch, she worried she was being intrusive and pulled her hand back. Helanza walked in and came to the other side of the cot to drip a few small spoonsful of a thin syrup into Kejanu's mouth. "He does not need much now," she said.

"Is this typical for aelves?" Delilah asked, "Can they all go into this kind of hibernation?"

"Only in extreme circumstances. I have only seen it once before," the healer said. "It was in a half-aelf who was beaten mercilessly within an inch of his life. He went into such a sleep. I fed him for three moons, secretly, until he recovered. Even afterward he would sometimes go into a trance-like state for days at a time. He became a great writer, though, and would awaken from his trances to write long scrolls and epic poems."

"Are you speaking of Gravenwell?" Delilah asked.

"Yes, but how did you know that?" The healer looked at her with curiosity.

"I stayed with him in Yonderlot for a few days. He told me about the secret society of half-aelves that existed in Hope so many years ago. In fact, he told me you would be able to tell me more about it."

"You have seen Gravenwell?" she exclaimed. "Recently?"

"Why, just a few days ago. I left him at the tower where he had been a most gracious host to me. At least I think it was a few days ago. My journey through the Whayer Wood and my injury have made my recollection of time a little fuzzy."

"Your Majesty, how did you come to be there? How is Gravenwell?" Helanza's typical reserved demeanor had vanished. She seemed more youthful and eager than Delilah had ever seen her.

"I was carried there by someone Gravenwell said was an aelf. I thought it was a unicorn, at first, and then I also suspected it may have been my brother. Why Gravenwell would think my brother was an aelf is beyond me. To answer your other question, Gravenwell is quite well. His beard is longer and he may be even lonelier than when he was a prisoner here, however he hopes to join his kin in Winnawater, that is, once another Keeper of the Tower appears." Delilah saw Helanza nodding with understanding as she relayed each piece of the strange information that should have left her as confused as it had made Delilah.

"Yes, that makes sense. It makes sense that Gravenwell would not know Jarvis, as he was imprisoned long before you both were born. Never meeting him, Gravenwell would have clearly identified Jarvis as an aelf as opposed to a human. Half-aelves are able to recognize others with aelven blood even when they have no outward aelven attributes."

"Aelven blood? Jarvis does not have aelven blood, though. Wait a second. I need to sit down," Delilah had reached the end of her endurance.

Xanfar, who had still been waiting by the door, ran to pull a chair up to the queen and brought around a second for Helanza. "You will forgive me if I must go. I am sure you will fill me in later," said Xan, and rushed off before either of the women could object.

"But he was half-aelf, Majesty. You need this information now. Before it would not have helped you. The King, your father, was not Jarvis' father. It was never known publicly and your mother worked to keep it a secret. The truth is that when your father came from the Bedooin lands across the sea to marry your mother, he brought with him his close friend: an Usiku noble and advisor, Lord Radyu. Your mother fell in love with Radyu, and he bonded with her instantly, as I am sure you have seen the Dusk Aelves do by now."

"A mate of souls," Delilah said.

"Yes, and neither of them could resist it. Despite Radyu's loyalty to your father, and despite your mother, Queen Zaryadne, being promised to someone else, their love bloomed. Zaryadne and Radyu made their connection instantly and consummated their love. It was like moths to a flame. They could not fight their attraction, despite it being wrong. In an act of honor to his friend, the king, and to the human woman whose marriage he jeopardized, Radyu self-immolated to protect them all. It was devastating to your mother and father both, as Radyu was a dear friend as well as an ally and advisor to the king. The marriage between your mother and father happened shortly after. Your father agreed to keep Zaryadne's secret and raise the child as his heir.

"As a Bedooin, your father was dark," Helanza explained, "and as a Dusk Aelf, so was Radyu. When Jarvis was born, no one suspected. Jarvis had a complexion similar enough to your father and no visible aelven features, so Zaryadne and Radyu's secret was preserved. It got back to Jarvis at some point who his real father was, though. This is why he became so obsessed with aelves and began to plot with the aelves to take over Hope."

"If what Jarvis says is true, my parents were going to throw him over the cliff to sacrifice him," Delilah said, "so in that way, I can see why he wanted to defend himself."

"Yes, this is true. It broke your mother's heart, yet it was well-understood that the Ancestors demanded this blood sacrifice to preserve the Vector. The legend went that the firstborn child of the monarch would need to be sacrificed when the Vector began to fail." Helanza looked saddened to recall this time.

"Helanza, please tell me: how is it that you know so much about all of this? I know you were my mother's personal healer. It was one of the reasons I trusted you when others were eliminated in... the Purge. How did you come to know these secrets?"

"I knew firsthand from your mother. She told me she was in love and had secretly given herself to Radyu. I knew she was with child even before she knew it herself. And, I knew it because I am half-aelf so if there had been any doubt about Jarvis' parentage, I would have been able to tell upon his birth that he was not a fully human child."

"You are half-aelf? Why did you never tell me?"

"You never asked. Although I am surprised you could not tell, with your new aelven accessory!" she said, gesturing to Delilah's ear.

"Oh yes, that. A gift from my half-aelf brother, apparently," Delilah said and shook her head.

"It will be as a gift, I am certain, although it may not seem so now," said the healer.

"From what I am hearing, it seems there is no doubt that Jarvis is part aelven. It seems all of Hope must have been crawling with half-aelves in the past!" Delilah exclaimed.

"No, not crawling. There were not many of us, yet we all knew each other and protected one another's secrets. Gravenwell's heritage was not a secret because his father had married his aelf mother. That made him more of a target because everyone knew what he was. They expected him to conspire and perform profane magick. Gravenwell and I are around the same age and were playmates. Before Gravenwell's mother was sent away, she told us stories that allowed me to figure out who my father was. Before the Gloom, travel between the regions was much less restricted. My father was an emissary from Winnawater that had come with a group of aelves to form alliances with those of Hope. Gravenwell's mother had been part of that mission and had stayed behind to marry her human lover. Apparently, there were several children born from that peacekeeping mission. My mother was the court healer, and she had worked closely with an aelven cleric from Winnawater. She never told me who my father was or that I was half-aelf, but Gravenwell's mother told me. I never confronted my mother about it. I let her keep her secret and learned all I could from her about herbalism and the spirits of plants. She died when I was not much more than a girl. Still, I was so advanced in my studies by then that I was able to walk right into her role as court healer, which I have been ever since."

Queen Delilah and the Encroaching Gloom

"But that was over 100 years ago!" Delilah said. It had never occurred to her that Helanza, whom she had known since she was a child, had never seemed to age.

"It is my aelven lineage that keeps me looking youthful," Helanza said. "It is not so for every half-aelf."

"Gravenwell says he was blessed with a long life, yet has looked old for most of it."

"It is true. He grew old while I stayed looking young, although we are the same age. I am pleased to hear my friend still lives and is safe, if trapped in a commitment as a Tower Keeper."

"Better to be a Tower Keeper than an eternal prisoner in a dungeon," Delilah said.

"It was how I knew you would be a good leader," Helanza admitted. "Although you were misled into killing some of the elite people who had surrounded your mother, most of them were corrupt anyway, so I did not mourn them. Yet you were a compassionate enough queen to set an old man free."

"And why did you not tell me about Jarvis' heritage before now? You have had my trust for fifteen years. Was it not something that you thought I should know?"

"Like you, I thought Jarvis had died. When I learned that he was still living, I watched and waited to see how this would evolve to implicate you. My goal has always been to protect you, Your Majesty. If I felt it would have helped you to know the truth about your brother, I would have shared it with you before. At the time you found out that he was alive and wanted to take over Hope, I felt you needed all your strength to wage war. It would not have helped to have the complicated piece of information about his lineage."

"I am always amazed when people think they are protecting me by shielding me from the truth," Delilah said.

"Since Gravenwell left Hope, I have kept my own counsel, Majesty. I have no friends. I have lived only in service to you while trying to remain true to myself. I assure you that I make my decisions with my inner compass guiding me and with loyalty to you foremost in mind."

"I am thankful for that, Helanza. It is just that I was so lost all those years. I took leadership because no one was left to do so. I may have made different decisions if I had known Jarvis was half-aelf. Ultimately, it does not change anything. It just fills in some of the missing pieces from the story. For one, it explains his allegiance to the aelves and their acceptance of him."

"Zsezskili du shlekven."

The voice seemed to come from thin air and it took a moment for Delilah and the healer to realize that Kejanu had spoken. They looked down and yet Kejanu appeared the same, embodying stonelike death.

"He does that sometimes," Helanza said.

"What does it mean?" Delilah asked.

"It is not traditional aelvish, more of an obscure dialect," Helanza said. "The closest translation, I think, would be: 'The Seven Goddesses of Death.'"

Deliliah shivered. "What could that mean?" she asked.

"I do not know, Your Majesty, but it does not sound good."

Delilah took her crutch and slowly walked to the barracks to find Olav. The grounds were empty compared to how they usually were. Even so, everyone she passed bowed and smiled, wishing her adoring greetings. She was used to being honored, yet now the soldiers' exaltations seemed even more heartfelt, as if the losses they shared enhanced their loyalty. She heard the ground pounding behind her and felt herself being lifted into the air.

"Ly-la!" Ook yelled, swinging her and hugging her close to his chest.

"Ook I am injured!" she shouted, her body crushed in his embrace. "Please be gentle."

"Sorr-ee, Ly-la," Ook said, putting her down.

"I am happy to see you, too," she said, reaching up to put a hand on his beefy shoulder and stopping when she saw the bandage where his arm had been repaired. "What have you been up to? Where are you staying?"

Ook pointed to one of the dormitories. "Ook Guard!" he said.

"You are officially one of the Guard now?" she asked, pleased that someone had thought to formally enlist him.

"Ook is one of our most valuable soldiers," Batelnut walked up and bowed to Delilah, who pulled the young woman up and hugged her. Batel seemed surprised to be embraced by her queen, yet hugged her back.

"I hear congratulations are in order, Sergeant," Delilah said.

"Yes," the soldier said, and colored. "One of my first acts as an officer was to make sure Ook was inducted into the Guard. He is part of my unit now," she said, reaching up to scratch Ook behind the ear. The ogred glowed.

"Lucky for you to have such a strong and loyal ogred on your team," Delilah praised, and now Ook blushed. The pair of them looked so young and bashful, Delilah thought. If she had not seen them at their fiercest, it would be hard to believe they had it in them to be ruthless soldiers. "I am glad you are both here. I was not able to properly thank you for your help on our mission and in escaping the Crystal Mountain."

"You were not able to thank us because you fell into the Whayer Wood," Batel said. "We were quite sure you must have died or at least must have been distorted by the Gloom. Although you do seem different somehow," the Guardswoman looked Delilah over and her eyes landed on her pointed ear. "Well, that is new, is it not?"

"Yes, I am afraid so."

Ook and Batel accompanied Delilah to find Olav. Delilah and Olav had only just begun conversing and Delilah was reassured that he was in good health when their conversation was interrupted by Doktora Chastice coming to the door. "Queen Delilah, you are needed in Verily," she said.

"Right now?" Delilah asked.

"Yes, you were summoned," the elder said and turned, expecting to be followed.

"In what kind of queendom does the Chief Scientist summon the Queen and not the other way around?" Delilah grumbled, and made a grimace of pain as she stood upon her bum leg. "Honestly, Doktora, I may not be able to make it," Delilah called after Chastice.

"Let me get Sethran," Batelnut said, and avoided Delilah's questioning look. "He is back at my quarters. I am sure he will be most happy to deliver you to Verily."

Batel's golden Centauri suitor arrived within minutes, looking as robust and gallant as ever. Ook helped Delilah onto the centaur's back. Then they were both blindfolded to be led by Doktora Chastice, who admonished Sethran not to squash her feet with his big hooves. Inside the entrance to the tunnel, Chastice removed their blindfolds and disappeared. The centaur trotted through the passageway to Verily in a fraction of the time Delilah could have walked even on a good day.

"Delilah!" Ilvana's shouts greeted her the moment they crossed the threshold and helped Delilah disembark. "You are safe!" Ilvana threw her arms around Delilah. They embraced and as the doctor pulled away, she reached out to touch Delilah's ear. "This is an interesting development!" she observed, checking Delilah's other ear to see if they were balanced or if only one had changed.

"I missed talking to you through the Nearth," Delilah confessed, as she had grown so used to speaking to Ilvana every day when they could use their crystals.

"That is why I asked you here!" Ilvana said, and pulled Delilah by the arm toward the Observatory.

"I shall be back in a bit," Delilah said to Sethran, who was already busily chatting with a few robust young monks who did not get to meet centaurs every day.

"I found a way to make our communications confidential," Ilvana said. "It is called a 'blocking stone' and it stops others from being able to listen to our transmissions. It is secure from one end to the other by transmuting the messages into something indecipherable to anyone who happens to hear them. Only those who are intended to receive the messages are able to understand what is being said. To anyone else, it sounds like crunching up parchment."

"How wonderful! I was worried we could never use the technology again safely," Delilah admitted. "It seemed like such a waste of all of our efforts to have it compromised and rendered useless."

"Those insidious aelves figured out how to tap into our Link. I should have anticipated it, really. I feel silly for not realizing they would be able to, with their sophisticated connections to the natural world. They are practically trees themselves, you might say."

"Trees that can kill," Delilah offered.

"Yes, I am sorry for that. I know you are probably feeling horrible after our defeat. It was not the way we planned for it to go," Ilvana shook her head.

"We knew the risks. I was too confident, though. I thought with the help of the pirates and centaurs, and definitely the Usiku, that we would prevail. Our allies took the hardest hits. The poor Usiku: their kind have been made practically extinct from that single battle."

"I hear their king is still in deathlike sleep?" Ilvana asked. "Do you think he will awaken?"

"No one can tell," Delilah said. She was tempted to tell Ilvana about the connection she had felt between them, yet unable to give voice to that while his status seemed so precarious. Maybe she would tell her about it if he awoke.

"Give me your hand," Ilvana said. They were standing at a table where Ilvana had laid out some sharp instruments.

"I guess I have no choice?" Delilah asked and held her crystal hand out to the scientist, who briskly wiped Delilah's palm with some strong liquid and sliced a small hole in the middle of the five crystals. Delilah sucked in her breath and looked away as Ilvana picked up a small dark stone with thin tweezers and tucked it under the flap of skin. The doctor stitched a few small loops of thread to hold the crystal in place.

"Not so bad, ay?" Ilvana asked and Delilah nodded and wiped the tears that had involuntarily come to her eyes from the procedure. "Mine has healed quite well already," she said, and showed Delilah where the dark spot of the crystal showed through her skin in the middle of her own palm. "I tested it out on Aaranon first," she said, and giggled.

Aaranon, as if on cue, entered the room carrying a tray of tea for them. "So nice to see you, Aaranon," Delilah said, and he bowed to her in greeting and left quickly.

"He is a little grumpy since I made him get the new crystal installed," Ilvana said. "We have had good results so far. I feel confident that the communications are private with the blocking device. I have sent our allies instructions to remedy the flaw in the design. We have tested it and actively had others try to intercept the messages. Once there is the blocking stone, no one can pick up on what is being relayed. We can finally use our crystals again!"

"Excellent work, Ilvana! Now I can call you with my crystals just to complain about my soup, like I used to," Delilah said.

"And the cook will not be able to intercept the message and get insulted!" Ilvana laughed. "Let us not wait until we are apart to talk, though," said the doctor. "I am eager to hear how the battle went for you... especially where you were in the time you were missing."

"And I am eager to hear what you know about the history of aelves in Hope," Delilah said.

"I thought you would never ask," said the scientist.

On the journey back through the tunnel, Delilah's mind was full of the information Doktora Ilvana had shared with her. It astounded her that there were so many secrets within Hope. The clandestine society of half-aelves was one of them. "Please do not tell me you are a half-aelf, too!" Delilah had exclaimed when Ilvana began sharing what she knew. The doctor laughed and reassured Delilah that she was certainly of a different sort, but had no aelven blood. However, she did know an extraordinary amount about the aelves in Hope that had remained underground, as many of them had made it to Verily for training. A few still lived among them, and some were dispersed into the populace of Hope. Ilvana calculated that with all the half-aelves who had stayed in Hope and had children, and then their children who had children, there were probably dozens of Hope's citizens who were a small part aelf, even if they did not know it.

Ilvana was intrigued to hear Delilah's account of the battles and the adventures she encountered after leaving the land of the aelves, including how she had gotten her irregular ear. Delilah had trouble thinking of it as anything but a deformity. The doctor was excited that Delilah seemed to have acquired some sharper senses. She wondered what other kinds of skills might be in store for Delilah in her future. Delilah proclaimed that she just wanted her old ear back, and could not see it in a positive light even if it came with enhanced senses.

Ilvana gave some insight into the meaning of the Seven Goddesses of Death. "In an old aelven legend," the scientist explained, "there are seven sisters who rule over death. A weaver learns that one of the goddesses is coming for her, so she finds a way to trick the goddess into taking a cow instead. In doing so, she unleashes a ripple effect of unintended consequences that impacts all she holds dear. The Seven Goddesses of Death became a metaphor for the consequences of actions that one does not anticipate. There is a rippling out of the small and larger impacts of those decisions that end up leading to strange and unexpected results that no one can predict." This description puzzled Delilah more than when she had thought it might refer to actual goddesses who were coming to impose death on her or others. Ilvana's interpretation did not answer any questions for her and only raised more.

By the time Delilah got back to the castle, she was tired and her body hurt from being jostled on the centaur, walking, and standing more than she should have. She asked for Helanza to send something up to help her sleep. The healer delivered the medicine herself. "You have had a long day, Your Majesty," Helanza observed, handing her the bowl of strong tea. Delilah nodded and thanked her before retiring to her bed, but only after retrieving the strange words Gravenwell had written on parchment that she had carried with her through the Whayer Wood. Helanza clutched the writing to her chest and ran from the room like a young lass. It did not take long for sleep to shroud Delilah's mind after the healer left.

Delilah heard her name being called. It was far away and she sat up in bed, trying to figure out where it was coming from. She stood up, wrapping a cloak around herself. Her feet got tangled in the fabric and she tripped and fell, her hands going right through the wall! She was dissolving through the stone, pulled by a force that felt like falling. She moved through each chamber as she passed the sleeping occupants, who did not stir. She fell down through floors and closed doors and into the lazarette, where she hung suspended, unable to make her body turn in any direction. Kejanu was lying there, as he had been that morning. Except now he had a rosier glow about his dusky skin and a thin halo of light emitting from his whole body, outlining him in the dark.

Delilah heard Kejanu speak her name, though his lips did not move. "I am right here," he said and his heart lit up. She could see the glowing red light through his skin, his heart pulsing with burgundy radiance. She could hear her own heart beating amplified in her ears, and felt blood racing through her body. Now she gained control of her movement and levitated above Kejanu. She hovered over his angelic face. It had none of the hardness she had seen at other times. There was only tranquility in his expression. She reached out and placed her right hand on his chest, just over his glowing heart. She felt its rhythm beneath her palm, forming a loop of energy that coursed through her hand, up her arm, and into her own heart and back again.

"I am here, Kejanu," she heard herself say, though her mouth had not moved. "I have always been here," she said. Kejanu opened his eyes and looked up lovingly into hers. He smiled the most grateful and tender smile.

Birds were chirping relentlessly. Delilah opened her eyes to see the bright light of morning spilling in her window. The dream had felt so real! She got up and dressed as quickly as she could while favoring her injuries, which seemed worse today than yesterday, most likely from the extra exertion. She went out to the hall and the Guard there greeted her: "Good morning, Your Majesty. You are looking rested!" She bowed her head in acknowledgment and went to pass the woman. "You are wanted in the lazarette, Your Grace," the Guard said, and Delilah stopped in mid-step.

"What? Why is that?" she asked.

"The Usiku King has woken."

Delilah rushed down to the ward, leaning heavily on the crutch, but the cot was empty. She tried the chambers next door where Helanza performed most of her healing arts. As Delilah walked in, her heart nearly stopped in her chest to see Kejanu sitting up, laughing and smiling. He was eating thin porridge as Helanza ground herbs in a mortar. Kejanu's face lit up to see her. His smile was the same serene look he had on his face in the dream. She intuitively understood that he had experienced the same vision, dream, or astral projection that she had. Whatever it was, they had shared it.

"Your Majesty," he said, trying to stand to bow, yet teetering weakly.

Delilah ran to him, dropping her cane in the process, and helped him sit. "Please, do not trouble yourself," she said. Her hand on his arm felt burning hot. She pulled away, embarrassed that she had touched him, yet he did not seem to mind. He looked up at her from his seat with such a joyful expression, it took her off guard. It was such a contrast to his vast seriousness before the war. "Your patient is looking much livelier today, Helanza," she observed. The healer nodded and smiled. "Your Majesty," Delilah spoke to the king, "I am sure you are aware of the losses to your army." She pulled up a chair beside him.

"Yes, I am aware," he said. His expression did not falter. He still looked calm and relaxed.

"I was so distressed to hear about the devastation," Delilah said.

"I appreciate your compassion, although death is different for the Usiku," Kejanu said. "We do not fear it as humans do. We know we go back to the earth and are cycled again through life in another form, so it is not such a tragedy."

"Is that so?" Delilah asked, wondering what he knew about the afterlife that gave him such easement.

"I learned much in my recent dormant state," Kejanu said. "I left the shell of my body to assist my people. I was able to travel with the fallen to accompany them into their next incarnations. I comforted them as we voyaged. We went around the world, through stars, and under the ground or ocean at times. I kept fellowship with each Usiku soul as it was pulled into its next life. I take comfort that I was able to make that journey with them as their king, to lead them to their next earthly forms. A few remained in spirit form, or merged with tree spirits or other lifeforms. They are all safe, though," he asserted. "I have no regrets."

"I am heartened to hear that," Delilah said, "but your whole culture, your entire people have been largely wiped out. Are there more Usiku in other realms?"

"There are a few Usiku shamans left in the desert land. There are other aelves like the

Queen Delilah and the Encroaching Gloom

Dusk Aelves, yet none exactly the same. Of the countless races of aelves, we are but one. Ultimately, none of us are any different. In spirit, we are not largely different from humans or beasts. Still, the Usiku are a unique persuasion."

"Yes, I have not heard of any like the Dusk Aelves. I mourn for your lost culture."

"We are not lost, Queen Delilah, and there is no call to mourn. There are many who remain, and each one is bringing our culture to their new homes, their new partnerships. It is like the seeds that scatter when the blossom dies, and dries, and blows in the wind. We are spreading differently now. You will be happy to know that some of the lost Usiku are already growing in new wombs: their essence will not be lost."

"That is reassuring," Delilah said. She could not help feeling wary of Kejanu's absent grief and considered that perhaps he was in shock.

"We think of death differently than you," Kejanu said, as if reading her mind. "It is why when one partner of a linked soul dies, we can bond so quickly with another. We know the soul is eternal. We never quite lose our love. We simply spin around and blend with others until we die and are reunited with them again in another place and time."

It had troubled Delilah that the Dusk Aelves could connect so quickly with a new being after the death of a mate, especially when they seemed to have such an intimate soul-connection. Still, it was probably much more practical than human grieving. She had to admit that in many ways the aelves were more sophisticated in their emotional makeup and their approach to life than humans. "I wish humans could let go of those we care for so easily," Delilah said. "I mourn for every soldier we lost."

"It is not that we let go of those we love," Kejanu corrected. "It is that we know that they are not truly lost and that we will meet again."

"And if there are so many that one could love, I wonder about those who do not find love early in life? If they can love anyone, why do they not find someone to love early on?"

"Some hearts are only unlocked by their true mate. I did not find love early on because my heart was waiting for you, My Queen." He said this while looking intently at her, directly into her eyes. Delilah glanced at Helanza who was busy pretending not to hear their conversation. "My heart was waiting for you my whole life," Kejanu continued. "My heart was waiting for you while I slept until you came to retrieve me. You have carried me in your heart as I have carried you in mine."

Despite Delilah being drawn to this beautiful aelf, something about the finality of what he was saying made her uncomfortable. She could not find a way to respond to him, so she looked down at her hands. "I am unsure how to take this profession, Your Majesty," she finally said.

"You will grow to understand it," Kejanu said. "Your heart will teach you."

She glanced up into his sincere eyes and wanted to love him if only because he seemed so confident. Instead, she got up and struggled to pick up her crutch. "I must go see to the Guard," Delilah said. "Please excuse me," and she turned and limped as quickly as she could out of the healer's chambers. She chastised herself as she walked through the halls and out the far entrance to the courtyards toward the barracks. Most recently she had regretted that she had not partnered and had children early in life and worried that she might die alone with no heirs. Now that there was one who, in all appearances, might be the love of her life, she could not get away fast enough. "I must be the stupidest queen alive," she berated herself.

Taking a sharp right, she left the path toward the barracks and went out to the orchards instead. She needed to be around trees, to breathe fresh air. With her newly shaped ear, being in the orchard made her tingle all over, as if she could feel the breeze in her own branches and feel their petals as part of her skin. She yearned for the wisdom of the forest. Aumenveill came into her mind and she realized it had been ages since she had spoken with him. She approached a cherry tree and placed her crystal hand on it. The stitch above the black stone was still quite tender. She put her hand gently on the trunk and invoked the old tree spirit in the Fallengrove forest.

"Queen Delilah," she heard Aumenveill's silken-gruffly voice address her.

"Great One, Aumenveill, I am relieved to hear your voice," she admitted. It was like a salve to her troubled soul.

"You did not think I was gone, did you? We tree-beings live for a long time. I am not going anywhere soon. You, on the other branch, have a fleeting human life, like that of a stablefly."

She laughed, in spite of herself. "It is true. We have barely any time to get anything done at all," she said.

"And yet, you are different now, are you not, my child? Have you not been touched by the aelves?" he asked.

"I believe so. I am not sure what it means, but my ear was cut by an aelven blade, and now it grows in a pointed form. It is quite disconcerting," Delilah said.

"Yet brings with it so many possibilities," Aumenveill mused.

"What does it bring? I am unable to get any clear answers about that," Delilah said, frustrated in the changes that had been imposed upon her.

"For one, you are probably more sensitive to the living things around you. You may have heightened senses, better reflexes, greater strength. For another, you may even have a longer life. It is a gift," the tree concluded.

"It does not feel like a gift. It was given to me without my consent," she pouted. "Why would someone choose to do this to me?" she asked, wanting to understand.

"Wait a moment, I will find out," Aumenveill said and went completely silent. Delilah shuffled and wondered just how and who he was plying for information and how far his connections reached. There were several long minutes where Delilah began to get restless and believed Aumenveill might not be returning at all. Then, his voice emerged. "Yes, it is a gift," he proclaimed.

"How is that?" she asked.

"You were marked as belonging to the aelves," the old tree said.

This did not appeal to Delilah. "I am not thrilled about the idea of belonging to anyone, much less the aelves who decimated my allies and a large part of my own army," Delilah said.

"No, you misunderstand," Aumenveill said. "It is a way of claiming you as one of their own, invoking the sacred authority of the aelves to legitimize you."

"Legitimize? I am legitimate. I am the legitimate heir to the Hope throne," she felt annoyed by the insinuation that she was somehow not authorized to rule.

"Again, you misunderstand, my child. Listen with your heart and your aelven ear, not with your human ear. You are sanctioned by the aelves to rule," he said.

This struck Delilah. Had Jarvis somehow given up his claim to the throne? She thought about how he and the aelven queen had come into the castle, taken up residence briefly, then vanished without explanation. "Aumenveill, do you know if my brother has given up his claim to rule Hope?

"It is not that simple," the tree said. "You may not like to hear this, but he is the rightful heir in more ways than one. What he has done is allowed you the authority to rule as an aelven queen on behalf of the aelves. He has not abandoned his claim: he has simply given you sacred aelven blood to verify that you are also permitted to rule."

"Well, how nice of him to give me permission," she said.

"Do not brush this off, Delilah. It is truly a blessing," Aumenveill said. "As is the aelven king who offers his heart to you. One thing I have learned in my very long life is that it is not wise to spurn the blessings offered to you by an aelf."

Delilah started at this statement, then realized how terrified she was. "I am scared, Aumenveill. I have grown used to being on my own with no family for half of my life. Now it seems the family I have is not what I thought it was. To be claimed by my brother and claimed by aelves is… too much!" Delilah began to cry. All the feelings she had purposefully tucked away over the last weeks bubbled over. The sobs coming up in her chest were foreign and painful, as if she was being physically tortured. Still, they came, great convulsions wracking her chest. A wail that she tried to subvert escaped her lips as the tears flowed down. She watched the water from her eyes fall to the earth, as if it were an alien substance that could not possibly belong to her.

The tiny droplets sat upon the surface of the ground and then sunk in quick gurgles below the soil. Within moments, small green shoots emerged from where her tears had fallen. Tiny white and blue blossoms appeared at the end of the curling wands of green spiraling from the ground. "You are blessed, Delilah," she heard Aumenveill's voice saying, and she was overcome with drowsiness. She lay down, still crying, and fell almost instantly into a deep sleep, her head among the flowers.

When she awoke, the sun was still high in the sky. She reached for her cane and strangely, did not feel the pain in her leg anymore. She pulled up her legging and was dumbstruck to see that the giant gouges in her skin, which had been puckered red and oozing, had completely disappeared! She stood up and looked down into the neck of her tunic to see that the wounds on her shoulder and arm were also gone. Her pointed ear was humming and vibrating, as if it were a separate lifeform attached to the side of her head. She shook her head and the vibration slowed and ceased. The small field of flowers that she had somehow manifested with her tears was alive. The blossoms were reaching up to the light, quivering with excitement.

What a strange day! Delilah thought. Just then, a disturbing sight caught her eye. It was the Vector at the far edge of the orchard. Whereas she had sometimes seen it flicker and jump, now it was bending, thinning, and even tearing in some places. At the edge of the Whayer Wood, small lacerations were forming and the dusky hue of the Gloom drifted through in wisps coming into Hope! Without thinking, Delilah grabbed the trunk of the cherry tree and sounded an alarm, summoning Xanfar, Ilvana, and Abbowhen: "We need to gather now! The Vector is failing! The Gloom is going to overtake Hope!"

"When the world goes awry and is filled with doom
We waver, worry, and assume
That our lives will falter, and fail to bloom
In a sad, silly world, filled only with Gloom."
-The Ghost Scribe

Chapter 13: The Seven Goddesses of Death

Ilvana had told Delilah that she was working on something to repair the Vector and should know within a few hours if she had a solution.

"I have no firstborn child to sacrifice, so that is not an option," Delilah had joked when she spoke to the scientist. In contrast to the regrets that Delilah had recently harbored about not having children, she now felt great relief that she was not faced with the impossible choice, as her mother must have been, to save her city or to save her own child. Delilah had relayed Jarvis' assertion that the aelves could find an alternative to repairing the Vector that would not require the sacrifice of a firstborn royal child. With this in mind, Ilvana had requested that any Usiku tribespeople, as well as any healers or shamans with aelven blood, should be sent to Verily. Kejanu helped to spread the word for those to be delivered by Doktora Chastice to the entrance to the tunnel of the hidden realm. Helanza was also summoned to Verily to assist the Doktora.

The Vector continued bulging and faltering in a way that was now obvious to everyone: occasional creaks, crackles, and rubbing sounds were heard echoing from the fringes of Hope, putting the whole city's nerves on edge. At the apex of the Vector, the bubble dissolved into the atmosphere so that if one looked up on a regular day, they would not even notice that there was anything between them and the sky. The clouds floated along with no mind to the sphere that contained Hope. If one did not know it was there, they would probably not even be able to detect its perimeter. In the odd refraction of light, or sometimes at the very edge, by the docks or in the orchards, you could see a little bend of light like a reflection off a piece of glass. Now, the perforations in the Vector looked like hot sugar when it melted and pulled apart, small holes and punctures making its contours visible to the naked eye. Rather than vanishing into the sky, the Vector stood out. It gave one the impression that they were trapped in an aquarium that was melting. Even though most of the residents of Hope had never left the city, they suddenly felt restless and constrained.

Now that her wounds were healed, Delilah decided to go out and greet her people, to reassure them, and to pay respects to their dead. Before the battle, she had been limited in where she went, as she had Guard following her everywhere. Now, she insisted upon going alone, although Abbowhen warned against it. She pretended not to notice the Guard who were secretly trailing her, showing up in the market or hiding down an alleyway. It was not a terrible thing to have people watching out for you, Delilah decided. She had enough surprises over the last few months that she knew feeling safe did not necessarily mean that one was safe.

She knocked on the door of Erigail's house. She was dreading seeing Oravica's wife, but when the woman opened the door and hugged her warmly, she knew she should have come sooner. "She loved you, you know," Erigail said.

"She loved *you*," Delilah said.

"Yes, but she loved you with her life. She would have given her life for you a thousand times over. She would have been annoyed that she only got to do it once."

"I wish she had not had to do it at all," Delilah said. "She died trying to save me."

"Of course she did," Erigail said.

"Do you know that when the Dusk Aelves lose a mate, they bond again quickly to a new partner?" Delilah did not know why she was telling the widow this; it was still kicking around, foremost in her mind.

"I have heard this about the ones who have returned from Raefenshire with the Guard. I know they are our allies now," Erigail said, "and yet I find that barbaric. How could one go from loving their spouse with all their heart and then just turn around and love another? I find it lacking humanity."

"They are not human, so I suppose that is appropriate," the queen contended. "I was thinking, though, that it might be a smarter way to grieve. Would it not be astounding to be so at peace with the loss of your wife that you could fall in love instantly with another? There is something primal about it, lacking the normal emotions we associate with mammalian love. Perhaps that is more adaptive; a better way to survive the harrows of the world."

"I do not want to adapt!" Erigail shouted. "I want Oravica back! I want her and I can never have her again, and I will spend the rest of my life wanting her!" Erigail broke down in tears and buried her head in Delilah's shoulder. The queen held her friend's wife and stroked her hair.

"I want her back, too," Delilah admitted. "A queen has few true friends, and she was my best."

Erigail sobbed deeply then took a few shuddering breaths. "If giving her life helped to save you, I know she would be satisfied," she said, stepping back from their embrace with a small strained smile to wipe her tears on her apron.

Delilah did not have the heart to tell Erigail otherwise. As she walked away from the widow's lonely cottage, nodding to passersby, she was overcome with the utter pointlessness of Oravica's death. It had not prevented Delilah from being captured and it did not help them to win the war. It was just a waste of a good life. She was filled with shame that Oravica had died for no reason. The burden of that inhabited her whole mind and sat on her chest, inhibiting her breathing. She remembered the turning point: the point at which all went to hell for them when she reached for the onyx skull, before she knew the statue was Jarvis, before she knew her allies were being systematically slaughtered on the battlefield. It was as if in the moment she had reached for the skull, the world had shifted and all went in the wrong direction. Until that point, she had been so certain of their conquest. She believed fully that she would get the skull, the Crystal Aelves would lose their power, her soldiers would prevail, and she would save Hope.

Then everything changed. Delilah sharply recalled the second that she opened her eyes as she reached for the relic and saw her brother's hateful eyes looking back at her. It had all turned when she had reached for the skull. The skull! Delilah spun around and almost knocked over a woman behind her carrying a basket of bread on her head. "Excuse me! I am very sorry," she said and rushed back in the direction of the castle. Outside of the castle walls were two giant pinwheel shoak trees that were probably at least 300 years old. Unable to wait until she was in the privacy of her own garden, she placed her hand on the tree to the left and summoned Ilvana.

"What is it, Your Majesty? We are quite busy at work here," said the Doktora.

"Yes, I am sorry for the intrusion. I need to ask Helanza something. It could be important."

"Well go ahead and ask her, she needs no stones for you to speak to her."

"Helanza?" Delilah had not ever tried to reach the healer through her stones.

"Yes?"

"Jarvis' father, Radyu?"

"Yes?"

"When he self-immolated, did he leave anything?"

"Like?"

"Like a relic. Other aelves have been able to crystallize their skull, which has become a source of power for their descendants. Did Radyu leave his skull as a totem?"

"It is possible. And if so, I would guess it would be your mother who kept it," Helanza said.

"Where might she have kept it? The Dusk Aelf skull that we found in the treasure room was from a different aelf, I am sure of it. My mother would not have put her lover's skull in with a pile of treasure," Delilah reasoned.

"No, she would have kept it close to her, someplace secret and near to her. Delilah, if we do find Radyu's skull, that could help us enormously here."

Delilah knew exactly where to look. Leaving the shoak, after thanking the tree spirit within, she rushed up to her own chambers. This had been her mother's bower when she had been queen: a private place where not even the king was allowed. The bed in Delilah's quarters had been her mother's, and it was where both Jarvis and Delilah had been born. Delilah had never had reason to change the furnishings or move the bed. However, now she used all her strength to shove the heavy carved frame inch by inch, scraping over the stone. As she suspected, right below her bed, an irregular shaped stone was set into the floor. With the edge of a fire poker from her mantle, Delilah wedged the stone up until she could lift it from its resting place. A piece of blue silk was bundled in the hole. Delilah lifted it carefully, knowing what it would contain. She was filled with awe when she unwrapped the stone, which was a deep midnight blue with sparkles like stars throughout its form, containing swirling dervishes like galaxies. There was no doubt that it was Radyu's skull. Queen Zaryadne had kept it close to her all those years, right under her own heart.

Delilah had Abbowhen send the skull, carefully packed in a chest, to Verily with a fast rider. Delilah hoped it would be the solution Ilvana and the aelves needed. She wanted to go to Verily to help, yet felt she would just be in the way. She suspected she would feel out of place among all the aelves and part-aelves, in spite of the fact that she might be part aelf herself now. Also, Kejanu was in Verily. Delilah was not ready to face him again yet. She had to have faith that the combination of the brainpower of her super-scientist and the magickal aelves would bring about a miraculous repair to the Vector, which was failing more every minute. She hoped it would not be too late. Delilah took her dinner outside in the garden and watched and listened to the Vector creak and grumble.

Xanfar walked out of the castle, looking up at the sky. "That does not sound good," Xan commented.

"No, it does not," Delilah agreed. "Did Calliwe go to Verily with the others?" she asked.

"Yes, he felt it was his duty," Xan said. "It is the first time we have been apart in days."

"And how is it for a bachelor whayerwolf to have so much closeness?" Delilah asked playfully.

"You know, not bad," he said, and grinned. "I think of Ferrashi at times, and I grieve for him. Calliwe is not Ferrashi, though. It is that simple. There is something very natural about our… relationship. There is no pressure, it just is."

"It sounds too good to be true," Delilah said.

"It is just good enough to be true," Xan said. "Delilah, I realized that I just want to be happy. I do not want to be alone anymore. Do you know the aelves are working on technology so that two men can have children together?"

"Truly! How fascinating. Men in Hope who partner just adopt if they want children."

"As it is elsewhere. Would it not be miraculous if we could create an aelven-wolf child? One of our own bodies?"

"Would you want that, Xan?"

"I never thought it was possible. Still, since Calliwe informed me of the scientific work that is being done, I have to admit the idea has appealed to me. I never thought I would be a father at all, much less have a child of my own fur with a man I love."

"It would be quite magickal," Delilah said.

"The aelves are good at that… magick," Xanfar said.

"Yes. Well, let us hope that they find enough to solve our present crisis. We can talk about you and Calliwe populating all of Fallengrove after we get through this," Delilah teased.

"And what of you and King Kejanu? Are there little half-aelf royal babies in your future, do you think?"

"Oh, Xan. I do not know why, but the thought absolutely terrifies me," she admitted.

"Really? I thought you were falling for him when we were in the mountains at Raefenshire. What changed?"

What did change? She had to really think about that: "He woke up, and he is so intense and intent upon being my soul-partner. I do not know why it troubles me so. I almost feel as if I have lost my agency, my choice." She continued, "If it is destined and we belong together, as he seems to think, that makes me feel… trapped." Xanfar laughed and Delilah looked at him with annoyance. "What?" she demanded.

"You are such a typical queen. Were you not just recently telling me how you wished you had spent more time on your romantic life so that you could leave a legacy for Hope? Now you are suddenly petrified by the idea?" Xan shook his head. "I think you just do not like to have decisions made for you, Delilah. You are an independent spirit. Running Hope from the time you were barely more than a child, who could you rely on except yourself? I think you are wary of trusting someone else to rule Hope by your side. You would have to share the crown. Kejanu is a king in his own right. To marry an equal might not sit well with you," he concluded.

"Could I be so petty that I just do not want to share the throne?" Delilah wondered aloud.

"I do not think it is pettiness, my friend. I think it is about safety. You would need to trust him completely, and that would be scary, indeed."

"I think about my parents, whom I always thought had a perfect marriage. Now I find that my mother loved another and the partnership with my father was carried through only after her lover's death."

"Calliwe was very excited to hear about Radyu's skull. Having it returned to the Usiku will make them more powerful and whole. It is one of the reasons they agreed to align themselves with us: they wanted to have an ancestral skull returned to them. It is not the same skull, yet it is just as important to them. Radyu was a shaman and a renowned sage in Usiku history. His whole family was prominent and held great power. His older sister, Malliwory, was a high priestess who was revered among the Usiku nobles. Malliwory was killed by a roaming troop of rhino-bears, so she was not able to self-immolate and pass on her skull to the tribe. The Usiku rejoiced to hear that Radyu's skull was retained, as he was considered a holy man in his own right. The Dusk Aelves believe it will give them the power back that they lost so many years ago when their ancestral skull was stolen."

"I hope that it does. Do you think this means that they might re-build their kingdom in the desert?"

"I do not believe so. There was talk of it being a sign that they should settle here, in Hope, where Radyu lived his final days and where his skull has resided all these years," Xan said.

"Xan, do you think the Usiku would support Jarvis taking over as monarch here? I mean, he is Radyu's son! What if the Dusk Aelves champion Jarvis' right to the throne? Once word is spread that Jarvis is the son of the ancestral aelf they revere, would they not back him to rule?"

"I did not think of that. It is not publicly known, but Jarvis could use it as a way to establish his right to reign."

"I am so tired of thinking of all of the things that could go wrong. I did that in my mind for weeks before the battle with the Crystal Aelves in Raefenshire and none of what I feared came true. It was all even worse than I imagined! Now I feel my energy is wasted if I let my mind be occupied by all that could rip us asunder when I need every scrap of energy that I have for whatever may come that will be completely unexpected." Delilah sighed and threw down her cloth napkin onto the ground in disgust. A Guard nearby ran to pick it up and Delilah held up her hand and leaned over to get it herself.

"You are right, of course," Xan said. "We probably do not have the ability to imagine what might come next. Our world is changing with new technology. The Vector here in Hope is in jeopardy. Who knows what may happen and how it will all turn out?"

"And what of you and Calliwe? Will you return to Fallengrove soon?"

"Calliwe has been invigorated with news of Radyu's skull. Before that, he insisted he wanted to go back to Fallengrove, get married, have babies. Now, well… I am worried he will want to stay in Hope with almost all of the Dusk Aelves who are left in the world. I wonder if his love for me will win out over his loyalty to his race." Xanfar sighed and then threw down his own napkin, laughed, and picked it up before the Guard could run to get it.

"What a sorry pair we are," Delilah snorted.

"Actually, we are quite fortunate, Delilah," Xanfar countered. "We have those who love us, and we are alive and in possession of great resources. Things have been hard. We lost a lot. Yet we are blessed still." His deep chocolate eyes filled with expression, and Delilah once again was struck by how human a whayerwolf could look when he was filled with emotion.

A large ruckus around the corner of the castle drew their attention. Ook came running out, practically knocking over several guard and a servant carrying a tray of tea. He zeroed in on Delilah and Xanfar and ran awkwardly toward them, his big frame not built for moving so fast.

"What is it Ook?" Delilah stood and reached out to steady the ogred as he stumbled and caught himself before falling on her. He took a deep breath and then mimed sniffing in a big smell, snuffing the air. "What do you smell?" Delilah asked.

"Zhom-boys!" Ook said. "Lots!"

"Lots of zhomboids? Where?" Delilah asked, looking around. Ook pointed back at the part of the Whayer Wood that circled around the meadows and orchards toward the barracks. Delilah grabbed her newly minted scimitar, as she had lost the one Xan had made for her at Raefenshire, and called over the nearest Guard. "Sound the alarm! Gather at the East Quadrant to defend against invaders!" She, Xan, and Ook ran across the grass toward the barracks, with Ook gesturing and leading the way. As they reached the fields where the Guard often enjoyed recreational games and practiced drills, they could see an alarming incision at the base of the Vector, the rippling tear illuminated against the dark backdrop of the Whayer Wood. The slice was a long, vertical opening, zapping with tiny sparks on the edges, each burst making the fabric of the Vector waver and flap. What Ook had smelled came into view, as ghoulish body parts began to grasp and feel around through the rift from the other side of the Vector and into the air of Hope.

Delilah turned to Xan as they ran and shouted, "See, I never could have imagined this in all my fantasies of what could go wrong next!"

Xan shook his head and despite the situation, his snout curled up in a toothy smile. He was going to enjoy this, Delilah realized. Then, with some surprise, she realized that she was going to enjoy this, too! Things that could harm her were so nebulous and invisible, and yet smashing zhomboids was something they could, perhaps literally for Xan, sink their teeth into.

A foot came through the opening, a torso, and slow, awful undeadish things began to pile into Hope. It was a confusing jumble of arms and legs, half-decaying bodies with corpse faces, eyeballs hanging out, and limbs that seemed askew from their joints. An army of the undead stumbled onto the field. Zhomboids are not the most intimidating Beasts, thought Delilah. They are slow and easily dismantled, and yet they are persistent foes. Several dozen of them could certainly cause some chaos. The floodgates seemed to be open as a throng of the creatures amassed upon the green.

"Attack!" yelled Delilah, and she and the gathering Guard ran at the crowd of whitish, foul-smelling flesh bags. Delilah began hacking away at the nearest ghoul, which stood as limbs fell around it, looking barely aware that it had nothing left to assail its prey. It just kept coming forward until Delilah sliced its head apart and it fell in two pieces to the ground. The next one was easier, falling after a giant swipe to its middle. It still dragged itself along the ground by its hands, but Ook came by and jumped on it with both feet. The ogred stomped in the zhomboid's chest and then kicked its head like a ball across the field. "Nice one, Ook!" Delilah complimented the ogred, who grinned widely.

As the wave of monsters came flooding in, the Guard handily dispatched each one without much difficulty. Delilah could tell the Guard were enjoying letting out their frustration on the creatures, easily conquering them in a way that had escaped them in Raefenshire. It was good for them to have some sport for a change, she thought. Things came to a halt when suddenly a few Guard backed up, shouting to each other and pointing. Some of the garish fiends wore armor that was decaying and falling apart. Delilah had not thought much of it, as she had gotten caught up in the slashing and dismembering. When she saw the Guard retreating with horrified looks upon their faces, she realized there was something not quite right about these zhomboids.

Word spread quickly through the Guard, and more and more stopped attacking and the crowd of fleshy corpses continued piling in. The Guard stepped back and away from them instead of moving forward to push the monsters back through the hole in the Vector. Delilah moved toward the closest group of soldiers who were pointing and shouting to one another. "What is it? Why are you not attacking?" Delilah demanded.

"Your Majesty. It is my sister! She was killed on the battlefield in Raefenshire. I do not know how, but she is there! That zhomboid is her!"

Delilah looked and realized that some of the faces, though distorted by death and decay, were familiar. Just then, she noticed a particularly familiar face among them. The beast was bent to one side with many holes in her torso. Still, there was no doubt that it was Oravica's swollen and disfigured face! Delilah now stepped back, too, and moved away as Oravica's monstrous being came at her, locking one of its bulging eyes on her. Delilah rattled through everything she ever knew about zhomboids, how they were animated from the dead by ghoulish magick, and how to kill them. Her mind raced to wonder: if these Beasts were trapped and contained, could they be repaired? Could you undo the damage and heal a zhomboid with magick? Not human healing, of course, but perhaps with aelven magick?

Delilah used her crystals to call out to Ilvana. Without any tree near, she simply trusted that the water vapor in the air would relay her plea.

"We are still busy, Your Majesty!" Ilvana's voice entered Delilah's mind.

"As are we. I will not keep you. I just need to know: is there any way to cure a zhomboid once it becomes undead? Can they ever be reversed and turned human again with any type of magick?"

"Zhomboids? No. There is no cure for a zhomboid. Once the organs and the flesh deteriorate, they can never turn human again. Even if it were possible to restore them, they would have a decayed body. Being brought back to life would inflict unimaginable torture."

"Are you sure? Nothing at all can be done?" Delilah desperately hoped for a different answer.

"There is only one thing to do with zhomboids," Ilvana said definitively. "You must put them out of their misery."

"Thank you, Ilvana."

"Is the situation there so dire? We are almost to a solution," affirmed the doctor.

"It is dire. Hundreds, maybe thousands of our dead have been somehow turned to zhomboids and are invading through a hole in the Vector. The Guard are losing their taste for this battle."

"We will work fast here. Kill them, Delilah. There is nothing else to do," the scientist asserted.

Delilah ran back to the group and began shouting: "I order you to kill these monsters! They are not the people we knew and loved! Our friends are gone! These creatures are not our loved ones. They are piles of animated flesh. Our family members are gone and there is nothing that we can do. Their current state is only prolonging their suffering. I order you to kill them now!" With that, she ran to Oravica's mutated form and sliced her head clean off. The body of her dead friend, poked through with holes and deformed beyond belief, kept coming at Delilah and she forced her arm to move again to cut it down.

Queen Delilah and the Encroaching Gloom

Seeing their queen slice apart her favorite officer gave some strength back to the Guard and they began to fight again, with less enthusiasm and sometimes turning their heads away when they made contact with decaying flesh, but still, they went in chopping and hacking. Ook, having little sentimentality for the dead Guard, kept up his bashing and kicking the flesh piles apart into stringy and powdery hunks. Xanfar also had little attachment to the creatures, and decimated dozens into ribbons with his claws. The whayerwolf did not seem to have much of a taste for their musty smell and flavor, though, and seemed to avoid chomping them with his deadly jaws.

With renewed vigor, they were able to push back the tide, leaving piles of rotted meat and limbs strewn about. With sustained effort, they pushed the moving creatures back through the hole. "Back you nasty beasts!" Delilah yelled, bashing them and shoving them. Her sword sunk through a chest cavity all the way up to her fingers, which bumped against dissolving flesh and rubbery bone as she pulled her weapon back with a slippery grasp. "These truly are the most disgusting creatures," she thought. She recalled the trollves assertion that they tasted like rotten chalk and gagged with the thought of it. Then, as if her mind had summoned them, she saw, chomping and gnawing at the back of the crowd, her old friends Herk and Harvey! They were busily eating zhomboids at the rear.

When they saw her, the trollves looked at one another with total shock. "It is our human meal!" Harvey said, pushing away the zhomboid meat he was gnawing at and coming at her, licking his toothy snarly mouth and sniffing toward her with his piggish snout. "Hey there, darlin'! How 'bout making my day and coming over here so I can eat you, why not?"

Herk followed behind, "It is mine, Harvey, I smelled it the first time, remember! You did not even believe me that there was a human!" Herk pushed zhomboids aside and climbed over fallen piles of bodies that had toppled over when pushed back through the entrance.

"Enough to share, Herk! This one is substantial! And, so fresh! Not rotten like these smelly ghouls."

The trollves were still on the other side of the Vector and Delilah stood there with her hands on her hips, daring them to come through where her Guard, Ook, and Xanfar were ready and prepared.

A giant reverberating sound suddenly cut through the air like a tremendous thunder clap, leaving a deep resounding echo in its wake. Another explosion blasted through the sphere above followed by a sound like crackling ice. Splinters appeared, like lightning spears, shooting across the concave surface of the Vector. Everyone looked up, including the two trollves, who had not yet stepped foot across the threshold. "I think it might blow!" Herk said, and the two began to scutter away, back into the darkened trees.

A shattering like Delilah had never heard made her grasp her ears, covering her head and forcing her to duck downward. Surely the Vector was crumbling and would crush them all! Then, like glass, millions of shards of the clear ceiling Hope had always known blasted in all directions at once. The sound of the shattering dome was like hundreds of mirrors smashed at once, so loud it was unbearable. The splinters rained down and Delilah feared they would all be cut to shreds. Yet the glittering diamonds just sparkled and evaporated, leaving streams of faerie dust in trails that reached from the top of the sky to the ground in a dazzling fountain.

All was silent. Then, as the air from all directions rushed in to fill the space where the dome had been, a sea current wafted in. They could smell the salty air from the ocean, replacing the putrid fumes left by the stench of zhomboids. Another breeze came from the direction of the Wood. The smell of the loamy forest was on the wind, air which had previously never reached Hope because it was blocked by the Vector's enchantment. Those who had crouched to brace from the falling sky stood slowly and smelled the amazing scents that had never reached them before. It was invigorating! And just as quickly as they were filled with reverence and longing for the smells around them, they looked toward the Whayer Wood. They realized that for the first time ever, nothing stood between them and the forest full of Gloom. A look of terror spread across the faces of the gathered Guard as they watched the deep shadows moving in the forest.

The Wood came alive: it was as if all the creatures and Beasts of the Gloom suddenly realized that there was fresh meat and nothing to keep them from it anymore. Among the trees, vampwhyrs, dessicators, flying undead dactyls, and whayerwolves appeared, along with trolls and trollves, and bands of ogreds and gobbelins, all with curious expressions, eagerly sniffing the air. Unrecognizable furry monsters with claws and fangs and ghostly floating apparitions appeared among the others and the group began to inch forward. They smelled the human breeze that rolled in toward them, pushed out among the trees when the vacuum seal of the Vector was broken.

Delilah yelled to her Guard, "Stand alert! Be prepared to fight with your life to defend Hope! We will not let these Beasts enter!" The city would be quickly lost, she realized. Even if they could fight off the dozens of creatures they could see, countless more would come behind them, pouring into the city. With no barrier preventing them from leaving the forest, they would keep going to devour all in sight. It was only a matter of time before everyone in the realm would be killed and eaten, no matter how valiantly they fought. Delilah felt so hopelessly lost in that moment. Her heart filled with despair for all they had gone through, all of their efforts, all the losses they had already faced and survived, to end like this? She was responsible and she had failed her people who were going to die horrific deaths, devoured by Beasts.

A buzzing in her palm drew her attention from her desperate thoughts. Her crystals! They were vibrating with a force Delilah had never felt before. Xanfar looked down at his own paw, where his crystals were embedded. Across the field, Delilah saw Abbowhen and other officers looking at their own hands with confusion. A low, tired, drawling rumble began, far beneath the earth. To Delilah, it suddenly appeared that the trees were talking to one another, branches rubbing against those of their neighbors, leaves rustling in velvety whispers to one another. Her pointed aelven ear began to twitch and ring. Light was running along the ground, as if power was coming up from the Nearth below.

The Beasts seemed to sense something. It took their attention from their intended prey and they looked toward the ground. Clots of dirt began to rumble and break apart, and then roots of light burst forth from the surface of the earth and began spiraling upward. Tendrils and shoots ejected from the earth in great volcanic streamers. All was buzzing with energy and twisting light. Shining coils of luminous and vibrating vegetation shot up into the air and scaffolded upon itself in an interwoven net to climb further still into the air. Up and up, it grew at lightning speed. Within minutes, a brilliant and glowing sphere of magickal plant-matter was appointed in the sky in the exact shape of the Vector. It was an illuminated globe of tangled and cris-crossed vines loosely resembling a fisherwoman's net. The Beasts of the Gloom, comprehending they could not cross this barrier, looked at each other with bemused expressions. As an alternative to what they thought would be an easy human snack, some began to attack and devour one another. More vulnerable critters ran away with the fiercer monsters in hot pursuit. Shrieks from the less fortunate creatures being devoured out of sight were the only remnant of the monsters' invasion. Soon, it was quiet again, with only the faint humming voice of the new, glistening vines of the dome, which was barely visible against the lightness of the sky above.

"Did it work?" Delilah could not tell who was speaking for a moment until she realized her crystals were vibrating and the voice in her mind was that of Doktora Ilvana.

"If what you intended was a wholly new Vector made of vines of light, then yes, it worked!"

"Yes, we intended something like that!" the doctor exclaimed. "We called upon the power of the Nearth and the network of ancient trees to assist us, yet we were not exactly sure what would form. It sounds like they have come through! We have the Great Trees and the Usiku shamans to thank for this."

"It is nothing short of a miracle," Delilah said. She was bewildered by how the story she had envisioned for herself and Hope being obliterated by Beasts had so quickly changed in only moments to one where they were safe and protected once again. "And the Gloom? It will not be able to encroach anymore?" Delilah asked.

"Neither the Beasts nor the Gloom should be able to penetrate the barrier," Ilvana asserted.

"Then it truly is miraculous!" Delilah exclaimed.

Cheers went out across the Guard as they realized they were safe, not only from the creatures trying to enter Hope, but also from the Gloom. A dense fog of it bunched up in clouds along the edge of the forest and yet could not cross the living, glowing Net.

"Ilvana, you have saved us," Delilah said gratefully.

"I hardly did it alone. It was an inter-species effort," the scientist said.

"Yes, but you had the ingenuity to bring all of the great minds and magick together to create this astonishing feat," Delilah said, looking up to the shining vault above. Sparks of energy from below the ground came up and glittered along the surface of the Net as it ran up the different pathways across its web and back down below the ground.

"And the Ancients. You must not forget them," Ilvana said. "The Ancient tree network was the key."

"Will it need any maintenance?" Delilah wondered, already looking to the future and when this marvelous accomplishment might fail.

"No maintenance, no human sacrifices," Ilvana confirmed with a laugh. "It is self-sustaining, built from the eternal power of the Ancients and the Nearth.

"Remarkable," said the queen, looking around at the happy and relieved faces of her army. "Please pass my congratulations along to the team in Verily. We will have a great feast in their honor when they return. And Ilvana, of course you must come, too!"

"I will see if I can make time in my schedule," said the Doktora.

Something was not right. As soon as Delilah entered the castle, she could tell that the energy in the place was disturbed. There was an intruder, she could feel it with her new heightened senses and in the air of the place, which smelled like aelves. Yet it was not the woodsmoke scent of the Dusk Aelves that she had come to associate with kindness and harmony. It was the sharp and cold smell of the Crystal Aelves. Delilah did not usually spend time in the throne room, yet her body pulled her there as she followed her uneasy intuition. It did not occur to her to get help. She simply followed the pull to investigate this unsettled feeling.

She walked into the throne room and somehow was not surprised at all to see her brother sitting on her throne. He was surrounded by Crystal Aelven soldiers, yet his queen was nowhere to be seen.

"Jarvis!" Delilah exclaimed.

"Delilah," Jarvis said. His tone was not filled with the hissing bitterness she recalled from when she had encountered him and was enslaved in the Crystal Mountain. Jarvis' whole demeanor seemed different, and he did not wear the skull helmet. He was relaxed and had a serene expression on his face. "I am glad to see you, sister," he said.

"I am surprised to see you, here, and upon my throne," she said.

"It is my throne, if you recall. You were quite busy fighting Beasts when we arrived. I presumed you would find me when you were through with your… travails."

"Yes, we have had a trying day, for sure," she said. With that, her exhaustion overtook her. Her fear of Jarvis and of what might come vanished in the realization that she could not stand to lose any more. She walked up and plunked herself down in the throne next to the one Jarvis sat upon. The Crystal Aelves gasped, as if she had done something scandalous, yet her brother just laughed.

"You seem to have given up, Delilah. Do you not want to fight me for the throne?"

"One throne is just as good as another," she said dispassionately. "I simply do not see the point in our rivalry anymore."

"So, do you acknowledge me as your King?" Jarvis asked in disbelief.

"We are both the rightful heirs," she said. "I see that now. You were intended to be the ruler of Hope and I became Hope's ruler only because of your absence. You were bequeathed it; I earned it. Which one is more righteous?"

Jarvis laughed again: "I see your point."

"You do?"

"Yes. I have had much time to think since I fell from the drakeon over the Whayer Wood."

Queen Delilah and the Encroaching Gloom

"Was it you who carried me to Yonderlot?" Delilah asked.

"Yes, you do not remember? You were quite impaired," Jarvis chuckled.

"I thought you were a purple unicorn," she admitted.

"Ah, the secret password," he said. "You were mumbling something about that."

"And my ear?" she asked. "Why did you cut me?"

"I blended my blood with yours to keep you safe. It was the same reason I brought you to Yonderlot. I needed to keep you out of harm's way while I attended to some urgent matters. I had to meet up with Nimevah to invade Hope."

"And that was your intention? When you tunneled into the castle?"

"I had dual intentions," Jarvis said. "I was still driven to claim my crown here, and yet I also intended to change the mind of my queen."

"In what way?"

"Queen Nimevah has been my heart and inspiration, the love of my life. I found out recently she has also been my captor," he said. "When I first fled Hope and ended up in Raefenshire, I was married to Nimevah and became King of the Crystal Aelves. I was given the ancestral skull as a crown to wear. It was a great honor to wear the relic of the Khattu. I did not realize it was also poisoning me. It was indoctrinating me with the beliefs of the aelves, making me bitter and hateful. I wore it for fifteen years. When I fell from the drakeon after the battle at Raefenshire, the skull also fell off, releasing me from its power. It was no longer infecting my mind. I saw clearly for the first time in years, and realized that I had been manipulated."

"And what was it that the queen wanted?" Delilah asked.

"She wanted to gain the territory of Hope and become its queen. You see how powerful the Khattu are. She could have taken it anytime she wanted, yet I was her ticket to taking it legitimately, through our marital alliance. They were only waiting for the right time after the failed coup. Fifteen years is nothing to an aelf. After I left you at Yonderlot, I rejoined Nimevah here in Hope and I expressed my feelings to her. I told her there had been enough bloodshed. She did not appreciate that sentiment and thought me a traitor for suggesting we abandon ruling Hope together. Her attitude toward me changed once I did not conform to her plan."

"But does she not love you?" Delilah wondered. Despite everything, she felt deep pain for her brother.

"I do not know. I was useful to her, I am sure of that," he said sadly.

"How awful," Delilah said, and reached her hand across the expanse between the thrones. The royal chairs were not set close enough together to reach Jarvis without him also reaching out. In that long moment that her hand lay exposed in the air between them, Delilah felt as if she had laid herself bare to be rejected again by her brother. Yet he reached out and let his hand pause for a moment in the chasm before grasping the hand of his little sister. They both sighed and after a squeeze of old affection, let their hands drop. The aelven warriors who were guarding the room did not blink or look at them as they spoke. Delilah gestured to them, "Is it safe to speak of your misgivings in front of them?"

"The Khattu are profoundly loyal. I am their King. I can do no wrong," he said with confidence.

"Jarvis, when you came to Hope and took over the castle," Delilah started, "why did you leave? Was it because of the disagreement with Nimevah?"

"Partly. We had communicated after I fell from the drakeon. Our plan was to meet up at Hope. Nimevah was expecting me to bring you so we could execute you in front of your people. It would give finality to your rule and help them to understand the inevitability of ours. When I arrived without you, Nimevah was furious. By then, I was having doubts about everything I had been thinking and feeling for years, since the poison of the skull was no longer affecting my mind. Nimevah was angry that I had lost the Khattu relic and that I had brought you someplace safe. She could tell that I was already thinking for myself without the skull and was no longer in agreement with her on everything. She insisted that we go find the relic and return once I had some time to 'reconsider my priorities,' as she put it. In other words, she wanted me to wear the helmet again, which would put me back under her control. So, we departed, with her intention to take possession of my mind again, to find out where you were hidden so that you could be returned to Hope to be executed there. By doing this, she intended to take the realm.

"And Doktora Ishlip and her kin? Why did you murder them?"

"I did not! They were alive when I left. I spoke to Ishlip, and without the influence of the aelves in my ear, I could see only evil when I looked into her eyes. I wanted nothing more to do with her. I refused to release her and her kin, as she begged me to do, so we left them locked in the dungeon."

"They were murdered by an aelven sword!" Delilah exclaimed.

"'Twas not my sword, nor anyone else who was with me. Doktora Ishlip and her kinswomen were alive, yelling for us to take them with us, when we sealed up the hole in the floor of the dungeon," Jarvis said.

A scuffle in the hall occurred and Kejanu entered at the spearpoints of several Khattu guards. A group of Dusk Aelves followed their king. At the back of the Usiku group were Helanza and Doktora Ilvana. The scientist carried a bundle of blue silk in her arms. To Delilah's surprise, Kejanu walked up to Jarvis and bowed before him. "King Jarvis," Kejanu said.

"King Kejanu," Jarvis said, rose, and bowed back to the Usiku ruler.

Delilah was baffled. Kejanu looked at her and nodded his head deeply, "My Queen," he said.

Jarvis announced: "King Kejanu, before we discuss anything else, I would like to re-invoke the Aelven Shield."

"Agreed," said the Usiku king. "The Shield has been broken, and must now be repaired."

Delilah practically fell out of the throne. "What?? King Kejanu, you are aligning with the Crystal Aelves again? After everything they did and even after they slaughtered your people?" She could not believe her ears.

"We are aelves above all else, Your Majesty," Kejanu said, his eyes not leaving hers. "We must repair the rift between the races. We need our alliance to be whole again."

Queen Delilah and the Encroaching Gloom

"And what of your alliance to Hope?" Delilah asked, incredulous.

"We will maintain that, too," said Kejanu, as if no conflict at all existed in this statement.

"Delilah, perhaps we may explain a few things," Ilvana said, coming forward. "We invited Jarvis to come back here. It was ordained by the Spirit of Radyu." The scientist took the sparkling midnight blue skull from the fabric and held it out to them.

"My father!" Jarvis said and ran forward to take the skull from Ilvana's hands.

"One moment," Ilvana said, and held out a palm. Jarvis stopped in his tracks and then turned to sit again. "We have important things that must be revealed," the Doktora said, "which is why we asked you here. While we were replacing the Vector, we used Radyu's skull to connect to the Ancients and tap into the power of the Nearth. We found a secret message in a deep chamber within the skull. It is not a physical thing, but an enchantment that was placed there. It was put there by your mother, Queen Zaryadne, perhaps for this very day."

"How would our mother know how to place such a complicated enchantment?" Delilah asked.

"I know exactly how," Helanza spoke up. "She was able to do it because I showed her how," the healer said. "She asked for my guidance and I gave her what she needed to be able to encode a communication within an object to be released later. I did not realize what she had intended until we came upon it as we were building the Net. Your mother did not place the message in the skull until after she passed over into the Spirit World and had moved beyond tangible things."

"What is her message?" Jarvis asked, his eyes filled with pain. Delilah wondered if he recalled their mother's last moments as she died at his hand, as Delilah did vividly in that moment.

"I will show you," said Helanza, and placed the skull upon the floor in front of the throne. She waved her hand above the skull and whispered a few words in an ancient aelven dialect. Helanza stepped back and a blue ray of light blasted from the top of the skull, making an upside-down pyramid of glimmering color. In the rays, a life-sized form appeared. It was their mother, Queen Zaryadne! She was dressed in a riding cloak of radiant blue with a longsword and tall black boots. She looked as strong and self-possessed as she had been in life, except in the light emanating from the skull, she was partly transparent, like a ghost.

"My children," the lips of the hologram image of their mother moved. Yet her voice came from the whole room, amplified against the curved stone ceiling. "I know you will find this message someday, and it is clear I have some explaining to do. By now, Jarvis, my child, my dear heart, you will know that your father was the great Usiku priest, Radyu. I regret that I was not able to reveal this to you while I was alive. I should have been the one to tell you that you had aelven blood, and that my husband, the king, was not your true father. King Yuli loved you so entirely as his son. Yuli knew you were not his, however we came to an understanding. It was important to him that you experienced his love as if you were his son. He kept my confidence, so I owed it to him to honor this request." Jarvis gulped upon hearing this. Zaryadne's voice carried across the ceiling: "You will know better now in your maturity what it means to be a half-aelf and the magickal blending of human and aelven traits. After you hear what I have to say, I hope you will also understand more about our intentions."

Jarvis shifted and looked uncomfortable, yet fully alert. Delilah leaned in to wonder at her mother's face, animated as if in life. The queen continued: "When the Vector began to fail, the Council put pressure on us to sacrifice you, Jarvis. They would not relent, and even suggested they would bring to question our right to sovereignty if we failed to fulfill our duty by sacrificing you to save the city. We knew that the need for the blood sacrifice of the royal heir was just a foolish myth believed by superstitious minds: the Ancients, as we knew them, would never require a blood sacrifice. It was unthinkable that the benevolent spirits of the earth would ask us to sacrifice our son, or make a blood sacrifice of any kind. We defied the Council and chided them for their ignorant beliefs. Instead, we planned to formally name you our heir, so that they would see we had full confidence in you and no intention of harming you.

"Doktora Ishlip had been coveting our power for years. She had served as my regent briefly after my mother died and before I came of age as the Queen. She never gave up thirsting for more control. After I was crowned, she had to step back from her prominent role. She undermined me and turned the Council against me, until all of my advisors questioned my authority. She had found out about Radyu somehow, and used the information to convince my Council that I was unfit to lead. She began to hatch a plot for a coup. Sadly, she determined that you, Jarvis, would be the best option to assist her in implementing it. The people of Hope would never have allowed Ishlip to rule, however they would accept our son and heir, if we were removed. Ishlip believed she could control you. She also thought your connection to the aelves would help them get the assistance they needed to heal the Vector. She knew no blood sacrifice was needed, and that only the ancient power that built the Vector could restore it again.

"She fed you information about your parentage and began making introductions between you and the Crystal Aelves. Ishlip had negotiated an agreement with Nimevah the Aelf Queen that once you were married and under the Khattu's control, that Ishlip would be appointed Chief Advisor to the Crown. You began to trust Doktora Ishlip because she told you the truth about your father, which we, regrettably, had not done. This helped her to gain your trust. Ishlip encouraged you to plot with the aelves. When she told you that we were going to murder you at the Cricket Moon, under the guise of a ceremony to formally appoint you as our heir, you believed her. Doktora Ishlip used her foul influence with the Council to conspire with them to back the coup. She convinced them that once we were eliminated, they could all have more power. They would then use your connection with the aelves to heal the Vector and gain their own advantage in Court. They were greedy and power-hungry, and could not resist the temptation of getting rid of us, as we were never easily under their thumbs. They believed they could manipulate you as a young and malleable new ruler and exert power and dominance over the aelves, who they believed would be slaves to them. They were sorely uninformed about the nature of aelves to think they could be so easily subjugated.

Queen Delilah and the Encroaching Gloom

"Unfortunately, they also underestimated the loyalty of my Guard." Zaryadne said. "Once Yuli and I were killed, the Guard, seeing your actions as that of a traitor and murderer, came to our defense to capture and imprison you. You were cornered on the cliff. Although we were dead by then, have no doubt that we saw everything. We saw you fall into the waves, and watched as the Guard—who are legally ordained to act in such situations—put the crown on Delilah's head and proclaimed her as the rightful Queen of Hope. Over the days that followed, we watched as Ishlip began to poison Delilah's heart against the other Council members. She was afraid the Council would reveal her role in fomenting the coup. She pressured you, Delilah, to have them all executed before they could expose her sinister part in the plot. It was easy to convince you, my daughter, that the Council had conspired against us, because they had. Delilah, my dear, do not shed any tears for the Council members you had purged. They were profane, every one: they would have turned on you just as easily as they did on us. The worst part is that Ishlip lived long enough to influence you further. Yet she, too, will meet her fate.

"Jarvis, I do not blame you for our deaths," Zaryadne said. "You were vulnerable to those you trusted who lied and exploited you. If we had been honest with you about your true father, you might not have gone seeking other counsel. If we had confided in you earlier, you never would have believed we were capable of plotting to kill you. What I regret most, more than our own deaths, is that your actions made you and your sister enemies. Neither of you knew the other's intention. Jarvis, you believed Delilah had been part of the plot and had conspired with us to kill you so she could become the heir. Delilah, you thought your brother murdered us over nothing more than a lust for power. These were inadvertent consequences of our decision not to reveal Jarvis' parentage from the beginning. Now I intend to put them right: the truth is, you are both the rightful heir. King Yuli and I had always intended to recognize Jarvis as our son and heir. Delilah, you are the only true child of the Queen and King of Hope, making you also a true heir. Which one has greater claim? Jarvis was in line to be King. Delilah, when Hope needed you, you became the ruler they yearned for. The question of who will rule is not in my hands. It is in yours, my children." Zaryadne paused for a moment to wipe a tear from the corner of her eye. "I hope that in learning that we were only ever concerned with your well-being and safety, you will find the courage to work together toward a resolution. My children, my dearest loves, this will be the greatest test of your characters."

The phantom version of their mother vanished and quiet fell over the hall. Jarvis and Delilah looked at one another. They shook their heads, trying to absorb all they had heard. It was a different mother than either of them had ever experienced. Zaryadne had always seemed so reserved, even cold at times. Yet now they saw how she had carried so many private burdens: a covert love affair, hiding the paternity of the heir to the throne, and hateful foes on her own Council who wanted her dead. Perhaps this had made her preoccupied and distant at times. She had a lot to contend with.

Jarvis stood up and took a step toward the skull. He crumpled and began to sob, his face buried in his hands, his body heaving with wretched lamentation. He was grieving them, Delilah realized. He was finally grieving their parents. All of these years, he had felt justified in his actions because he believed the lie that they were going to sacrifice him. Now, his whole worldview had been flipped upside down. He had murdered people who had loved him and had tried to protect him. Delilah watched as it tore through her brother's fragile heart. The others in the chamber stood somberly, with eyes averted and heads down.

"I have a question," Delilah said, trying to be respectful of her brother's grief, yet still puzzled. "I would like to know, Jarvis: if you did not kill Doktora Ishlip and her family, then who did?"

"It was I," the voice surprised Delilah. It was her healer, Helanza, who stepped forward with her head bowed to offer her confession.

"But... why?" Delilah stuttered.

"Because I hated Ishlip for years," Helanza said. "She imprisoned my lover, Gravenwell, and kept him in the dungeon for decades. I loved your mother, Deliliah, yet each time I would go to her to beg to have Gravenwell released, Ishlip would interfere. She and the Council would take a stand and Queen Zaryadne would not take the risk of their displeasure. I think Zaryadne never fully believed that Gravenwell had committed no crime—he had been put in the dungeon during her mother's time and she only knew what was told to her. Zaryadne was never confident enough in his innocence to invoke the wrath of the Council." The healer looked at her queen. "Delilah, when you took the crown, one of the first things you did was defy Ishlip to set Gravenwell free. I knew then that I would be loyal to you always.

"When the aelves took the castle and then disappeared, I saw this as an opportunity to enact the justice that Doktora Ishlip deserved—not just for Gravenwell, but vengeance for Zaryadne and Yuli, and for the evils she did to Jarvis and you, Your Majesty. I did not want to risk the aelves coming back and setting them free before they were properly executed, so I took things into my own hands."

Delilah was dumbstruck. "But it was an aelven sword!"

Helanza reminded her: "Yes, and I am half-aelven. I do not use my sword often, but you can be assured that my weapon is of aelven craft."

Delilah shook her head. "I understand your actions, Helanza. The traitors were destined to be executed anyway, yet it was not your right to deliver that justice."

Abbowhen stepped forward. "Your Majesty, with your permission, I will escort the healer to the dungeon." Several Guard grabbed Helanza's arms as if she might resist, yet she did not. They began to lead her out.

"Wait!" Delilah heard her own voice, although she had no idea what she might say. "Bring her back here." The Guard led Helanza to Delilah, and the healer kneeled before her queen. Delilah took a breath, then spoke: "Helanza, you have violated our code to have taken this action upon yourself. I am ready now to mete out your punishment." Abbowhen offered Delilah her sword, yet the queen ignored it. "Helanza, you are hereby banished from Hope! You will go to Yonderlot. There, your punishment will be to become the next Keeper of the Tower. You will stay there until the day when you are released from that duty. You are to go now. Guard! Bring her to the docks and give her a boat to ferry herself to Yonderlot."

The Guard looked at one another, and Abbowhen gave Delilah a bewildered expression. However, in a moment, they pulled Helanza to her feet and began to lead her toward the door. As they reached the doorway, the healer turned to look at Delilah. The crystals in Delilah's palm tingled and she heard Helanza's words in her mind: "Thank you," before she was ushered away.

"Well, this has been a tremendously draining and overwhelming day," Delilah said, turning to her brother. "I know we must resolve this little "Ruler of Hope" thing. I must admit, though, I am totally exhausted. What say you, brother? Shall we sleep on it and resume our conversation in the morning? Your chambers have been left untouched all these years. Please, let us eat and sleep and talk in the morning after we have had time to rest and reflect."

"Why yes, sister. I think that is a truly inspired idea." With that, Jarvis picked up Radyu's skull and placed it on top of his head. "Look at that," he said. "It fits me perfectly."

Throughout the night, the Crystal Aelven soldiers and Sister Guard dealt with one another civilly, as if they had not just been at war. They were even seen going through exercises in the courtyards together along with the Usiku warriors. In the morning, Delilah, with her officers and the aelves, gathered again in the throne room. The queen sat specifically in the secondary throne that she had inhabited the day before and awaited her brother. Jarvis entered, with Radyu's skull still affixed to his head.

"Good morning, brother. I hope you slept well in your old chambers," Delilah said.

"I did not sleep much at all," Jarvis said.

"Well," Delilah said, "I am well rested. I can say today with a clear mind that after all that has happened, I can only come to one conclusion: we must rule Hope together, if you are willing."

"I have received a message from my father," Jarvis said, plopping down on the throne.

"Oh?"

"In the night, I put the skull on the table beside my bed. I was half asleep in a trance when Radyu came to me. He called me 'son' and told me what I needed to do," Jarvis swallowed on the word 'son' as if he was holding back a flood of emotion.

"And what is that?" Delilah asked, concerned that Radyu would demand Jarvis be placed on the Hope throne, as he had been denied when Zaryadne spurned him for Yuli.

"I must go back to the desert to the land of the Usiku. Our tribe is almost extinct. We must rebuild our realm and our race there. I will need those who know the old traditions, who can help to re-establish our sovereignty in the old way. Any Usiku who want to come with me, and their partners—human or otherwise—are welcome. We will be a small, yet powerful nation and become whole once again. King Kejanu, will you come with me to rule as our monarch?" Jarvis stood to ask the King this question and Kejanu stepped forward from the gathered crowd.

"No, King Jarvis, I will not be joining you in the desert," he said. He looked at Delilah as he said this, which made her heart pound faster. She dropped her eyes to the floor. Kejanu continued: "I give up my claim to the Usiku throne. You may have it, King Jarvis, if you care to lead the Usiku people, as our esteemed ancestor, Lord Radyu, has suggested you might.

My path leads elsewhere."

"I accept the Usiku crown," Jarvis said, and with that, the Usiku in the room bowed to him. The Crystal Aelves looked confused, unsure of where this left them, with their king abandoning his post to govern a Dark Aelf outpost in the desert.

"Jaaaaarrrrviiiiisssssssssssss!!!" the sound came echoing through the castle as if it came thundering down from the sky.

"Oh no," said Jarvis.

"What is it?" asked Delilah, already suspecting the answer.

"It is Nimevah. She has come for me," Jarvis said, with something like terror in his eyes.

The Crystal Aelves bowed as the aelven queen swooped in as if on a cloud of ice: her pale skin glistening, white blonde hair flowing behind her like a current of wind, and a pale silver cape billowing behind her. A six-pack of female aelven guard followed her entrance. They all wore silver embossed leather armor. Nimevah wore the same, and it moved with her like a second skin on her lean body. She was a sight to behold and Delilah caught her breath with how impressive she was. It was no wonder her brother had fallen in love with her, she thought.

"King Jarvis!" Nimevah shouted in her musical aelven accent that sounded like tinkling bells. "I have suffered from your intransigence long enough. You will return to Raefenshire immediately. As for Hope, we will take the city imminently after we have settled our affairs at home." Her eyes grew wide as she seemed to just notice the dark blue skull on her husband's head. "What is that on your head?" she demanded.

"My father's skull," Jarvis informed her. "I reclaimed it as well as the right to rule the Usiku people of the Great Desert Plains in Erithea."

"And what of your role as King of Raefenshire and the Khattu Aelves? What of your duty to me as my husband?" A small quiver in the queen's voice betrayed her angst with being defied.

"As all those in this room as my witness, I sever our ties as husband and wife at this very instant. Aelven Law allows me to do this, and that is my wish. So mote it be." Jarvis' voice was confident.

"No, that is not allowed!" Nimevah practically shrieked. "*I* am the Queen, and I will not permit this! My word goes above the law." She bounded up to Jarvis and hissed in his face: "You are my husband still and nothing can change that!" Delilah felt fear and anguish for her brother. "Take that skull from your head," Nimevah insisted. "I have brought the Khattu relic with me," she took the old skull helmet from a bag at her hip. "You will put this on immediately." She held the skull out to Jarvis, glaring at him.

"No," he said simply. It was quiet and firm. He no longer seemed worried.

Nimevah began to shake all over and shouted a stream of aelven words at Jarvis, so fast that Delilah could not understand them, however the eyes of the aelves in the room grew wide.

"My Queen," a soft voice interrupted the flow of the aelven queen's abuse, and she turned to see who was speaking. It was Kejanu. "We are in a serious dilemma, all of us," said the aelf in his soothing, calm tone. "I would like to propose a solution." Nimevah stood listening, her graceful head tilted slightly toward the Usiku king. He continued: "The Usiku and the Khattu have long been allies. The Aelven Shield has always been stronger than any conflict. Our recent war is over. We must heal the Aelven Shield. While it is clear you do not wish to release your claim on this man, he is only a half aelf. Perhaps your realm and your monarchy would be stronger with a fully aelven king on the throne."

Nimevah looked at Kejanu curiously. "What do you propose?" she asked.

"I give myself to you, Queen Nimevah, as your husband, if you will have me. Together we will heal the Aelven Shield and rule Raefenshire, as well as restore alliances with the Usiku. Your former husband has agreed to take on the leadership of the desert region, and we will be assured of peace if we work to maintain his friendship."

Nimevah and all else in the room were speechless. The queen sized up Kejanu, who stood at least a head beneath her. Still, he was a strikingly beautiful aelf, and she appeared pleased with what she saw. "Yes, I will accept this. You will wear the Khattu skull relic?"

"After I have the Usiku sorcerers remove the charms that are placed upon it, yes, I will. There is some foul trickery within that object, Your Grace, and I will not deign to wear it until it is pure and restored to the ancient magick for which it was intended."

"Hmmmmph," said Nimevah, yet she handed off the skull to Kejanu, who handed it to a nearby Usiku priestess.

Kejanu bowed to his newly betrothed. "I will meet you in Raefenshire in two days' time," he said. "Then we shall be married and rule the Khattu lands together."

"And what of Hope?" Nimevah demanded. "I will not give up my claim here. I can attack and take this weakened city whenever I want." She sounded like a petulant child.

"We will discuss that after we are married and I am crowned King of the Khattu," Kejanu said, and bowed again.

The aelven queen, apparently appeased, spun dramatically and left the room with her six guards shadowing her movements. She held her head high without any acknowledgment of the others in the room, not even a glance toward Jarvis. It was only after Nimevah had left that the implications of what had happened sunk in. Delilah realized that the man who had proclaimed his love for her was now betrothed to her fiercest enemy. She looked at Kejanu, who nodded solemnly in her direction. The gnawing pit of fear that had sat lurking underneath all of the other horrors she had experienced over the last days dissolved. A weight lifted from Delilah's chest and she felt lighter and freer than she had in months.

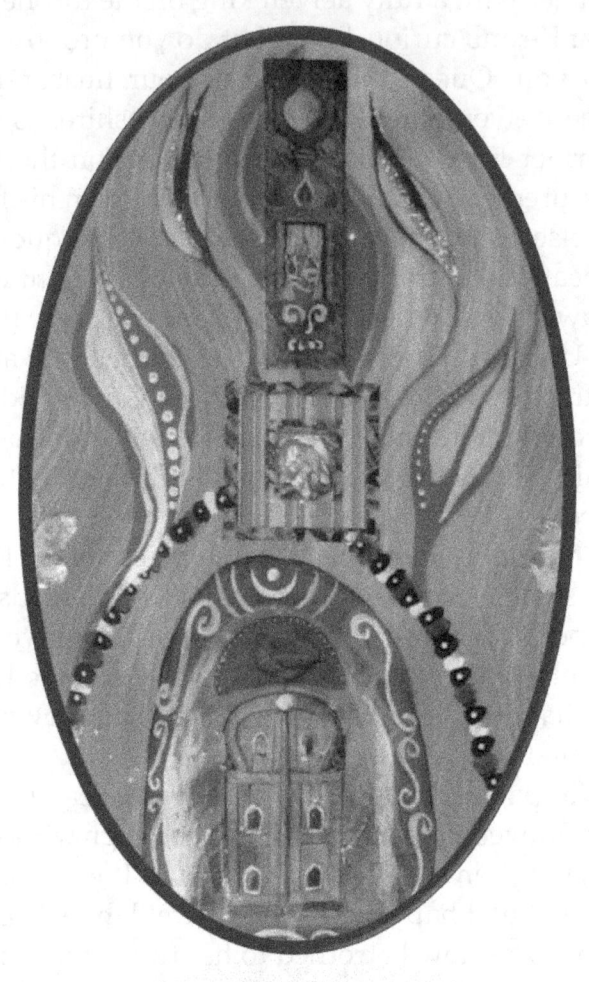

"I wish I could tell you all would be well
That no human would again turn Beast
I wish I could tell you there would be no more hell;
One must have Hope at least."
-The Ghost Scribe

Chapter 14: Impermanence

Delilah walked in the orchard, morning light filtering through the filigree of foliage. The trellised dome shimmered on the horizon, rising in front of the Whayer Wood like a piece of green lace arching across the sky. Sparks of light ran up from the ground, revealing how the bubble of the Net above was connected and powered by the Nearth below. The magickal barrier's iridescent curling vines and leaves were barely visible against the sky. It shimmered just when the light hit its entwined layers or when the wind fluttered its tendrils. It was a breathtaking work of pure science and nature, those forces that the aelves blended so beautifully.

Leaving no time for ceremony, Jarvis had gathered up the Usiku and their partners who wanted to travel to the Great Desert Plains to rekindle the spirit of the Usiku Nation. He had hugged Delilah warmly before departing, Radyu's skull still upon his head. He told her he was sorry for all the pain he caused her. Delilah told him it was all water under the bridge. She asked him to keep in touch with her through the Nearth.

Ilvana had returned to Verily shortly after the spectacle with the skull when Delilah's mother had appeared, so she had missed Nimevah's visit. Delilah had spoken to the scientist through the Nearth early that morning. The Doktora was shocked by Jarvis' proclamation that he was called to rule the Usiku and his abrupt departure. She was even more surprised by Kejanu's declaration to offer himself to Nimevah to satisfy the pact.

"You have to admit, it is an elegant solution," Ilvana complimented the former Usiku king.

"Yes, it solves several problems at once, including that he had a depth of feeling for me that he realized I do not reciprocate. I admit, I find him appealing. I would have loved him if I could," Delilah said, feeling slightly incompetent for not returning the love of this glorious man.

"You will not be alone your whole life, Delilah. You have many years ahead of you to partner, have children, and enjoy a family," Ilvana said.

"Or, it will be as it always has been: the people of Hope are my family. This realm is my legacy: my primary obligation." Delilah doubted more than ever that she would find love. If a startlingly attractive aelven king had not roused her deepest passions, who possibly could?

"Allow yourself room to be surprised," the scientist consoled.

"And what of you, Ilvana? Will the great doctor ever find love?"

"I am built for laboratories, experiments, and mastering Qi-Kai, but not for love. It is not in my essential design," she said, with no regret in her tone.

"Well, you might leave yourself room to be surprised," Delilah said, and they laughed.

As Delilah returned from her course around the perimeter of the Net, nodding to the Guards who were doing their rounds in the other direction, she felt her crystals begin to tingle.

"Aumenveill!" she said when she recognized the greeting of the ancient tree.

"You have been quite occupied, Queen of Hope," said the tree in his grumbly centuries-old voice.

"Yes, I am sure you have heard about the Vector and the miraculous Net that has arisen from the Nearth to replace it?"

"Why yes, dear. It was the collaborative work of the aelves and all the ancient trees in our network across the earth, even under the sea. We were all *rooting* for you, so to speak," he said, then chuckled a slow, self-amused guffaw.

"We are so fortunate that you and the other Ancients helped us," she said sincerely.

"You are part of us now, your spirit is woven into those branches and leaves, same as we are. We are all connected."

Delilah felt this as she walked back to the castle, the tingle of every tiny shoot of grass, ever tangle of nettle and every fuzzy branch of the briars. She felt them all as if she was feeling the tiny hairs upon her arms. Her aelven ear buzzed and she looked up to see Kejanu coming toward her, his compact frame moving with the grace and musicality that she so admired of the Dusk Aelves. "My Queen," he said, bowing to her.

"King Kejanu," she said, bowing back.

"I am no longer a king," he corrected her. "At least temporarily until I take the crown of the Khattu."

Delilah nodded at the truth of this. "You have given up much," she observed, hoping to find some way to apologize.

"Perhaps. Or perhaps this is how I can best demonstrate my love for you, Delilah. I can save and protect Hope by marrying Queen Nimevah," he said, "while also restoring the Aelven Shield. I realize that your feelings for me are slow to evolve. Our paths are connected: I have seen that in your eyes and in your heart. Yet maybe it is not as your soul's mate that I can best serve you and the love I feel for you," he said, his tenderness and sincerity overflowing in the emotional tone of his voice.

"It is a great sacrifice," she said.

"No, not a sacrifice: a duty. We have a duty to those we love, and sometimes it does not look the way we may wish it might," he said.

"Regardless, I am humbled by your selflessness," Delilah said.

"We will find a way to keep the peace between our two nations: aelves and humans. This is the reason royals have always intermarried, is it not? To keep alliances and forge peace."

"The aelves seem so much better prepared for this kind of logic," Delilah said. "I have much to learn from you."

"Do not forget that you are partially one of us now," he said and reached up to brush the tip of her ear. The tingle that ran down Delilah's whole body surprised her, and she thrilled unexpectedly to his touch. "We are One whether we are together in partnership or not," he said.

Xanfar and Calliwe were returning to Fallengrove for a brief period before journeying to Erithea to assist the Dusk Aelves in reforming their nation. Lord Xanfar would have the adventure he had been seeking in his youth, and perhaps would play a part in helping to repopulate the depleted aelven realm. A few of the Centaurs were staying in Hope with those who had ensnared their hearts. Batel's golden love, Sethran, who had carried Delilah to Verily when she was injured, asked Xanfar for permission to stay. Xan felt he had no claim on the Centaurs. Ultimately, they were mercenaries and free to go wherever they chose. Xan held no hostility toward any who chose a different path, especially after drawing them into the losing battle at Raefenshire. He felt he owed it to them to give them his blessings in whatever brought them joy. Batelnut and Sethran celebrated with an impromptu joyous wedding. Sethran wore a golden saddle and his bride rode in on his back, looking magnificent in shining ceremonial armor and a pair of bright green silk pants. Delilah realized she had never seen Batel out of uniform before.

Delilah officiated the ceremony, where she wound a green and gold braided cord about both of their joined wrists. Great cheers rose up among the guests, who threw sprigs of rosemary and junebark berries. Afterward, there was much revelry, feasting, and dancing. The Usiku who stayed behind showed off their fantastic musical prowess. They were joined by several of the freed dwarves, who turned out to be exceptional musicians. After all they had been through over the previous weeks, everyone seemed to need a release. As much as Delilah was grateful to see her people celebrating, she longed for quiet. She went to Batel and her husband and kissed them both, imparting upon them the gift of a cottage away from the barracks that she had fitted with a door large enough for the centaur to pass comfortably.

Instead of heading to her bower, Delilah climbed the stairs to the viewing tower. She had loved the Keep when she was a little girl; it had given her such an expansive view of the city, the sea, the tower across the bay in Yonderlot, and of course, the dark spooky woods. She would stare for hours, imagining the lives that were being lived in the dwellings on the close winding streets of Hope and the creatures who inhabited the Whayer Wood. It was almost like being able to venture out into the world herself. Delilah could see the festivities and heard the music drifting up from Batel and Sethran's celebration. She saw Xanfar and Calliwe, along with the rest of the party returning to Fallengrove, saying their goodbyes before heading into the forest. The Net parted as they approached and sealed with sparkling light after they passed through it into the Wood. Delilah had privately said her goodbyes to her wolfen friend earlier in the day, and yet felt a sense of loss seeing him leave, as if they had not had enough time together.

Kejanu had departed after their brief meeting. He said he would be in touch to let her know what he was able to negotiate in terms of a treaty between Hope and the Crystal Aelves. Delilah felt that everyone was leaving, which was partially true. A wave of pensive solemnity overtook her. She felt lonely, and yet utterly at peace. For the first time in months, she was not afraid of being attacked or worried her brother would try to kill her and take the throne, or preoccupied with the possibility of the Vector failing and the Beasts overtaking Hope. She looked to the tower in Yonderlot and wondered about the reunion between Helanza and Gravenwell. What Delilah would have given to see the look on the Ghost Scribe's face when his old love came up from the cliff face to tell him she was the new Keeper of the Tower!

Although Delilah indulged herself momentarily in feeling somewhat sorry for herself as new partners joined and old partners reunited, she also felt that all was right in the world. She was exactly where she was supposed to be. As it had always been, she was most comfortable alone. She knew in that moment that she had made the right decision in staying by herself all these years. It would have been easy to fall in love with the pirate queen or to pair up with Kejanu, if she were so inclined. Yet, she was a solitary person, raised without the comfort of playmates or even affectionate maternal love. Jarvis had been her only connection in childhood, and of course, Gravenwell, who had plied her with stories and had won her loyalty with his kindness.

The wind picked up from the ocean and gusts of salty air reached her, even as high as she was in the tower. The weather had been fickle all day, gusty and cool one moment and then scorching sun the next. It was reminiscent of when the seasons transitioned and the harvest rolled in, yet they were in mid-summer. It was unusually tempestuous. When the crystals on her hand started buzzing, Delilah almost missed it, watching the wind tossing the treetops around in all directions.

"Jezschmel!" she said, when she heard the Pirate Queen's voice in her mind, a bit frantically calling her name.

"Delilah, there is something very odd going on about the ocean," Jezschmel said, urgency in her tone.

"The weather is strange here, too. What is happening?"

"You will not believe it. First, there were vigorous currents and strange blasts of wind from every direction. Then the sun came streaking through the clouds, unlike any rays of sun I have seen before. They were… rainbow colored, is the best I can describe, rays of light in every shade."

"How magnificent," Delilah said. Just then, she noticed glowing light on the horizon of the ocean. Color pooled around clouds of many different hues. It was like a sunset, except even more varied, with purples, pinks, greens, and yellows, deep reddish saffron and moody dark indigo. "I think I see it here. The colors of the clouds are spectacular!"

"Well, that is not the strangest part," Jezschmel said. "When the light touched the surface of the water, it made the Gloom evaporate! The rays came down and touched the smog—it just sizzled and disappeared! I am telling you because I hardly believe it myself: at this very moment, there is not a single speck of Gloom left on the ocean!"

"That is impossible!" Delilah said. Yet as she proclaimed this, color-filled clouds drifted in from the sea. Light streamed in radiant tinted columns and rolled over the edge of the city. Vibrant shades shifted on rooftops and all became a silky haze of pastel light. The rays came closer and passed over top of Delilah, turning her skin a dusky rose as it passed. It moved swiftly on, over the orchards and fields. She turned to watch its path. As it crossed the threshold of the Net, its bright face eviscerated the shadows of the Whayer Wood and turned it ablaze in beaming technicolor. Delilah watched as the light touched the purplish shroud of Gloom. As she watched, the Gloom turned inside out and evaporated into the air above in tiny smoke curlicues. The light continued its journey, all Gloom in its path disappearing within the luminous glow. "Jezschmel!" Delilah gasped, "The Gloom is vanishing here, too!"

Just then, Ilvana's voice chimed in to join them. "Women, we are witnessing something spectacular," the Doktora said. "After plaguing our world for 100 years, today is the day that the Gloom has perished. The Age of Gloom is over!"

Jezschmel laughed and so did Delilah, mostly because there seemed to be no appropriate reaction to this stunning news. Delilah heard shouts of joy from the wedding party below, and realized they too were witnessing this astonishing transformation. "It is unbelievable," Delilah said. "I truly never thought I would see the day!"

"Yes," said Ilvana. "It has been with us our whole lives!"

"Speak for yourselves," the nebulously ancient Jezschmel said, and the three of them hooted with excited abandon.

"What does it mean?" Delilah asked. "What will this mean for communities that have been solitary and trapped, surrounded by Gloom! They will be able to travel, share culture and scientific knowledge. Imagine the discoveries that may have been made in small isolated communities that may now be revealed!"

"It is invigorating to think of, for certain," Ilvana said, "yet we must also consider the negative repercussions. What will this mean for the Beasts of the Gloom who are no longer protected by the Gloom, and will surely venture out into the rest of the world?"

"Our Net was created just in time," Delilah said. She realized at once their good fortune. At the same moment, she became cognizant that the other nations across the world would be put in peril once the Beasts had nowhere to cluster and hide and would begin to roam free. It could be a terrifying time for many realms.

"Perhaps we could share the Net technology with other queendoms?" Ilvana said, thinking quickly. "We could help them to create their own Nets to keep the Beasts from coming in to invade them."

"We must convene with the Ancient Trees as soon as possible," Delilah said. Rather than the end of an era, the end of the Gloom could mark the beginning of unprecedented danger.

Jezschmel yelled out, "There! It is a giant sea mongrel! Ladies, I must go. We may have some Beasts from beneath the waves to contend with. Without the Gloom atop the sea, we can now see better what lurks beneath the waves. It is… troubling," the pirate said, and bade them farewell.

Ilvana and Delilah ended their conversation with a plan to summon a great conference of the Ancient Forest Beings the next day. Delilah stood at the edge of the tower. She could see out over the Wood in a way she never could before. Creatures moved among the trunks of trees and flying Beasts dove in and out of the canopy. All that had been concealed by the Gloom before was now revealed.

Delilah put her hand down and felt the shaft of her scimitar, comfortable in her grip. Her weapon's leather binding rested against her skin. She sighed and then tipped her head back and howled. Down below, members of the wedding party heard her and returned her call, howls echoing across the lawn. Whayerwolves from the Wood joined in the jubilant song. The future was completely unpredictable! Things could go awry in so many ways yet held so much promise of excitement and adventure! She was once again at the helm of her queendom.

She thought to herself: "I was made for this."

About the Authors
Niko Peone & Nikki Pison

Nikki is a writer, psychologist, and artist. At seventeen, she fell in love with a boy named Jason who loved Dungeons and Dragons. Jason became the father of her first child, Niko, who was named after Jason's favorite character in a D&D book series. Niko has D&D in his DNA! When Niko was a little boy, he loved to be told stories. Nikki wanted to raise an egalitarian boy, so she changed all the heroes in common fairy tales to be strong women. At night, she would make up long tales for Niko. His favorites were about a warrior queen named Delilah. Delilah solved problems by rolling up her sleeves and talking to others. She had compassion for ogres and trolls alike, yet she knew how to bust heads when necessary!

Naturally, Niko became an extraordinarily good storyteller and Dungeon Master. A few years ago, he told Nikki that he wanted the two of them to write a book together containing stories from the Queendom of Delilah for a more adult audience. *Queen Delilah and the Encroaching Gloom* was born. Niko started a D&D campaign to strengthen the bonds of the story and test whether people really enjoyed the world and the characters within it. As it evolved, he painted the backdrop of the story for Nikki, who then filled in the scenic touches, dialogue, and mystical sci-fi narrative. Niko let her know when more bloodshed was needed! What started as a bonding time for mother and child almost 30 years ago has persevered as a creative link between mother and adult son. We hope the magick of Hope has entertained you, and perhaps even made you cherish the Nearth beneath your feet.

The authors would like to express special thanks to our friend, Nic Schoonbeck, for his insightful and detailed editing advice.